We All Will Be Received

LESLIE VRYENHOEK

Breakwater Books
P.O. Box 2188, St. John's, NL, Canada, A1C 6E6
www.breakwaterbooks.com

**A CIP catalogue record for this book is available from
Library and Archives Canada.**

We acknowledge the support of the Canada Council for the
Arts, which last year invested $153 million to bring the arts
to Canadians throughout the country. We acknowledge the
financial support of the Government of Canada and the
Government of Newfoundland and Labrador through the
Department of Tourism, Culture, Industry and Innovation for
our publishing activities.

Printed and bound in Canada.

Breakwater Books is committed to choosing papers and
materials for our books that help to protect our environment.
To this end, this book is printed on a recycled paper that is
certified by the Forest Stewardship Council®.

For Russell

PART ONE

1977

DISAPPEARING WOULD BE AS SIMPLE AS SLIDING OFF THE edge, as stretching one leg forward and following it over. Dropping from sight.

She'd been working up to it for a long time, for hours maybe, shifting her limbs and resettling her hips like a restless sleeper, stealing a little closer to the edge with each shift. Beneath her, the bedsprings had cried out with every small advance, but now she was on the verge, a foot already toeing the air. Just one more move, fast and certain, and she'd be gone.

She closed her eyes and let all the air seep from her lungs. Reached one arm forward. Counted it down.

Counted it down again.

And this time, she did it. She went over. Kicked her leg out, twisted and plunged to the floor.

She heard a soft one-two thud as her toes and palms touched down, then heard nothing but the rushing, loud and louder, that filled her ears. Panic, she thought, or adrenaline—were those the same things?—she didn't know, but it calmed her to wonder it.

She stayed low and still, forehead to the floor. Pulled air through her nose to feed her hammering heart. The motel carpet smelled like wet boots and gas station toilets.

When the noise in her head subsided, she could hear he was still snoring and she began counting again, pacing the rhythm of his guttery breath—the sour whine as he inhaled, the pause, then the roaring exhale. She'd been marking that cycle for a long time, for all the eons it took her to take the plunge, to escape the trough in the mattress that wanted to keep her in his orbit.

Finally she lifted her head and opened her eyes. It was darker down on the floor, but a blade of light bisected the room near the foot of the bed. Slake had left an inch-wide gap in the curtain the last time he'd peeped out. He was loaded by then and careless, or else he wanted the harsh white motel sign for a nightlight.

That light dead-ended at the bunched mound of her t-shirt lying just inside the bathroom door. Her favourite t-shirt, powder blue with cap sleeves and a gentle V of a neckline, and she felt a small tug of regret for having to leave it behind. Near the foot of the bed, just beyond that slash of light, she could make out her khaki jacket, arms spread wide where she'd let it fall. She wanted to leave that too, to get away from it as fast as she could, but her wallet was in the pocket and her ID—a driver's license, an old library card—would tie her to this. To all of it.

Crawling so close to the floor it was more like slithering, she crossed through the sharp blade of light, gathered the jacket to her chest with one arm and then listened for a moment before making her way around to Slake's duffel bag. He'd left it lying open alongside the bed—along his side of the bed—easily within his reach.

She rocked back on her heels to look at him, hoping to read the depth of his sleep in the slack line of his mouth, but his face was turned away and cloaked in darkness. His chest was bare and for a scant second, she saw what she'd liked about him—the breadth of his shoulders, the taut line down to his wrist. His right arm was thrown wide, his hand dangling off the bed not a foot from her head. He wouldn't even have to sit up to grab a handful of her hair, to drag her back onto that squalling bed.

But maybe he wouldn't bother pulling her up. She could make out his knife on the nightstand. Maybe he wouldn't even check to see who it was before he struck. Next to the knife, the glint of his car keys and the shape of his watch. She wanted to reach for that, for the watch, wanted to calculate how soon the sun would rise. Wanted to be far enough away before dawn—assuming dawn was even out ahead of her, that she could creep her way out of this dark place.

Tylenol. That's what she planned to say if he opened his eyes. Where the fuck's the Tylenol, baby?

He'd grunt an answer or maybe just point impatiently, but then she'd have to take some. She'd have to swallow it down and get back into bed and by then he'd be awake, waiting for her, maybe pissed at being woken up and wanting something to rock him back to sleep.

She slipped her hands into the duffel bag, its leather worn soft and silent, and rooted out what might weigh her down—a tube of Prell shampoo, a beer opener, his jeans. Two bottles of Labatt's Blue wrapped in one of his filthy shirts. She felt those before they had a chance to clank together and knew he must have forgotten he had them; otherwise they'd be as long gone as the two-six of rye he'd put back earlier.

She lifted out his unzipped shaving kit. Inside, a razor and blades, his bone-dry toothbrush, an empty pill bottle. Slake had sold almost the whole store in Sault Ste. Marie—cashed in before they'd torn out of there.

She ran her hand around the bag's interior, hoping to find a few stray Quaaludes. Thinking it might be nice to have some handy, but then she remembered the tranquilizers were on the table behind her, next to the empty rye bottle, because Slake had washed back a couple of them earlier.

Take it easy Elvis, she'd said, hoping to inspire him to swallow a few more.

Slake rarely dipped into the drugs, special occasions only. Like wiping your ass with cash, he said. Besides, I need to stay sharp. Half the time he was drunk when he said that, well past the point when the booze slurred his speech and made him overconfident. Usually they were alone by then, tucked away in a dingy room in some bleak strip of a motel along the highway, and the worst that would happen if he got too loud was a dull thud pounded on a neighbouring wall.

But they hadn't been alone tonight. Slake had wanted to celebrate, to knock back a few now that he'd made the big delivery and collected his cash. Now that the job was coming to an end. And she'd felt like celebrating too, knowing she'd be back home in a day or two with just enough time to say sorry—Sorry for taking off like that, and can I get that money you said Dad left for my tuition?

Home, and free to get on with her life.

There was nothing left in the duffel bag but a flattened brown paper bag, her clothes, a hairbrush, and all of Slake's money. She could feel rolls and rolls of it, wrapped in elastic bands. Loose bills, too—folded flat or else wadded up like they'd been jammed in fast. She pinched a few of the folded ones, slipped them into the back pocket of her jeans. Then she laid her jacket over the money, tucking it so it concealed what was underneath and folding one of the arms to hide as much blood as possible.

She shouldn't have clung to the damn jacket. She should have dropped it at her feet or thrown it out the window, anything else, but she'd been too dazed as they'd raced into the night, Slake speeding more than usual, taking curves so fast her shoulder collided again and again with the car door. Still, she didn't brace—she just hugged that jacket against the wide, wet circle of blood that soaked her t-shirt.

By the time they'd stopped at this motel, the shirt was glued to her, stuck fast just below her ribs.

As soon as they were in the room with the door bolted, Slake had cracked the rye and grabbed the pills. She'd gone to the bathroom so she could strip without him watching her, but once she'd peeled off the blood-stiffened powder blue shirt, Slake was beside her at the sink. When she flinched away, he didn't seem to notice. He just tore into a bar of soap and cleaned his knife, the blade glowing in the dull bathroom light, then washed his hands more thoroughly than she'd ever seen him wash before.

Take a shower, he said. And then he didn't say anything else, not for more than an hour, not even when she didn't shower, just put on a different shirt but kept on the same dirty jeans and shoes.

It was unusual, Slake keeping quiet for so long, so she knew he must be shook up, too. When he finally did start talking it had nothing to do with that night, that place, or anything else that had passed between them since they'd met. It was a story from his childhood, a fishing trip, his father or someone like his father, someone who made him hopeful and then made him angry. Convoluted, impossible to follow—not that she was trying. She was just pretending to pay attention, small snatches of his narrative needling in around the crowd of images in her head.

The sound of waves. He said that a few times before he got caught up describing the barb on the end of a fishhook. He kept repeating that detail, circling back to it. The barb, he slurred. The hook. He was fucked up by then, not even talking to her. Not even in the room with her. Which made it easier for her to slip back into the bathroom with the cup of rye he'd handed her and pour it down the sink. He was too far gone to notice that she wasn't keeping up, that she was staying sharp—so sharp she'd pretended to pass out with her shoes still on.

Under the bed, she lined up Slake's things—his jeans next to the shampoo, his beer beside the shaving kit. All of it waiting right there for him. Everything but his money. She didn't leave any of it, not even enough for breakfast or a pack of cigarettes. She thought about that briefly, about whether he'd be even more furious if he was hungry, but she decided the two bottles of Blue would fill him up until he figured out what to do. Or until he caught up to her.

The leg closest to her head jerked hard, making the bed shriek. Her breath caught like a balled-up fist in her throat and she willed herself to move, to get up and run—run dammit, run now, before he's got you—but she couldn't. She could only huddle, shrinking against the floor like she could make herself invisible while that locomotive roared through her head again.

Long seconds passed before the rushing quieted, before she could hear that Slake was still snoring, deep and loud. She followed the rhythm of it, in and out, timed the metal zipper's rasp to the steady waves of his caustic breath.

Slowly, she stood, hoisting the bag in one motion. When the next wave began to crest, she took two long steps to the door and slid the chain, eased the door open just enough to slip out, bag first, then pulled it shut behind her.

Outside, the cool air smelled of lake. She sucked it in like she'd just surfaced after a very long time under water.

Walking past where Slake had tucked his Trans Am behind a copse of bushes and new spruce—off to the side and hidden, he thought—she saw the way Vacancy glinted scarlet off its taillights. Saw, too, that once she stepped from the motel's shadow, she'd have no cover. A double-barrelled spotlight mounted beneath the eavestrough lit the parking lot from corner to corner. But it was highway or black bush, so she plowed straight ahead, watching as her long shadow stretched out across the asphalt in front of her. Waiting for his hand to seize her arm the way it had hours before.

She could still feel the bruises from that grip on the arm she kept bent at a stiff angle so the duffel bag wouldn't knock her juddering knees. She moved steadily forward, her back braced to meet a sharp blow between her shoulder blades.

When her Keds came down on the side of the highway, the stir of loose gravel was barely perceptible over the racket of katydids in the ditches, the low bass of frogs beyond. She couldn't remember which direction they'd been heading when they'd pulled into the parking lot, but she didn't care. Direction didn't matter—it was erasure she was after.

Pavement beneath her, she picked up her pace. In seconds, the darkness swallowed her whole.

FOR A LONG TIME SHE WALKED DEAD CENTRE DOWN THE DARK highway. A crescent moon had risen above the trees and it cast just enough light that she could make out the painted amber line.

She'd started to run when she'd hit the first level straightaway, but she'd stumbled. After that she'd made herself slow down, each footfall steady and measured. She didn't want to twist an ankle, didn't want to be limping when he caught up to her. Walking slowly, however, gave her more time to think and what she was thinking about, now that she was beyond Slake's immediate reach, was what lurked beyond the road in all that blackness. Bears. Mostly she was thinking about bears and what she would do if one came ambling out of the woods.

Maybe she should have taken her chances back at the motel. She knew how to handle Slake—or she'd thought so, anyway, before yesterday—but she had only vague notions, things she'd heard as a kid, about how to survive a bear attack: lie down and play dead, rise up and act fierce. Run like hell. She didn't know which was the winning strategy, but she set down the duffel bag and leaned over to make sure her shoelaces were tied tight, just in case. That's when she heard it.

Faint but growing stronger, the distant whine of an engine. He was already after her.

First a wave of relief, as if the thing she was fleeing could be her salvation from this perilous dark. Then something else: fear. A jolt of adrenaline drove her to the side of the road where the shoulder fell off at a sharp angle. She dropped the bag on the incline and grabbed at the long grass to keep from sliding too far down. The engine stayed constant, still far enough away that she wondered if sound travelled further in the absence of light, and then she thought no, he's just moving slowly so he can peer into the woods. She moved down into what seemed like thicker cover, branches scratching at her bare arms, her heart beating so hard she could feel it in her throat.

Finally, headlights, wide and high. A semi-truck. She had to scramble fast to get upright, grab the bag and get out to the road. She finger combed her hair and tilted her head so it hung down, so the headlights would catch the long blonde of it. Thumb out.

The truck took so long to stop that she thought it wouldn't and when it finally did, it was well past her and she had to run a long way to catch up. Just as she reached the truck, the door flung open and the driver looked at her through thick lenses, looked her over good, then looked in the sideview mirror to make sure nothing was coming up behind him.

You coming? he said.

She put the duffel bag on the floor, pushed a six-pack of Coke over to make room on the seat and climbed in. The cab was warm and it made her realize how cold she was. Still, she sized the man up before she shut the door. He was more thin than fat, with a slight paunch resting on his belt buckle and hair like a ball of steel wool. There was no weapon she could see, and the sleeves of his plaid shirt were buttoned at the wrists. That seemed like a good sign and anyway, nothing worse would happen to her in the cab of his truck than what Slake would do if he caught her with all his money.

The driver asked what the hell she was doing out here—was she lost or in some kind of trouble, and she said, No, just taking a road trip, and shrugged like being in the pitch black of nowhere was just one of those things. But she could tell he didn't believe it.

Once they were up to speed, he asked where she was going and she said Ottawa because it was the first thing that came to mind. She hadn't come up with anything close to a story and she was just glad she'd guessed right, that he didn't say it was the wrong direction. Instead, he asked why Ottawa, was she from there? She pretended not to hear him and hoped he wouldn't ask again. He didn't get a chance. Another voice, loud and rough, jumped in between them and scared her half to death. The driver reached down to grab a CB transmitter, hauling it close to his mouth before he started talking. She relaxed. Now, at least, his attention was focused on that conversation and not on her or the bag at her feet.

She listened intently, wishing she could decipher the code he was using. She knew breaker, breaker because everyone was saying it these days. She knew what smokey meant, from the movie, and she knew he must be talking about her because he kept saying I got a ten-twelve, a Goldilocks, but she couldn't figure out exactly what they were saying about her. It was all gibberish and going too fast, numbers standing in for words and words coming together in strange ways and one thing meant another.

Then he was saying, I don't know either but it's turned me into a yo-yo, and he was going on about a fucking trap, and the other voice was getting faint like it must be moving further away until eventually the driver gave up, dropped the transmitter into its holder and told her if she wanted a Coke to go ahead and help herself. She did, then asked him for a cigarette. He said he didn't smoke, but he wanted to know what she thought of them changing all the road signs practically overnight like that, and had she ever seen such a waste of money and time?

She shook her head and he saw she had no idea. A minute later, he pointed to the side of the road, arm extended so his finger was right in front of her face. She followed the line of it, saw 90 whiz past.

See, they're changing all the signs now to that metric system. Every time you pass one, you gotta try to remember the last one, wonder are they telling me to speed up or telling me to slow down?

She took a long drink of Coke, noticed how the fizz felt like it was scouring her clean inside. Ninety is fifty-four, she said.

Is it? Well you're pretty quick. I suppose they taught you that in school. He said it like he thought she was part of the *them* who were changing the signs. Well hell, he continued, they didn't teach me that. We never learned any of that metric shit. Goddamn government's sure not thinking about those of us driving our old rigs out here on the roads.

She turned her head away fast so he wouldn't see her grin. She was thinking about Slake waking up hungover, broke and alone, and having to learn the metric system.

The driver kept talking. And those guys who haul South over the line—they can't ever get used to it. They'll be going back and forth, back and forth, doing the math until their brains burst. And nobody even knows when the States is gonna change over.

Her Coke was empty and she wanted to throw the can out the window, but then she spotted lights in the mirror, getting closer. The driver was rolling out his theory, how they were forcing people to buy newer vehicles that had both kinds of speed on the dash. That's what this is all about, he said, and he looked over at her to see if she agreed. Saw, instead, that she was fixed on the sideview mirror. Somebody chasing you? he asked.

She turned to him and smiled. Just watching out for smokey is all, she said, and bent low to drop her empty can and get another Coke as the car behind caught up and pulled out to pass them.

While they drove on toward dawn, she converted speed limits for him, repeating the formula when they passed a sign until he got it, until he could do the math himself or else had just memorized the equivalents. She didn't get why he cared so much—his speed never quite climbed up to the limit, and she found herself rocking forward like she could make the truck go faster. She kept looking in the sideview mirror, kept filling with terror every time she saw lights gaining on them, but it almost always turned out to be another truck.

When they stopped in the morning, she took a hard look down the road and another around the parking lot before climbing out of the cab and following the driver into a truck stop diner. She ordered a glass of Tang and a cheese omelet and waiting for it, decided she was hungrier than she'd ever been.

As she scraped the last of the cheese from her plate with a fork, her driver pointed to the payphone. You got parents or somebody who might be worried? But he let it go when she told him she was older than she looked and nobody, nobody at all, was worried about her.

She didn't know if that was really true and for a split second, she remembered the feel of hands on her face, remembered her stepmother, Carol, saying softly, Of course you'll stay here. This is still your home, honey, and we're your family. That's what your dad would want.

But that was just after the funeral, everyone still dressed nice and acting proper, the house anchored with the weight of lingering mourners—her stepmother's friends, an aunt in the kitchen. Shiny shoes on slippery floors, nothing you could trust.

Slake probably thought that's where she'd go—back there, back home, and he knew exactly where that was. He used to hang around the 7-Eleven until her late-night shift ended, take her for long drives in his car, the deep rumble of the engine and his arm draped around her shoulders a kind of haven, equal parts exhilarating and seda- tive. She'd only known him a few weeks before he'd asked her to come with him to Ontario. His cousin had a friend who had a good business and Slake said he could make a lot of money in just a few weeks, maybe a month, and they could have some fun, too.

Plus, it's fucking beautiful there, he'd told her. You'll be blown away.

And she'd said sure just like that. Sure, and Slake's face lit up like he'd never really thought she'd go along.

Now, she figured the best way to keep Carol and her half-sister safe was to stay far away from them, to keep them out of it.

As soon as they were back on the road, she pretended to sleep, head bent forward with one fist tucked under her chin. Pretended, and then really slept. Slept right through the endless chatter on the CB and didn't wake up until the truck came to a full stop. They'd pulled into a gas station off the highway and judging by the light, she could see it was afternoon. The driver said he was filling up before making the turn for home, and he should probably go it alone from here.

She started to gather up her duffel bag. Hey, he said, how about a thank you?

Then she noticed that he'd parked off to the side where no one else was parked. She didn't know what he knew, or what he suspected, or what he might do if she refused, so she gave him a hand job without argument, without giving him time to demand anything more. She took care to let him spray all over his bunched-up shirt. Then she jumped down out of the truck with the duffel bag while he was still gasping.

From there, she caught a ride in an orange Pinto with a pollster heading for Ottawa who wanted to know what she thought of Pierre Trudeau. When she said she didn't know anything about politics, he said, No, I mean do you think he's sexy? My wife says he's sexy, but I think she's nuts.

She said she couldn't see it either, which made the man smile and pat her thigh like she was his best girl. Then he said, What about me?

What about you?

You think I'm sexy?

She said she had to pee first, then she'd show him how sexy he was. He took the next exit, decided he'd take a turn in the washroom, too, and while he was gone she hauled out her bag. Climbed up into the nearest truck without even waiting for an invitation.

The driver raised a stiff hand like a cop halting traffic. Please, she said, just a little way and I'll get out.

He looked over at her then, let his hand fall to the seat. I'm going all the way to the mill in Corner Brook godforsaken Newfoundland, he said, but you let me know where you want out. He raised his hand again, this time just to hold up one finger. Only thing is, I don't speak French—you speak French?

She shook her head.

Then we don't stop in Quebec. We don't even slow down. And I'm Jerry by the way.

Thanks for the ride, Jerry. I'm going to Newfoundland, too.

If he'd noticed that she hadn't offered a name, he didn't remark on it. He just nodded and pulled out onto the Trans Canada Highway, saying, Well it's a great coincidence that we met up then.

After a few minutes, she picked up the *National Enquirer* lying on the seat next to her and started to flip through it. She didn't get very far before Jerry asked whether she believed it.

Believe what?

He ran a big hand through his slicked-back hair. The King, he said. Elvis. D'ya think Elvis is really dead? Because some of them newspapers say he's not.

She looked down at the stack of tabloids on the floor by her feet, then had a hard look at her driver, at the way his mouth was canting down toward a loose jawline. A hound dog face, she thought and suppressed a smile.

He leaned into his topic. Some people are saying the story's made up, that Elvis faked his death—you know, just to divert attention so he could slip out the back door and disappear. Have a normal life for a change. Now wouldn't that be rich if he got away with it.

They drove in silence just long enough for her to read the main article—*Elvis is Alive!*—before Jerry said, See, it kinda makes sense. Hell, I figure maybe he's got himself a ride on one of those NASA things—the Voyagers. Maybe Elvis is tucked into one of them Voyager space probes they sent up the last few weeks, and now he's heading for the far edge of the solar system.

Shit, she'd hitched a ride with another kind of crazy. She looked in the rearview mirror. There was no Slake in sight, just a truck far, far behind them, and she thought about saying she'd changed her mind and needed to go back west, could he please stop to let her out. But then they passed a highway sign and she saw it was in French and she knew there was no getting out of this truck, not for a while. Anyway, a little conversation was a small price to pay in exchange for a free ride, so she asked if he really thought that was possible.

Hell, I'm only kidding around. When Jerry laughed, the sound came from deep down in his belly. I mean there's no oxygen in space and besides, I doubt Elvis could fit into one of those little capsules these days.

What are they, anyway, these space things you're talking about?

Jerry told her all about it then, all about NASA and its new space explorations, about how they were sending probes to take temperatures and pictures and other measurements and figure out if there were any other beings living on other planets. And figure out if there was any place for people to go.

You know, like someplace new we could go and live.

It was at least more interesting to her than Elvis, dead or alive, so she thought of more questions to ask. After awhile she realized she didn't need to prod him. Jerry would just roll along filling the air with words. Soon he was on to signals getting picked up from outer space.

They call it 'the big ear,' he explained, and it's been listening for sounds from space for years. But suddenly it picks up something, some kind of extra-terrestrial radio signal. Freaky, isn't it? That was last month, just before Elvis died.

Behind them, the sun was setting. Jerry rubbed a hand on his cheek, scrubbing at the shadow of stubble that could have been a sideburn if he'd ever let it be.

That seems like quite a big coincidence, he said, now that I think of it. Maybe somebody was calling the King home.

Next Jerry told her about some spaceship called *Enterprise*, named after a TV show, but this spaceship was real and it had just taken its first flight.

And that's called a space shuttle, he was telling her, meaning it can shuttle people out and around space. I'll tell you what, twenty-five, maybe even twenty years from now, we'll have colonies in space and we'll fly there just like we're catching a jet airliner.

She thought about how she'd only been gone from home for a couple of months, but it was like she'd missed the whole world changing.

Jerry was grinning wide. Hell, that's a job I'd like. Maybe I'll be driving an intergalactic cargo ship before too long. Like that—what's his name? Not Skywalker, the other one, Solo something. Did you see that *Star Wars* movie?

She hadn't. She and a couple of friends from work had planned to go see it on a Saturday afternoon, but then she'd cashed her paycheque, thrown a few clothes and a hairbrush in a paper bag and climbed into Slake's car. She was far, far away from Winnipeg by the weekend, so she'd missed that movie.

Greatest movie ever, Jerry said, and he told her all about it—told her the whole plot and all the best lines, and it was like he was telling his own story. Like he'd created it or maybe even lived it, and she closed her eyes so she could picture it better.

When she opened them again he wasn't talking anymore, not until he saw she was awake. Then he patted his stomach and said, We're out the other side of Quebec. You hungry?

After they'd both ordered a burger and a waitress had sloshed coffee in their cups, Jerry leaned back in his side of the booth and asked, What's in Newfoundland?

She shrugged. How the hell would she know? But her legs felt a little jumpy.

He studied her. I mean, what's taking you there?

I guess you are, she said, resisting the urge to overplay it with a wink. I gotta powder my nose.

She stayed in the bathroom a good while, longer than she needed to, long enough for their food to arrive but not, as it turned out, long enough for Jerry to arrive at a new topic.

You ever been to Newfoundland? he asked before she was even back firmly in the booth.

I'm starving, she said, and took a bite of burger big enough to jam up her mouth for a long minute.

Jerry watched her chew. Okay, he said, cocking his head and looking something like wounded. It's none of my business. I was just curious.

She nodded and forced a smile around the dry bun and greased leather of the patty, washed the mouthful down with coffee and said, Yeah, me too. Just curious, I mean. I never seen it, but I heard it's nice.

Jerry laughed then, fast and loud, letting go of the thick fry he was swiping in ketchup. Newfoundland's a lot of things, he said, but I've never heard it called nice before.

What's it like, then?

Depends how you look at it, he said, turning his attention back to his fries. It feels most times like it could actually be the middle of nowhere, but folks there swear it's still the centre of the universe.

So which is it? While Jerry considered the question, she grabbed the unlabelled bottle of ketchup and banged on its side until it produced a good-sized gob on her plate, another gob on what was left of her leathery burger.

Little bit of both, I guess, he finally said. A small place up against a big ocean on the one side, a big country on the other. Rock and a hard place, you might say, but it's had its moments. Used to be quite the strategic locale before jet fuel and modern telephones and such—not so much now. He paused long enough to finish his own burger. Though of course there's still the fishery.

Fishing. That sounded right—that's what she remembered from geography. A fishing place.

She mopped ketchup off her plate with the last bite of her burger. You always lived there?

He shook his head. Born in Toronto, moved there when I was fourteen. My parents couldn't wait to get home, back to the grandparents and the cousins and the cool air. At the time, it felt like I'd been plunged into purgatory.

But you still live there—you must like it, right?

His eyebrows shot up and down so fast she didn't know what to make of it. He looked at his watch, then grabbed up the single bill the waitress had slapped on their table, saying, We better haul out if we're gonna catch our boat.

Boat?

Yeah, the ferry I mean.

She looked at him blankly.

Jesus, girl, you at least know it's an island, right?

Sure, she said. Of course.

When they got the cash, she pulled out the few bills she'd stuffed in her back pocket but Jerry waved her away with the wallet he had in his hand. So she just stood off to his side while he paid and that's when she saw it. It wasn't the big headline on the front page. Still, it was the one on the top left side—the one your eyes got to first: *Pair sought in murder investigation.*

She started to lean in, but Jerry had turned and he was watching her. She pulled back and faked a yawn, looked blankly ahead so he'd know she was bored beyond all reason.

Before they even got back in the truck, she asked him to tell her more about space travel and his plans.

HOURS LATER AT THE FERRY TERMINAL IN NORTH SYDNEY, darkness firmly entrenched, she and Jerry stepped down from the truck and went to look out over the water. He lit a cigarette, then lit one for her, too, and they stood quietly together, listening to the waves.

I never seen the ocean before, she finally said. Never.

Jerry blew a mouthful of smoke out toward the water and told her this wasn't really the best way. You want to get somewhere quiet, somewhere where it's just you and the land falling off into the sea, he said, so you can see how huge it is. How it keeps on rolling forever.

He flicked his spent cigarette away, took off his jacket and draped it around her bare arms. She gathered the jacket closer and smiled her thanks. It occurred to her that she hadn't looked, not for hours, to see if Slake was coming up behind her. That she hadn't felt this safe for a very long time.

The ocean's a lot like space, Jerry was saying. There's so much of it, you could go out there and sail around forever and never see it all.

She leaned on the truck, stuck her arms properly into his jacket and laced her fingers together behind her head. The overhead lights reflected off the water and it was as calm as a swimming pool and as dark as ink.

Colonies in space, Jerry was saying. I'm telling you, the world is about to change more than you and I can even imagine.

And then he spotted it.

He straightened, shot an arm overhead, index finger pointing to the heavens. Look, he said, see the one that's moving—that bright one there?

His finger made a slow arc. Her gaze followed.

That's gotta be one of them satellites, he said. Satellites, you know, that receive signals from one side of the world and beam them to the other, so we can see something that's just happened a half a world away.

Dawn searched the sky until she found it, the small, bright point trekking across the heavens, and the sight of it pulled her up straight, too.

One day, we'll all get to go up there, Jerry said, and we all will be received.

Together, they watched in silence until it vanished.

Jerry lit two more cigarettes and handed her one. I sure hope they hurry up, he said. I can't wait to be driving around up there.

They both blew a thick column of smoke toward the heavens, smudging the stars, believing that they were looking out into a whole and foreseeable future.

_2012_

ETHAN WROTE A MESSAGE ACROSS THE BATHROOM MIRROR, his index finger slick with shaving cream. He didn't know what made him think to do that, to scrawl a secret message in the steam. Exhaustion maybe, from getting up before sunrise to start another long shift, or leftover exhilaration from the night's lovemaking after such a long drought. Either way, it was just an impulse—unplanned, uncharacteristic but genuine.

Hours into Ethan's shift at the hospital, Lana would climb out of the shower, the curves she tried to flatten with pilates glistening with droplets—this is how he pictured it, her glistening curves— and see his declaration on the newly re-steamed mirror: _You are so beautiful._ Her smile would spread like sunlight racing across a field when a cloud moves aside. That's how he remembered her smile, the way it seemed when they were first together. And maybe, Ethan thought, maybe she'd wipe the mirror clean with a towel and using some potion he couldn't quite conjure, some cream or gel from the drawer, she'd write a message back to him. Love re-emerging like an invisible code between them.

Except that's not what happened. That's not what happened at all.

When Lana stepped out of the shower and saw the words scrawled across the mirror, she grabbed the hairdryer—the heaviest thing within reach, the closest thing to a weapon—and she held it high over her head, peeked into the hallway then darted to the landline. Someone's in my house, she whispered to the 9-1-1 operator. Hurry!

Then she fled, straight down the stairs and out the front door, leaving the hairdryer at the threshold and clutching just a damp bath towel to her chest against the sub-zero chill. It hadn't snowed for days, so the sidewalks were clear and dry. Her bare feet barely suffered on the frigid concrete at first. She pounded on consecutive doors until finally, the older woman in the townhouse at the end of their row let Lana in, gave her a robe and poured her a cup of lukewarm coffee to calm her nerves.

The police cruiser was at the curb before Lana called Ethan at the hospital. But just then, Ethan was in the middle of a scan, was making sure the dark mass he'd seen on the screen didn't show up on his face. So Lana went to voicemail. By the time Ethan heard the message, the cops had scoured their townhouse top to bottom, turning up less than a trace of an intruder.

Lana couldn't explain why her head had gone that way, why it hadn't even occurred to her that Ethan had written that message. They didn't laugh about it—not that night and not the next. Maybe it was all the violent crime she ingested, all that CSI and *Criminal Minds*, the bodies-on-slabs television she couldn't get enough of.

Ethan Windexed the mirror twice and hoped that would erase the whole incident.

But days later in his mother's kitchen, as he reached for the one decent knife in the place, he heard Lana say *So—*. And in that single syllable, Ethan knew she was about to tell the story of the message on the mirror, and he knew that in her re-telling, it would pass from minor incident to family lore, from miscalculation to that *thing* he'd once done.

He kept his back to them as he listened to Lana's matter-of-fact delivery, tried to focus on the knife in his hand, the way it seesawed smoothly through the cranberry-lemon loaf. His mother, Pauline, bought the same loaf every week, set it on the edge of the counter in its plastic wrap waiting for Ethan and Lana to arrive. And every weekend, he stood at this counter and cut that damn loaf into eight even slices. Pauline insisted. Ethan, she said, cuts so straight, makes each piece so precisely *equal*—her tone taking on just enough of an edge that he knew she was making a point, laying her tolerant forbearance against his inability to handle her crooked slicing. And maybe she did have a point. He could recall complaining, once— years before—about her slanted style, about pieces of bread too thick on one end to fit into the toaster.

The sixth slice fell sideways as his blade landed on the cutting board and Lana's bare feet hit the frigid concrete in her re-telling. I didn't even know how cold I was until I was safe, she was saying. Ethan heard the echo in her story as the knife descended again.

When he turned to deliver the loaf, he saw his mother had heard it too, that she was mentally holding their stories up side-by-side: Lana, near-naked and running down the street, banging on doors; Ethan, six years old, escaping through a small window wearing only his dirty, torn underwear.

Lana, finding safe harbour in a strange woman's home, just like Ethan.

He placed the loaf in the centre of the table and sat down heavily in his usual chair, fixed his eyes on the coffee in his cup. One of them—Pauline or Lana—had put too much milk in it while his back was turned. He wanted to jump up and pour the whole damn thing down the kitchen sink and tell them to stop doing that. He wanted to tell them that it wasn't the same, not at all—that he hadn't knocked on any doors, for one thing. That Lana hadn't been in any danger, for another.

He lifted his cup to take in a mouthful of lukewarm coffee, but he couldn't because now in his memory he was running, his socked feet slapping the street. Just running, with no destination in mind. Certainly not knocking on any doors. It was the woman who saw him—saw him out her window from who knows how far away. Then she was running too, out into the street in her housecoat, intercepting him. Bringing him inside.

She'd recognized him right away, of course. His picture was everywhere by then.

It was a full-on publicity push and he's sure his mother still has some of the posters—posters on which his initials, *E.T.*, were printed in the same style as the movie poster. The round face of a little boy—grinning, teeth missing—replacing the cinematic full moon. The message, also borrowed from the movie, read HELP ETHAN TURNOWSKI COME HOME in all caps.

Ethan reached for a slice of the loaf, glad for the sweet tart of it, the oil it left on his fingers. The glue of it in his mouth.

Lana was saying she'd never met that neighbour before, but she supposed she'd have to make a point of being neighbourly now, show her gratitude. A bit of an aside, and Pauline leaned forward, every inch of her urging Lana to get on with it. Rapt, Ethan realized, because she didn't yet know who'd written that message on the mirror.

You have to give it to Lana, he thought. She tells a good story.

Ethan never had the chance to thank his rescuer, doesn't even know the name of the woman who took him in and locked the door and called the police, then gathered him up in a blanket and held him on her lap, saying, It's okay, you're safe now. Who hugged him tight until his trembling stopped and then gave him chocolate milk, cold and syrup thick, in a coffee mug. He remembers that, the chocolate milk, even more clearly than he remembers the police officers and their uniforms, the guns on their belts. And he remembers his parents hurrying into the hospital, everyone bawling. Or maybe he just thinks he remembers that tearful reunion; maybe it's one of those memories that gets planted afterward and flourishes from regular repetition.

Lana, at least, has the grace of clear and full recall, every detail of her fear carefully conjured and recited for his mother.

Ethan has no such thing. He doesn't remember most of his thirty-four days in confinement. Macaroni noodles and canned peas—he remembers those—and a few of the assaults. Flashes really, nothing in its entirety.

It's not like he's blocking it; he knows what happened to him. He gave as complete a statement as a six-year-old can, and he went for counselling for months until the counsellor told his parents he was fine, that he didn't need to keep talking about it. That it was time to just let him have a normal childhood.

He knows that from the re-tellings, too.

But there's one thing he's certain of: Lana knew his mother so she knew better than this.

Ethan was considering a second slice before Lana finally got to the punchline. Got to, It was Ethan. For an instant, he thought his mother might topple right out of her chair and he reserved a hand to catch her, but then she settled back as Lana repeated his name. I mean, she said, glancing his way, what was I *supposed* to think?

Pauline reached across the table, bypassing the loaf, and took Lana's hand, but she fixed her attention on her son. You of all people, Ethan. Her voice a low simmer. What were you thinking? You really should talk to someone about why you're acting this way.

Acting this way. A curious phrase for his mother, proud as she was of her career on the stage. When she was younger, she'd performed all across Canada—twice at Stratford, she never failed to mention that—though she'd never appeared on television. Not until Ethan's kidnapping.

Days after he went missing, the cameras showed up. Local news first, then the national crews and even a few from America. On day six, someone—the police? Pauline? someone— decided a press conference was the best thing, a chance for Ethan's parents to make a public plea. Except Frank, Ethan's father, was too busted-up to speak so he'd sat stone-faced, leaking tears, while Pauline pleaded for their boy's return.

I was a complete wreck, too, of course. Pauline always made sure to emphasize this when she told the story. Beside myself with worry, so afraid—those phrases, in that order, every time—but thank god I'd had my training. I knew what I had to do, how to *act* to save my child.

Her passionate plea aired repeatedly, right across the country and down through the U.S. She has a videocassette tape with nothing else recorded on it but two news items: the full plea as it first aired, and a story about Ethan's return that carried a short clip of it. Ethan had seen the clips so often—though not for the first time until he was ten or eleven—that he could rattle them off verbatim.

For decades, Pauline kept an old VCR hooked up to the TV in case someone hadn't seen her finest work or wanted to see it again. Three years ago, she had that tape digitized. Now it was easier than ever to show it off.

It was important to her, Ethan knew, that everyone understood what a brave pioneer she was in the field of desperate mother love. Knew, too, that it was unkind to think that, that the whole episode was harder on her than it was on him. Still, he was tired of the re-telling, of having to watch her tearful television debut, of having to pretend she was the sole reason he squirmed through that tiny window.

Ethan broke a slice of loaf in two and bit into the right half while he studied the left. He could feel his mother's eyes on him. But when she spoke again, it was Lana she addressed. There's no reason for you to be embarrassed, she said. You did the right thing, getting out of there. I'm just glad you're okay.

Then she reached over and took hold of Lana's other hand.

Ethan washed his mouthful down with cold coffee and took in the scene. Six untouched slices of cranberry-lemon loaf on the table; his mother and Lana, holding hands.

That's when he knew he was leaving.

1977

MARGARET LOOKED UP FROM HER NEWSPAPER WHEN HER cousin's big rig pulled up out front. Through the window she watched a girl climb down from the cab of the truck, reach back to withdraw a dirty duffel bag, then wave at the driver, at Jerry, before making her way toward the inn. She wasn't familiar, wasn't from around here—Margaret could tell that much from the slender height of her, the long-boned limbs, the serious knob of her chin. The young thing moved slowly, as if fighting a strong current, and the duffel bag thudded twice against Margaret's brand-new door with its oval of glass before the doorknob turned.

Margaret turned back to the newspaper, didn't even look up when the girl arrived at the counter, not until she actually spoke.

I'd like a room, please. The cheapest one you've got.

Margaret blew out a stream of menthol smoke and gave the girl a thorough going over while she folded up the newspaper and set it aside. It wasn't like Jerry to deliver trouble right to her doorstep.

And how do you plan to pay, my love? She leaned forward as she asked it. No smell of marijuana, not a whiff of booze. That was something, anyway.

Cash. I can pay cash—up front, every day I'm here if you want. To make the point, the girl pulled three crumpled twenties from her back pocket and laid them on the counter. Then she set the duffel bag on the floor at her feet and looked down—looked as if she wanted to crawl inside it. Margaret saw her hair was greasy and lank and when the girl looked back up, she saw her eyes were ringed with fatigue.

Rooms are all the same price, Margaret said, as long as it's just you in there. But I see anybody else go in, the price goes up—then you go out. This isn't that kind of place.

I just need a place to sleep, the girl said, her voice choking to a thin reed. Tears welled up in her eyes then, surprising them both.

Behind Margaret, the phone on the wall rang. She excused herself, grabbed the receiver and walked through the doorway into her office, pulling the cord taut.

JERRY'S COUSIN WASN'T AT ALL SURE ABOUT GIVING HER A room, that much was clear. He'd told her to say he'd brought her, told her the Blue Iris Inn was the best place to stay in Corner Brook and that Margaret would be inclined to give a good rate to someone he'd dropped at her door. But she didn't want to ratchet up her debt to Jerry any higher, so she'd skipped that and gone straight to cash.

Probably a mistake. She knew how she must look, filthy from so many days on the road, wiped out by so little sleep. She wished she'd slept a few hours on the ferry like Jerry had, but the churning and the chatter and her own anxiety had kept her awake. She'd spent almost the whole crossing outside by the railing, watching the sun rise and then watching the land rise out of the water. Once they were off the boat and back on the road, just as she'd drifted off in the truck, Jerry had decided to stop for breakfast. She'd drunk enough coffee then to chase off any chance of sleeping after that—but there was no chance anyway, since Jerry kept up a constant barrage. It wasn't his near future in space he was on about though—the ferry crossing had grounded him. Instead, he was all about the past, about old battles with the French and how people here divided themselves up by affiliation to an old country most of them had never even set foot in.

He hadn't seemed to notice that she never showed any interest, that she'd stopped listening not long after he'd started talking. Wide-eyed but dazed, she'd just stared out the window at the telephone poles along the side of the highway, the constant dip and rise of the wires that strung them all together.

Jerry's cousin came bustling back in, saying, Let's get you registered. Sliding the guest registration book and a pen across the counter, all hospitality and business now.

Registered.

She looked down at the book, at the words *Name* and *Address*. She doubted Slake would think to come looking for her in such an unlikely place. Besides, it was an island. She'd crossed water and isn't that what you did—what escaped captives and people plagued by demons did?—they crossed a body of water so nothing could sniff them out. So no evil could follow.

Still, she didn't feel safe, standing in this small hotel lobby. She felt scraped bare by the older woman's scrutiny, chilled right through and there was nothing for it, her jacket still in the duffel bag, still branded in blood. Thinking of it made her realize it wasn't all such a long-ago dream. Made her feel stupid, too, for not having flung the jacket overboard in the night.

Outside, she could hear a murmle of voices and they sounded like she felt, like they were deep, deep underwater. She straightened up and stamped her feet, trying to drive off the exhaustion. She just needed to stay on her game for a few more minutes. As soon as the older woman turned her back to study the room keys on the wall, she looked around the Blue Iris for something that might sharpen her focus.

Behind her, the only windows were curtained in off-white sheers. Wood-panelled walls swallowed the dull daylight. On the long wall to her left, two posters interrupted the panelling. She focused on the first, a nature scene pasted so flat to the wall it could almost be a true passage to a serene pond and the leafy green forest beyond it. Beneath the image, in blazing yellow, *There is virtue in beauty*.

The words ruined the whole effect.

The second poster, further down from where she stood, was nowhere near flat. It rippled and flexed as if it had once been soaked, was pulling away from the wall in so many places that it had to be planning a slow escape from this inn. It was Tony Orlando & Dawn, the three singers posed and captured in black ink lines. Some kind of concert poster, and she stared at it until Jerry's cousin, key in hand, cleared her throat.

My name's Margaret, she said, setting the key down and taking up the pen that still lay on the registration book. What's your name, dear?

Dawn. A barely intelligible squawk. Margaret held the pen poised, didn't look up.

Dawn. Louder, definitive this time. My name is Dawn.

Okay my love. The pen landed. I'll just put that down for now.

Margaret wrote the single syllable neatly into the book and if she suspected it was a lie, she never let on—not that day or that week or ever—and she never asked for more information. And Dawn wasn't sure whether Margaret had proffered a kindness, or decided it was none of her business, or if she just had no interest at all in knowing more.

A STEADY TRAFFIC OF BOOTS AND THE SCRAPE OF LUGGAGE pegs had worn a dull, dove grey path down the centre of the hardwood floors at the Blue Iris Inn. The whole building canted north but Dawn was too exhausted to notice it as Margaret led her down the long hallway, past a steady rhythm of closed doors with brass numbers until they arrived at the door in the furthest back corner of the first floor. No brass number—no number at all—just a blank door that opened into a room that only fit a single bed and a bedside table with a lamp.

The room was smaller than any of the ones in the shit motels where she and Slake had stayed. A complaint was rising to her throat.

There's a full bathroom just there, Margaret was saying, pointing to the corner. So if this will do, you can stay three nights.

Dawn nodded, set down the duffel bag inside the doorway. This'll do, she said.

When she was alone, she pulled the drapes shut, plunging the room into a premature dusk that made her feel safe again. Then she stripped off her filthy clothes for the first time in days, unwrapped the single bar of soap in the room and climbed into the shower.

She soaped her hair, wishing for shampoo, and her face, then let her hands travel her torso until she felt it—something that wasn't her, a texture that wasn't skin. She looked down, bent a little to see past her breasts. A patch of dried blood the size of her palm on the flat of her stomach.

All this time.

She backed up against the wall, scrubbed and scrubbed at it with her hand in a fist, careful not to get it caught under her nails.

When she was sure it was gone, she washed her hands and her hair again and then every inch of her body until she knew she was clean all over. Then she stood and let hot water course over her—stood there until she was too tired to stand, her mouth hanging open and her knees jellied.

Naked except for the towel pulled like a shawl over her shoulders, she sat on the edge of the bed and considered the duffel bag. She might still have a clean t-shirt buried in there, but she couldn't bear to open the zipper.

Next to the bed, the numbers on a digital clock clicked forward, all of them flipping at once with a distinct *tock*. It was one o'clock in the afternoon. Dawn let the towel fall to the floor, slipped between the sheets and fell into a hard, empty sleep.

Minutes later, or what felt like minutes later, she was jolted awake by voices nearby. Disoriented, not able to think where she was, she listened. A door, not hers, opened and then closed with a thud, muffling the voices behind it. Silence again, except for the tock of time moving forward.

She opened her eyes.

Daylight nuzzled in along the edges of the drapes. The room came back to her and with it, her place in the world. The clock said five-thirty and she assumed it was evening, then wondered if she could possibly have slept all the way through until morning. But no—she still felt profoundly tired, though exhaustion was running a distant second to hunger.

She needed something clean to put on, some money, so there was no way to put it off any longer. She went straight to the duffel bag and pulled the zipper, fast.

Lifting out the jacket, she saw there was more blood than she'd remembered. She dipped two reluctant fingers into a pocket and pulled out her wallet, then rolled the jacket inside out. Didn't matter. The blood was worse on the inside, where it had pressed against her sodden shirt. She wished again that she'd left it behind or thrown it off the ferry, and she wondered if bringing it here left a trail that cancelled out the cleansing of a water crossing.

Back in the bag, she found her one clean t-shirt and pulled it over her head, slipped into a pair of panties that at least looked clean. Everything else, the few items of clothing she'd brought along, were filthy. She made a small pile of laundry, noticing that her only other pair of jeans was even more tattered and splattered than the ones she'd been wearing.

Once she was dressed, Dawn picked up the duffel bag and dumped all the money onto the bed. Several loose bills fluttered out first and then six fat rolls, each held by a couple of elastic bands, thumped onto the bed. She eased the elastics off one of them, surprised to discover it contained a mash-up of denominations turned every which way. All the rolls were like that, and she wondered if that's how the money had come or if it was a sign of Slake's style, as inconsistent as everything else about him.

She couldn't know for sure. She never saw the big deals, the times he'd delivered all that PCP she wasn't supposed to know about. The first time he'd made her hide, made her slide down real low in her seat. She'd listened as he deconstructed the trunk to get at the stash, listened to the slam and the distant voices. Impossible to discern. Slake was more nervous when he got back in the car than he'd been before the deal.

After that, he always left her in a restaurant or a motel, told her to wait there in a voice that said don't argue.

But she saw plenty of the smaller sales, the sideline stuff in parking lots and back halls, and she never understood how Slake knew if he was being paid the right amount. Occasionally he counted the money carefully, silently mouthing the numbers. Usually, though, he just pocketed the bills without looking at them.

And sometimes—a few times—he rubbed a wad of cash between his fingers and said, No, I don't think so, man.

Then he got the fight out of his system.

The first time she saw him lose it, shift from sanguine to violent in seconds, she wasn't even surprised. It was like she'd known he had something dark inside him since the day he'd burst through the door of the 7-Eleven and asked, Is this guy bothering you?

That guy had been bothering her—hanging around, leaning over the counter to say something gross, coming back to buy one more thing—so she'd been grateful for Slake's interference, for the way his height and swagger gave him authority, the way his long dark hair and leather jacket suggested menace, even if all he did was ask a question.

She separated the ones and the twos from the fives and tens and twenties, smoothed each bill as best she could, remembering her father's money clip, how he sometimes refused a bill at the store if it was too rumpled. Wondered if maybe that's what she was doing with Slake in the first place, looking for that kind of certainty, for someone with a firmer grip than a grief-stricken stepmother who had her own kid to cope with.

Anyway, Slake's appeal was obvious. It wasn't just his looks, his confidence—it was something about the way he paid attention to her, like he thought she was essential. It had been easy to turn away when he had to throw a few punches to move things along.

That last time, though—she couldn't look away. She'd ended up right in the middle of it, bloody and screaming for them to stop, then shoved aside, helpless and stunned by Slake's knife, the body on the ground.

She shook off the image, counted the money again, making thousand-dollar piles as she went. When she was done, there were nine full piles and over a hundred dollars besides. It was more—much more—than she'd expected, and she sat on the edge of the bed with her hands over her face until she got used to the idea of it.

She rolled each thousand-dollar pile and secured it with a rubber band, used a leftover band to secure the braid she wove in her still-damp hair. Slid the last hundred-and-seventeen dollars into her wallet. She hid the rolled thousands beneath her dirty clothes in the leather duffel bag and set off to find some food. She wanted McDonald's, the familiar taste of a Big Mac and fries to make her feel like she hadn't drifted so far from the known world, but she couldn't see the golden arches and when she grew tired of looking, she settled on A&W. After she'd eaten and talked herself out of a second order of onion rings, wiped the grease from her fingers, she went back outside and looked around.

She wanted to walk and see more of the town, but a wind had come up, the air chilly in a way that said summer had packed up and moved on. So she folded her bare arms over her breasts and looped back around toward the inn.

And that's how she found the laundromat—by chance. By scent, really, her nose picking up the distinct smell of detergent, of diffusing hot lint. Then she saw it through a window, the wall lined with five washers, the opposite with five dryers, just one person inside and a sign on the door that said *Open 8 to 8*. She hurried back to the inn, stuffed the bloody jacket into a paper bag and put everything she wasn't wearing on top of it. Then she raced back, stopping at the adjacent store for a box of detergent and a jug of bleach, a handful of coins.

Inside the laundromat, there was no one else now, every machine open and empty and still.

The washer was filling, a sweet chemical steam lifting from it after she poured in the detergent. She looked over both shoulders— still no one—and pulled out the jacket, leaned with it into the tub, soaking the dried blood under the washer's spray. Then she poured detergent straight onto the fabric, onto the stain that was as big as a splayed hand and surrounded by smaller islands of blood. She scrubbed the fabric together the way Carol had taught her to wash away the shame of stains on her underpants.

But this blood, embedded in the heavy canvas of the jacket and so long dried, barely budged. Which made her think about how advertising lied. Made her open the bleach and pour the smell of swimming pools—of someone holding onto her midsection and promising she wasn't alone—into the suds.

Eyes watering, Dawn dropped the jacket into the stew and slammed the washer lid to shut the smell out.

She threw all the rest of her clothes in a separate load, stayed right beside the machines until they'd spun themselves still. When she peeled her jacket from the wall of the washer, she saw that the bleach had lightened it to a sickly celery colour—a pale imitation of itself that only made the blood more obvious.

She crammed it all in the same dryer, plugged in coins and stood watching the round and round tumble and fall. And she thought about going back. About going home and coming clean.

She could go to the police. I know who did it, she could tell them. It was a guy named Slake.

But then she imagined the rest of that conversation. Is that a first name or a last name? they'd ask, and she'd have to say she didn't know. She only knew Slake. He'd told her his full name once, but she hadn't bothered to hold onto it. She didn't know where he lived, either, or how to get in touch with any of the people he'd had business with on the road. She just knew what he looked like—like the guy in those cigarette magazine ads, the same kind of sexy dark eyes and mustache, but with longer hair. And that might help the cops understand what she was doing with him, but then they'd have more questions and she didn't have any good answers. The truth sounded so flimsy—I never did any of the bad stuff. I just went along for the ride.

She could say she'd been taken against her will, that she'd been looking for the chance to get away. She could make that sound true because it felt true, even though she couldn't think of a single time when Slake had actually threatened her, couldn't remember ever mentioning that she wanted to go home. But she had been afraid he wouldn't let her leave if she asked—and she'd been afraid enough to leave in the middle of the night. So she figured she could embellish, could make it seem true enough that she'd been a hostage.

But then she remembered that Patty Hearst was in jail, and everybody knew she'd really and truly been kidnapped. She hadn't just climbed into somebody's car because he seemed cool and he was good looking, and he thought she was beautiful.

Anyway, the police would only care about what she was doing while a murder was happening right in front of her. And what if she caved under questioning, told them all of it? The first part of the truth—I just stood there and watched—that would sink her before she ever said, When I saw he was stabbing the other guy, I tried to stop him. And I tried to help—there was blood all over me from helping.

Accomplice. The first time she'd heard the word, on one of those detective shows she and her Dad used to watch, *Colombo* maybe, she thought it had something to do with being accomplished. By the end of the episode, she'd figured it out. Accomplice meant you went to jail, even if they never found the guy whose actual hands had done the actual killing.

She pulled one piece of clothing at a time from the dryer and folded it, building a small, neat stack until, at the last, she pulled out the jacket. It was still damp at the collar and along the seams and the blood was every bit as unmistakable as before. She bunched it up and stuffed it alone into the paper bag.

Cradling her clean clothes against her chest, she stuffed that bag into a garbage can behind the laundromat and walked, feeling lighter and less chilled, back to the inn.

The next day, she went shopping. She bought a pair of straight-leg trousers and a button-down blouse in a colour she thought might be called lilac, a striped turtleneck and a matching plaid skirt so long it almost covered her knees. The clothes cost over thirty dollars and were unlike any she'd ever owned before. She wasn't even sure she liked them, but she thought they made her look mature and reliable. Employable.

When she walked out of the store, the cool air hit her. She turned around, went back inside and tried on a trench coat—navy blue with white piping and a wide belt, the kind of thing her stepmother might wear. She had the salesgirl cut the tags off so she could wear it out. Next, she bought a pair of tan boots with a wedge heel. Then she crossed the street to the beauty parlour.

The hairdresser clipped a smock around Dawn's shoulders and began to unwind her braid. She sunk her hands deep into that long dark blonde hair and asked, You want the Farrah cut?

Dawn blinked at her in the mirror.

The woman pointed to a poster of three women with feathered hair and gleaming teeth. Like that? She was gesturing to the blonde in the middle. Most people don't got the hair for that. But yours, it'll work.

It looked like a style that attracted attention so Dawn shook her head. Shorter, she said, less fussy.

The woman shrugged. Suit yourself. Wings or bangs?

Later, Dawn's new wings blown dry, the stylist smiled at her in the mirror. There now. Tweeze your eyebrows and put on some makeup and you'll look just like one of them angels.

Dawn doubted that, but she stopped in the drugstore anyway and spent the last few dollars she had with her on a pair of tweezers and some pink lipgloss. That left just enough change for a pack of Doublemint gum.

Walking into the inn, she caught sight of herself in the door's oval of glass. The longest tips of her hair barely grazed her shoulders now, and the fullness of the layers and wings made her face look narrower, more defined.

Behind the reception desk, Margaret laid on her best hospitality smile before she realized she was looking at Dawn. Well now, she said, you look like a brand new person.

2013

SPENCER PUSHED AWAY FROM HIS DESK AND SPUN HIS CHAIR sideways so he was facing the window. He liked to look outside while he stewed.

The snow had started to stick, was coating the cars in the parking lot, and the sky was the concrete grey that announces winter and plenty more of it out ahead. He almost added it to his list of grievances, the shovelling and scraping while his fingers lost all feeling, the persistent ache in his leg—but then Spencer thought of Denny. Thought of how excited the boy would be. Thought that if the snow kept coming and stayed sweet and light like this, they could get out the snowshoes and the toboggans and make a mythic winter weekend of it.

He'd need to buy marshmallows. He'd need to make sure Janet had packed all of Denny's winter gear when he picked the kid up tonight. Scratch that—of course she would. She was like that. The think-of-everything type. He wanted to kiss her in anticipation of the snowpants she'd think to pack, the extra pair of mittens.

But then he remembered she was setting boundaries these days. She'd been clear: co-parenting only, mitts off. He'd wanted to kiss her so bad when she'd said that.

Wanted to kiss her like he used to before the barricades went up, to slide a finger inside the dark ringlet of curl that hung down beside her cheek. She wasn't even his type, really, with all that fuzzy black hair and those dark eyes, but she'd hooked him at hey, and that barb was still planted deep.

Shut that down. Focus on Denny. Denny on his way home from school with his ridiculous Elmo hat and his rosebud of a tongue stuck out to catch the flakes. Eyes wide.

Daddy, it's hard to watch the snow—it keeps getting in my eyes.

Was he four when he'd said that? Three? This was the problem with being an old dad. Spencer imagined younger parents with nimbler brains could hold all those details in their heads. But he was getting too old to hold onto details—or else he was just too full up on them, his RAM overloaded so the good stuff, the stuff that's supposed to matter, kept getting pushed out.

And that, Spencer was absolutely certain, was because of Harve. Harve and his details. Fucking Harve, who insisted on making things so much more complicated than they had to be.

Harve wouldn't last a day on the inside, Spencer was sure of that.

This morning's bullshit was just one more example, right down to the way Harve had strolled into Spencer's office, hands in his pockets, and stopped just inside the door. Stood there. Spencer wondered if he'd learned it in business school, how to stand in a doorway, looming large and silent until enough attention came your way. Spencer had wondered that for a full twenty seconds before he'd lifted his eyes from the grant application he was pretending to proofread.

You know where we've never held the annual meeting? Harve's hands emerged from his suit pant pockets with a flourish.

Nunavut? Spencer said, as much hope as joke.

Harve pocketed his hands again and dropped his voice half an octave. Newfoundland, he said. Let's do it in Newfoundland this year.

Harve had a thing about holding the annual meeting in a different province every year. Have to spread it around, he claimed, as if everyone across the nation was eagerly anticipating their turn, holding their collective breath and hoping this was the year Redempt-Ed would show up with its sixteen-and-a-half staff members to gun up the local economy and bring meaning to some heretofore insignificant city.

But at least Newfoundland was somewhere interesting, somewhere he hadn't seen, and Spencer was excited until Harve emailed over the budget—not a dollar more than they'd spent to meet in Regina the year before. Spencer knew it would be hard to do anything half-decent on that budget even before he checked the price of flights. Then he saw it would be impossible.

Spencer delivered the bad news in the hallway. Can't do it, not for that much, he said to Harve. Airfare alone—.

Harve had cut him off with a curt reminder of the hit they'd taken in the federal budget. And then he did that octave-drop thing again, said, What we can't afford is to be seen as one of those central-centric organizations.

Spencer must have looked unconvinced, maybe even a little dangerously disgruntled, because Harve took a full step backwards before he lifted a hand and waggled his finger. I know you, my man—you'll make it work.

Central-centric, for fuck's sake. Never used to have to worry about that kind of shit, Spencer wanted to say, but he'd bitten it back like he'd bitten back every back-in-the-day comment he'd wanted to make for years. Which only made him long more for the days when Redempt-Ed was a grassroots group with a one-room office and a couple of borrowed classrooms. Spencer knew for sure Doug

Baxter—Bax, he was called—never meant for it to grow into this when he started the organization back in the feel-good nineties, when society still had enough faith in rehabilitation to put some public money into a fresh idea.

Bax was a short, square box of a man with a fast laugh that reminded Spencer of crushed gravel pouring from a dump truck. And Spencer heard that laugh every time he looked up to see the portrait that Harve had hung in the boardroom—Bax in all his lopsided glory. The painting was done by some long-ago Redempt-Ed art student and it wasn't great, the eyes not quite right, but Bax was unmistakable because of the scar that wandered across the bridge of his nose and off toward his ear.

Harve had found the painting in a drawer and he'd had it matted and framed. But Harve had never met the late, great man, and he had no idea just how ludicrous Bax would find that. When he got bored in meetings, Spencer sometimes looked up at that portrait and thought he could hear Bax calling out—I've been framed!

Spencer was the last one left who'd actually known Bax, so he was the last one who knew both the official story of Redempt-Ed's origins—an epiphany in prison, spurred by witnessing a comrade's suicide—and the true story. The truth, Spencer thought, was better—was just a man with a notion that most crime was fueled by boredom and what he called a lack of life literacy, so it could be prevented. Bax had scraped together a little funding, most of it from his mother, and started to offer classes. Basic, useful stuff—money management, menu planning, government services—but also aspirational classes like painting and creative writing.

The whole thing was barely off the ground when Spencer got out, and he was stalled with no direction at all. Reporting in to his parole officer, banging away on roofs in the summer and trying to earn a buck with odd jobs in the winter. Bored senseless. Starting to think fondly of the prison library and his old pals inside.

It was Spencer's parole officer who suggested he take some classes, handed Spencer a photocopied sheet that said Redempt-Ed across the top.

He took a money management course first, just to be compliant, but he liked Bax so much he signed up for the creative writing course. When that course was over, Bax invited Spencer for coffee and hired him to write grant proposals.

Now Redempt-Ed was national, chapters in every province and territory, a United Way darling. And some of that—maybe a lot of that—owed to Spencer's gift for selling, for making a compelling argument with a smile. For seeing what was possible and making it happen, then telling the story in a way that made generous believers out of even the tightest twats. He'd cut his hair short and bought a suit that fit properly. Mastered database management. Even learned to golf and then kept his feelings about that kind of land use to himself. All in service to the cause. But now—well success came at a price, big surprise. Ten years ago, he got along with everybody he worked with, all the other ex-cons who got a second chance at about the only place that would give them an office job. If he didn't like them all, at least he understood them. At least they spoke the same language.

On Spencer's last performance evaluation, Harve had written *Needs to spend more time blueskying.*

Out the window, there wasn't a speck of blue sky. Spencer watched a car on the side street lose its back end and start to slide sideways. He wanted to see it spin a full, perfect arc but the driver managed to pull the wheels straight again. Then Spencer thought maybe there was just nothing left in the world that was graceful and wild.

It had all gone in the shitter after the Board of Directors decided to expand the hiring practices. Keeping the mission intact, the memo said, while securing the right skill sets. About a minute later, they'd hired Harve and his MBA to serve as CEO because suddenly, Redempt-Ed was the kind of place that needed a position called CEO.

Harve had slithered right into the role and filled it up like it was never non-existent. And even though Spencer was upper echelon— even though his business card read Director of Development and he'd just landed another million-dollar grant, even though he'd been here *since the beginning*, Harve treated him like a fucking administrative assistant when it suited him.

And if there was an annual meeting to plan, it suited Harve fine.

Nothing Spencer could do about it. He had a kid now; he needed a steady paycheque, and there was nowhere else he could go. Other fundraisers he knew wrote their own tickets, bouncing from one non-profit to another—from Lungs to Symphony, Symphony to Heart and Stroke—their salaries growing by leaps and bounds. But even though Spencer got his share of calls from headhunters and more than a few straight-up offers, there was no way. Once, he'd taken the bait, gone for a first interview and then a second. They were down to the handshake when the interviewer said—offhand, like it wasn't an issue—that they'd just get a criminal record check and then they'd make the offer official.

Spencer had laughed, and then when he saw the guy was serious, he'd reminded him where he worked. Said of course he had a criminal record. And just like that, all the smiles evaporated along with the offer.

For a few days, Spencer had kicked himself for revealing it, told himself to keep his big mouth shut next time. But of course it wouldn't matter. His record had been keyed in with all the rest of them. No matter how they liked him, or needed his skills, one background check later and they'd all be turning his resumé over on their faux-wood laminate desks and imagining the headlines: Millions missing from fund after slack-ass hiring committee brings in ex-con.

Still, he knew he'd hit it lucky in life, managed to slip through that narrow fissure of opportunity before it closed up behind him. Knew he could be selling used cars or reshingling roofs like the guys he'd hired to do his own roof two years ago.

Spencer used to go talk to the classes, try to give those guys something to shoot for. He loved that part of the job, sitting on the corner of a desk at the front of the room, telling them his story. Making it inspirational. Here I am, one of you—a murderer, for god's sake—who's come out the other side and is making a decent living.

But that was back when. Back before the fucking tattletale internet put a lie to even the faint hope of starting over. Now, if one of the instructors asked Spencer to come in and speak, he made up an excuse. He knew those guys would smell the bullshit on him before he ever opened his mouth. And he knew that the way things were now, short of an official pardon, every ex-con in the classroom would be stuck swinging a hammer on a roof, bang bang, no matter how straight, how sober, or how skilled at math he'd become.

Denny. He was supposed to be thinking about Denny, about the weekend they'd have. The now of it, because the now of it was the all of it.

That was another thing he knew—before long, Denny would be old enough to find out, and Spencer and Janet had never decided how they'd do it, if they'd tell him or wait until he found out somehow, maybe on the internet by accident, or from one of those fucking dead-girls-of-days-gone-by stories that popped up every now and then on a slow news day.

Fuck, he should have changed his name. He should have married Janet and taken hers. If he'd thought ahead—if he'd seen not just a baby coming but the boy he'd grow into—he'd have done things better.

Too late now to change any of that.

Spencer reached down and rubbed his knee, the ledge along the bone that throbbed with the dropping barometer. This wasn't the

time to be worrying about what details he might have changed. He
had other details to worry about.

That's what Harve was always telling Spencer—I need you to
look after the details so I can stay focused on the big picture.

Spencer swung around to his desk and typed *cheap authentic
newfoundland inn* into the Google search, gave the enter key a sharp
rap with his middle finger. He knew they had to stay close to the city,
but maybe he could make this interesting, find something a little
scenic, a little rustic, even if it had to be bargain rustic.

He didn't know the geography, not at all, so he just started click-
ing his way down the links. The third click took him to a website that
hesitated before opening like it was considering just how much to
reveal. Slowly, a picture of the place filled his screen.

It was a strip mall of a motel, clad in white vinyl with a half-
heaved parking lot for a front yard and a copse of spindly evergreens
barely visible behind. Spencer shoved his cursor up to the back
arrow but before he could click again, that image slid away and a
new one took its place.

The air went hot in his lungs. And then it left him in one long,
slow whistle.

1978

DAWN WAS DRAGGING THE HOOVER DOWN THE LONG HALL OF the Blue Iris when Margaret found her. Phone call for you at the front, Margaret said, and bustled back to reception before Dawn could ask a thing. Dawn's mouth went dry. She couldn't think of a single reason someone would be calling her that didn't mean trouble, but she left the vacuum in the hallway and went to reception to take the call because there didn't seem to be a way not to, especially with Margaret standing right there, pretending not to listen.

Turned out it was just Jerry—Jerry who never called, who always came by and came in, every single time he passed through town. He said it was his cousinly responsibility to check and see if anyone needed anything from the mainland. Margaret, always head and eyes into the accounts, or folding towels, or checking somebody in or out, would say, Jerry, lad, you don't have to bring your rig down here and block up the place—you could just phone me.

But Jerry didn't. He never called, not until that early August morning when he wasn't even heading to the mainland.

Dawn, he said as soon as she picked up the receiver. I'm taking you on a scenic drive tomorrow.

Embarrassed for both of them, Dawn laughed. Then she reminded Jerry she had work to do, that she couldn't just take off in his truck for a week. And Jerry said, No, that's not what I mean, maid. I mean just the day. And then he told her he'd already arranged it with Margaret and he'd given his cousin hell, besides, for taking advantage, for not letting Dawn have even one day off a week.

Dawn had never thought about asking for a day off. She didn't know what she'd do with it, for one thing, and she thought Jerry should probably stay out of it. Her arrangement with Margaret wasn't even a real job, just an agreement they'd made soon after Dawn had arrived.

It was like pure good fortune, the way Margaret's housekeeper had quit just like that. Dawn heard the whole conversation while she was standing at the reception desk, waiting to pay for another few nights because she still hadn't figured out her next move and was starting to see how any move at all was next to impossible. And then she heard the woman say, I got work in that new fish plant in Burgeo and I'm leavin' the weekend.

And Margaret said she wouldn't like it, so much standing in one place, and the woman said she didn't care. They're building us a new plant and it's closer to home, and I miss Mom.

Dawn made sure Margaret caught her straightening a picture in the lobby not five minutes later, and by the end of the day Margaret and Dawn had made an arrangement. It meant Dawn still lived in the little room at the end of the hall but now she wasn't paying for it. And she could eat whatever was available in the kitchen, plus Margaret gave her fifty dollars every two weeks—a twenty and three tens, which Dawn folded and tucked into the front pocket of her Levis. It was enough to buy what she needed, which wasn't much, just books and shampoo and winter gear—and it got easier and

easier to forget that she only had a first name and a blank slate
for a past. After several months, it even got easy to forget about
the duffel bag, zipped shut and pushed so deep under her bed it
touched the wall.

Jerry, Dawn said into the phone, I don't think—

But his mind was made up. I'll pick you up in my car after breakfast and take you to see some sights, he said. Margaret and I both
think it'll be good for you to get out. And then he hung up.

Dawn looked over at Margaret, but the older woman kept her
back turned and her hands busy sorting paper that was probably
already sorted, so there was no point even throwing a dirty look.

The next morning, Jerry showed up in a Chevy Camaro, a car
Dawn hadn't known he owned. She thought he seemed younger,
but also somehow lesser, behind its wheel.

The car had an 8-track cassette player and it was playing Elvis.

I was just thinking, Jerry said as he pulled away from the inn,
that it's almost the anniversary of his death, which means you been
here almost a year.

Dawn couldn't help but laugh at that, the way Jerry twinned her
arrival with the departure of his rock hero, but if he noticed he
didn't react.

As soon as they were out of town, he rolled into full tour guide
mode, saying everything he could think to say about the topography
and the plants they passed, occasionally sprinkling in some history
like he was narrating an educational film for junior high students.
He'd turned the music down so low there wasn't any point in having
it on, the King reduced to such a slight bump and hum that he might
as well have been a wasp in the backseat.

Dawn started to worry that maybe this was Jerry's idea of court-
ship. Of seduction.

She knew he was well over thirty, maybe even edging close to
forty. He'd never told her his age and she hadn't asked, but he talked

about the late fifties the way Dawn thought about 1973, and when
sunshine fell on his arm as he drove, she saw how his skin had a
slight ripple that hers didn't, how the coarse hair on his forearm
seemed faded and heading for grey.

She kept her eyes focused on the scenery and tried to feign just
enough interest that he wouldn't be either embarrassed or encouraged.

She was twenty now. Her birthday had slipped past her unnoticed in June, and she felt somewhere between all grown up and
impossibly old. Still, she couldn't understand what some women
saw in older men—or why older men believed she would want their
loose, puckered skin up against hers. But they must imagine she did,
because almost every week some guy even older than Jerry would
glide up behind her in a hallway at the inn, put a familiar hand
on her shoulder and then slide it down her back. She'd learned to
whirl around fast, before he got too close, to keep her expression
completely neutral when he told her his room needed attention.

Where are we going, Jerry?

You been here a year, so I figure it's almost a crime that you
haven't seen any of the scenic glory that is Gros Morne.

Dawn had no interest in scenic beauty—she'd seen enough trees
and rocks, rocks and trees during her months with Slake to last her
a lifetime, but Jerry was excited enough for both of them and she
figured she owed him at least some pleasant company on a sunny
day, so she even made an effort to pay attention.

When he told her about the roads, how new they were—how
just twenty years ago the only way in and out of most places on
the island was by boat, Dawn got caught up in it the romance of it.

Jerry glanced over at her. You have no idea, he said, what a long,
drawn-out nightmare winter can be out here when you're cut off
from the world.

Dawn wanted to tell him she was from Winnipeg, that she knew
all about long, hard winters, but she couldn't remember if she'd

ever told him she was from somewhere else, so instead she sent him off in a different direction by asking whether there were trains. That turned out to be an expansive topic, one where the history of transportation steamed straight into Jerry's favourite topic of all: how people—and especially people here—weren't willing enough to throw open their arms and eagerly greet the future.

Sure, trains were a great thing in their time, he was saying, but they're finished now, on their way out. So of course all of a sudden, he said, people want to talk about the railroad like they couldn't get enough of it. Well don't you believe it, Dawnie. Those trains were slow and expensive—plus, the tracks here were narrower than in the rest of Canada. You couldn't even move a boxcar to the mainland without changing its wheels.

While Jerry steamed on, Dawn wondered what had made her think of trains anyway. Her knowledge of them was nothing, was all arm's reach, was the distant sound of freight trains as they rumbled through Winnipeg, blasting their song like a ghostly warning, indecipherable and always, always done before you quite got attuned to listening. Her only other acquaintance was through her mother, through the slow locomotion of stories she'd told her only daughter while she was dying, random pieces of a narrative that was going nowhere fast. There'd been a trip through the mountains and across the prairie after the war—though Dawn wasn't sure in which direction, her mother a young child and only able to remember the moon out the window, the silhouette of the mountains and the relentless sway of the train. There were stories, too, of one line that went to Winnipeg Beach on Saturdays, teenagers travelling to dances. But all of those stories were faded now, bits missing, curled up at the edges and full of people no one could identify anymore.

Jerry indulged in a long, pointed sigh, then shifted, one butt cheek at a time, to resettle in his seat. Things run their course, he was saying. Good roads and lots of 'em, that's what we need to keep this place moving into the future.

When she didn't reply, he kept on like he had to convince her.

I'm not kidding you, Dawnie, I could bring a load halfway across the country and deliver it right to the customer in the time it'd take a train to get it here from St. John's. Why people want to stay bogged down in the past, I don't know. Some folks hate progress just for the sake of hatin' it.

She was looking Jerry's way, nodding to make him think she was listening, but all of her attention was pulled past him, drawn out the driver's side window and fastened on a sickly, tan-coloured lump of parched land. She thought industrial wasteland—a phrase she figured she'd learned from Slake. Then she thought corrosive, and wondered what she'd do with all the words she had stored up in her.

Jerry, she asked, what the hell is that?

He looked over at her finger, pointing toward his window, then turned and looked out that window.

That, he said, and his voice deepened, is the famous Tablelands.

She shook her head, meaning she hadn't heard of it, or hadn't paid any attention anyway.

What you're seeing there, he said—his official touring voice now—that's the Earth's mantle. A very rare sight on the planet. Not the crust, mind you, the mantle.

He glanced over to see if Dawn was getting it, if she understood the import of what he was saying. And she did, kind of; the terms were familiar, but the significance eluded her.

Jerry looked delighted. She knew there was nothing he liked better than to fill in her blank spots, and he paused just long enough for Dawn to wonder why it was that every man she met shared that trait.

He started with continents.

Jesus, Jerry, I know about continents—

And those continents sit on plates, he said. You know about plate tectonics?

She nodded, yes. Emphatically.

Well right here, millions of years ago, two of them plates collided and pushed the earth's underside—the mantle—up over its thin skin.

Jerry had taken his hands off the wheel to demonstrate collision, lift, rollover—so artful she thought he must have practiced it.

Jerry, hands back on the wheel, was saying, If you think of scraping your skin—

Can we stop? She could see they would soon outdrive it. I want to get out and go look.

With his careful lesson disrupted, Jerry's face drew down, all of it concentrating at his pursed mouth. Dawn imagined words piling up like sticks at an impasse in a stream. He didn't look angry, more like confounded, and she realized it was the first time she'd ever seen him look anything but wide open.

He relaxed his foot on the gas and turned to look at the Tablelands, then checked his watch. Finally he said, How about on the way home? I got something in mind first, for lunch, and then we'll come back this way. We'll still have plenty of daylight.

Dawn sagged back in her seat and folded her arms. Jerry turned the radio back up, louder than before. Elvis sang, Don't be cruel. Neither of them spoke again until he pulled over in a small bulge of gravel that stuck off the road and must have been intended as a parking area.

End of the line, Jerry said, let's stretch our legs, and he walked around the back of the car and opened the trunk and pulled out a basket. An actual basket, with handles and a latch.

Shit Jerry, you got Toto in there?

Jerry laughed his deep, booming laugh and Dawn noticed the sky seemed a more brilliant blue than she'd seen in forever, and she smiled and followed him into the woods.

They didn't go far along the path, just far enough to be surrounded by trees. Jerry seemed to know where he was going, the spot he wanted and when they got to it, he pointed to a dome of exposed rock, flat-topped and sitting low. Voila, he said, nature's picnic table. Have a seat, my dear.

He took out four identical sandwiches, square slices of orange cheese layered inside square pieces of white bread, and Dawn imagined Jerry's thick fingers carefully peeling the plastic film from those thin cheese slices. There was an apple for each of them, too, and four cans of Pepsi, and Dawn told him it was the best picnic she'd ever had. A slight, slight breeze flitted through the tops of the pine trees, stirring up the turpentine smell that the hot sun had released. And that smell sent Dawn right back to Northwestern Ontario. To Slake.

They'd been just two days on the road when Slake took a detour, left the car alongside a wall of rock and grabbed her hand to lead her up a path just like this one. It was a slow-rising slope between tall pines, more of an incline than the prairie had ever shown either of them. The air smelled acerbic, smelled something like her father's shelves in the garage, and that smell grew stronger as the day warmed. They kept moving for what seemed a long time, not fast but steady.

She was a few feet behind Slake on the narrow trail and he stopped so suddenly she almost tumbled headlong over him as he went down to his knees. When she met him there, near the ground, his face was inches from a flower that looked like an old pink balloon.

Moccasin flower, he whispered like the name was a secret. I wanted to see if there was a bee inside.

There wasn't, near as they could tell, but when she reached for the flower he chased her hand off. Careful, he said. Just leave it. And then he stood and started up the path again before she could ask him how he knew that flower's name.

It was nearly an hour of walking before they emerged at a high point in the woods. They were breathless by then, breathless and sweaty and horny. They fucked standing up on a broad slab of stone, Slake holding her hips while she bent forward and studied a splatter of mint-green lichen at her feet. Afterward, they sat on the rock. She picked at the lichen like it was a scab while Slake dissected a pinecone. Then he decided they had arrived at the perfect moment to sample the Quaaludes.

We should know what we're selling, right? That's just good business, he said.

He reached for his jeans and pulled a few tablets from the front pocket. She knew then he'd planned it all along, since he kept the pills, hundreds of them, wrapped in a plastic bread bag and tucked inside a Ritz cracker box buried with their things in the back seat. The box bulged slightly, which she thought was a dead giveaway, but Slake didn't worry much about getting caught.

We've got it easy, he told her. It's those guys who cross the border who have to worry. They're the ones breaking the big law.

He tossed a white tab toward his throat and threw back his head, swallowing hard so his Adam's apple leapt dramatically. Then he handed her the other pill. When she shook her head, Slake bit it in half and pushed one portion into her mouth. She could barely work up enough saliva to get it down. They lay side by side on a smooth stretch of bedrock, naked and silent and holding hands, waiting for the show to begin.

She could feel herself blurring, growing less solid until, with the afternoon sun on her skin, she felt like she was made of wax, like she was melting onto the smooth rock beneath her.

Beside her, Slake lay perfectly still. She shifted onto her side. He was looking at her and not looking at her, his eyes glazed and even more black than they'd looked in the fluorescent lights of the 7-Eleven. Her finger began to trace his nipple. She watched it circle, round and round with no purpose at all and it struck her that she'd like to slide inside him and stay there—that if she could only find the perfect angle of entry, she could feel this liquid and shimmery forever.

They must have slept. The sun had passed to the other side of them and when she opened her eyes, Slake was crawling away on his hands and knees like a toddler, like a supplicant. She thought maybe he was going to be sick but he kept going, kept crawling until he reached the place where the world dropped out of sight.

When he got there, he peered over and then reared back like he'd been stung. Come over here, he shouted without even turning his head. She struggled to her feet, wobbled. Saw the ground was getting too far away too fast, so she dropped back to her knees and crawled the rest of the way toward the edge.

As she came up beside him, Slake whispered, Fuckin' amazing. And then she saw it too, the steep plunge, rock separated from rock as if an enormous axe had cleaved the earth. A deep V of a gap that narrowed as it went, disappearing into darkness maybe thirty feet down. Light from the sun at her back shone only on the far side of the chasm, which leaned away on an angle. Though it looked to be just a wall of rock, there was life down there, trees that somehow held on, growing nearly parallel to where they'd set their roots, determined to find some sky.

The wall beneath them was straighter, was soaked in shadow and so sheer a drop that she knew nothing could grow there, nothing could get a toehold.

She stared into the chasm until it lost its wonder—until it, too, became just another expected bit of scenery.

Do you say crevice or crevasse? she asked Slake.

Her voice jolted him from whatever reverie he'd fallen into. He reared up and pushed her, gave her just enough of a shove that she felt herself pitching forward into that gap, even as he pulled her toward him with his other hand. Her reflexes were dulled, her gasp coming after she was already well caught. Slake laughed and pushed her onto her back, onto a rough blanket of lichen and pine needles.

I say gorge, he said, and plunged two fingers into her still-slick pussy, pumping away, leaning in close to watch her face until it was clear she was just going to stare, glass-eyed, up at the sky. Then he pushed those same two fingers into her mouth and fucked her, fast and hard and still so close to the edge of that cliff, and she surprised them both by getting into it, by bucking and shouting until he collapsed onto her with a groan.

It was after that, while they were getting dressed, that Slake said he loved her. Just that, an arm coiling around her and those dark marble eyes trying to look soft and earnest.

When he said it, I love you, she kissed him, her lips and tongue still tingling from the tranquilizer, and he sighed and said it again, but this time he added that he loved how she could look so innocent and act so dirty.

Then he said, I want to watch you with another girl. I bet you'd get into it.

She pulled her shirt on and didn't say anything.

By the time they were down the rocky path, back in his car and back on the road, the rippling magic of that place and that pill had dispersed, leaving behind a dull ache that coursed from her head into her limbs, pooling in her fingers and toes so she wanted to keep bending and flexing them to shake it off. Her mouth filled with cotton worse than any hangover she'd ever had. And all of it, combined, made her want to pull open the door and just roll out as Slake tore up the highway. To just let herself fall sideways and away.

Jerry touched a can of Pepsi to her arm and the cold, wet metal made Dawn jump.

Sorry, he said. You're a million miles away. You okay?

Yeah, she said, just thinking. This is a nice place.

Jerry nodded. Special place, he said, reaching into the basket and pulling out a tall red can. So special I'm gonna share my special stash with you. Ever had these? They're a newfangled kind of potato chip.

Course I have, Dawn said and took the stack he offered, fed Pringles into her mouth two at a time, remembering how good they tasted.

Jerry looked deflated. Right, he said. Guess if I can get 'em on the mainland you could too. Never seen 'em here, though, so I always bring some home.

Dawn rubbed the salt off her greasy fingers and reached into the can to get another inch-high stack of chips. They were more than half gone, and as her hand disappeared past her wrist, she thought about how deep those cans were. How no one would suspect there was anything down at the bottom, under a stack of chips, but more chips.

Hey Jerry, she said, will you bring me back some next time? A couple of cans anyway. I'll pay you for them.

The Pringles had made a slick on Dawn's tongue that even Pepsi couldn't wash clean, and all she wanted was to get out of the woods. Jerry seemed disappointed to be leaving so soon but he went along, packed it all in the trunk and headed the car back toward the Tablelands.

Once they were up to speed, he reached under his seat and came up with an 8-track cassette, still wrapped in plastic.

New music, he said, handing her the cassette. Figured you might get tired of listening to Elvis. You heard of this guy?

Dawn turned the cassette over and laughed. Everybody's heard of Bruce Springsteen, Jerry. He's, I don't know, he's the Elvis of now, I guess.

Jerry shook his head. I doubt that—nobody's the King but the King. But I'm glad you like it.

I don't know if I like this one, she said. It's new. She slipped a
fingernail under the plastic seam to free *Darkness on the Edge of Town*
from its packaging.

She'd been crazy for Springsteen since the first time she'd heard
"Thunder Road," and she'd bought all his earlier albums and now
she half blamed him for the whole mess of her life—all that *Born
to Run* romantic shit she'd listened to, over and over in her room
until she was convinced that climbing into some strange guy's car
was the finest of ideas.

Dawn rolled her window all the way down and leaned her head
out to let the wind blow her clean, but she couldn't stop the memories from playing on.

Slake had meant it—the part about wanting to see her make out
with a girl. Weeks later, both of them half cut, he walked her down
an unlit street in Thunder Bay, scouting for just the right one. The
rough edge of that, its baldness, surprised her. Slake had always
been romantic with her, was always talking about wishing it could
be just the two of them forever, without all the complications of
business and other people. But she knew he'd made a lot of money
on the last run and she figured he was feeling flush, and maybe this
was his idea of celebrating.

That one, Slake said, and she turned to see a small native girl
standing by herself at the curb. She could have been twelve. She
certainly wasn't more than fourteen.

She's a kid, Slake. What's wrong with you?

She is not—she's working, see? She's not a kid, she's a hooker—
probably been doing this for ages.

She shook her head, started to walk away, but Slake said, C'mon,
at least let's go talk to her.

No way, she said again but he kept insisting until the only way
to get him to stop was to tell him, Look, she's ugly. I'm not making
out with no ugly girl for you.

They walked back to their motel in silence. Slake was simmer-ing—she could feel it coming off him from an arm's length away. Even when he fucked her that night it was just that, fucking, not so much as a kiss before or after, and she fell asleep thinking maybe it was over, maybe he didn't love her anymore, and she started won-dering how she would get home.

He was just as sour and silent the next day. It bucketed rain so they stayed holed up and drinking beer because they had no busi-ness to take care of. Late in the afternoon, he left the room and came back with a big bucket of Kentucky Fried Chicken, and he kind of grunted to let her know that she should have some too, and then he turned on the television and watched a baseball game. The TV's vertical hold was shot, so the picture kept rolling, sometimes getting stuck halfway so the batter's legs were at the top of the screen and his head and shoulders down below. Half the time his bat was miss-ing altogether. Slake just kept watching like he didn't notice until the seventh inning, when he suddenly got up off the bed and slammed his hand against the side of the TV. The picture didn't budge so he yelled Piece of shit! and kicked the plug loose from the wall.

Then he opened a bottle of rye and poured them both a glass full, no water, no mix. She started to shake her head but the look in his eye said she should just drink it. And then he poured her another and offered her one of the last Quaaludes, which she thought might be a peace offering, but which she really didn't want.

Suit yourself, he said, and slipped it back in the bag.

She was pretty wasted by the time she finished her second glass of rye and she laid back, realizing that she hadn't been outside all day, that she hadn't put on anything besides a t-shirt so she didn't even have to take anything off before she fell asleep.

She only half heard Slake leaving. She had no idea how much time had passed before his hand was shaking her.

I got something for you, he said.

She opened her eyes. The room was full of late-night northern dusk, and at first she could only make out a shadow standing next to him.

I picked the prettiest one, he said. And don't worry, she's eighteen—I asked.

She tried to focus but she couldn't make out a face, could just see a silhouette, a sharp chin and jean jacket, a short denim skirt and folded arms. Slake gave the shadowy figure a nudge toward the bed and said, Let's go.

She felt cold metal buttons against her forearm, the weight of a body beside her. Slake was on the other side, pulling her t-shirt up to her neck and she wriggled, wanting him to stop, but it only had the effect of helping him lift it.

Tell her what you want her to do, baby, he whispered. When she didn't, Slake did, directing the action in a flat voice like he was telling someone how to place product on a shelf.

She might have passed out completely if he hadn't shaken her and asked if it was good, if she liked it. When she opened her eyes, Slake was leaning over her, watching intently, his face inches from where a strange mouth was slurping at her nipple.

It felt like nothing. It felt like she was completely numb to everything but how the undulating bed made her feel like throwing up. Slake turned his face so it was an inch from hers. Tell me how good it feels, he said. She understood then what he needed from her, what would make this end, so she said So good, and Yeah, and she moaned like she was expected to. And then she fell silent again, slipping just enough below the surface that the sudden touch of a hand between her thighs made her jolt. The hand drew back and Slake said, deep and quiet, Use your tongue—that's what she likes.

The girl pulled away. You didn't pay me enough for that.

Slake stood up fast, pulled cash out of his wallet and let it fall on the bed. His other hand tried to coerce what he wanted.

Hot breath and then waves of nausea washed over her, so intense now she couldn't help but draw her knees up and plaster a hand flat over her mouth. She heard a mumbled conversation at the foot of the bed, a zipper, then the bed lurched and a sharp chin drove into her kneecap. Her eyes flew open. When she raised her head from the pillow she saw clearly the face of the girl Slake was fucking. Saw the eyes looking back at her, but not at her. Not at anything. They were blank. Hollow. Hollow like a long dark tunnel that led straight to nowhere.

It was over in seconds. Slake collapsed into the jeans caught around his knees, resting his head on the foot of the bed. She felt the weight along her legs lift away and minutes or seconds after that, the door slammed.

She scrambled off the bed then, her knees rubbery and almost giving out, and staggered to the bathroom. Pulled the door shut and turned the lock before flicking on the harsh white light. She expected to be sick but when she caught sight of her reflection in the mirror, everything in her went still. Her skin was ash, the colour of burnt pages, and she was naked except for the t-shirt still caught around her throat.

She stayed in there a long time, long enough for Slake to start calling to her and then stop calling to her. Long enough that she hoped he might be asleep. But when she lay back down on the bed gingerly, pulling the sheet tight around her, Slake leaned over and kissed her cheek. She turned away from him, barely breathing.

Don't be jealous, he said. She didn't mean anything to me. It's you I love.

JERRY ROUNDED A BEND IN THE ROAD AS FAST AS SLAKE EVER would and Dawn turned away from the window to look over at Jerry, trying to imagine him wanting to watch his girlfriend make out with another girl.

She was glad when they stopped, glad for a strong and steady wind blowing across the Tablelands, for the surreal butterscotch of the rock and how much this terrain was unlike any she'd seen before.

Dawn wanted to go in a long way, to get up high and see how far it went, but her shoes weren't made for climbing and rocks kept slipping away underfoot. She might have scrabbled on but it seemed like Jerry was having trouble catching his breath, so she stopped and asked him for a cigarette, and they sat and smoked on the rocks, not very high up at all and just downstream from a thin waterfall.

Jerry pointed to a shallow pool near his feet. The water was milky and a froth of sandy-looking bubbles crowded along one edge. I read somewhere, he said, that those bubbles are actually the start of new rocks. Dawn leaned over to get a better look. Frail beginnings, Jerry was saying. But she couldn't tell at all if that was true.

And then another frail thing caught her attention. The landscape had looked so barren from a distance, as if scorched by some harsh chemical—yet just there, poking up between the rubble of rocks, she could make out a spray of white blossoms. She stood, took a few steps and her eyes refocused. Then she saw the whole secret garden—the fine shoots of grass bending in the breeze, the tiny flowers that shivered like stars, and just a bit further on, a splash of pure yellow.

Jerry was right beside her then. I wish I'd brought a camera, he said. It would be nice to get a picture of you out here.

When Dawn looked at him, he was holding his hands to his face, pretending to snap a photograph. Click, he said, click.

She smoothed her hair but the wind just threw it around again. Hey, she said, don't show those pictures to anybody. I look terrible.

He stepped toward her then, hands at his side but not settled there. My love, you don't know how to look terrible.

Dawn backed away, an involuntary reaction but an instinct she was glad for. This didn't need to get complicated. I guess we should be heading back, she said.

Jerry looked away, looked off toward the rise they hadn't climbed as if he was reconsidering it, then said, Guess so.

Dawn led the way, Jerry following at a distance that felt both relief and rebuke. When the ground leveled out, she chanced a glance behind her, saw he had stopped and stooped down for something. She waited then while he closed the gap between them.

Here, he said, extending a hand. You should have a memento of your first trip to the Earth's mantle.

Without meeting her eye, he handed her one of the butterscotch rocks, thumb-sized, smooth and dark on one side. She smiled without looking at him, tucked it in the front pocket of her jeans and after that, they walked more or less side by side the rest of the way.

At the car, he asked if she wanted to drive. I always drive, he said, but sometimes I think it would be nice if somebody else got behind the wheel so I could look around.

Dawn churned through all the ways that could go wrong before she said, Sure, I'll drive.

Too late—her fleeting hesitation had caught Jerry's attention like the flicker of an animal looming on the side of the road. He swerved.

You even know how to drive? You got a license?

She said of course she did, but he wanted proof then, wanted to see her driver's license and she could picture it, lying at the bottom of the duffel bag, the name on it all wrong and the damn thing expired. She didn't even know why she'd kept it.

I don't want to drive anyway, she said, heading for the passenger side. I like it better when you do.

Jerry climbed into the driver's seat like always. While he reversed out of the parking spot, he told Dawn that everyone should know how to drive. I can teach you, he said.

Jesus, Jerry, I told ya I know how. My dad taught me when I was sixteen.

Taught her because he wanted her to be useful. That was the word he'd used—useful, meaning he wanted her to go to the grocery store, pick up drycleaning, get a job. Everyone at school talked about driving like they'd sprouted wings, and she could only imagine their smiling parents tossing them car keys and telling them to go have fun. But fun was no longer a word in her father's vocabulary, not when he was talking to her, not once he had Carol to keep him company and a new baby daughter gathering up all his affection.

Jerry had pulled up to the highway but hadn't pulled out yet. He was studying her. That's the first time I ever heard you mention a family. So where is this father, what's he at?

Dawn could tell Jerry had been looking for just this kind of opening to wedge his thick black boot into, to force open the door into her life. She considered lying, but the true answer was straightforward enough.

He's dead. And my mother. They're both dead.

Jerry started to turn toward her, but then looked back at the road and she could tell he was uncomfortable, like he thought it might be a murder-suicide or a fiery car crash—something sudden and unspeakably tragic.

Cancer, she said, heart attack. Eight years apart.

Oh. Jerry settled back in his seat and pressed down on the accelerator and didn't say anything more until he had the car up to speed. Then he said, So you're an orphan?

I never thought of it like that, but yeah, I guess I am.

Me too, Jerry said. Me too.

He didn't tell her anything else about that and she didn't ask. The silence lasted almost the whole drive back to Corner Brook, lasted until Dawn was so unnerved she started to prompt him, asking him where he'd grown up—Hamilton until he was fifteen, then Deer Lake—and how long he'd been driving truck—lotta years now—and if he'd ever been married.

Engaged once, didn't turn out right. Hard at the time, but I'm glad for it now. I wasn't ready to settle down...back then.

Dawn couldn't tell if he meant to emphasize it like that, meant for it to sound like he was saying more than he was saying, but she decided against asking if he was ready to settle down now. No point opening a door she had no intention of walking through.

When he pulled up to the Blue Iris Inn, Dawn said thank you too quickly, and she leapt out of the car without a backward glance.

Later, when she was getting undressed, she pulled the small rock Jerry had given her from her pocket. Such a foreign sort of stone from such a strange place. She thought of the bubbles along the edge of the puddle and decided she liked the far-fetched idea of that cauldron, of new rocks forming from a milky sheen.

She saw then how over the whole of the last year, she'd been thinking about her life here as some kind of fictitious and temporary state, like a dull dream she'd slipped into and would soon rise out of. But she could see there was no easy way to turn around and go back home. In fact, there was no way at all. The tracks had been torn out right behind her.

She set the rock on the little table beside her bed, nudging a paperback copy of *The Other Side of Midnight* to make room for it. Thinking this is the ground I'm standing on now.

And then thinking she didn't even mind. There was nothing calling her back to where she'd been before, nothing that tethered her to anything. Nothing except an expired driver's license, which she retrieved from the bottom of her money-stuffed duffel bag.

There were matches in the hotel ashtray. When she opened the matchbook cover, the inside flap told her that she could be anything she wanted, that she could train at home to be a bookkeeper or a television repairman. And in the bright flare of a lit match, even those future paths seemed glorious.

She held the flame to the corner of her license. It took four matches for the official, coated cardboard to catch but when it did, it went up so fast she was afraid of burning her fingers. She raced to the toilet, hovered until she saw all her particulars disappear in the flame, then dropped the torch into the bowl and flushed it all away.

Later, unable to sleep, she caught herself singing snatches from one of those new Springsteen songs. *Adam raised a Cain.* And she thought if this place, if Corner Brook, Newfoundland, was east of Eden—and why not?—then it was where she'd been cast and where she was meant to be.

In the glow from the clock, she could make out the little rock on her bedside table. She picked it up and rubbed her thumb across its one smooth surface. It was the only souvenir she had, the only object that gave her any history at all. She had no other mementoes and no photographs either, nothing that tied her to anyone or anything she was before.

And all she had to do was keep it that way.

PART TWO

1979

MARGARET WAS IN A STATE, ALL BUSTLE AND FLUSTER, AND she needed Dawn to stop vacuuming and watch the front desk again while she ran an errand. This time, it was picking out the stationery, getting the printer going on those invitations. And it was urgent like every one of Margaret's errands were, now that the wedding was just a few months away.

Dawn had already made the mistake of asking why the wedding couldn't just be moved a little later, seeing as it was happening at the Blue Iris and they weren't booked up solid for September.

Don't be stupid, Margaret had spit back. Any later and my bride'll be as big as a house.

The bride was Margaret's youngest, Andrea. Dawn had come across the two of them discussing the wedding details a couple of times—come across them accidentally because Dawn had developed a habit of wandering in the late evening to escape the confines of the little room that felt, more and more, like a solitary cell.

The first time, she'd watched them from just outside the dining room. It was obvious, even from a distance, that this wedding was a party Margaret was throwing, that Andrea didn't care what colour the napkins were, or who sat where, or whether the meal was chicken or beef. The next morning, Dawn found them again, still hashing out the menu as if they'd been at it all night. Andrea spotted Dawn, locked eyes with her, and then Dawn saw that what Andrea really wanted was for every one of the guests to choke on whatever meal Margaret finally settled on.

Dawn had seen all that, yet somehow she'd missed the circumstances of Andrea's situation, assuming the bride-to-be was always that shape—the shape they used to call buxom—that she tended toward doughy like her mother, even if she was half a head taller.

Margaret leaned over the reception desk to grab her purse. Don't know how soon I'll be back, she said to Dawn. Depends on the fight we have. That child's always been more trouble than the other two put together.

Bustling out, the door wide open, Margaret turned back to Dawn. Trade the lot of 'em for one more like you.

She pulled the door firmly shut and the turbulent air finally settled. Then Dawn looked down at the reservation book and there wasn't a breath in the place.

She spent the next two hours just watching the closed door, steeling herself for disappointment. There were so many variables—age, height, eye colour—and ten months had passed since Dawn had flushed away the charred remains of her driver's license. She'd been hoping ever since. Lately, she'd started to wish she'd christened herself Mary or maybe Linda. Seemed like there was one of those through the door every couple of days.

It was almost four when the reservation finally arrived. At a glance—and that's all Dawn dared, a glance—the woman looked to be not much older and only a little heavier, her hair a shade darker. But Dawn knew it was eye colour, impossible to fake, that mattered most. She didn't have the nerve to look up as she slid a registration card across the desk. She could feel the artery in her neck pulsing, put a hand to her throat to hide it and focused on the pen as it filled out the registration card. A simple, sloping signature. *Dawn Taylor.* An address in Guelph.

Ontario, Dawn said, because she had the feeling she should say something.

Yes—but I was invited here. When Dawn Taylor said that, it sounded like a confession, like she thought she needed to declare a good reason for arriving in such an unlikely place.

Dawn looked up then, looked straight into slate-blue eyes that absolutely glittered with enthusiasm. She knew she was behind in offering the usual hospitality, the smile that confirmed this guest's importance, but she was afraid her lips might quiver. Afraid she might make herself memorable in some way.

It didn't matter—Dawn Taylor needed no smile. She understood her own importance. I'm giving a presentation at the college, she said, her left hand making an emphatic gesture in the wrong direction as if the actual whereabouts of the little college were beyond her concern. When she did, the sun caught on the diamond ring she was wearing—a ring that suggested she wouldn't be needing her name much longer anyway.

Dawn finally offered that smile and turned to get the room key. Margaret had marked #215 beside the reservation, but Dawn reached for #221. End of the hall, no one nearby. After she'd handed over the key and pointed to the elevator and Dawn Taylor was out of sight, Dawn sank down into the wooden dining chair Margaret kept behind the counter and tried to think of what to do next.

She left in the morning without a word to Margaret— left without making any beds or changing any towels—just ducked out the back door and got in a cab and it was only once the Blue Iris was out of sight that she dared to pull out Dawn Taylor's driver's license and take a good look.

She'd barely slept, imagining all the ways she could get this done and all the ways she could get caught. Twice, she'd gone to stand outside 221, listening. Wondering how heavy a sleeper Dawn Taylor was, if there was a chance she'd sleep right through a break-in. But in the end she didn't have the guts, not until she saw Dawn Taylor in the dining room bent over a spread of papers, the pen in her hand hovering and her lips moving as she read. She looked up just long enough to order breakfast and bent again over her presentation.

Dawn had gone straight to 221 then. The purse was open on the unmade bed, the wallet nestled at its bottom. She found the license front and centre, a birth certificate in a separate fold. Behind that, unexpected, a creased and yellowing piece of paper with an official crest at the top. It was a certificate of Canadian birth abroad. Dawn Taylor was American born but a Canadian citizen, and that dual identity felt exactly right to Dawn.

In the cab, Dawn studied the license. Dawn Taylor was born in 1951, which made her almost eight years older, and she was saddled with the too-distinct middle name Marica. Dawn slid the license from its plastic sleeve and pulled out the very sharp pencil she'd swiped off Margaret's accounting ledger. She worried away at the final digit of the birth year just enough with the eraser, then drew a few careful lines.

At driver licensing, her hair pulled back into a high ponytail to hide her blondest outer layer, she filled out a form and made sure to pick the wicket where a middle-aged man would serve her. Handing him the pilfered license, she said, I just moved here and I don't have a car yet. I plan to buy one soon, but I don't know what kind to get.

He told her he drove a Chevy and they were good cars, and then he asked if she wanted new or used and he went on about horsepower and handling. She nodded and prodded him with new questions and by the time he was done checking over her details and signing off on her license application, they'd agreed that the Chevy Nova was probably exactly the right car for her, and he'd okayed her hair colour as light brown and 1957 as her birth date and her middle name as Marie.

He handed her a temporary Newfoundland license—the permanent one would come in the mail—and gave her back the old one so she could keep it for posterity. Later, before she returned it to her namesake's wallet, she erased the pencil marks she'd made, leaving just a faint shadow she couldn't remove.

2013

Cheryl should have left before the rows all around her filled in, but she realized it too late. Realized it only after the whole lecture theatre had packed up, eager bodies pressing into every seat and then, when the seats were gone, lining both sides of the theatre, standing two to a step, shoulder to shoulder with their backs pressed against the wall.

They'd oversold the tickets, that was clear. Cheryl knew someone in a back room was worried about how the media would cover the carnage if a fire broke out and the exits were blocked. She'd watched the minions who were sent out to impose that firing squad stance so the aisle was open.

As the lights dimmed, Cheryl edited herself: The time to leave was before I got here.

A man in a beige cardigan, pencil trousers and red sneakers—Attempted Mr. Rogers, Cheryl thought, what a crime—was laying into an introduction, slathering it on like mayonnaise at a cheap diner. And then he was praising the audience too, just for being there. For making the effort to *be there for the kids*. Before he stepped away to make room for the main event, he paused. Gazed seriously out into the crowd. Said, I need to remind you to please make sure your phones are turned off.

Cheryl had noticed the signs on her way in—signs in the lobby and on all the doors—bright red letters: no phones please. Above the words, a slashed-through image of a cell phone that looked like it had stumbled right out of 1999. But the man at the podium must have thought a significant portion of the audience couldn't read or grasp basic pictograms, because he didn't leave it at that.

Not just silenced, he said, I mean off. I mean turned off and put *away*. Another pause, another smile. It's a habit we all need to get better at, right? *For the kids.*

There was a flurry of compliance, women leaning down to rifle in purses, the few men in the audience contorting to get at their pockets. Beams of dying light and the faint humming of phones going dormant.

When the audience looked up from its task, the woman they'd all paid so much to see was striding to the podium. Hands came up in unison to applaud and Cheryl went along with the crowd. In her peripheral vision, she saw backs peel away from the walls, bodies clog the exit aisles and then she understood that no one was getting out of here until this was over.

Why the hell hadn't she anticipated how crowded this theatre would become? The speaker had sold so many copies of her book *Don't Break the Egg: The Delicate Shell of Youth* that she'd gained a cult following. People called her the Egg Lady and other people knew exactly who that was. Cheryl hadn't read the book—or any book like it, ever—but she'd read a lot about it on the internet during the hour after hour she'd spent trying to figure out what the hell she'd done wrong with Jenna. Those hours, at least, a respite from the hours Cheryl spent trying to get stories about herself—stories that didn't contain phrases like *racial slur*—to appear sooner in a

Google search, to push that specious story lower until it fell right off the front page of every search. Late at night, exhausted, she sometimes just spent hours seeking out examples of careers that had been demolished, then resurrected. Also, examples of parents who were doing even worse than she was.

Right. That's why she'd come. The slim hope of finding answers, of getting some assistance and, please god, maybe even a little redemption, some small suggestion that her daughter's self-destruction wasn't all Cheryl's fault.

The Egg Lady hadn't said a word yet, but she was holding an egg up over her head, the distinct white oval poised between her index finger and her thumb. An actual fucking egg, extra large from the looks of it. She walked around the podium, egg aloft. Walked right to the edge of the stage and for one glorious instant, Cheryl thought she might hurl it into the crowd.

Instead, the woman leaned down and placed the egg just there, perilously near the stage's edge, and let her hand hover over it until she was confident it wouldn't roll. Then she stood upright, walked back to the podium, leaned into the microphone and said, Friends, please—don't break the egg.

Thunderous applause. The room shook with it. Cheryl thought she saw the egg twitch and she must have, because someone in the front row leapt up and moved into position to save it should it start to roll toward the drop-off. Eventually the Egg Lady held up her hands to stifle the applause. When it was quiet enough, she leaned again into the microphone and said, addressing the vigilant protector of the egg, Thank you, friend—you are obviously an excellent parent.

Cheryl wished the speaker had said *eggcellent*, a fleeting thought before regret washed over her. Obviously she should have taken a seat in the front row so—

Stop it, that's ridiculous. Obviously that eggcellent parent was a plant, was all part of the show. Cheryl took out her phone and

Googled the phrase *egg lady excellent parent,* but none of the top results spoke to these rehearsed antics. Cheryl went back up to the search bar, typed in *cheryl hayworth.*

Award-winning filmmaker excuses use of racial slur was still top of the charts.

What was the point of even trying? It was never going away. And while Cheryl was distracted trying to bury those shameful search results, her own daughter had been left unattended, free to find a starring role in her own online nightmare.

#WorstMotherEver

It was pure chance that Cheryl had spotted an ad for this event while scrolling through a news story about her ex. She'd clicked the ad on impulse, bought her ticket right then before she had a chance to change her mind. She should have bought a ticket for Miguel, too.

No, she should have handed her ticket over to him, let him, the sanguine stepparent, come listen to this shit. Let him figure out what the hell was wrong with Jenna. After all, Jenna still liked him, still called him up every couple of days just to check in—or maybe, probably, Cheryl figured, to complain about what a crazy bitch her mom was. Cheryl couldn't be sure what, exactly, they talked about since she never let herself hover outside Jenna's closed door, listening.

One thing Cheryl knew for sure: Jenna hadn't told Miguel about her online escapades. And she'd made Cheryl promise not to tell him either, which was a sign, at least, that Jenna felt some remorse. And Cheryl honoured that promise, though it meant she had no one to talk to about it. She sure as hell wasn't telling her sister or her parents, and she wasn't exactly replete with good friends these days—not unless you counted the social media kind, the ones who didn't know anything about her now, but remembered her from college and sent a useless stream of U2 videos and stupid memes they thought she would surely adore.

Anyway, even if she'd told Miguel, begged him to come here with her, he couldn't. He was off filming in Honduras this week and fucking his production manager, Cheryl knew, and since she was here and she was the only actual, sacrificing, all-in parent Jenna had, she needed to knock off the smirking and start to listen to the Egg Lady. Needed to stop listening with that part of her brain that was always looking for the weak spot, the crack that opened into the real story behind the self-made expert who was bobbing her head at the podium as if nodding at her own genius. Bobbing her head like—

Ha!

Cheryl battled the urge to get out her phone, search to see if anyone had already dubbed this crazy woman the Chicken Lady. She wished she'd made Jenna come along so she could whisper it in her ear and they could snicker. But of course she hadn't told Jenna or anyone else she was coming to this. Because come on, ridiculous.

Come on, listen.

Young people are both fragile and perceptive, the Chicken Lady was saying. If you show anger towards a young person, you're sending two messages: they're not good enough, and you've abandoned them in favour of your own selfish emotions.

Nod, nod. Nod. And this time, not just from behind the podium. Cheryl looked down the row to her left, and then to her right, noting how many bobbleheads she'd have to squeeze past to escape. When the woman next to her met her gaze, Cheryl rolled her eyes and whispered, Didn't everybody's parents yell? The woman scowled. Cheryl turned back to the stage and wondered if she was being defensive. Maybe she'd been damaged by her parents' yelling in ways she didn't know about, and maybe that linked to the damage she'd done to Jenna, which was responsible for the way Jenna was behaving. Maybe it was proof of bad parenting, rolling her eyes at good parenting advice. She crossed her ankles and tried to listen harder.

But she couldn't get past the bobbing. In front of her, a sea of heads all moved in unison as if listening to some catchy tune.

Was there enough light in the room to film this? She tapped record on her phone and held it at forehead height, held it there for several seconds, hoping, until the woman to her right nudged her with an elbow, hard, and pointed to the end of the aisle.

Shit. Some kind of uniformed security person was pointing at her, waggling his finger like parents do—or used to, anyway. Shaking his big, beefy head. She couldn't make out much else, except his presence was enough to have pushed a wide swath of sideliners sheepishly back against the wall. Cheryl nodded and dropped the phone into her lap. She could feel hot disapproval emanating off the woman who'd elbowed her.

At least her phone could still record sound, she thought.

Five seconds later, she stopped recording. What the hell was wrong with her? When she'd been a new parent, a lone parent without even a grandparent nearby to rely on, Cheryl had been desperate for the kind of wisdom she could get here. Once, she'd even tried to banish the word no from her home after watching an afternoon talk show. No was a poison dart of negativity that retarded a child's development, an expert explained from an immaculate TV-set living room. No was a slammed door, a full stop on possibility.

At the time, Cheryl had just wrested herself, fully and finally, from any contact with Jenna's father. It had taken more time than expected, though she'd started even before she was pregnant. Exhausted from struggling to escape that velvet cage of mediocrity, she was wide open to the TV expert's message because just then, possibility felt like air returning to a pearl diver's lungs. But never saying no to a headstrong toddler turned out to be much harder than it had sounded. Cheryl had tried anyway—tried for months— turning the full force of poisoned negativity on herself when she caught herself failing at it.

Now she regretted all that effort. It turned out *no* was the one word her daughter absolutely needed to have in her vocabulary.

Cheryl needed better advice than that and she needed it urgently. The Chicken-and-Egg Lady, she knew, was about to lay out the rules for parenting and Cheryl needed to concentrate. She needed to hear those rules. Except the right phrase had just popped into her head.

She turned back to her phone, typed *egg lady lays an egg on stage* into the search bar. Boom, there it was—an exact match in a Sacramento headline, a description of the same performance that Cheryl was watching, right down to the helpful, spontaneous friend in the front row.

That was it. That was exactly the problem—it was too easy these days to be exposed. And what Cheryl and Jenna were both suffering from was too much exposure.

Young people are difficult, the Egg Lady was saying. They shape shift and they rebel—but that's their job. Now I'll give you the recipe for doing your job, for helping them take flight.

Cheryl's head was nodding along with every other head in the theatre, but it was the words *take flight* that had captured her attention. Into her phone, she typed *interesting trips off the grid*.

1982

MARGARET WAS STANDING NEXT TO DAWN AT THE RECEPTION desk, checking over the expense report. Sliding her pen down the column, punching numbers into her electronic adding machine, then returning to the print-out to make small ticks beside the numbers she'd already punched. Every five or six numbers, she'd lift her head and sniff the air like a wild animal who sensed danger. Then she'd bend again to her task.

Dawn knew what it was about, that sniffing, and it made her aggravated, made her fingers clumsy on the keyboard. Twice now she'd had to hit escape, to back out of the report she was trying to create and start fresh, the blinking amber cursor as accusing as Margaret's pointed sniffs.

Can't see how that damn diddlebox makes anything faster, Margaret said. It was the first thing she'd said to Dawn all morning, and that silence, too, was an accusation. Normally while they reconciled the monthly report, Dawn was obliged to listen to a stream of patter, to the details of whatever elaborate family function Margaret was planning. And Margaret had plenty of time to plan now that Dawn and the computer had completely taken over the reception duties.

And the computer—well that was Jerry's fault.

Jerry had bought a personal computer the first chance he'd got, bringing it over to the island in a box marked IBM, strapped into the same seat Dawn had arrived in years earlier. Within months, Jerry had started exhorting Margaret to get one too, and get with the now of modern business. Virtues of the new age, he kept saying.

Margaret resisted for months but Jerry kept it up—and kept trying to drag Dawn into his camp at every turn. When Sears started carrying them, Jerry brought the store catalogue to the Blue Iris and waved it in Margaret's face. If these machines were for sale at Sears, he argued, she could hardly deny this was the wave of the future.

A week later, he brought over his IBM and set it up—free of charge, he said. Then he crawled around on the floor for a while, wrangling a viper's nest of cables that ran to the monitor and the printer. When he straightened up and shook the stiffness out of his legs, he was beaming. Now I got an excuse to go buy myself the newest model, he told Dawn over the desk.

Margaret said it was all too much for her. Said she couldn't keep up, couldn't possibly master the blinking cursor and tab key and data entry regime, though Dawn could see it was nothing more complicated than filling out a form the right way. She tried to train Margaret, tried to ease her into it using familiar pen and paper language, but they'd both given up and Margaret had given Dawn the job full-time—a real salary job, with a raise and a paycheque that Dawn deposited into her bank account.

Opening that account had been her next big step after her driver's license had arrived in the mail. Dawn had walked down to the bank in the afternoon with that license in her new wallet, resting against the stolen certificate of birth abroad. She'd kept the certificate, figuring she might need it. Figuring it wouldn't be missed for a while—at least not until that other Dawn Taylor needed to cross a border.

Alongside her new identity, Dawn carried four hundred dollars in cash to the bank. It felt to her like just the right amount—like the life's savings of a young woman who was new in town.

She'd taken pains to look her best, had rehearsed what she'd say and practiced her signature, but she was too nervous when she got to the bank to go straight in. She had to walk the full length of the block, suck down a cigarette in each direction, before she felt steady enough.

Her anxiety was unwarranted. Within minutes, a smiling teller handed Dawn a passbook with her account number written on the first page. After that, it all got easier. When an iron-haired woman blocked her path at the entrance to Sears and offered Dawn a free umbrella to apply for a credit card, she applied. Two weeks later her card came, accompanied by a letter about her credit limit, which they'd based on Dawn's own exaggerated estimate of her income.

Next, she risked applying for a social insurance number, figuring she'd need it if she was ever to move beyond cleaning hotel rooms for cash. She'd doctored the birthdate on the certificate and dabbed it with bleach, hoping to fade some of Marica from sight, but the bleach ate a hole right through the paper, leaving just Mar. In the government office, the clerk pointed to the hole, her face a mask of disapproval. Dawn had to clasp her hands together to stop them from trembling when she said, Sorry, I should get a new one. It says Marie.

The clerk couldn't take her word for it, of course, so Dawn had to take out her driver's license to prove it. After that, the paperwork was done without another question.

Dawn memorized the details of her new identity the way she had when she'd used someone else's ID to buy beer underage. She practiced responding to her name and rattling off her new birthdate, and she read up on being a Capricorn—which would never have been her first choice—in case she ever had to fake it. She even invented a backstory—her Pennsylvania birth, the family's immigration to Canada, all of it—and trained herself to know how old she would have been at significant moments in history. Dawn conjured a whole memory of how she'd heard about President Kennedy's shooting, what her made-up teacher had told the class, and she rehearsed it until it seemed like a real memory to her. When no one ever asked, when even Jerry never offered a theory on JFK's assassination, she raised it with him just so she could get the story off her chest.

After that, she stopped rehearsing. People knew she came from the mainland and that was enough information for them, even if *mainland* was so broad it could mean just across the gulf or clear over on the other side of the continent. For that matter, it could mean the south of France or the far side of the moon. Nobody cared about specifics. All anyone ever asked Dawn was what had brought her to Newfoundland, and did she love it?

Everyone just believed Dawn was who she said she was, and so after a while, she believed it too. Believed she was Dawn Taylor, age twenty-five. She didn't even mind losing more than a year, could see how that time might be fouled by bad choices, dumb choices—and she'd certainly made enough of those in the year since she'd moved out of the Blue Iris and into an apartment of her own.

It was an uphill walk to her new address, but everything about the place was downhill. It was bigger than her tiny cell of a room at the hotel, but it felt just as claustrophobic. Rundown and gloomy, the few small windows coated outside with grime. Still, it was all she could afford on what Margaret paid her, and Dawn had decided not to use her secret money—Slake's money—until she had a solid plan, some direction for this life she was inventing. Even though she had a whole identity and a bank account to go with it, she kept that money rolled up inside a couple of Pringles cans and tucked at the back of her only kitchen cupboard.

There were two bars on the street that served shift workers all day and into the very smallest hours of the night. The raucous talk, revving engines and occasional brawls kept Dawn awake or else woke her up, but it only took a few months for the noise to turn from a nuisance to a lure. She started stopping at the bar after work—no matter what time work ended. Stopping for a single drink just to get a feel for the place, to have a conversation that didn't involve handing over a key or calling a cab or fixing some shortcoming, real or imagined. After that drink, she'd go home and change out of her starchy white hotel blouse, eat a late dinner and try to settle into a book.

But if she got restless—and many nights, she did—she went back across the street again and stayed longer. Sometimes, she didn't leave until last call and sometimes, she didn't leave alone. The night before had been a night like that, and Dawn had come to work hungover and unshowered—not for the first time.

That's what Margaret's sniffing performance was about. Dawn figured she must smell like last night's debauchery. But she also knew Margaret couldn't afford to fire her—that she'd never find someone else who'd work almost every day, sometimes twelve hours a day, for such a minimal salary.

Dawn watched the printer do its work, the print head marching back and forth across the paper a relief from Margaret's pinched up, disapproving expression. The rhythm of it was soothing and the sound drowned out the oppressive quiet.

While she was stripping the perforated edges off the last report she'd printed, she looked up from the paper in her hand to see Margaret scrutinizing her.

I suppose it's lonely for you, no people and whatnot here, Margaret said before Dawn could look away. I'll get someone else to work the next Sunday shift and you'll come for a proper holiday meal at my place.

Jerry picked Dawn up and drove her over to Margaret's house for Easter dinner. On the way, he gave her a rundown of who was who—names and connections, branches and twigs of a massive family tree. When he propelled Dawn through the living room, his hand on the small of her back to steer her through the labyrinth, Jerry repeated what he'd said to her in the car—all the details about who was connected to him and how. And each time he introduced her the same way. This is Dawn Taylor, he said. Said it time and again without once offering an explanation of who she was or how she fit.

Dawn smiled her hospitality smile, smiled hard, and fought the urge to shake loose of Jerry's grip, kick his knee out and make a run for it. All she wanted was to be back at the hotel, back where strangers spelled out their particulars and expected nothing but a key in return.

When Jerry had finally exhausted his introductions, he went to see about getting a drink, leaving Dawn caught in the midst of his impossibly gnarled family tree. She looked down the length of the set table, which ran the whole of the dining room and cut across half the living room, too. There must have been twenty-six chairs. Two card tables leaned against the wall, ready to take the overflow.

She'd known to expect a crowd, known that the Bakers and Bennetts were all about the big family gathering, about making a fuss over every possible occasion, every holiday and birthday and anniversary. They'd even had a massive early morning family breakfast on the occasion of Prince Charles and Lady Diana's wedding. Jerry had invited Dawn to that event, but she'd told him she wasn't getting up before daybreak just to witness history and eat waffles with strangers, and maybe that's why this next invitation was so many months coming.

As soon as Jerry was out of sight, a short woman planted herself in front of Dawn. She had coppery hair—henna, Dawn guessed—and she was Margaret's sister. Or maybe she was another one of Jerry's cousins. Or both. Anyway, the woman had an urgent look on her face, and a question, which she asked at high volume.

Now Dawn, what is it your mother cooks for Easter back on the mainland? A ham or a turkey?

Dawn had never anticipated a question like this, and she was keenly aware of the sudden hush in the room, the faces turned her way. Turkey, she blurted, though she really wasn't sure. All she remembered of Easter from her childhood was chocolate in the morning and then a jittery funk that lasted all day. But she could remember that her father had once tried to cook a turkey. Or they both had, because that's what they did, learned how to cook things together—pot roast and pineapple chicken, recipes from her mother's old *McCall's* magazines, a side of mashed or boiled until they discovered Minute Rice was easier. But Dawn didn't offer those details, didn't say anything after turkey.

So she'll have a turkey on today then, the woman said, and Dawn shook her head and said, No. No, she's dead.

All around her, every head turned in her direction, every face open and staring. She felt like a rare specimen in a jar or else like a celebrity caught in a scandal, microphones pointing and cameras flashing. She forced her lips into a stiff smile.

Poor lamb, one of the older aunts pronounced from the couch, setting off a murmur of sympathy. Well you'll get a proper meal tonight.

Dawn wanted to bolt but there was nowhere to go—she was surrounded on all sides with that massive table dead ahead. And then Andrea appeared at her shoulder, leaned right into Dawn's ear and said, Follow me.

And Dawn did, followed Andrea as she wove expertly through the crowd and down a hallway of shag carpet and closed doors until they got to one that was a few inches ajar. Somewhere in the hall, Dawn had come back to herself enough to notice that Andrea had a squirming baby slung over one shoulder.

The room was dark and Andrea plopped down into an armchair without turning on a light. In the dimness, Dawn saw her haul up

her shirt and then the bra that covered one bulbous breast. God
they're a handful, aren't they? Andrea said as she attached the baby
to the breast, and Dawn wasn't sure if she meant babies or all those
relatives, so she didn't respond. She was too busy working out her
escape route—first from this room, then from this house.

Jesus, you look like a scared rabbit, Andrea said. I'm not gonna
eat you. I'm just out of my tree with nobody to talk to, and I can't
feed her out there with all the uncles— Andrea tilted her head
toward the door, the living room, the uncles— I mean, imagine the
scandal of it. Not that they wouldn't expect it from me.

Dawn's eyes had adjusted enough to make out Andrea's pale
round face, the big round eyes looking up at her. Expecting something, though Dawn couldn't guess what.

Figured we keep seeing each other around, Andrea said, so we
should get to know each other.

They hadn't, in fact, seen each other for years, not since Andrea's
wedding—the bride an explosion of satin and lace, her enormous
skirt starting just high enough to hide the baby bulge. Margaret the
overbearing mother-of-the-bride, the restaurant staff near out of
their minds trying to get dinner out on time. And Dawn in a trim
white blouse and black skirt carrying trays of hors d'oeuvres, struggling to navigate the over-abundance of family, hobbled because her
skirt was too long and too narrow.

The only words Dawn had ever exchanged with Andrea before
this was when the bride had waved Dawn over to get more of those
sausage pastries.

I'm Dawn Taylor, she said finally. And though she'd just heard
Jerry say the name twenty-five times, it suddenly felt treacherous
on her tongue.

Oh, I know who you are. You're Jerry's girlfriend.

Dawn gave her head an emphatic shake. I'm not, she said, and
Andrea laughed, a peel of ripe delight that startled the infant in her

arms. I know—that's why I said it. She paused to resettle the baby
back on the breast, then asked, So what brought you here?

Jerry did, I guess.

Another peel of laughter, hard to resist. You're funny. But I'm
serious—why would you come here? And why would you stay?

It was Dawn's turn to laugh, and she did her best to make it con-
vincing. Just looking for something…different, I guess.

I'd say you found it. Andrea flipped the baby over into her other
arm and shoved her other nipple in its mouth. Dawn watched in
fascination, and then pretended not to be watching when Andrea
caught her at it.

You get good at this after you do it a million times, Andrea said.
She pointed at the bed and told Dawn to sit down. Go ahead, you
won't bother him. I swear he wouldn't wake up if you sat right on
his head.

Only then did Dawn notice a small figure asleep on the big bed
that dominated the room. The little boy, Jacob—Margaret had
shown Dawn about a hundred pictures—curled on his side, fully
dressed, shoes and all, lying still on top of the bedspread.

Dawn perched carefully on a corner and asked what the baby's
name was. She recalled it was a girl but couldn't think if she'd ever
heard a name.

Tara Elizabeth, Andrea said. After my Aunt Betty, the only one
of the whole crowd I like.

Tara—like the plantation?

Andrea grinned. Tara, because frankly my dear, I don't give a damn.

Dawn glanced over at the little boy. The only sign he was even
alive was the occasional slight wiggle of the pacifier in his mouth.

Andrea smoothed a hand around the curls on the infant's head.
I guess you know all about me and my troubles?

Dawn did—knew enough, anyway. After the wedding storm
had passed, Margaret had settled down for a while. There was the

excitement of the baby, of course, a holy grandson, and Margaret was thrilled and no longer minded so much how he got there. But then Margaret went across to St. John's to see the little guy and came home all worked up because Andrea was pregnant again.

Getting on like an old Catholic—I thought you girls knew how to prevent this sort of thing. Margaret said it like an accusation, like Dawn was somehow culpable just for being the same generation.

And then all the drama and fuss over Andrea's marriage ending, Andrea showing up at her mother's when she was seven months pregnant, a toddler in tow and no real explanation why. Telling Dawn about it, Margaret had wondered aloud if there was another woman, one without so much encumbrance. But anyway it didn't matter—to Margaret's mind, this was all just another way her youngest had come up short. I know better than anybody that girl's hard to live with, she'd said. She hasn't shut up since she learned to talk. How she'll manage now with two babies and no man around to feed them, I don't know.

But of course Margaret did know, because she'd already put in an offer on a house not far from her own—one of those new, modern, vinyl-clad bi-levels with a full apartment in the lower level.

Andrea pried the baby off her nipple with her pinky finger. The baby's head lolled away and lay still as a doll.

Hardly seems fair, Andrea was saying, you knowing so much about me, and me hardly knowing a thing about you.

Even in the darkened room, Andrea's gaze was like a laser beam and Dawn thought this seemed like the perfect time to duck out, to take her chances back with that big crowd. But Andrea was up on her feet, leaning toward her. Plopping the baby in Dawn's arms like she was dumping a sack of flour onto the counter. Dawn instinctively made a cradle, even while her mouth made a noise like a protest.

If Andrea heard, she didn't react. She just got busy fastening her bra and pulling down her shirt, talking the whole time. Dawn wasn't

listening, though. She was smelling the baby, remembering the way
her stepsister had smelled when she was this small. A smell Dawn
thought of as goodness even back then, even when she hated the
idea of her dad having a new daughter.

Fine, don't tell, Andrea said, both hands busy riling up her mass
of wavy hair. So you work at the hotel and you live in a shithole, and
I guess that's all I need to know.

Dawn heard shithole, pulled her nose up out of the baby and
stared at Andrea, whose hair was now as wide as her shoulders. She
didn't have to ask who'd told Andrea that. Jerry was the only one
who'd ever seen Dawn's place, and only because he'd insisted on
dropping by with a housewarming gift—a spider plant that had died
a few months later from a lack of sunlight or else a lack of nurturing.
Now she was glad that plant was dead.

The sound of chairs scraping back drifted into the room. Dawn
stood and passed the baby to Andrea. Sounds like it's time to eat,
she said, and left without another word.

When she emerged into the living room, blinking from the bright
lights, Jerry waved her over and she wedged into the empty chair
next to him, the plate there already more than half full of the turkey
and cabbage and potatoes he'd dished out for her.

She was spooning carrot wheels, glistening and sticky, onto her
plate when Andrea sauntered out of the bedroom alone, empty
handed, and took the last remaining seat directly across from
Dawn. Dawn focused on her food, shovelled a big load of turkey
into her mouth.

We've been talking, me and Dawn, Andrea said as she dropped a
dollop of potatoes in the middle of her plate. I've decided she's not
half as bad as I thought. So yes, Dawn is gonna live downstairs and
we're gonna be roomies.

Proper thing, Jerry said, and Dawn's jaw stopped working, a wad
of turkey still heavy on her tongue.

Well I'm glad that's settled, Margaret added from where she loomed at the head of the table.

Dawn looked from Jerry to Margaret to Andrea, who was drowning her plate in gravy, but she couldn't catch an eye. Then she looked down the whole length of the table at all the Bakers and the Bennetts bent over their supper plates, the sound of knives and forks and chewing filling the space, but no one looked up, not until a piercing wail came from the bedroom down the hall.

DAWN WAITED UNTIL SHE WAS BACK AT WORK BEHIND THE desk, sure-footed and necessary, to let Margaret know she had no interest in moving just now. Go have a look was all Margaret said. And once Dawn did—once she saw the place was open and new and clean, that she had a separate entrance, her own kitchen and bath—she decided it might be okay for a little while.

At the end of the month, Jerry helped her move what little furniture she had to bring: a spindly table and two chairs, a mismatched mattress and box spring and the striped armchair, cat-scratched and seat-worn, that she'd plucked off the curb on garbage day. After they'd hauled it all in, Dawn looked around and saw that what had filled her last shitty apartment looked haphazard and ridiculous here.

I guess there's a few garage sales in my future, she said, and Jerry told her to buy herself something new once in awhile. Then he took her hand. It's a big favour you're doing us, taking on Andrea like this.

Dawn wanted to know what the hell he meant—wanted to say hang on, that wasn't the deal—but Andrea was already hollering down the stairs and then barreling through the door that separated Dawn from the rest of the house. She hit the brakes when she came to the impasse of Dawn and Jerry. I'm ordering pizza, she said, her voice still close to a holler. What do you want on yours, roomie?

And Dawn saw she was in it now. In it, and there was no stepping out.

1986

THE PHONE RANG JUST AS DAWN WAS DRIFTING BACK INTO something close to sleep. Her eyes flew open. Quarter after one on her bedside clock. She shut her eyes again, counted the rings. Four, five, six. Silence. She flipped over and levered a pillow over her head to block out the mid-afternoon sun, muffle the noise coming from upstairs. She could still hear Andrea shouting something at Tara, could hear the raw edge in that, the impatience she knew could ramp up to something angrier.

She should get up, go help. Tara always came home from nursery school full of evil spirits. But Dawn had been avoiding upstairs all morning, and her door was uncharacteristically closed, locked for the first time she could remember, and she figured she should keep it like that. Figured everything would go more smoothly if she just had a little more sleep.

She closed her eyes again. The phone rang again—eight rings this time, something insistent and pleading in every one of them. Dawn curled her hands into fists and kept her arms crossed against her chest. She knew it was probably Margaret, calling to see if she could come in, or else it was Derek—or Darren—or whatever his name had been. Was.

Or Jerry. Probably Jerry. Tuesday was the equivalent of Dawn's Sunday, and he was home this week. Sometimes he called just to chat.

But Dawn didn't want to talk to Jerry any more than she wanted to talk to anyone else. When the ringing ceased, she reached her hand out and took the phone from its cradle, laid it on the table and waited for the alarm—the short, sharp jabs of warning that accompanied a phone disarmed—to start and then stop. Shut her eyes tight.

It was Jerry's voice that woke her. Almost two now, and he'd come in the back door, called out to her from the landing, his voice like a hollowed-out tin can. Dawn knew something was wrong, that something terrible had happened and she was on her feet before Jerry shouted up to Andrea. Turn on your TV, he yelled, and Dawn heard a boot drop to the floor and his socked feet hit the stairs. Going up, which gave Dawn enough time to strip off her nightshirt and pull on a sweater and pants before she followed.

Climbing the stairs, she could hear the TV—a kind of muffled drone—but nothing else. No voices until she was almost to Andrea's kitchen. Then she heard Jerry again.

That's it, he was saying. That's the end of everything right there.

Andrea was leaning against the door jamb between the kitchen and living room, facing the television. Jerry was on the couch, watching too, one hand on his head like he had to hold it to his body. And Tara was at the kitchen table, fingerpainting blueberry yogurt across a plastic placemat. Spotting Dawn, she grinned and plowed her hand back into the yogurt tub, grabbed up another fistful.

Andrea glanced over her shoulder, her gaze omitting Dawn on its way to the little girl. Tara Murphy, smarten up!

Dawn heard the warning shot—knew Andrea only attached the name of her missing-in-action ex to the children when she was livid.

But she didn't say anything else, didn't make a move to stop the four-year-old's art project. She just turned her back on Tara and Dawn and fixed her eyes on the TV again.

And so Dawn did, too. She saw a space shuttle lifting off, the usual technical reportage, a dry voice giving the command to throttle up. She recognized it for what it was. She'd seen another launch a few years earlier because Jerry had a party when Sally Ride took off—the first woman traveling in a shuttle some kind of good omen, it seemed, for Jerry's dreams. Dawn couldn't remember much about that party, except that Jerry kept rewinding his VCR footage of the launch and calling out, at just the right moment, Ride, Sally, *ride!*

Her eyes moved from the television screen to the back of Andrea's head, to Tara, intent on her masterpiece, and back to the television screen. And then a sudden burst of smoke, unexpected, and Dawn understood why they were all here.

Did it—

But she didn't need an answer. Two trails were moving up and away from each other like the curling horns of a beast.

They finally send a civilian up and this, Jerry said, this is what happens.

Dawn went to stand beside Andrea, to watch the whole loop, from liftoff to disintegration, again. To see the shuttle explode into ribbons of smoke. And when it did, she flinched, then wondered what it was—that thing that made us hope, loop after loop, for a different outcome.

The image on the television changed to the spectators. Andrea raised a hand to cover her mouth, her elbow resting then against Dawn's upper arm, though Dawn was certain she didn't realize it.

Sweet Jesus, Andrea said. Just look at her.

Her voice broke and Dawn turned to look across the small space between them. Are you crying?

Andrea flapped her hand loosely toward the TV. The mother—she started to say. Behind them, a wet smack as the yogurt tub hit the floor.

Dawn turned from the TV, grabbed the washcloth from the counter and wiped up the mess—face, table, then floor—while Andrea stayed where she was, sobbing now, noise and tears and snot, the whole works. It wasn't until Tara wrested away from Dawn in a loud protest that Andrea tore herself from the screen.

That teacher's mum, she said, heavy voice cracking as she snatched the washcloth from Dawn. Didn't you see her? Like she knew all along. Like she was just waiting for the worst and—well there it was.

Andrea wiped at her eyes with the cloth, leaving a smear of blue yogurt along her cheekbone that looked like a fading bruise.

Dawn looked over to the TV but they'd looped back to liftoff. I don't get what you mean, she said.

No, course you don't, Andrea said. Big surprise.

Dawn kept her eyes trained on the TV, watching things blow apart. Struggling to keep her arms at her side and not cross them into a shield against the driving point in Andrea's voice. This, Dawn knew, was about the other night on the couch—the couch where Jerry slouched now, his feet straight out in front of him like he'd been shot.

On the couch. Dawn and Andrea both drunk on cheap wine—the wine a prerequisite for watching the porn video they'd rented because Andrea had never seen one. Dawn not even sure who started it, all of it happening in what seemed like one rolling move, the coming together of tongues and fingers, so much urgency and those empty wine bottles right there within reach. Dawn disoriented when she woke up the next morning still on that couch, her head thumping, all the rest of her aching and sore. Andrea already up and dressed, staring down at her. So that was ridiculous, she'd said as soon as Dawn opened her eyes.

Dawn had struggled to pull her body out of the sinkhole of the cushions, eyes closed against the light or else against Andrea's broad, beaming face. God, I feel disgusting. That's what Dawn had said, all she'd said, before she took her pasty-mouthed, shaky self down to her own bed.

And it would have been fine—would have become just one more inside joke that nobody else got—if the rest hadn't happened. Days later, back on the couch. Late. A Dennis Quaid movie playing out its final moments. Andrea and Dawn both making a show of salivating over his lanky good looks and then Andrea slid over and brushed her fingers along Dawn's forearm.

Dawn had stiffened and leaned as far into the arm of the couch as she could. She was still watching the TV but she was losing the thread of the movie. Andrea, she said. We're not doing this.

You got a better offer right now? But Andrea was already pulling away, was already hardening to stone. Was already up on her feet and leaving the room, not a sound until she slammed her bedroom door.

The movie was over and the credits were rolling and the wine was empty, so Dawn had gone downstairs and struggled to make sense of it. Everything turned her on these days—music, wind, the sound of water dripping from an eavestrough. Everything. And it could be so easy, Andrea right there, willing. Why not?

And still.

And still she'd gone to the bar last night. Line danced. Brought home Darrell—yes, that was his name, Darrell—and had made sure Andrea heard it. Heard all of it.

Not that Darrell was a viable option, or even a better one, but it was all Dawn could think to do. After he was gone, she'd spent the morning regretting it, worrying that she'd gone too far, that she'd drawn a line with fire instead of chalk and burned her own house down.

And now this. Dawn turned to look at Jerry. He'd stopped watching the TV and was staring instead at the signed photo of Priscilla Presley that he'd picked up on his first visit to Memphis the very week they opened Graceland to the public. Jerry had given that picture to Andrea, saying he couldn't believe the resemblance, and Dawn and Andrea had laughed about it a million times since.

The picture still sat where Andrea had propped it on a side table, but now it was bent and torn, so mangled by sticky little fingers that it no longer bore much resemblance to Priscilla, never mind Andrea.

Dawn caught Jerry's eye, and he came to stand beside her to watch the Challenger explode again, to watch the fallout spiralling down. On his face, Dawn could see his grief and it was a bottomless well, so she let him place a hand on her back to steady himself.

They won't do it again, he said. Not with a civilian, not for a very long time. They'll keep sending things into space, but they won't be sending people.

And then Andrea was there, planting herself on the other side of Dawn, and Jerry was still talking, saying something about them damn satellites looking down on all of us who'll never get up there. And Tara was winding around and through Dawn's legs on her way to some new mayhem, and Andrea was pointing to the screen saying, Look now, her—that teacher's mom—see the look on her face?

And then she turned to Dawn. But you can't see it, because you're nobody's mother. Because you don't belong to anybody and you don't love anybody.

They were inches apart, and Dawn saw the twitch at the side of Andrea's mouth—a twitch that gave away Andrea's pleasure at knowing how her words scalded. Dawn felt seared right through.

She turned back to the TV. There was commentary now, a promise of experts on air soon who could make sense of what it all meant, but the picture was still the same. Liftoff. Dawn saw that massive burst of fire, the immense energy needed to overcome gravity. And she felt the air lifting, a warm wave of relief washing through her. She and Andrea had wounded each other now. The universe was in balance.

She smiled a little, turned away while the shuttle was still intact. Said I guess *Days of Our Lives* won't be on today. I'm gonna go take a shower. And she went back downstairs, leaving Andrea and Jerry to deal with the fallout.

2013

Look, Ethan told Lana six weeks after he left the message on the mirror, it's clear things haven't been right between us for a long time.

But as soon as he said the words, he realized it wasn't clear, not to her. Not at all. She disagreed—deeply—with his assessment of their relationship and that grew more evident over the ensuing weeks, intensifying in the hours of dissection that dragged like flint across bone. Reverberating in the hoarseness of Lana's voice, in the scrape of her chair legs on the floor.

And of course Lana told Pauline before Ethan found the chance—or, more truthfully, before he'd worked up the nerve—so all he could do was play catch up, try to corral the mess with his mother into one neat pile. It's an amazing opportunity, he tried to tell her. A chance to work where I'll feel useful. I've always wanted to go somewhere more—. Here he fumbled, could only come up with the word interesting, when what he meant was different, further afield. It didn't matter, because he could see Pauline was determined not to understand.

You should be glad I'm not going halfway around the world, he said, and waited to see if that sunk in. Funny, I thought you'd be proud that I'm stepping out of my comfort zone.

But Pauline just kept saying nothing, just fidgeted with a button at her cuff so that Ethan could see she was neither glad nor proud—she was what Ethan thought she always was: concerned. And that concern looked like it had always looked, like he was letting her down.

He considered that they had planned it, Lana and Pauline, their tag-team disappointment. Ethan felt so beleaguered he might have backed down and stuck around, at least for a while—but just as he was about to raise the white flag, Lana made her own sudden reversal and announced the break-up publicly. Maybe she'd realized, finally, that he was right and it was over, or maybe it was a tactic, a slap meant to clear his head and set him straight again.

It was a slap anyway, and her timing, he thought, no accident. They were both at home, moving delicately in a kind of queasy, early-afternoon truce. He'd gone to his study, so she knew he was online. First, she changed the relationship status on her Facebook account to *It's Complicated* and then minutes later, like she'd given it some thought, to *Single*. Each time, Facebook leapt to notify her friends. And her social media posse rallied. Condolence messages and emoticons poured in, along with a slew of questions.

Ethan had never seen so many question marks in one place—some posts were nothing but question marks, all lined up and heavily armed. Facebook's algorithm responded to the flurry by making sure more of Lana's friends, many he'd never even heard of, got in on the action.

Ethan knew what must be coming, but still he couldn't bring himself to duck and cover. Some kind of sick curiosity held him there, waiting for just how caustic it would be. He was probably one of the very first to read it—to read Lana's post, her long and frank, bitter and righteous explanation of how much she'd given, how little he'd tried. He read every word of it and then, convinced he must have missed something, the part he might recognize as actual reality, he read it again.

After that, he tried not to look at the comments surging in beneath her screed, but it was like watching a train wreck and somehow, he was both inside the train as it left the tracks and far above it, watching as the whole thing buckled and twisted and caught fire.

— *Can't believe it. He seemed so normal. Was he cheating on you?*
— *I know, right?! I considered that. Also brain tumor and drugs. I'm so exhausted from trying to figure him out and help him.*
— *Fuck him! Time to help yourself.*
— *Someone else??!!*
— *He says no but I think maybe...*
— *They always cheat. fuckers. HUGS!!*
— *You always said you thought he was emotionally cold*
— *Yep—didn't think he was actually cruel.*
— *your better off, Lana*
— *Probably. Just awful to know I wasted 4 years of my life.*

And on it went, Lana's replies coming fast and steady. Ethan began to see her as the conductor, orchestrating it all—every ping and shout out, every scrap of vitriol, all the caps-locked curses and hugs and emojis fully in her control.

He remembered once overhearing his sister and two of her friends talking about a break-up. They were all in high school then, and some guy had broken up with one of the friends. They were taking him apart—everything the poor bastard had ever said or done—ripping him to shreds in absentia. Ethan's bedroom was next door and the girls were ramped up, loud and animated. Venomous.

He couldn't recall the words, exactly, but he remembered thinking I'm not supposed to hear this, it's just for them, this comfort for a wounded friend. He'd learned the word catharsis in English class, but that was the day he understood what it meant.

When Ethan told his closest friend and only real confidante about Lana's post and the reaction to it, the friend called it Facemob mentality. Get out fast, he advised Ethan, before they come with the torches.

But Ethan didn't get out fast enough. He kept watching, reading, checking threads as they piled up. He was waiting for something— someone to leap to his defense, maybe, or else a clear accounting of his crimes.

And then a woman whose name he didn't recognize posted the comment he hadn't known to expect, and Ethan exed out of Facebook fast and backed away from the computer like it was in flames.

So here it was, Carrie Morris all over again. When Ethan was seventeen, Carrie sat two rows in front of him in biology. He could still picture her amber pony-tail curling at its shiny end, swinging just slightly when she walked out of class. He was crazy for her. When he finally got next to her at a party, she'd dropped her hand on his thigh casually, like it didn't mean anything, but Ethan could feel the warmth of it through his jeans. Turned out she was crazy for him, too. He'd felt like he couldn't breathe he was so happy, and for a few months they were inseparable. And then he found out, and he was never sure how, exactly, he realized it. Must have been a comment that led to a conversation that led Ethan to understand Carrie Morris considered his famous, tragic past to be his greatest appeal.

They went on for a few months longer, but he couldn't get back to the shiny place they'd been, the place where he believed she loved him like he loved her, without pity.

The day after they broke up, Ethan asked his parents—casually, because he'd practiced how to ask—for the name of the woman who'd let him into her house. That's all he wanted, just a name and a street address, a way to say thank you. An idea had crept into him that she had given him something—something remarkable. That it was her blanket and her chocolate milk that had made him okay.

But Ethan's parents wouldn't give him the name. His mother said they couldn't recall it, not after all this time, and then she made him go back into counselling. Things seem to be lingering, Pauline told the counsellor at the first meeting while Ethan sat, all lanky six feet of him, between his Mom and his Dad on a floral couch. He's too angry too often, she said, and it was clear she thought it was caused by that small sliver of his childhood and not by all the years since.

Counselling had turned out to be just the right thing—not because they talked about Ethan's past but because that counsellor wanted to know where Ethan was headed, what plans he was making. And no one had ever wanted to talk to Ethan seriously about that—about his future—before.

Carpentry or something like it, he said first, like his dad. He wasn't sure about that, but he knew he wanted to do something substantial, something that made a difference for being done. Control and purpose but not fame and glory, the counsellor said. Is that it? When Ethan nodded, she considered him long enough to make him self-conscious. Then she leaned so far forward her glasses slid down her nose and she said, her voice low and grave, that he should think seriously about looking further afield. That there was danger in sticking close, danger in following footsteps just because it's all you know.

Anyway, she told him, a good student like you can chart his own course.

And so Ethan did. He got scholarships and went away to college where no one knew him or knew about him, and it was as if finally, he really had escaped.

Then, halfway through his first year of medical school, his father was diagnosed: ALS. Lou Gehrig's disease. The living coffin. It began with his voice, his tongue growing clumsy, his larynx unresponsive. But who would notice that Frank Turnowski was talking less than usual? It was only after he started having accidents at work, after he found himself unable to lift things or to trust his own hands on the lathe, that Pauline dragged him off to the doctor. She called Ethan even before it was confirmed.

Even so early in his studies, Ethan knew enough—knew there was no hope. And he hated that his father's doctor had played it down, had talked about potential new treatments and best-case scenarios, leaving Ethan to tell his parents just how dire it was. Sorry, he said, there's really no hope. It was the first time, of course, he'd ever said that to a patient, and after the words left his mouth, it was interesting how it felt. Like he'd pronounced it and made it true.

He took a leave from school at the end of the term and moved home to wait it out. His sister was finishing college, far across the country, and no one asked her to come back because everyone knew she wouldn't. No one asked him to come, either—not in so many words—but he knew it was expected, knew he should, even if there was nothing useful he could do.

But it turned out there was. Frank Turnowski, his tongue tied and his body shutting down, suddenly had a great deal to say and no way to say it. It was Ethan who did the research, who made the calls and found the equipment and when it arrived, worked with the technician to hook it up and find out how it worked. Then Ethan sat down with his father for the first time in a decade.

By then, Frank could do little more than twitch a few fingers to choose letters, the pace painstakingly slow at first, but he'd spent a lifetime training his hands to fine details and he was a patient man. Slowly, and then a little faster, he made words and sentences and whole ideas—even jokes—appear onscreen. Every day the software got a little better at predicting what would come next, at anticipating whole words and then whole phrases from just a few letters.

Predictive software, the technician had called it, and Ethan had never seen anything like it.

Pauline had no patience for it, for sitting hour upon hour while her husband twitched his way through the story of his life, all the memories he'd stored up, the opinions he'd formed. But Ethan was willing. He knew his father's fingers would fail, and then his lungs, too. That this was a limited time engagement. And there was something else—he suspected his father was happy, maybe happier than he'd been in years, though Ethan had no way to measure that. For all he knew, the mood behind that expressionless face was just a foggy, flat plain brought on by the pain meds Frank took for muscle cramps.

One evening, while Frank slowly flicked out a drag racing story from his misspent youth, Ethan looked toward the window. The sky was shot through with crimson from the setting sun, and he realized these were the first real conversations he'd ever had with his father. That in the large and inexorable company of death, they'd escaped the narrow rules that had defined their relationship since Ethan was a boy.

The next morning, something was off with Frank, something more than usual. His colour was all wrong and he wasn't interested in communicating, not even to tell them what was happening inside. Ethan called the doctor's office and the receptionist put him on hold for a long time. When she returned, it was just to say Mr. Turnowski doesn't have an appointment until Friday. Ethan insisted, so she put him through to a nurse who said if you're so worried, call an ambulance.

So Ethan did—Pauline watching, standing in front of him with her hands on her hips like she needed him to remember she was the one in charge.

Frank was dead long before he reached the hospital. When Ethan called the doctor's office to cancel that Friday appointment, the doctor himself came on the line to offer his condolences. Ethan told him it was a heart attack, that's what had killed Frank, and the doctor said, Well that's one way to do it—sometimes you just get lucky.

Ethan hung up.

A week later, he watched his uncle stumble as he made his way to the front of the church to deliver Frank's eulogy. At the podium, he looked watery and uncertain. Ethan put it down to grief and nerves and he made the mistake of staying to listen as his father's brother erased every grace that death had granted.

It was fine at first, Uncle Mike talking about a young Frankie who was happy, who grew up strong, who loved his family and was loved in turn—but then the eulogy veered, and Mike was talking about the kidnapping, about how it had poisoned Frank. It might have been that Lou Gehrig's disease that killed Frank, he said, leaning heavily on the podium now, but a sickness like that doesn't come out of nowhere.

Slurring. Definitely drunk. Ethan saw it for what it was and tried to close up his ears before he heard the rest.

That sick bastard didn't just take away Frank's son—he destroyed Frank's spirit. That's what made him so weak. That's what really killed him.

Pauline, crying the exact right amount of silent tears, had placed the whole of her hand on Ethan's forearm, pressing down as if she was afraid he might leap up from the pew. But he didn't leap—he stayed through it all, and then stayed to make small talk at the reception. Over and over he heard some variation on what a blessing it was, Frank's death. Thank goodness he isn't suffering anymore, one woman said. Ethan recognized the woman—a neighbour, from across the street. While she talked on, her tongue riddled with the remnants of a date square, Ethan thought about all the months when Frank was sick, how this woman had never come across the street to visit, not once.

By the time it was all over—Frank in an urn and Pauline more or less functional, Ethan at least used to the way grief snuck up on him from all directions—medical school was off the table. Ethan hadn't just lost a year, he had lost the desire to be the one who presumed or pronounced anything. It was the technology that interested him now—CTS, MRIS—all those waves of the future, precise and objective in their execution, if not their interpretation. He got trained and certified across the board, could peer deeply, thoroughly into any patient yet never had to be the one who delivered the bad news.

He was lousy at that anyway, judging from this breakup with Lana. Maybe if he'd anticipated it, the fervour of her anger, he'd have tried to circumvent it rather than heading straight into it. But he'd let himself get sideswiped because Ethan had believed Lana was the most rational person he'd ever met.

This was long after Frank's death and after *Mystic River*, too. After that movie stirred up a fervid fascination with the boys who'd fallen prey to pedophiles. After Pauline had called Ethan near hysteria, pleading with him to tell her if that's what it was really like.

Ethan had seen the movie, too, and he'd spent a month preparing, rehearsing what he'd say when the call finally came. It blindsided him anyway, made him want to scream, There are no fucking wolves in me! But he'd managed to flip his phone shut before anything like that escaped his mouth. He'd learned that to his mother and people like her, denial sounded exactly like proof.

It wasn't that Ethan was blind to the possibility of lingering effects. He'd studied it, read all the research, poured over the first-person accounts and the novels. Listened to the experts. He knew he was supposed to be messed up and for a long time—maybe for forever. And sometimes he'd catch himself wondering what was wrong with him that he felt so fine.

And then he met Lana, both of them safely on the other side of thirty. A few months in, when it was starting to solidify, he knew he had to tell her before she met his mother. There was always the risk of exposure, that videotape at the ready. He gave Lana a clear, succinct account with lots of room to ask questions. She had a few but not many, and she pulled a blanket up over both of them and said, We don't have to talk about this, not ever, if you don't want to.

Lana had never said another word—not to Ethan—about it, and she'd laughed along with him when Pauline had converted the videotape to digital so she could be sure it would last.

When Ethan opened Facebook again, the comment that had sent them running had 37 Likes, but no response yet.

— *You said all along he was damaged. Well he's proven it. Time to move on.*

Damaged. Ethan snapped out of his paralysis, realized he didn't need to wait for Lana's response. He unfriended her, which seemed a necessary but strange thing to do, since they still lived under the same roof. Then he went straight to the Air Canada website.

After that, the rock was rolling down the hill and there was no stopping it. Soon the disentangling, the subletting, the last round of tears and recriminations were all behind him. He shipped what he figured he'd need out ahead, clothes and boots and books mostly, and stored everything else in his mother's basement, her consent a terse nod with no easing of the tension between them.

It was all forward motion now, nothing binding him to a past he wanted no part of.

2010

You could have fought it, Dawnie. I don't understand why you didn't. It was your house sure as it was anybody's.

Jesus, Jerry, this is why I'm not going with you on any long drives. I'm not listening to this all the way up and back.

In truth, it was only one of about a thousand reasons why Dawn was planning to make the trip alone, but Jerry had spent the better part of two weeks trying to talk her into letting him come, first in person then over the phone, calling from his truck at all hours, from anywhere out along the Trans Canada. When he did, the sound was so clear she'd hear the hum of his tires on the road, rain hitting his windshield. And she'd picture him behind the wheel looking not as he did now, grey-haired and paunchy, but like he had three decades earlier when she'd climbed into his truck that first time and he'd seemed so old to her.

Thirty-one. He'd been just thirty-one when they'd met.

Jerry, you gotta stop calling me. I'm trying to get stuff done here.

Like what, at this time of night? What could you possibly be doing?

And when she told him she was packing glassware or china, crinkling the newspaper into the phone for effect, he'd say that didn't sound so all-consuming, and he'd start in again, all the same lines of attack.

Listen, I was thinking, why don't we go over to Deer Lake this weekend—I saw a couple of houses for sale on the internet. Nice looking places, decent yards if that's what you want, and all close to shopping. You won't get that out there in the middle of nowhere.

Dawn tore a broadsheet in half along the centre crease before replying, laid a glass down on one half. Jerry, I told you before, I'm not moving to Deer Lake, shopping or not. You're the one who always told me there's no deer there, so that's on you.

She had the cordless phone tucked between her face and her shoulder and if she wasn't careful, her jaw would push buttons as she spoke, beeping out half of what she said. This time, her cheekbone hung up on him. But like always, Jerry called right back and picked up right where they'd left off.

You won't find much up the coast, either, just a whole lot of nothing but moose. You'll have no options, you move that far out.

Jerry was a skipping record stuck in the groove of baby don't go.

I'm not looking for options, she told him again. I just want a view and some quiet.

You got more quiet around you than anybody, Dawn. Too much of it and all it does is make you sadder. A pause, and then Jerry was yelling. Yeah, fuck you too! Not you, Dawnie—another driver showing me he doesn't much care for my driving. Can't speed up to get out of his way, see, cuz they're watching me.

Who Jerry, who's watching you? Grateful for the change in topic, for the endless entertainment of Jerry unguarded.

Company, that's who. They got all this goddamned monitoring in the truck. Watching my speed, tracking when I stop and when I go. Before you know it, they'll be checking on how much I eat and burp and fart.

Uh huh. She shoved more newspaper into her favourite mug, twisted as much as would fit around the handle.

Used to be a man was trusted to get his job done right, without somebody breathing down his neck every minute of the day and night, he said. Anyway, I keep telling you, you're gonna feel better soon. Won't be long before you're out the other side of this sorrow.

For over a year, Jerry had been telling her that and it wasn't true, not yet, and she couldn't see how it ever would be. But maybe, holed up in a place like Flower's Cove, she might find some kind of solace. It didn't have to be precisely Flower's Cove, either. She had no idea what the place was like, but she'd seen the name on a map and fancied it enough that she'd looked it up online, found a picture of a rowboat leaning in a field of flowers near the water's edge, a lighthouse in the distance.

Flower's Cove. She imagined a small, pointed house, a table at a window looking out toward the ocean. She could sit at that window all damned day and frame up arrangements of the flowers she'd been pressing between the white and yellow pages of every phone book she could get her hands on, going back almost twenty years. It would be enough, she figured, just to pass the time and maybe make a little money selling the framings.

But when she'd finally told Jerry the plan—late night, after a few glasses of wine drunk from one of the coffee mugs she hadn't packed yet—he'd brushed away her idea like it was already ash. And he was still on it now.

It's the wrong thing for you, Dawn, all that time inside your own head. You'll sink right into it and never climb out again. Trust me, I know what I'm talking about when I talk about loneliness.

Dawn passed the phone from her right ear to her left to even out the crick in her neck. You know, Jerry, she said, you've got a pretty good opinion of your opinion for an old man whose whole experience of the world is trucks and video games.

There was a deep silence over the line. Even the road noise was gone. Then Jerry said, Never you mind Flower's Cove, my love. It's Savage Cove for you, that's where you belong. I'm home Wednesday. I'll take you up on Thursday.

She wanted to tell him to go fuck himself, that she wasn't sorry at all for saying it and she'd be making the drive on her own. But then she heard Andrea saying, Be kind to Captain Jerry—he loves you so.

It had come out of nowhere, that line. A snowy January night while they were doing the supper dishes and Andrea laid a southern belle's lilt over her Newfoundland accent. The result was mucky but Dawn heard it anyway, heard what Andrea was going for, the *Gone With the Wind* reference and all its deathbed connotations.

Dawn had lifted her wet hands from the sink, suds ringing her wrists, and said, Stop doing that.

It wasn't even the first time that day. It was as if Andrea had made a decision without consulting Dawn at all, and now she was intent on delivering every damn dramatic line she could think of to announce her imminent demise, to shore up her conviction.

Dawn had turned to look down at where Andrea sat drying the dishes. She wanted to lay her warm, soapy hands on Andrea's beautiful, bare, shining head. She wanted to say, You're having a hard time right now but we'll get through this.

Instead she said, Please, just stop it.

Andrea pushed herself up from the chair. No Dawn, you stop it. Then she threw the damp dishtowel to the floor and said she had to go lie down.

Dawnie, you still there?

Over the phone, Jerry could sound so bereft.

Yeah, I'm here. I'll see you Thursday Jerry.

DAWN WAS PICKING JERRY UP AT HIS HOUSE IN STEADY BROOK so they could make the drive north in her little car. It was a small victory, eked out only because she insisted Jerry wasn't driving all the way into Corner Brook to fetch her and then retracing his steps. No way would she go along with a plan that stupid, even if it was only ten minutes up the highway.

She missed the turn. She was looking the opposite way, noticing how the scars cutting down the hillside were more pronounced on a sunny day in deep summer, with the trees at their greenest colouring in all the ski runs. Jerry had complained the lights were getting brighter on the ski runs every year. They hardly used to bother him at all, he said, but now he swore even when he was standing at the back of his little A-frame looking out at the river, the glare off those lights made it hard to see a star or anything like it.

When Dawn had called him on it, asking if that wasn't just the price of progress, he'd reminded her that not every change is an improvement.

When she realized she'd missed the turn, Dawn considered just skipping Jerry, just continuing on up the road without him, but she doubled back and pulled into the big driveway that let him drive his big rig in and out without disturbing the neighbours too much.

She was half an hour later than they'd agreed but he still made a play of keeping her waiting. Why don't you take yourself for a nice walk around the neighborhood while I finish these dishes and wait for the dryer to finish, he said, and she knew what he was up to. She'd seen the For Sale sign on her way in.

In answer, Dawn plunked down on the couch in the living room and surveyed the room. It looked just the same as it had the first time she'd seen it, not long after he'd bought the place. The black leather couch took up the same space as the black couch that had preceded it, and it faced a television that was wider and flatter but

still canted on the precise angle as the last TV and the one before
that. Between those two anchor points sat the very, very same
chrome and smoky-grey glass coffee table. And Dawn still thought
that table was as ugly as she had the night she and Andrea had come
to Jerry's party, held in honour of his new Atari game system, and
they'd drunk peach schnapps in orange juice, their glasses leaving
sticky rings on the glass top while Jerry and his friend Bill, the only
other person at the party, battled for supremacy.

That was the night Andrea had run outside and Dawn had found
her doubled over in the front yard, a spray of hot orange puke hitting
the cold snow, strings of it dangling from the hair hanging around
Andrea's face. Once she was empty, once the heaving stopped, Dawn
had helped her inside and cleaned her up and got her tucked into
the little single bed in the spare bedroom—a bed Dawn knew must
have been Jerry's when he was a boy. And the whole time, Andrea
was saying I love you, Dawn, I love you so much.

All night Dawn had sat there on the floor, leaning against the bed
and trying to stay awake, afraid that Andrea would suffocate in her
own vomit like celebrities did on the news. In the morning, Dawn
had dragged her aching body up off the floor and gone to get them
both a glass of water, and Andrea had taken two sips and said, God,
my head. I just want to die.

You ready to go?

Dawn looked up from Jerry's ugly coffee table to find him looming, looking overly concerned and more impatient than she could
ever remember seeing him look before. She glanced around the
room to get her bearings. There was a newer desk on the far wall
with a massive computer screen on top and a big CPU underneath.
Jerry was the only person she knew, maybe the only person period,
whose computers kept getting bigger.

Above the desk, a framed ink drawing of Elvis that Jerry had
picked up on his last visit to Graceland.

He hooked the keys from the palm of her hand and she didn't protest.

Eventually, Dawn thought, eventually everybody gets what they wished for.

THEY DROVE IN SILENCE FOR THE FIRST WHILE, WINDING their way through the splendour of Gros Morne National Park, Jerry steering one-handed and Dawn staring out the passenger window at the exultant peaks and spectacular vistas. It was July and hot, and the electric blue sky and the denim blue sea were both making promises that summer could go on for a long while. But by the time they hit the north edge of the park, the sky was dulling, fading into a lighter blue and then a flat brushed steel. The trees were short and gangly now, kept low by the constant wind, bent from its endless badgering and Dawn felt shrunk down too, her great plan diminished. Small.

They passed into Parsons Pond and Jerry finally spoke. Now here's a place, he said. Surely this is far enough down the road to suit—got plenty of oceanfront views and a bit of convenience, but plenty isolated enough, too.

Keep going, Dawn said, her eyes scanning the ocean. She was wondering if maybe she'd see a whale, though she had no idea what a whale might look like. She'd never seen a whale. Jesus, thirty-three years in this place and she'd never seen a single thing, not anything that looked at all like the tourism brochures.

You can live in a place your whole life and still not know anything about it. She heard Andrea say that, remembered Andrea saying it once a long time ago. Saying, You know the places you go and how to get around, how the weather feels and the air smells, but you don't know anything about its history or its inner workings. I mean sure, there's a museum—but have we ever gone there?

And so they did, they went there. A blustery, grey March day but they dragged themselves out into it, made the effort. Walked all through that museum and took their time, looked at all the artifacts and read all the plaques. And six years later—seven years? eight?—Dawn can't remember a single thing about it.

Jerry hadn't spoken for an uncharacteristically long time, for long enough that the trees were shrubs by any reasonable standard and every bit of blue was erased from the sky. Then he said, February. You gotta think about February out here, girl, because it only gets bleaker from here.

And it was bleak, but maybe that's what she was after. The further they drove, the more comfortable she felt, like the bandages around her ribcage were being loosened.

Three hours into the drive, they stopped to stretch their legs and eat the lunch Dawn had packed. Jerry tucked the car over on the side of the road and pulled two folding lawn chairs from the trunk. He carried one in each hand while she carried a bulging Sobeys bag in one hand and a two-litre of Pepsi in the other. They sidestepped, crab-like, down a slope of scrabbled rock toward the water, crossing a carpet of juniper until they arrived at a flat, smooth shelf of rock the colour of pewter that ran like tarmac into the sea.

A sandwich and a fruit cup restored Jerry enough to set him back to nagging. Small towns are no good, Dawnie, he said. Everybody knows where you went and who you talked to and what you had for supper last night. You don't want everybody knowing your business.

You're forgetting, Jerry, I got no business. There's nothing for anyone to know.

Jerry knew it was true, but he ignored it and kept on anyway. Listen, he said. It's one thing to keep your own counsel. It's another not to have a soul who even cares what you're counselling on.

Dawn rolled her eyes and drained the syrup from her fruit cup and Jerry, seeing that he was shouting into the wind, started in from another direction. You're still in shock, not thinking clear. This is all just a reaction to your loss.

Dawn shook her head. It had been seventeen months and she'd gone through her share of reaction, senseless and hard. But she was past that. She could leave the house now without being struck by an urge to turn and rush back in again. And anyway, she had no choice but to leave now, and to leave for good. In just over a month, the house wouldn't be her home anymore.

It had never been Andrea's house, not really. It had been Margaret's all along and her death had made it part of the estate, divvied it up equally between her three kids. Of course nobody was going to call in their share while Andrea was alive. The benefit of being the family fuck-up, Andrea called it. She could stay forever, as far as they were concerned, especially because both of her siblings lived on the mainland now. They'd barely come home for a week when Margaret passed, and not even that long when Andrea died.

Funeral family, Dawn thought then and still thought now. Always arriving after the fact.

Maybe that was unfair. Probably that was the kind of reaction Jerry was talking about. A reaction to the gut punch of it all, to having been the one who helped Andrea to the bathroom and who called her kids when it was time for them to come home. Who washed the bedding when it was all over and then rolled it up and stuffed it into garbage bags because it was just too sad to keep.

It wasn't lost on Dawn that if she and Andrea had been having sex all those years, if they'd been lovers instead of friends, she'd have a claim now. Blood and sex, that's what counted.

Sometime after the funeral, one of the brothers or else one of the kids must have remembered it was their house, that Dawn was a squatter and they had an asset to dispose of. Maybe they got on a conference call or met on Skype, because Dawn got an email saying she was welcome to stay in the house for a time (unspecified) if she'd fix it up, paint it, modernize it enough so it would fetch top dollar in this market. All very impersonal and nobody suggesting that they were fronting any money at all for the renovations, or even saying just what it was they expected to have done.

That message came from the oldest brother's email but it was signed from all of them—the brothers and their wives and also Tara and Jacob, who owned a third of the property between them.

Dawn had expected to hear from the kids after that. Both of them living in St. John's now—Tara finishing nursing school and Jacob finishing nothing, ambling from job to job, working in the restaurants that were suddenly blooming like dandelions along every sidewalk in that city, fed by the new spring of oil money and easy credit that suddenly made culinary adventure a requisite for living there. Neither was planning a return to Corner Brook except to tie up the loose ends of Andrea's estate and sign whatever had to be signed to get their inheritance.

They hadn't come back at all since Christmas. And why would they? With their mother gone, the only connections left for them on the west side of the island were a few old relatives and Dawn. And Dawn was no relation, no real tie at all.

Jerry was still talking. Sure, she'd find a place dirt cheap up here but how, he wanted to know, was she planning to finance this purchase when she hadn't worked in two years and the house she'd lived in forever had been sold out from under her and she hadn't inherited two nickels after being there by Andrea's side all that time?

I told you before, Jerry, the money doesn't matter so stop talking about it. I've got my savings.

It had taken her years to deposit it all, to empty the Pringles cans she'd filled with the duffel bag loot. Accounts in two different banks, each getting a little more, a little more every few weeks so no one would get suspicious about a hotel helper's cash stores. And she'd barely touched it since, living on what she earned and living cheap—except to add a little more to it and move it into safe, solid investments recommended by her financial manager at the bank. She'd told Andrea about it, said it was an inheritance from her father. Said they could use it for anything, anything at all they needed, but nothing so necessary had ever come up. So it sat, earning interest year after year until it had grown into a decent sum, though the growth had slowed to glacial in recent years.

Jerry brushed crumbs from his thigh and spoke without looking at her, which she thought might be a trick he used to manage her, or else a habit developed from all those years of talking while his eyes were on the road. And once your savings are gone, what then? There's not a lot to do up here, you know, unless you've got a boat or you're a Viking.

Dawn handed him another sandwich, pale pink ham jutting out the sides, the yellowest mustard staining the crust.

That's it, is it? You're a Viking? Jesus, Dawnie, I always knew you were hiding something from me. Jerry took a big bite and talked over the bread. Those blue eyes, that braid—well I'll be damned. All these years and you never told me.

Dawn might have laughed if she hadn't noticed them just then, two bent indigo heads, petals fluttering against the grey rock. Jerry was saying something about renaming her Helga that she didn't quite catch because she was already up on her feet.

Hey, toss me the keys, Jerry, would ya.

When she came back clutching a phone book, he pointed to it. What's the vintage on that one?

She squinted at the cover. 2008, she told him. Why?

Didn't know they still made 'em, that's all. Guess you don't get one if you don't have a phone connected to the house. They'll stop soon enough, I imagine—they can't be cheap to produce.

Dawn thought about phone books as she walked across the outcrop. It hadn't occurred to her that something so standard, so omnipresent and essential, could just disappear. And then she couldn't remember if a new one had shown up on the doorstep this year. It made her pause in mid-stride. What if they'd already stopped—what then? What could replace the weight of it and still offer the thin, uncoated pages so suited to desiccation?

She dropped the book, put one knee on it to keep it from fluttering open in the wind. The smooth rock that met her other knee where her jeans were nearly worn through was warmer than the air. She studied the flowers—two blue flag irises that had pushed up through a crack in the sheet of rock like poster children for determination, like proof that life would always find a way.

Irises were tricky to press well, but not impossible. Dawn had pressed a few into flawless specimens over the years.

Both flowers were in the prime of their bloom, straddling the middle ground between purple and blue, white fans on their petals reminding Dawn of the eyes on peacock feathers. She'd take just one and leave the other for someone else passing this way to admire.

Dawn moved the phone book to where her body could shelter it from the breeze coming off the water and flipped it open to roughly centre. Flipped it open to the unexpected discovery of Andrea's round, flowing script, to ink circling the number for a clinic, its name unfamiliar to Dawn and giving nothing away about its nature. In the margin, *No* and *6* and *fuck* were written in an achingly familiar, grade-school-perfect cursive.

It came to Dawn that this was probably the last phone book Andrea had ever opened, that she would have been gone months before its replacement arrived. And so maybe, this was the last number Andrea ever circled, the last page Andrea ever annotated.

Dawn flicked the blade open on her knife, carefully severed one blue flag from its stem. Set it on the page beside Andrea's blue ink. She cut the second flower clean off, too, and laid it a distance away, arranging both so it looked as if they were thrusting their tongues toward each other. Then she carefully closed the book.

Let's go, she called to Jerry as she strode back to where he still sat, looking out to sea. I'm ready for what comes next. And I'm driving this stretch.

THE SKY DARKENED AS THEY HEADED NORTH ALONG THE coast, occasionally spitting rain so Dawn had to keep turning the wipers on, then off when they started to squeak against the dry glass. Jerry suggested turning at the road to New Ferrole, but Dawn said they could stop on the way back if she didn't find what she was looking for at Flower's Cove, and she pressed a little harder on the accelerator to make the point. Which only made Jerry say he intended to stop plenty on the way back, no matter what she'd found. He'd show her that she didn't have to go so far to get a fresh start.

She wanted to explain that a fresh start wasn't the thing, not exactly—that she wasn't thinking about starting. That she was thinking about stopping. All her life was behind her now, all the things she might once have wanted were like the trains that no longer ran here—long departed and forgotten and the tracks pulled right up out of the ground. She thought of herself as a helium balloon floating away, utterly untethered.

Untethered. It's what she'd always been anyway—Andrea's word, what she'd called Dawn as they'd lain naked in the desert. One of their last Thelma and Louise trips to the American southwest, one of the last times they'd sunsoaked themselves under a cerulean sky, Andrea going on about staying there in the desert forever.

Dawn had been listening for rattlesnakes and not really listening to Andrea at all until she turned onto her side and cast a shadow across Dawn's face. We could, she was saying, just start a whole new life. Hunt jackrabbits for dinner and never tell any of them where we are. What do you think of that?

I think you'd make it three days before you had to find a phone and check up on the family and the gossip back home.

No way, I'm done. Fuck the lot of them. Now that Tara's leaving too, I got no reason to go back there.

Tara's leaving?

Didn't I tell you?

Dawn couldn't remember the last time she'd seen Tara, or asked about her, or even heard Andrea mention her name. She didn't know what had happened, exactly, that had pushed her so far outside the circle when for so many years, those kids had tried to pull her in with their sugar-coated hands. But that was before they were teenagers, before their moral outrage when they realized Dawn was fucking a married man—a classmate's dad—in her basement suite. Before she kept it up for years. Andrea said they'd outgrow it, and maybe they had. Maybe the distance now was normal, was just about growing up and growing apart. Anyway, no point lamenting it now, in the desert, with the sun scorching her knees.

She plans on staying with Jacob until she can afford a place of her own, Andrea snorted. Can you imagine that?

But Dawn couldn't. She knew even less about Jacob. He'd been gone since he was sixteen and moved to St. John's to finish high school. Moved away from Andrea and moved in with his dad, who was suddenly ready for the responsibility of fatherhood. Andrea saw the irony but Dawn knew it bothered her, too, the way Jacob could just switch sides like that, only come around at Christmas, only call on Mother's Day. Still, Dawn suspected some part of Andrea was glad for Jacob, for his escape from the family's clutches.

It's more than time that girl went on her way, Andrea was saying. Jesus, I had two babies at her age. Now I'm washing my hands of them.

What about your mother? She's not going anywhere.

Andrea flipped onto her stomach and made a pillow of her arms. Fuck my mother most of all, she said.

Margaret was dying, or at least that's how it seemed. She was in chronic heart failure, taking a handful of pills morning, noon and night. Supposed to be on oxygen, too, but she wouldn't use it when anyone else was around. Most of the time she seemed like a flashlight whose batteries were running low, her beam too weak to point in any direction. Which only made Margaret more determined to point and direct, and it was her baby, her only daughter—the one near enough to check on her daily—who was taking all the jabs.

Teddy and the rest can figure out what to do with her, Andrea said.

And then Dawn knew this was only a fantasy, since Andrea had had to beg just to get one of them to come home and take a short stint looking in on Margaret. She'd started by calling Teddy, who lived closest and seemed the most likely candidate. When that hadn't worked—Not my thing, he'd said, sick people—Andrea tried her older brother and his wife, then looped back to Teddy. Told him she had tickets to Reno so he could make his own choices, but she was going.

Okay, Dawn said. I give you four days, then, before you run out of lotion and we have to leave the desert in search of Jergens.

Well hell, we can make the occasional trip into Walmart for supplies and chocolate.

High overhead, a plane bisected the sky, leaving a long white contrail in its wake, a wrinkle across the sky. Dawn watched the sharp line dissolve into cotton fluff before she said, Don't forget, the rental car's got that OnStar tracker.

What the hell do people want that shit for? Did nobody see *Thelma & Louise*? Anyway, we'll get our own car. Maybe a camper van.

Dawn rolled onto her stomach, checking for snakes and scorpions and any small sharp shards of rock before she did. Jesus, Andrea, she said, you really are thinking this through.

Andrea sat up and promised god yes, she was. She tipped her head back so sunlight washed her features away and said, I envy you, Dawn, no family and all the bullshit that comes with it. No one defining you with their expectations.

You could just tell them who you are, Andrea, instead of going into hiding.

It wasn't the first time Dawn had suggested it, but maybe it was the last.

Andrea turned her head away so Dawn couldn't see her face. Trust me, she said, hiding out in the desert is a much easier choice.

Dawn shielded her eyes to study Andrea, to see if she was as serious as she sounded. But Dawn's eyes landed first on the side of Andrea's right breast, where sand had formed an arc around a small crater. A dimple really, like someone had stuck a finger into a meringue.

Hey, Dawn said, do you know you have an indent there? Pointing.

Andrea only pretended to look. Well you can't expect the girls to look flawless forever. And don't change the subject. I'm serious about this. I figure you can teach me how to be untethered.

But Dawn hadn't felt untethered then. In fact, while Andrea brushed the dirt from her back, she'd felt wholly tethered. It was only after Andrea was gone and her will executed—Dawn herself the executor of Andrea's puny estate—that she understood how flimsy the ties lashing her to any ground.

Fat raindrops began to spatter the window as Dawn drove past the sign for Deadman's Cove. By the time they reached Flower's Cove and Dawn steered the car into the small settlement, the air had turned colder and Dawn was wishing she'd brought along a sweater. What came next was all disappointment—nothing for sale, nothing looking as she'd imagined it would and a steady downpour that made her want to stay in the car and keep moving.

We're up all this way, Jerry said. Might as well push on, go visit your Viking relatives at L'Anse aux Meadows. We can stay in St. Anthony overnight.

He said St. Anthony the way the locals did, the *th* abridged like it was stuck on the back of his tongue.

So Dawn pushed on, but she wouldn't have if Jerry had told her what came next, how the road turned away from the water and crossed the peninsula, nothing to look at but bog and alder and desperate scrawny spruce muscling their way toward the road. The next time she looked over at Jerry he was blessedly asleep, his head pressed against the passenger side window and his mouth hanging open.

The sky was low and the only things with any stature across the whole vista were the telephone poles, flexing their muscles along the shoulder of the narrow highway.

They really are everywhere. Dawn meant to say that to Andrea—silently, in her head—and she only realized she'd said it aloud when Jerry startled awake.

He wanted to know what, and he was looking around for some keenly interesting thing.

Telephone poles, that's all, Dawn said. Go back to sleep.

Andrea was always on about those poles and the wires strung along them. She spent twenty years at the phone company, starting as soon as Tara was in school, working first as an operator connecting collect calls and looking up numbers until they automated that and moved her over to payroll. Twenty years and everywhere they went, Andrea pointed out those poles. Look, she'd say, here too. And Dawn would call her a company man, and Andrea would launch into her tirade. People talk about the railroad, laying all that track sea to sea, but nobody talks about how they had to put up all those poles and string 'em all together, she'd say. And not in a straight line, either, but branching off to every home, tying everybody together.

Across the vast open Nevada desert, there they were. Driving across the island to St. John's to visit the kids, there they were. Halfway up Signal Hill to see where Marconi received his radio signal, there they were again, stopping only when the houses ran out.

Once, on the way home from St. John's, they'd passed a truck parked just off the highway, its trailer loaded down with poles— massive poles, all uniform in length and circumference. All bigger than anything Dawn had ever seen grow on this island. Where, she'd asked Andrea, did they find wood that tall and sturdy and true?

But Andrea had no clue. That's not my department, she'd said.

Jerry didn't close his eyes again, didn't go back to sleep. Instead, he watched those ubiquitous poles whip past his window like he'd never seen them before. Dawn expected him to say something, to call them relics of a soon-to-be forgotten age, but Jerry was keeping his own counsel.

When Dawn drove past the turn-off to St. Anthony's airport and there still wasn't any sign of civilization outside the damn telephone wires, she asked, Where the fuck's the town, Jer?

Soon, was all he said—but soon wasn't soon enough and there was a whole lot of the same nothing. And then they came to a small outcrop of rock, a squat little group poking out amid the trees, the first for miles. Someone had spray painted GRACE! on the first one they passed. The next one read BARRY LOVES ~~SARA~~ GRACE.

S'pose it was Barry or Grace who did that? Jerry asked, and Dawn said it was Sara. Sara was sick of the both of them, figured they deserved each other.

It was practically the last thing they said to each other until they'd arrived at a hotel and said goodnight in the hall.

THE MORNING CAME ON SO DREARY THAT NEITHER FELT LIKE taking in any of the sights or paying a visit to L'Anse aux Meadows. It's a thousand years old, Dawn said over corrosive coffee in the hotel lobby. What could possibly have changed since the last time you were there?

Jerry grinned. Now you're gettin' it, he said. There's no point wandering around in the past.

So they put their sick-of-this-trip selves back in the car, Jerry at the wheel, and pointed it south. Music? he asked after a minute. Dawn declined, and they drove in silence save the occasional slap and squeak of the windshield wipers Jerry had set to intermittent.

Dawn fixed her gaze on the side of the highway and if she was thinking, she didn't know about what. The constant painted line, the blur of black spruce passing on the periphery, the damn wipers, it all had her hypnotized. And then there it was again, BARRY LOVES ~~SARA~~ GRACE and GRACE! and Jerry shouted *Shit!* and hit the brakes. Hit them so hard Dawn's seatbelt locked tight across her shoulder and drove her back into her seat.

Jerry was sucking air in hard and when Dawn looked at him she saw he'd gone white. She thought he must be having a heart attack, but then she saw it, too—a big moose sauntering diagonally toward the highway's edge, oblivious. Oblivious to its near demise and to theirs. She watched it amble into and out of the ditch while Jerry pulled in another full breath, the car thrumming at a standstill. The moose stopped, sniffed the air, then continued up a slight rise and jogged slightly left to skirt an obstacle.

Jerry, Dawn whispered, look—

Yeah, I saw the little fucker.

More colour was returning to Jerry's face than had left it.

No, not the moose. *That*—

Faded, half-hidden by new poplars crowding in around it, was the painted plywood sign announcing The Tumble Inn. And nailed to that, smaller, a realtor's sign: For Sale.

The inn itself was out of sight, half a kilometre up an overgrown gravel road that led to a paved parking lot.

More like the Tumbledown Inn, Jerry said, but Dawn was out of the car before he'd shifted into park. He wasn't wrong. The place had obviously been empty a long time, but its white siding still lined up straight and only one of its faded green shutters had come loose.

Windows intact, nothing boarded up, and Dawn peered in the front door before she tried it, twisting and tugging though she knew it must be locked.

After that, the day picked up speed—back down the highway toward St. Anthony until Jerry caught a signal on his phone and reached the real estate agent. A long wait for the agent to arrive, Dawn and Jerry sizing up the outside. The building was much longer than it was deep, but the front reception jutted out just enough to save it from looking like another bland strip of a motel.

As she struggled with the lockbox, the agent warned them about the smell of things that had been closed up for a while. But inside, the smell wasn't as bad as they'd been made to expect, despite the dust and the obvious signs of mice on the wide plank floors.

Dawn took it all in. There was a large room off reception with linoleum floors and an old fridge, propped open, a wide white stove with four coil burners and three chrome and vinyl stacking chairs, unstacked. Down the hall, past the green formica counter that served as the reception desk, a bigger room, this one heavy with wood. The plank floors were darker, not as worn as the ones in the hallway, and three walls were lined with wooden shelves, floor to ceiling, some of them still filled with paperbacks and magazines. At the back of the room, the biggest woodstove Dawn had ever seen.

The electricity had been unhooked for months, the agent told them, and the daylight trickling through two small, grimy windows was puny. Jerry took out his phone and pressed the torch. When he shone it on that massive stove, the enamel glowed a deep hunter green.

Sold, Dawn said, and both Jerry and the agent looked at her like they thought she was serious. Jerry said, Now my love, you'll need to get the place inspected, top to bottom and corner to corner.

Dawn cut him off. I thought that's why I brought you, she said. To inspect the place.

The agent put up her hands, palms open like she was used to dealing with marital discord, and suggested they take a look at the guest rooms. Only she called them suites—Why don't we look at the suites?—and she led the way down the dark hall.

Furniture intact in the first three, all of them a decent size half-way between the biggest and the smallest rooms at the Blue Iris. A wallpaper border in each—the exact same one Dawn had pasted up in one room in 1989. She was managing the Blue Iris by then, though Margaret had recovered enough from her first heart attack to start sticking her nose in again. She approved of the dusty pink that Dawn had painted all the guest rooms, an empty room each day until it was done. Dawn trying, just then, to fill the nights when there was nothing good on TV, to keep busy so she could ignore how she keened with desire that outstripped the pool of local losers. When she showed Margaret the border she'd tried out in #114, Margaret said it was nice but maybe not worth the effort in every room and could Dawn please stop changing things without talking to her first. Later, Dawn wondered if it was just that—her wallpaper misstep, a whiff of the kind of mismanagement that would cost Margaret money—that made Margaret decide a year later to get out of the business altogether.

But this wouldn't be like that. This wouldn't be someone else coming in to stomp on Dawn's ideas, to make her do things like they'd always been done before. For the first time ever, the place she poured her energy into could actually belong to her.

And that's as far as she got in her dreaming before they entered the fourth suite. There's trouble, Jerry said, pointing to the moisture on the back wall, the ceiling buckled above it. But Dawn didn't need Jerry to point it out. She had a nose—she could smell mildew and rot.

Okay then, she said, meaning I guess we're done here. Meaning let's go. But Jerry was taking his role as inspector seriously, using the bright beam from his phone to scrutinize the problem, stepping up close to it, pressing a finger here and there, and then stepping back.

Let's talk about the plumbing, he finally said to the agent, tucking his phone back in his pocket and missing Dawn roll her eyes.

She left Jerry and the agent in the kitchen, peering under the sink, and wandered down to the furthest guest room, the fifth and biggest, the door barely ajar. The room took a deep breath when she entered, then held it as she closed the door fully. A darker room than the others, nothing in it but gloom and one small, low table painted a flat white and pushed against the wall where once, it must have sat bedside. She ran three fingers over its surface, surprised that not even dust had found it there. In one corner, the wallpaper border had let go, folded over itself and come to rest against the wall.

Dawn stood listening but there were no whispers. Nothing. A kind of quiet that might be called blissful, in another place.

She crossed the room to the window where heavy, blue and yellow flowered curtains were closed with such finality that not even a crack of daylight slipped through on any edge. In one movement, two-handed, she threw open the curtains.

She threw open the curtains. An unusually bright day, sunshine splintering off new snow, hard angles of light rushing into Andrea's bedroom. Behind Dawn, a question.

Who are you?

Andrea's voice like a shadow song, muddy from the drugs. Not a whisper, exactly—quiet like that but deeper, more compelling.

Dawn looked back toward the bed, thinking the sunshine must have cast her in silhouette. Too harsh probably, but Andrea loved the sun, and this was the first of it in days.

It's just me, she said. It's Dawn. Is that too bright?

Andrea's eyes beamed out from the loose, soft tissue around them. Her skin honeyed—not yellow but heading that way. A waxy sheen where the light caught it. Her body doing the opposite of what Dawn had expected, not shrinking into its collapse like Dawn's

mother's had but puffing out against it. Something even more fragile in that expansion, like a marshmallow swelling from heat. But
Andrea's eyes, even with the haze of painkillers, still recognizable
when she surfaced. And she was all there now.

I know it's you, stupid. She lifted her head from the pillow. I
mean tell me your real name, who you were before you got here.
What happened to you.

Dawn edged toward the bed. How are you feeling? Do you need
anything?

Oh for Christ's sake, just tell me. What does it matter now?
Andrea's voice the strongest part of her.

It doesn't. It's ancient history now.

I know that. I'm just curious is all. Please.

Dawn fussed with the covers, retucking them at the bottom of
the bed, watching what her hands were doing. Funny, she said, keeping her tone light, you never asked before.

It was true. Three decades and not once—not once—had Andrea
ever asked anything directly about her life before she crossed over
on the ferry.

Figured you'd talk about it someday, then after awhile I just forgot to ask. You were just you. At least until—well, who the fuck
can't get a passport?

There it was. The tone that couldn't help but be an accusation,
that said you wouldn't and now here we are. This.

Dawn breathed in deep the sweet-sour smell of sick that was
exactly the same as it had been with her mother. She knew this
might be their last day together in the house, maybe their last
hour—the kids already in town, staying with cousins, a palliative
care unit yawning open to take over and see Andrea out.

Dawn lay down on the bed, fit her head into the hollow of the pillow she'd brought up from her own room so she could sleep beside
Andrea, be nearby if the pain worsened or the fear was too much.

She placed a hand on Andrea's skull where the hair, even still, was making a valiant attempt to come back in fine wispy curls, and she spoke the name she hadn't spoken in thirty years.

Rosie, she said, the feel of it still familiar on her tongue but shaky, scraping the way the pencil had when she'd first learned to write it. My name was Rose, Rosie, before I came here. Rosie Benson.

Rosie? The last syllable leaving Andrea in a wheezing whistle. You know I really hoped you were going to say Louise.

Dawn laughed a little, despite herself. Her hand stroking Andrea's forehead, trying to rub away a line she knew was permanent because it had been there for twenty years. You liked me best as Louise, didn't you?

Andrea looked toward the window. I loved you best all the time, even when you broke my heart.

I never meant to.

Relax, I got over it. You never were my type anyway. Andrea coughed and swallowed hard, looked back to Dawn. Besides, you were right. It was better to love each other like this. It lasted longer.

She closed her eyes but kept talking. Tell me more, she said. Tell me the whole story of who you were and why you came here.

Dawn couldn't see why it mattered, but she couldn't see any harm in it either, not now, so she laid out the bare facts of her young life—told Andrea where she was born and when, about her mother and father and the streets where she'd lived, the name of her high school. The cat that was her first and only pet. Then Slake, that long summer, how it seemed romantic at first and how she ended up scared, desperate to get away. She left it vague like that, didn't mention the night Slake killed someone right in front of her. Too hard to explain and too upsetting for Andrea to hear.

Besides, Dawn realized, her gaze running along the sharp angle where the wall met the ceiling, she'd forgotten almost all the details of that night. The surprise of that forgetting, the pause in it, gave her a chance to check on her audience. Andrea was still right there, eyes wide open again.

I had to get away, Dawn said. Disappear.

Andrea closed her eyes and finished the story. Then along comes our hero Jerry and gets you out of there.

Well not exactly, Dawn said, prickling at the fairy tale revision. I took off in the middle of the night, hitched a couple of rides and ended up in Jerry's truck. You know the rest.

Andrea studied the popcorn texture of the ceiling for a long time—for long enough that Dawn wondered if Andrea was remembering a long-ago pledge she made to scrape the ceilings smooth. An apology forming on her tongue before Andrea spoke again.

I always thought, she said, it must be more dramatic than that. There has be something else, or why hide all these years?

Dawn flipped onto her back so she could look at the ceiling, too. Deciding. Well there's one thing, she finally said. When I was leaving, I took his money. All of it. All the money from the drugs. So I figured if he found me, he'd kill me.

Andrea turned to the window, to where the light pulsed in hard, and started to say something, the syllable *You* distinct before a convulsion took her, caused her limbs to curl into the pudding of her body, the air rushing out and out and out of her, then a sucking noise as she tried to pull some back in.

Dawn bolted up to her knees, brought a splayed hand down on Andrea's shoulder. Leaned into her face and said, Hey! Blood pounding out the number for 9-1-1, one foot heading for the edge of the bed, for the phone on the dresser. Her hand on it before Andrea's body relaxed into a real breath and her voice came on strong again.

Don't you dare dial nine-one-one, she said. I won't have those bitches talking about me. Swollen fingers wiping one eye. So all that money you have, it's *drug—*

That was all she managed before another convulsion took her. Dawn understood then that this was not an emergency. This was a fit of laughter. Andrea was laughing at Dawn and for once, for once in all these years, the hilarity was not contagious. It eluded Dawn; she couldn't find the jumping-on point to take the ride. Instead, she was gauging the effort, noting how much energy went into each fit and peel. Thinking how it had to be drawing down Andrea's reserves the way revving an engine burns up fuel.

Thinking how it must be killing her.

It took a long time before Andrea was composed enough to speak, her tone still laced with mirth. My Jesus, that poor angel— Jerry's *poor angel*. That's what my mother called you. Said you just have to let her live downstairs, *poor angel*.

No she did not.

You thought it was my idea to have your skinny ass hanging around all these years?

I guess I did.

Dawn feeling the sting of not having known, but Andrea just breezing along to the part that interested her more.

And Jerry, she was saying, acting like he'd bravely rushed in and rescued the damsel in distress. Telling us he'd pulled you out of a bad spot and it was nobody's business what, but we all had to protect you.

A single note of laughter escaping Andrea, rusty and offkey. And there's you—sticking it to the big bad wolf all by yourself.

Dawn was still on her knees but now she rolled back to her heels. Hey, I never told him I needed—

Doesn't matter what you told him, Andrea said. You know you can look at somebody with those sweet blue eyes of yours and the story you tell, whatever story you tell, is true.

Dawn, unsure if that was meant to be an accusation, was already wishing for a way to wind it all back now, to untell it even before

Andrea said, Oh Jesus, I can't wait to see Jerry's face when he finds
out he isn't a hero, that he just drove the getaway car.

Dawn rigid. You can't tell. Promise—

Jesus, I'm not tellin' anybody, you know that. Andrea lifted a
hand halfway to Dawn's face, then let it fall back to the bed. I'll take
your secret to my grave, Rosie Benson.

Dawn stiffened, drew her lips together and pressed down hard.

Andrea looked away then, her expression soured. Fuck you,
Rosie Dawn, she said. That was seriously funny. Look, you can't
be hanging around here anymore if you won't even laugh at my
jokes.

Dawn did try to find a laugh then, but she failed and a terrible
silence fell between them. She closed her eyes against it and when
she opened them, Andrea was studying her. A tear had escaped one
eye, was meandering through the puff of her face toward the pillow.
What are you gonna do without me, Dawnie?

Ssh. It's okay. You don't have to worry about me.

Who will you talk to?

When do I ever talk? It's always you talking.

Andrea smiled but another tear was already on the loose. Jerry,
you'll have to talk to Jerry. Don't forget about Jerry.

Dawn managed a smile. As if he'll let me. She reached over, used
her fingertips to gather the tears that were tracing jagged paths
across Andrea's face.

You know— Andrea's voice reduced to a whisper now, barely
more than the shape of breath and mouth. You know you can just
keep talking to me. I'll try to stick around close and keep the conversation going. But for god's sake girl, promise you'll get out of this
town and take me with you.

Dawn nodded, her throat closing around any promise she might
make. Clouds gathering thick and fast in Andrea's eyes while outside, the sun streamed on.

DAWN BLINKED, SQUINTED TO BRING A BAND OF DISTANT
spruce into focus, then stepped back from the window at the Tumble
Inn. She left the curtains open and hurried to find the agent. To say
she'd take the place, rot and all.

But Jerry wanted to go have a talk about it, and they drove back
to St. Anthony. Over lunch, his chowder got cold while he went
on about money and financing, about how expensive renovations
were. He said it like he didn't know she'd spent the last twenty
years redecorating other people's houses. When she reminded him
it was her field, not his, he warned her again about unanticipated
risks and faulty wiring. It was only when he finally saw that her
mind was made up that he tucked back into his bowl and scraped
it clean.

By morning, they had a deal—much less than the seller wanted,
though more than Jerry thought Dawn should pay. Still, she could
afford it. She put down a deposit, grateful for bank machines and
cell phones and all the invisible lines of the modern age that made
things happen when they needed to. She'd take possession just as
fast as the land title could clear.

On the drive back to Corner Brook the cloud thinned and the
light was different, better, so they stopped again at the Tumble Inn.
Dawn walked one way around the building, Jerry the other so they
met at the back, then continued on so they met again at the front.
The sun finally escaped the clouds altogether as they walked to the
edge of the property by the road, straight toward the rock emblazoned with GRACE!

Dawn turned to look at the shitty inn she'd bought, but Jerry
stood with his hands in his pockets facing the highway. I've been
thinking about getting off the road, he said. I'm just a couple of years
from my pension and pretty soon I'll be growing barnacles on my
ass. Anyway, what I'm saying is I'd be happy to hang it up a little
early and help you out up here.

Dawn was only half listening. She heard the thing about barnacles and heard help you out, but she wasn't adding it up. She was too busy thinking about window dressings, about art for the walls and the kinds of pies she could commission local bakers to make. And then she saw Jerry was looking at her with wide, bright eyes, his hands folded together in front of his belt buckle like a school kid. His mouth twitching.

What, Jerry, what's the matter?

I have a request, he said. Now, keep an open mind—

Oh Jesus, what now?

It's just a suggestion.

Jerry, for god's sake.

Well you could. I mean if you want, if you agree that the Tumble Inn is a terrible name—

She did.

Then would you at least consider calling it Graceland?

Her smile was unexpected and broad.

Hell yes, Jerry. Yes I will. I'll definitely call it Graceland.

2013

Sue picked Spencer up just after seven, the sun barely up but the morning clear and the air unusually warm for March. He'd come outside five minutes early so he could have a smoke, but she pulled up before he had it lit. He was barely in the car, barely had time to think how Sue was the one person he could count on, before they were tearing up his street.

I printed a map and directions, he said, holding it out like he thought she could look over at this speed.

I made coffee, help yourself. Sue made it sound like it was a contest and like she'd won, hands down. And I've got the GPS—once we're out on the highway, you can plug in the address and it'll take us right to the door.

I like a map, he said. I like to know where I'm going before I get there.

Takes all the mystery out of it, if you ask me, she said. Pour me one too, would ya.

Spencer laid aside the driving directions and wedged one of the coffee mugs between his thighs, reached for the thermos at his feet. He knew this meant they wouldn't be stopping, first thing, for donuts, and he told himself not to sulk. Sue was, after all, doing him a huge favour.

Sue was public relations—the best hire Spencer could remember in years. She was funny and frank and he trusted her. Redempt-Ed had snagged her from Heart & Lung and damn, the woman could spin a story. He'd gone with her on several interviews before this, and even details that made him flinch ran off her like water. She just stilled her pen, nodded, asked the exact right next question and ended up with something so seamlessly genuine that you couldn't even see the scar where her scalpel had removed the malignant bits.

When he'd asked her to do this interview, he'd expected Sue to say she was too busy, to point out what a long drive it was. Instead, she told him to go ahead and set it up. She didn't have to do that. This was Spencer's pet project, not part of any official strategic plan, but when he'd pitched it to her—pitched her on interviewing one of Bax's old writing students, some former bad-ass who'd become a best-selling novelist—Sue was all in. She got it right away, how Spencer could use it to leverage funding for the creative writing courses that had been cancelled in favour of straight literacy and the fundamentals of grammar.

And he was grateful for it. Grateful for something that kept him focused on work—that kept him from going back, again and again, to that website and staring at that picture, trying to define what was truth and what was just wishful thinking. Deciding one day he was absolutely right and the next, that he was dead wrong. Thinking crazy thoughts that were better left unthought. He couldn't go spending time and money he didn't have chasing some ghost of a dream, not when the dream he should be chasing was his family— was getting Janet back in his arms, getting back to watching Denny eat his cereal every single morning.

Spencer had taken all that crazy energy and focused it instead on this author, this interview. After more than a month of dogged determination, he was almost fed up with the bullshit. And then came the message from some bigshot agent: the author had agreed to do the interview and sit for a few photos, but he'd only give them one hour on a Wednesday afternoon. So they were racing to get there, and Spencer had to lobby Sue hard for a break, for the chance to stretch his legs and fill his empty belly. They had plenty of time by his calculations, but Sue was all business and no dilly-dally. Eat it in the car, Menard, or it leaves without you.

Haven't seen this before, he said when they were back underway. Your drill sergeant side.

I'm a serious traveller. She pulled the sunglasses off the top of her head and pressed them firmly against her face to make the point. After we're done, I'll buy you a nice meal at some roadside motel with a diner. Promise.

I'll pass, thanks, he said. Let's just get it done and get home.

He thought he said it casually enough, without a trace of anxiety, but Sue must have sensed it in his voice. You afraid of what'll happen, she asked, if we're alone in a motel?

Just not a fan of roadside motels is all.

Sure, that's it, she said, and they both laughed.

There'd never been anything like that between them—not a hint of flirtation. Sue was much too young for him, for one thing, and happily married, to hear her tell it. But when she'd first started working at Redempt-Ed and they'd become fast allies, Spencer would go home and tell Janet something funny Sue had said or some great thing Sue had done.

Then one morning, Janet told him to hurry up and get to work. I'm sure your work wife will be wondering where you are. When she said that, Janet had a streak of dried snot on her cheek and wild hair from trying to sleep next to a sick four-year-old all night. Spencer thought she must be jealous, that she was feeling insecure, and he'd moved to reassure her. Told her there was nothing going on behind closed office doors.

Just go to work Spencer, she'd said then, cupping her cheeks in her hands like her neck couldn't hold up her head any longer. You wear me out.

After that, Spencer tried hard never to mention Sue at home again, leaving her name out of even the best stories. Not that it had mattered. The forces that had been at work against him for so long—Janet's father and all the friends who'd hated Spencer before they even met him—they wore Janet down more than Spencer ever could.

Spencer shoved his seat back as far as it would go in the little car and stretched his legs out in front of him. Let me brief you on this guy and his work, he said.

Sue held one hand out toward him. I'm briefed, dumbass. All you have to do is carry the camera, sit quietly and let me do my job, same as always, she said. Here's our exit—tell me where to go.

Spencer's printed directions took them straight to the house in Sudbury, no problem. It was a surprisingly modest bungalow with a bright red door and a cracked chimney, and they were half-an-hour early. Spencer thought that would be okay, but Sue disagreed. She peeled away from the curb and took them on a tour of Sudbury's suburbs until she'd managed to get them lost, and they had to use the GPS to find their way back to the house.

WHATEVER SPENCER HAD EXPECTED—BUTLERS AND WATER in crystal goblets with lemon wedges, maybe, or a natty man with books everywhere and glasses that slid down his nose—it wasn't this. The author was wearing slippers, torn track pants and a death metal t-shirt, a leather jacket tossed over it like he had a persona to maintain. He opened the door and ushered them in without a word,

schlepping down the hall to the dining room as if he was already
tired of them the minute they'd rung the bell.

There wasn't a minute of chit-chat, either, just straight down
to business and thank god Sue was on her game. She really had
done her homework, but her subject was impossible. The author
was alternately hostile and mumbling, clearly high on himself but
full of pauses and stalls when it came to talking about his past. That,
and he swore so much, made so many coarse comments to Sue, that
Spencer wasn't sure they'd get a single, clean quote from any of it,
never mind the feel-good story they'd come for.

So you had a rough time after you got out? Sue asked, trying to
lead her subject onto some kind of path.

The author grinned. From the corner where Spencer sat like he
was an over-protective boyfriend, Spencer could see it was deliber-
ate, meant to evoke Jack Nicholson in The Shining.

I promise I can show you a rougher time than your suit-and-tie
choir boy over there.

Spencer almost cut in right then, almost called the whole thing
off, but Sue was on it. She didn't flinch, just pointed her left thumb at
Spencer like she was hitchhiking his way and said Him? You robbed a
couple of gas stations, am I right? But that one— her thumb jerking
emphatically now— he killed a girl. He's a killer.

Then Sue leaned away and set down her pen, looked her latest victim dead-on and said, I think they kicked him out of the choir for that.
But let's talk about you, and how you managed to get off losers' row.

BACK IN THE CAR, SPENCER SAID HE'D TAKE A HUNDRED
struggling drywallers trying to make good over a successful jackass
like that. Said he couldn't imagine they got anything worth coming
all this way for.

The magic is all in how you put it together, Sue said and started
the car.

Once they were back on the highway, she told Spencer she'd worked as a radio reporter. I always struggled with how much to edit, she said. There's always a lot of uh this, and umm that. False starts as they gather their thoughts, you know, before they say the thing they really want to say.

Sue pulled out and passed a slower car at a speed that left Spencer breathless. When they were clear of it, she slowed down and continued. I'd listen to the tape and try to decide how to cut that, whether to include all the uhs and ums or just keep the part where they were articulate.

And what would you decide? Spencer asked.

She shrugged. It depended.

On what?

On whether I liked the guy, or I thought he was an asshole.

THEY DECIDED TO TAKE THE NORTHERN ROUTE, AND SUE insisted on driving the whole way. Spencer didn't know if that was because she liked driving or because she didn't trust him behind the wheel, but he was happy to be a passenger. He leaned his seat back as far as it would go and dozed off for a bit.

When he woke up, they were driving through a provincial park, the terrain suddenly so familiar to Spencer in the afternoon light that it catapulted him back to another long drive. Something about the low clouds and the monotony of rocks and trees, the rhythmic splat of bugs on the windshield. Just him and Sue on an empty road, and the confines of the car like a confessional.

I'm not, you know. Spencer tipped his seat to upright. I'm not what you said back there. He blurted it before he thought it through, before he turned to look at Sue. When he did, he saw she knew exactly what he meant, so he said it more emphatically. I'm not a killer, I'm not that guy.

Well you should know then, Sue said, there's some nasty rumours going around the office.

She never took her eyes off the road ahead, but her face shifted and her lips rolled together and then it looked like she wanted to throw the car into reverse. When she finally spoke again, her voice was sad. I'm sorry, Spence. I shouldn't have said that. I know you're not that guy, and the past is the past. I know that's the whole point of all this.

She glanced at Spencer, and even with the sunglasses hiding her face, he could see she really was sorry.

Spencer looked out at a stand of tall, dead evergreens, their bare limbs a study in futility. There was so much he wanted to say that it all piled up, a jumble of syllables on his tongue. He was trying to sort it out—to start at the right place and make his way through it sensibly—thinking of this as the dress rehearsal for how he'd tell it to Janet when she was ready to hear it. But Sue wasn't waiting for his story. She had her own piece to say.

When I first took this job, I wasn't sure about it, she said, whether or not I wanted to spend my time making bad guys look good. But then I met you and you're like—like the poster boy for People Can Change. You know that, right?

Spencer watched a speed limit sign zip past, and he reflexively looked at the speedometer. Sue was twenty clicks over, and he wanted to tell her to back off but she was still running on.

Look I get it, you're not who you were. But Spencer, you have to know it's a big part of your appeal. You're the fucking embodiment of hope—for all of us.

Spencer pressed his tongue to the roof of his mouth. Don't worry about it, he finally said. It's fine. But you should watch your speed.

And he went back to looking out his window at that haunted landscape, blurring as it passed. Making up his mind.

2011

THEY WERE DOWN TO THE WIRE, DOWN TO THE LAST DETAILS
with less than a week left before Graceland officially opened its
doors. Already she had two reservations for opening weekend, half a
dozen more for later dates. The website Jerry had set up for her was
so simple it was stupid, just six photos and two paragraphs, an email
address and a phone number. No reviews and no stars and yet people
found it and were willing to pin their holiday hopes on the place.

For nine months she'd poured all her energy and almost all her
money into transforming the Tumble Inn into someplace worth
getting to. It wasn't just that the building and grounds had been
neglected for years—though they had been. To Dawn, it seemed as
if the previous owners had lost their nerve right from the start, had
backed down from any big plans and stuck to mediocrity, like they
didn't want to be seen to be putting on airs.

Or else they just ran out of money, Jerry said, sidling past her
with an oak chair in one hand. He set it down next to the row of
mismatched old chairs Dawn had collected over the months, two
of them still clamped where the glue was drying.

Jerry looked around at all of it, at the sea of old furniture piled in the dining room and waiting to be placed, then turned to face Dawn. You're furnishing this whole place in broken dreams—you know that, right?

They'd argued over aesthetics a lot in the beginning, Jerry trying to talk her into spare and sleek, into Swedish furniture sent over from the mainland. Easy to order online, he said, and I'll help you put it together. When Dawn protested, said, Wasn't the guy who founded IKEA a Nazi or something?—a story she half-remembered hearing on the radio—Jerry got fed up.

Christ, Dawnie, everybody's got a past. That's nothing to do with furniture.

But Dawn didn't agree. The past had everything to do with furniture. Besides, tourists weren't coming up this coast looking for sleek, modern styling. History, archaeology, geology: that's what the guidebooks were promising, no matter what Jerry thought.

She won the battle. It was, after all, her inn, bought with her money, and she'd never asked Jerry for his help. That was his choice. He'd insisted, retired early, traded both his big truck and his fast little sportscar for one good-sized pickup truck with a cap. Then he'd ordered two bumper stickers online, pasted *What would MacGyver do?* on one side of that truck's back end, *What would Captain Picard do?* on the other.

He claimed he was happy for the change in perspective, for the chance to be part of something new taking shape. But he kept up his protest nonetheless, grumbling whenever he was loading what she'd bought—a walnut sideboard, an ornate trunk, a hand-carved pine stool. So many lovely orphans, things left behind when a house emptied out. Things that must have carried no sentimental value at all, or too much of it.

Dawn had to fight her own sentimentality when it came time to empty the house she'd shared with Andrea. She thought she'd keep most of the furniture and appliances since neither of the kids had an interest in any of it, but in the end Dawn gave more stuff away and sent more to the dump than she piled into the back of Jerry's pickup. One load, that was it, and half of it taken up by her mattress and box spring. The trunk of her car full of glassware and dishes, the medicine cabinet an afterthought, its contents dumped into a shoebox.

After she got settled in, her little bit of furniture a perfect fit for the living quarters behind the kitchen, she started in on the rest. Went room by room, lists proliferating on every available surface. Feeling some days like this was the absolutely best thing she'd ever done, and others like she was in way over her head. Going for walks across the boggy barrens all fall and then heading back to tackle some task she felt sure she could figure out how to finish.

Jerry found a local guy who agreed to help out long as it was cash and could be done long before crab season opened. Dawn said no. No way. Said she wanted somebody who could do the job right, not somebody's nephew making a stew of things. But Jerry promised her this was one of those guys who could put the arse back in the cat, so she gave in. Paid him in cash and only knew him as Berg, and in a couple of months he'd shored up the sagging southeast corner where the water snuck in and repaired the rot, and he'd put in all new plumbing besides.

Shame, Jerry said, just a shame we're losing those skills.

For somebody so wed to the future, Dawn noticed, Jerry was starting to get a hell of a soft spot for the past. She didn't say anything about it, though, because she was tired of the bickering that had flared up between them since they'd started working together on the renovation.

It was a relief when Jerry decided he'd prefer to spend the worst of the winter somewhere not so disconnected from the world. That gave Dawn almost four months on her own, and she'd spent them in a kind of a humming fugue, baseboard heaters turned up on bust so she could plaster and paint each room, ceiling to trim. When her energy flagged, she put on a mixed tape Andrea had made for her in the eighties, in the fractious days when music seemed like the only thing they had in common. The tape was stretched to a warble and twisted in two spots where it lapsed, mid-song, but Dawn was so used to its flaws she sang right through them. When the music ran out, she flipped the cassette over and pressed play and turned it up even louder, let it wail so that all through the busy months of that winter, the music did the mourning for her.

She refinished the big dining tables they'd picked up at an auction—all different, all sturdy as hell—and ripped out the linoleum in the kitchen. Scoured and painted the plank floor. Board by board, room by room. Falling in love with the whole damn place.

The only thing she didn't love about it was the name. There wasn't a day that went by that she didn't regret the name, even rail against it, wishing she hadn't made that off-the-cuff promise. She wanted more than anything to have spent the winter months imagining unique and appropriate names for this haven she was building. To be bouncing those names off the audience that was Dead Andrea, her ever-listener, hashing it out until they agreed on a perfect fit. But she'd made a promise to Jerry in that singular moment of elation when everything seemed possible. Now she couldn't see any way to recant. Especially because she needed Jerry's help—and she especially needed it for the website, which she had no idea how to make and which he was so fond of telling her was essential, was the very backbone of Graceland's future.

Now it was deep spring, and Jerry had sold his house in Steady Brook and bought one in St. Anthony, and he was around all the time, talking at her. Adding to Dawn's panic because he wouldn't shut up and focus. Wouldn't let her focus, either, wouldn't let her concentrate on all the things that needed to be done. His mood was every bit as peevish as hers, but still he wanted to hover, rub up against her like he was starving for some friction. Like he couldn't just pick up a screwdriver and get busy.

Dawn put her hands on the chair he'd just set down and shoved it over three inches to make a point about wasted space. For fuck's sake, she said, can you just go put the last door on its hinges.

They'd salvaged five solid doors from a vacant house the week before. Dawn wanted to replace the hollow-cores that swung so light and flimsy on all the suites, so she'd taken out an ad in *The Northern Pen*. Right away she got a call from a man who said he knew an empty house just down the road from him, no owners to speak of that he knew about, so he would let her have every door in the place for fifty bucks cash.

She'd planed them all to a perfect fit. They were sanded and painted, and now she could hear Jerry down the hall tapping the last hinges into place. They just needed new doorknobs and sliding bolts to make her guests feel secure. With that done, she could finally start hanging things.

She'd start with the pressed flowers she'd framed—blue flags and harebells, a buttercup and the rare Long's braya—hang one beside each of those newly installed doors, the namesakes for what she'd call each room.

And then she'd tackle the artwork. She'd spent all of February and March finding it, asking around and paying close attention to bulletin boards and hand painted roadside signs to find them—find the painters and photographers and rug hookers who might agree to display their work. They all looked at her blankly when she'd mentioned Graceland, but they lit right up when she told them it used to be the Tumble Inn. Then their shoulders would drop, and they'd say, Oh, Ray's old place, and they'd ask a few questions about her plans there. After she'd given them a quick rundown on how she was bringing the place back up and told them again no commission—none, really—that she just wanted to have some local art, they gave her a few of their pieces. Trusted her with them and trusted that if she made a sale, they'd see the proceeds.

She figured it might be because they'd trusted Ray. He was one of their own, a man who'd tried his hand at hospitality after the fishery closed, and maybe that trust had to go somewhere after he walked away so it transferred to Dawn along with the title. She believed that until someone asked her which side of the Taylor family she came from, and she discovered hers was a common surname on this coast, and then she knew people trusted her only because they thought she had roots in this place and a right to be here. That she'd come home.

The shine came off all of it then, off all the generosity and the wonder. It was just another kind of fraud, made worse for being so unexpected. She stopped collecting; anyway, she had enough for the walls and most of it was passable. Most of it was exactly what tourists would want to see—moose silhouettes against spruce, iceberg watercolours in nearly the right shade of Windex blue. She'd lined them up along the wall in the room she called the library and left them there like convicts awaiting their hanging.

And then Sylvia showed up at Graceland, black-gloved and empty-handed. She found Dawn trying to caulk a smooth seam in a dining room window, disrupted the line by announcing herself in a loud voice.

I heard you were looking for art to sell.

The caulking gun jumped and the line went jagged when Dawn looked around to see the woman. Tall and fierce, bright pink lips and white hair perfectly coiffed—coiffed the only word Dawn knew for that hairstyle.

I got some paintings you might like, and I'm happy to hand them over on one condition.

Dawn smoothed out the line, wiped her fingers clean of caulking, capitulated to Sylvia's single, long-lasting request. Sylvia went outside then and returned with three big acrylics. She lined them against a wall in the reception area and Dawn saw each was another angle on life seeping from the crevices in barren rock, all of it rare and unexpected.

I call them Struggle and Triumph, Sylvia said, from my Burnt Cape series. This one's the cinquefoil—blooms here and nowhere else in the world.

Then Sylvia helped herself to a tour of Graceland that culminated in the library, where she studied every last piece of art that Dawn had collected. Dawn showed her the pressed flowers she'd framed, and Sylvia leaned over them for a while, looking closely, her pink mouth set firm.

You should bring these along when you come—we also do a bit of a craft circle, Sylvia said, standing up. Though I suppose there's not much skill to this.

And then she was on her way, heading purposefully for the door. She paused in the doorway just long enough to say, It's every Wednesday, mind you, so long as it's not a holiday.

Sylvia's paintings were Dawn's first introduction to Burnt Cape. Just a stone's throw away but she'd never bothered to go there. When she finally did—months later in the warmth of a summer day, Jerry holding down the fort—she saw the grey scrabble of the limestone barren was like a different kind of desert. But Sylvia had got it wrong—there was no triumph here, only desperation. Only the charred remains of something once lovely and vibrant now feigning its death and letting just a bit of its former glory seep out through the cracks.

Dawn sat for a long time on the scrabbled rock, running her fingers over a small patch of green that tufted up from between the rock, letting the ceaseless wind off the water drag a torrent from her eyes.

But the day Sylvia had brought those paintings, Dawn was still a novice at rare and unexpected. And the next day, Sylvia came back with a fourth painting, this one a spray of deep green against the grey of rock, dots of yellow and white that had to be flowers.

Might as well have this one too, she told Dawn. It's meant to be Fernald's braya, but you go ahead and tell folks it's the more famous Long's braya from down the coast. I swear only their maker can tell those two apart.

Dawn had looked at the painting dumbly until Sylvia said, Girl, you gotta know about these things to be a proper ambassador for us.

And then Dawn understood that what she'd mistaken for generosity was something even more potent. It was hope. People were putting their faith in the salvation of tourism.

The province was flush with a new prosperity, the kind everybody had stopped believing in when the fish were gone but was ready to embrace again the minute the oil boom began. A compulsory optimism had taken hold down south and crept slowly north up the peninsula, and now people talked about tourism like it was some kind of miracle cure for a dwindling population.

If it was, then Dawn had bagged an ideal location. Graceland rested midway between St. Anthony airport and the actual town. She had a rack of pamphlets beside reception that attested to just how many attractions there were—hiking trails and ecological wonders, whales and icebergs in season. But those were just extras. What really drew people was the nearby northward jag of blacktop that delivered tourists straight into a mythic Viking past. L'Anse aux Meadows was an international sensation, the self-proclaimed point where east and west reconnected after millennia of wandering in opposite directions.

On a good driving day, you could get from Graceland to Vinland in well under an hour, spend the whole day wandering the resurfaced sod huts and watching costumed guides tend the fires, feeling like you'd undertaken a grand expedition, then zip back to a comfortable inn and slide between soft, clean sheets.

Dawn was putting her faith in those tourists, too. This renovation had cost so much more than she'd expected, and she needed the business. And something else—she wanted it. She was tired of her own company, of having no one but Jerry and Dead Andrea to talk to. She had developed a sudden and earnest nostalgia for the years she'd spent at the Blue Iris Inn, for the strangers who arrived carrying skis or guitars or small rectangular briefcases full of god-knows-what. A regular whiff of accents and intrigue, yet now she couldn't remember a single interesting conversation, not even the ones she must have had with the guests she found herself drinking across from or waking up next to.

Maybe she'd been too young or just too damn cautious, but she could see now she'd missed out on enjoying it, the kaleidoscope of encounters that had been her everyday life. From this distance, it all seemed a shimmering miasma of missed connections. She didn't have a sharp memory, not until the moment Margaret told her she'd sold the Blue Iris, the whole of it, to a chain hotel that had sniffed out its potential.

And if they ask you to stay on, Margaret had said, you refuse. You've been here too long already. Standing in one place you didn't even choose is no way to live a life.

Dawn knew that Margaret was mostly talking about herself, but she also knew there was no point debating it. Margaret played the family—all of them, even Andrea—like an elaborate game of chess. Played both sides, moving the pieces expertly so they all stayed in play but knew they could, at any moment, be kicked off the board. Since Dawn had been practically adopted, dragged along like one of the kids to every dinner and brunch for years, she had no choice but to play along. She left the Blue Iris when it changed hands, despite a good offer, and for two years after, she completed paperwork at the paper mill—a job that even thinking about, all these years later, filled her nose with the stench of bleach and rot.

She'd quit even though she didn't have a single other prospect, and that's how she ended up painting houses—insides, not outsides. Not that she would have minded outsides—the money was better—but she knew most people considered it men's work since it required a tall ladder and a strong arm driving the scraper.

At first, Andrea was out of her tree over it, kept saying, It's not a real job, Dawn, it's just a job you made up. You don't even have benefits.

But it took off, demand keeping up with the home reno shows and the decorating websites, with all that seductive promise of a whole new life, starting with your living room. Within a few years, Dawn was out-earning Andrea, who spent her days helping people connect across blind telephone wires while Dawn spent hers helping them reinvent the way they wanted to be seen.

And she was good at it. It got so she never needed to tape, not unless someone wanted pinstripes, and she could finish a room in a day, moving agilely, skirting the guts of the room—the furniture and artwork and knick knacks she'd taken apart, piled up and shrouded in heavy dropcloths. And when the painting was done, she put the room back together. That was the pay off. That was a game of Tetris, and she carefully forgot the way it had gone together before so she could put it together some other, better way. A value add that pleased more clients than it pissed off.

She realized then that people were blind to their stuff the same way they were blind to themselves and everyone around them, so habituated to how things were arranged they missed even the most obvious opportunities for transformation.

Dawn had no intention of falling into that trap now, not here—not in Graceland. Not in the first place she could ever call her own.

DAWN WAS ON HER HANDS AND KNEES TRYING TO THREAD A long screw into a bronze doorknob. She didn't hear Jerry come up behind her until he spoke.

Just try it, he said. You'll be surprised what you can find out.

Dawn fumbled the screw and it fell to the floor, rolled under the half-open door. She had to crawl around to get it. When she came back, she said, No, and could you please get out of my light.

Jerry had acquired a new passion over the winter, a new reason to needle Dawn. She'd been telling him no for months. No thanks. No it's okay. No really, not interested. At first, she'd tried to make a joke of it—Stick it up your own ancestors, Jer, I'm not playing—but he hadn't laughed and he wouldn't let it go.

She figured he wasn't trying to make her heart race or her mouth go dry. He just wanted someone to share his new passion, this fresh adrenaline fix he got from tracking his lineage back and out just as far as he could, every branch and twig exposed. Twice in the winter, he'd even driven all the way to St. John's to paw through parish records at the Provincial Archives.

When he told her about it, he used the word satisfying in just about every other sentence. He was delighted with how his tree had taken shape—all the crowd he knew or knew about, plus a far-off tie to British royalty, an Earl of some import. A much closer connection to big pots of old Newfoundland merchant money. Finally, when he wouldn't stop bragging about those monied third cousins, Dawn lost her patience with it. That's all them, Jerry, she said. None of that is you.

He hadn't mentioned it again after that, not until this.

You might have all kinds of people out there who want to meet you, he said. Cousins you don't even know about.

So what? she said. The screw missed its slot and she had to slide it out, try a new angle.

Orphans like us, Dawnie, it matters.

This time, the screw caught. She twisted it in with her fingers until she was sure it was secure, then picked up the screwdriver, puzzling over what he'd said, letting it wind down through her to

see if it would grab onto something, some latent need for distant
relatives she didn't know she had.

Jerry didn't say anything, just watched her install and tighten
down the latch plate on the jamb, then close and open the door to
make sure everything worked. When she stood up and moved to
the next room, he followed her, tight as a shadow while she tore a
perforated strip from the molded plastic packaging that held the
new doorknob. She managed to pry open one small corner, but the
packaging otherwise held fast. She could hear Jerry breathing use-
lessly behind her, could almost feel his breath on her neck.

She whirled around to face him, to tell him to go to hell. But in
that unguarded instant of movement, Dawn caught a glimpse of
something in Jerry she hadn't noticed before, something the shape
and shade of lonesomeness.

You could find a family, Dawn, he said, and reached out to take
the package from her resistant grip. Reconnect with your past.

They stood facing each other, Jerry wrestling with the packaging
now and the two of them not an arm's length apart yet at absolute
opposite ends of the world. It wasn't just the impossibility of it
all for her. She wanted to tell him that she just didn't get it, why
someone would want to track down scraps of shared DNA and call
it a connection. The whole genealogy craze seemed to her like just
another new age way to vacuum up money and waste time—she'd
told him that, months ago, but he'd shrugged it off and told her to
give it some more thought. She hadn't, but clearly he had.

Aren't you even curious? he asked as the package finally opened
in his hands.

Dawn lifted the doorknobs from their perfectly formed nest,
snagged the little bag of hardware and left Jerry holding an empty
plastic shell. I'm over fifty, she said, lining the opposing knobs up
and bringing them together through the hole in the door. If I don't
know who I am, a cousin I never met can't help me now.

Jerry smiled but it was the kind of smile that carried only pity. Don't be so sure, Dawnie.

The two halves of the knob engaged. She let go of one side and reached for her screwdriver, but she'd set it down beyond her reach. Stretching for it, she yanked the knob, just a little but enough that its opposite half dropped to the floor with a bang.

Dawn didn't move, one hand still holding one knob in place, the other arm extended in the opposite direction, fingertips just grazing the screwdriver. She let out a slow, sizzling breath. You gonna give me a hand with what needs to get done, she asked, or you just gonna stand there making me tense?

After all the doorknobs and locks were in, Jerry installed light fixtures in bathrooms while Dawn walked from room to hallway to lobby to room, trying to decide where each piece of art belonged. Talking aloud the whole time, explaining why she thought here was no good and there was better, listening for Andrea's opinion. They both agreed the two small prints would be perfect at the end of the hall. As she drew the hammer back to sink the first nail, Jerry stepped out of the Buttercup. I shouldn't have left you alone all winter, he said. You've gone so stir crazy it's got you talking to yourself.

Dawn clamped her lips together, drew back and struck the nail square on, felt it dig into the stud she'd marked.

She was always talking to Andrea now, every day when she was alone and had something worth telling. Before, it had been Andrea who did most of the talking, but over the last few years Dawn had gotten better at it. Practice, she supposed, had loosened her tongue—that, and not being interrupted all the time. Dawn didn't know if a person could be dead and still be there, listening, but she kept the conversation going all the same, just like she'd promised to, and almost always she heard Andrea's response so clearly it was as if she was standing right there.

Dawn picked up the next nail and Jerry watched her sink it before he disappeared into the Harebell. They worked in different rooms, passing each other in the hall without meeting eyes for the rest of the afternoon. After he said goodnight, Dawn put on the kettle and listened to his tires crunch down the gravel driveway. Then she took her tea, a hammer and a tin of nails into the big room she was calling the Library. She didn't have nearly enough books to fill its walls of shelving yet, but she was getting there. She'd arranged comfortable seating for six around the big woodstove and she planned to hang the best of the art in there.

She had the hammer in one hand, a seascape in the other but Jerry had left the computer on again—the one he'd set up for guests to use—and its glow was a distraction. She went over to shut it down, but instead sat and typed her stepmother's name into the Google search bar.

Curiosity, she knew, was a hazard. But really, what could it hurt? People searched for people all the time, trying to connect for all kinds of weird reasons.

Carol's obituary. It hit her like a hammer on the thumb, like the knee-buckling pain of what we do to ourselves when we're not paying attention. Carol was dead—and why not? She'd be at least seventy now, and Dawn should have expected it, yet she hadn't even considered the possibility. Instead, she'd held onto an image of a much younger woman—held onto exactly the picture they'd used in the obituary that showed up first in the search. Carol's face frozen in time, as if people are most themselves when they look their best. An unsmiling photo of an untroubled woman, taken not long before she'd married Paul Benson and found herself saddled with a spiteful stepdaughter.

That picture sent Dawn right down a rabbit hole into a past she didn't know she still carried. It was a place she would have liked to show Jerry, maybe just to spite him or maybe to prove that she'd never learned to be good at attachment.

Her parents were transplants to the prairie, no family nearby, and she was an only child back when that was just asking for trouble. Once, she'd overheard a neighbour tell her mother to adopt, for heaven's sake, if she couldn't have another one naturally. Her mother had smoothed a hand over her own pale hair and nodded in that tight-lipped way she did when she disagreed but didn't feel she should say so.

But then her mother was sick. It came on fast and people stopped dropping in altogether and started dropping their voices when they walked past the house, like they were afraid they might attract cancer's attention. That left a lone ten-year-old in charge of the patient while her father went to work. All that long summer she helped her fast-diminishing mother to the toilet, wiped her down and cleaned her up and brought her food to eat that almost never got eaten.

School in September came as a relief, a return to normal that lasted just two weeks before her mother, hospitalized finally, took that last turn and the principal's faraway voice interrupted class to summon her over a scratchy PA system.

After the funeral, after a brief parade of casseroles and bundt cakes and other people's mothers smoothing her unbound hair, she and her father had each other and no one else to rely on. And that was fine, because they had a tacit agreement to be reliable, and neither ever had to worry about when the other would come through the door, or whether they would hold up their end of the bargain. They stopped going to church, saving Sundays for sleeping in and taking turns choosing how to spend the afternoon. They went to the zoo a dozen times and the horse races nearly as often, and before she was thirteen she'd seen an R-rated movie and knew how to golf and how to caddy and how to curl.

So it was a shock when her father broke ranks—when he introduced a third to their Sunday twosome, a woman as close in age to his daughter as she was to him. A bigger shock when he announced Carol was planning a church wedding.

Dawn couldn't bear thinking about it. Not how she'd acted then, or at the wedding, or a year later when she'd refused to hold her fresh-from-the-hospital baby sister. Not the way her father's smile had fallen away after he'd tried to remind her it was what she'd always wanted, a sister, and she'd spat back, *That was a long time ago, and I meant a real sister.*

It was Carol who'd try to smooth things over then, running interference like always, saying, *It's okay Paul, just give her some space.* Wanting everyone to relax long enough to get used to things, to let the path between them open up naturally over time. Carol was big on stepping back, stepping aside, never wanting to overstep until she'd stepped so far out there was no chance of making anything like a real bond. Dawn could see now how Carol must have tried, how aggravating it must have been. Dawn had made the same sidesteps with Andrea's kids a million times, afraid of coming too close, of interrupting or interfering. She stepped back and away so regularly that most times she wasn't even in the same scene.

When she was a teenager, they sometimes made her babysit while they went out for dinner or to go curling. They didn't know she mostly loved that, a ready audience in her arms as she cranked the volume on some album the adults wouldn't understand and spun her laughing little sister around the room. Her father and Carol always home too soon, and one of them always slipping her a couple of bucks, covertly, out of sight of the other so no one could ever say, *Jesus, you think she should be paid for looking after her own sister?*

She was seventeen the Saturday she stayed out all night, coming home when dawn was nudging the dark to find her father sitting in the living room, no lights on, seething. She'd been too stoned to care that he'd been worried, staying silent and barely listening while he lectured her, softly, trying not to wake anyone else. The next day,

Sunday, she'd stayed in her room, only coming out to pee and drink water from cupped hands.

On Monday morning, her father was still angry but in an unfocused way, his face the colour of storm clouds, beads of livid sweat breaking out all over him. Still, she wouldn't say she was sorry. Wouldn't even say, It won't happen again. Just left for school and put her father out of her mind until she heard her name scratching out of the PA system, knowing, even before she made it to the principal's office, that she had killed him.

Ancient family history, she thought. But no. Not even that now. Not a family or a history—just a scatter of memories fanned out and fading like Polaroid snapshots.

She read Carol's obituary out loud to the empty rooms around her, to Andrea, surprised to discover how many organizations the woman had volunteered with, how many honours she'd received for those efforts. More surprised to see her own name—her old name—in official print. It followed her father's name, which followed the words Predeceased by.

She waited for the blow of that and when it didn't come, she said, See, I'm dead too. Said it out loud but heard no answer.

She went back to reading. Felt a small tug of—what? not happiness exactly, but something nearby to it—when she saw that in that other world, the one she'd departed, there was still a half-sister and now three nephews besides.

Dawn closed the page and then the browser, left the computer, went to stand at the picture window she'd installed on the back wall so guests would be able to look out into the wilderness. The sun was setting behind a copse of ragged spruce. Its glow had burned away the trees and left just blackened silhouettes in their place.

Blood relations, Dawn was thinking, and not a soul who would ever think to look for her.

PART THREE

2013

THE GREAT NORTHERN PENINSULA, JUTTING FROM NEW-foundland's west coast, marks a tectonic divide, the Appalachian chain's end. It's the place to go if you're after icebergs and whales, if you want pictures of picturesque fishing villages or endearing moose and plenty of them.

Cheryl delivers the whole speech again, intoning it documentary style, summing up every tourist website she'd perused while planning their escape.

Why, there's even an ancient Viking settlement—

Silence from the passenger seat.

What the hell was the point in training a kid to be your side-kick if she wandered off halfway through adolescence? She wants Jenna to laugh, to join in and lay it on a little thicker the way only she could. But halfway along the 400-kilometre highway that some clever marketer had branded the Viking Trail, Cheryl has begun to suspect it's pointless, her attempted enthusiasm. She might as well give up and shut up and let Jenna sulk in silence.

If only it was complete silence, without the agonized groan every time the fifteen-year-old watched the bars of her cell service drop away, her connection to the world vanishing.

In all her guidebook recitations, Cheryl had avoided any mention of the peninsula's great big cellular blind spots.

Stop—Mom, stop!

Cheryl hits the brakes hard, glad they're alone on the highway, no one following a scant car length behind like there'd been earlier in the day.

Pull over for a second—

What's wrong?

I've got three bars!

Cheryl steps on the accelerator. I told you, we're not stopping every time you hit a signal. Now give it up and look around at the world for a while.

Jenna holds the phone up, rotating it left and right to maximize her reception. Groans again. Slams the phone into the cupholder, crosses her arms and glares out her window. Minutes of silence before they pass the sign for Nameless Cove.

Are you fucking kidding me?

Cheryl considers a rebuke but she's never been much for policing the language—her daughter's or anyone else's. She opts instead to say, That means we're getting close—can you check and see how much further?

Jenna unfolds the map they bought in a gas station after they disembarked from the ferry. She locates Nameless Cove and calculates the distance to her mother's red X, which is only a best guess. There's nothing there to help pinpoint the motel's exact location—no town, no circle, no star—just a nearby confluence of two roads, one heading for water and the other taking a slow hairpin toward St. Anthony.

There's still, like, a hundred kilometres to go, Jenna says. How do you even know this place exists, anyway?

I saw it online—pictures look nice. I think you're gonna like it.

Cheryl can see Jenna's unconvinced, and she can't blame her. The speed drops again to sixty, then fifty, and that just means there's more time to take in the latest cluster of off-white, vinyl-clad houses—all the same bungalows and bi-levels repeating all the way up this highway. All the same houses that Cheryl saw in every suburb across the country when she was filming *The PI Files*. She recognizes that there's more intrigue and drama going on in these little settlements than appears on the surface—but she also knows it's the same old intrigue and drama as everywhere else.

Next to her, Jenna's losing patience with the map, edging toward a kind of fury Cheryl knows too well. Cheryl tells her to unfold the whole thing and start over again, and she thinks she's delivered the message in exactly the right tone. But Jenna pulls the map wide in one vehement motion, and Cheryl's certain the shoulder punch she's dealt is no accident.

Before she can react, Jenna leans away from the map and reconsiders it. Hey Mom, did you ever notice it looks like Newfoundland is giving Canada the finger?

Cheryl feels the air lift and thin in the car. She glances at the map that Jenna has angled toward her. Yeah, Cheryl says, it does. And hey Jenna, did you know that the moose on this peninsula vastly outnumber the humans?

Whump. The air congeals again.

Oh god, is that why you wanted to come here—so we could see some stupid moose?

No, you idiot— Cheryl catches herself, tightens her hands on the wheel and readjusts her tone. Starts again. No honey, I mean I want you to help me watch for them—so we don't actually see the first one as we're smashing into it.

Jenna accordions the map into some semblance of folded, throws it over her shoulder into the backseat and stares straight ahead at the road, arms crossed again. Vigilant or pissed off, Cheryl can't tell but it doesn't last anyway. A minute later, Jenna is looking down at her phone again with that foul look on her face.

Cheryl's so glad she had the foresight to book them separate rooms. They've been twenty-odd hours now in close quarters, the time spent on the ferry the only chance to move out of striking distance, and Jenna's not the only one who's miserable about it. But Cheryl is determined not to turn this into what it always turns into lately—the two of them like cats on the same turf, backs up and making an ungodly racket. In her head, she repeats the lines she heard in that crowded theatre: Anger is not nurture. A raised voice can do as much harm as a raised hand.

Sarcasm is the coward's slap.

The Egg Lady had rolled out that last one as Cheryl was being escorted from the theatre. Security had caught her filming again and they'd come for her, all menace and immediacy—made her bang and barge her way down that aisle while the voice from the podium carried on.

Still, Cheryl was trying, at least off and on, to heed what she'd heard that night. It wasn't just what the Egg Lady said—it was the certainty with which she'd delivered those nuggets that had Cheryl running back over every time in Jenna's life that she'd shouted, or worse, slammed a hand down on a smooth, flat surface to ground her rage. She can't think about it—the anger, the tone, the satisfying smack of her palm on a countertop—without thinking that she was the one who cracked her daughter wide open.

But sarcasm? Christ. If even a smart, sharp remark is abusive, then every damn thing Cheryl has said to her daughter, going back at least ten years, has been an assault.

In which case she hasn't just cracked the shell, she's pulverized it and scrambled the insides and left the whole mess on the sidewalk to rot.

But hell, if the Egg Lady has left a lingering impression, well so has Cheryl. She recorded the whole thing, her forced removal. Captured it all: the mid-sentence pause of the Chicken Lady—head still bobbing well after she stopped speaking—then the heads turning her way. The irritation on face after face as Cheryl squeezed down the row. And finally, the clincher—the brutish hand of a wannabe cop coming down on her narrow shoulder to steer her from the hall as if she wasn't already leaving.

Cheryl had packaged it up in five segments, making sure she got the balance right between humour and outrage, and sent it out like a serial drama over Instagram and Twitter. She worried a little about the quality, but the low light and the jerkiness only seemed to lend credibility. Even Miguel, with all his high standards, had sent a two-word *Nice work!* to her inbox.

Her little mini-series was equally popular with those who loved its take-down of a celebrity guru and those who loved watching someone get dragged out of an event for not turning off her phone. But the whole thing really gained traction when the anti-coddlers—a faction Cheryl hadn't known existed—shared it all over their sites. And then the CBC called, and the story went national and finally, something had pushed Cheryl's unfortunate word choice off the front pages of Google.

She's survived the firestorm. Now all she has to do is rise from the ashes.

A whisper draws her attention back to Jenna and Cheryl sees her daughter is hunched over her phone, holding it two-handed just inches from her face. Her eyes are closed and her lips are moving and Cheryl thinks Jesus, no. Sex is one thing, but please, not religion.

She's relieved when Jenna opens her eyes to find her prayers unanswered. She slams her phone back into the cup holder, leans her head against the passenger window. Stares out toward the marshy landscape, its undulating beigeness punctuated by a few stands of beleaguered evergreens.

Cheryl focuses on the road ahead, the bigger picture. There's got to be something up here to do. And cut off from their troubles, holed up and rested, they can find some common ground. Negotiate a truce. Maybe even have a rational discussion about moving, about getting out of the murky small pond they've both been swimming in for too long and finding some big, clean water to start again.

She reaches over and nudges Paul Simon back into the CD player, advances straight to "Graceland."

Ooohh, not again, Jenna groans and that groan is so perfect that Cheryl wishes she had it on tape—wishes she'd thought to record this whole trip, in fact, right from the minute she announced they were going.

Come on, lighten up, Cheryl says. We're almost there—let's try to have some fun.

If you love this song so much, why didn't we go to the real Graceland instead of some faux place in the middle of nowhere?

Cheryl smiles at the idea of a faux place and sings the line about poor boys and pilgrims. Then stops singing to say, You know, Jenna, maybe this is the middle of somewhere—did you think of that?

Cheryl knows it's not. Knows, as a destination in the first weeks of spring, that northern Newfoundland has little to recommend it. When she'd told Jenna to pack a bag, that they were leaving in a few hours—a sneak attack designed to counter resistance—Cheryl had pitched icebergs and whales though she knew they were too early in the spring for either of those, and she knows the Viking site at L'Anse aux Meadows isn't open for weeks.

But sightseeing isn't the point. She considers this a rescue mission, a way to make up for all her shitty parenting, to be fully there instead of texting it in from some other location. To snatch her kid away from those—

She almost thinks those *savages* but catches herself. That word's already caused her enough trouble. Yet when she tries to come up with another word, one that has the same punch, she's stymied. And then she's sidetracked, searching her lexicon for words that attach to sharp beaks and claws, that mean those kids are ripping my daughter apart. But she can't find the word she wants and she can't take on those other kids, either—at least not until she knows who they are, until Jenna stops protecting them. All Cheryl can do is get her own kid off grid long enough to shake her loose of social media, rescue her from the black hole that threatens to suck her in—

No, not suck.

Cheryl chokes back a laugh and lets her hands pick up the beat on the steering wheel, her body loosening up to the infectious music. She thinks Jenna must be feeling it too, that maybe she's starting to bounce a bit, but then Cheryl looks at her daughter's face and sees she's still wearing all the accumulated misery in the world.

Jenna picks up her phone and barely blinks at it before she drops it into her lap. It's like the dark ages up here, she says. There's no reception at all.

Cheryl cranks the volume and leans over as far over as the seatbelt will allow. She waits for the song to tail off. Well maybe even texts will be received, she says, in Graceland.

NOW DON'T RUN AT YOUR PARTNER, DAWN, SYLVIA SAYS FROM across the table.

Dawn has no idea what that means, but Sylvia's tone makes her lean back in her chair to reconsider her cards, reconsider why she does this to herself every week.

We need some fresh blood. That's how Sylvia had phrased the invitation the drab March day she'd shown up at Graceland with paintings to trade. Three paintings to start, in return for an infinite number of Wednesday afternoons at the card table. In her naivety, Dawn had heard *fresh blood* in the most mild way, and since she knew they'd just buried one of their regulars, she'd agreed. She was thinking it might be nice to have a regular thing to do, a social afternoon with some women who were actually alive.

But you'll have to teach me, she'd said. I've never played 120s before.

Sylvia said, Course, girl, we can teach you.

When Dawn thinks of that moment now, she's sure she sees a shark's pearly whites glinting in Sylvia's thin pink smile.

Dawn was always so good at cards. As a kid she held her own at cribbage against the grownups and she'd won as much as she'd ever lost at blackjack. And once, a million years ago, Andrea's brother had dubbed her the Queen of Hearts. But this game with its highs and lows and shifting rules made Dawn feel slow-witted. It took months before she could follow both the cards and listen to the steady stream of conversation.

It's not the cards she comes for anyway—it's what goes on at the dining room table. It wasn't true, what she'd assumed, that they needed a replacement to round out the game. Most Wednesdays there's six of them and sometimes, like today, seven. Women slide in and out of the game and those who aren't playing are clustered around the bigger table, working on their mats, hooking traditional designs and inventing new ones, pointing out each other's master strokes and flaws and talking incessantly about their usual lives.

Dawn prefers that table now to the cards, even though she isn't hooking—not here. They've taught her the basics and maybe they've given up, because they don't tell her anything now. They just let her sit and watch, though she rarely adds anything to the conversation. She just takes it all in, rides along as the talk gets personal—sad, then raunchy, then sad again—and it feels delicious, feels like she's eavesdropping through an open window.

Not that she was so keen on it at first. So much of it was just trivial gossip about everyone who lived, now or before, in a hundred-mile radius of Wanda's house, where they always meet. But lately, Dawn's been able to follow more closely, to listen more carefully and she's decided the sum of the chatter is greater than it seemed. That put together, it might amount to an elaborate code for understanding modern civilization and the world in general—though when she'd said something like that to Jerry last week, he'd only looked at her funny and asked Isn't that what Google's for?

From behind her, Dawn hears, You got that scan yet, Wanda?

Next to Dawn, Wanda pulls her cards in closer. Postponed till next month, she says. Apparently the fella with the x-ray vision took off, so they're all backed up over there.

They like to keep you stewin', don't they?

Fine with me. Wanda plays a card. I'm not looking forward to it, having all those doctors peeking around in my cubbies.

They'll know all your secrets then, girl.

A round of laughter, but not from Wanda.

Secrets have gone the way of the dodo, dear. That was Mary, her voice distinctly high and strangled to Dawn's ear, like she has trouble catching her breath. I'm learning things about my granddaughter from Facebook I never wanted to know.

You're on that Facebook, too? Wanda asks. What's the good of it, anyway?

World's changing girl, you got to keep up.

World's always changing but look outside— Wanda gestures to the drapes she keeps drawn to block the draft— Always looks about the same to me.

No comment then, everyone staring down into the work at hand.

It's Agnes, from the far end of the dining room, who breaks the silence. Have you seen what that new crowd's up to, the big B&B down around? Supposed to be the thing.

Sylvia lays down the four of spades, shooting Dawn an inscrutable look, then says, That's the granddaughter of Miller who worked at the cod liver oil factory back in the day.

Oh, well that's better then, Agnes says.

Not sure it is. Sylvia's chair creaks as she speaks. Been gone her whole life and come back all high on the locally grown and the wine, I hear. Got an education—

Dawn plays the ten of spades—high card, no trump—then moves to claim the trick, knocking Sylvia off-track in mid-sentence. Dawn! Lowest card takes black, Sylvia says. I tell you this every week.

Dawn pulls back, feels her face redden. Sylvia goes back to what she was saying. Apparently she's got an education in wine.

Knows which goes best with parsnip then? That was one of the Beths, and it makes the room laugh but Dawn misses the joke because she's concentrating on not screwing up again.

God love her, it's risky, Agnes says from the other table, pouring all that money into the place and bringing in a big chef—it's a lot to think people want to come all this way for a nice meal.

It's the first time Dawn's ever heard the women talk about tourism, and she wishes she could hit the pause button on the card game long enough to listen closely.

Have you seen them, those ads the province is getting on with? Mary asks, her question dying away in her lack of breath.

Like we've all got nothing better to do than prance around on the edge of the rocks with our laundry blowing about, Wanda says. She lights a smoke, her first of the game, and produces a flowered saucer from god knows where. Dawn reaches down into her sweater pocket and draws out her pack. This is the only place in the world, she's sure, where a person can still smoke inside and though she'd never do it at Graceland, Dawn takes full advantage here at Wanda's.

Beth, the other Beth, is shuffling. Tourism, she says without looking up from the cards, is the new colonization.

A murmur of assent runs through the room, a muttered harmony like a congregational Amen.

Outsiders buying up the best and telling us what tune to dance to, just so they can bring in the steady dollar, Agnes says. Nothing new in that.

Beth is dealing, cards flying fast and sure, when Dawn looks up to find Wanda and Sylvia are both staring at her. It's Sylvia who reaches across the table, lays her hand over Dawn's. Of course we don't mean you, dear, she says. We know you're one of us—the Taylors have been around here for centuries.

Sylvia's hand is sheepskin soft but it sends a jolt through Dawn, a near-painful shock of human touch after so long with none. In that electric instant, Dawn's mother is alive and Margaret is alive and Carol is alive, like some ancient circuit of touch has been activated, and then Andrea is there, too, leaning over Dawn's shoulder like she did when they were in Nevada and Dawn played a little casino blackjack before they hit the desert. Andrea is leaning over her and she's whispering, Oh yes, they do mean you. And you better play your cards right or they'll tear you out by the roots and toss you off the nearest cliff.

Sylvia has withdrawn her hand to pick up her cards but Dawn still feels the tingle of it in the absence of its warmth. When she looks at her own cards, they're lousy and there's just nothing she can do now that will please Sylvia.

By the time Dawn arrives back at Graceland, a load of groceries and liquor to show for her day, the shadows are growing long. April is just days away but the chill of winter still permeates the place and when she calls out into that heavy stillness, there's no reply.

Still no reply when Dawn tries to strike up a conversation as she unloads her groceries in the motel kitchen, no saucy remark when she lines four bottles of wine up on the counter in her own quarters. And she thinks maybe Jerry's right. Maybe she's just been talking to herself all this time—and maybe it's time to stop pretending Andrea's right here, standing beside her, approving and disapproving in equal measure.

But if Dawn does stop, she'll only have this silence, pressing in at her from all sides. Apart from Wednesday afternoons, she's got no one else to talk to.

It's been two weeks since she opened for her third season, but there hasn't been a single guest yet and she's got no reservations. Slower every year, this business, so dead now she told Jerry not to bother to come down and cover the desk like he usually does on Wednesdays. No one's walking in, she told him, and if someone calls they can leave a message.

But of course there's no message, no blinking, no beeping. Nothing. Nowadays the phone only rings if Jerry's got something to tell her—and lately, all he wants to talk about is Nancy.

Jerry found Nancy online, one of those internet dating sites that promises to deliver an ideal match. And this time, he's sure it has. They've been seeing each other steadily since the first date, one or the other of them making the long drive to spend a day, and then a day and night, and now a couple of days and nights every week. Dawn has met Nancy twice, though the first time was so brief it hardly counted, just a quick introduction when Jerry had dropped by Graceland to show Nancy around the place. Dawn had worried for just a minute that afternoon that they might actually ask to rent a room.

The second meeting was even more awkward, a come-get-to-know-my-girlfriend lunch during which Jerry desperately tried to toss them conversational ropes.

Nancy here, she also worked at the mill in Corner Brook back in the day. Maybe your time there overlapped?

It hadn't, and Nancy had even less to say about her young mill years than Dawn did.

They came to the same stuttering standstill when Jerry pointed out their shared propensity to read books and made something of a big deal after they ordered the same meal. So it was a relief when the food came before Jerry got around to pointing out their similar taste in hairstyles. That day, both women had clipped their long hair back in a barrette set at the base of the skull. Blowing on her chicken tenders, Dawn had wondered why she'd expected a woman just seven years older to have a sprayed-in-place bouffant and bright red lipstick. Nancy had bare lips and bright, clear eyes and the only artifice Dawn could spot was her perfect manicure.

Even Nancy's warmth was genuine. She'd rescued the whole lunch time affair by making a joke out of how hard Jerry was trying. Then she leaned across the table and suggested to Dawn in a mock whisper that maybe the thing they had in common was Jerry, and did Dawn mind answering a few questions.

Dawn steeled herself, but all Nancy wanted to know was if he was always so dear or if there was something lurking, some monster in his closet. Dawn didn't even have to answer, because that unleashed a wave of affection between the new couple and it was clear they wanted lunch to be over so they could get back to being alone.

A week after that lunch, Dawn decided her long hair was dragging down her features. Who the hell, she wondered, walks around wearing the same hairstyle decade after decade? She had it cut short—really short, a little layering around her ears so it fell back the way hair did when wings weren't just for maxi pads—and she knew Andrea would tell her it was a big improvement.

Dawn goes to build a fire in the woodstove. While she waits for it to get going, she looks around at what she's made of the library, at the paintings on the walls and the books on the shelves. Every book she's ever read or owned, plus all the ones she bought at used book fairs and library clearouts and garage sales. All that substance of size and shape and colour and texture—and all of it just for her. She's almost filled those shelves with books, and she's filled the space between the books with pottery and pictures and the whale vertebrae that Jerry brought her from god-knows-where. In the centre of one shelf, she piled all the rocks she gathered over the years from the Tablelands, propped a postcard against them. She meant that to be a conversation piece, but the conversation never got started.

It's rare for guests to stay more than a night, two at the most. Most of them are here to get to the sights well beyond this place, not to read a book in a beautiful room next to a roaring fire. If they come into the library at all, it's just to stop inside the entrance and log into the computer, do their business and go on their way. Sometimes a guest might look over the books or flip through a magazine while they sip coffee first thing in the morning, but there are no impromptu salons, no long discussions between strangers. There's a stack of board games on a shelf, but no one has ever played a board game in here.

Board games and books. It was never going to be about that. It was always going to be about ratings and comments, about the websites where people had free rein to grumble. The pillows were too hard and the muffins were too dry, the water tasted like sulphur and all the restaurants were too far away. She wished Jerry had never told her about those websites, had never started printing off the comments and bringing them to her attention.

Think of it like constructive criticism, he told her. I'm trying to help you here.

But it didn't help. She bought new pillows and started adding applesauce to her muffin mix and Jerry brought in an all-plastic water cooler with a big blue, gurgling jug set on top. Guests smiled cheerfully at checkout and said everything was grand, then they went online to say there was nothing to do, that the weather had sucked and the place had no wifi and the next time, they'd stay somewhere closer to town.

And it didn't matter that Jerry was right when he told her it was a minority of opinion, that people only posted when they wanted to complain, because it was equally true that other people looked at those sites when they were making plans.

Her bookings had steadily declined after the first busy season.

Dawn drops a log onto the nascent flames in the stove and picks up her book, but she can't concentrate. She's thinking again about stars—about the stars she doesn't have and desperately needs, the points she's lost in the guidebooks. Twice she's had visits, two different outfits, and both times she's been told the same thing: people like carpeting under their feet. They want a TV in their room.

So far, Dawn has resisted. For one thing, she's got too much muscle memory of having to keep all that carpeting in the Blue Iris clean. For another, she can't believe anyone comes up the northern peninsula hoping to catch up on their shows. She did put cheap area rugs next to the beds, but it's been three years since she looked at a TV screen so she doesn't even understand what it is they're missing.

She just knows she needs those stars if Graceland's going to thrive—and since she's burned right through all her money, it has to. Which means Dawn is going to have to give up, give in to Jerry and get a satellite dish like he's been telling her right from the start.

Dawn's sick of Jerry getting his way. She's already let him set up an online reservation system she doesn't trust and load the website with about a million pictures of every damn room from every possible angle, Jerry walking around with his fancy phone in every season to capture every scrap of light and shadow while Dawn ducks out of harm's way.

All that effort—his and hers—and for what? She asks it aloud to the unmoved air in the library, but she gets no answer. This new, deeper silence still holding its ground.

The fire's burnt back on itself, gone out, and it makes Dawn wonder how anything ever burns down accidentally. She kneels to start again, twists up page after page of the lifestyle section, lays a crisscross of birch bits on top of the paper.

She's just lit the match when she hears the front door open.

CHERYL HAS THE CURTAINS SHOVED SIDEWAYS JUST ENOUGH to let daylight pour in. It's a blue-sky morning, the sun right there and bright, but the window is filmed over with everything that latched onto it during the winter so the light is diffused. Still, it's enough to illuminate a hair sprouting on her upturned chin and one of those fine, long black fuckers lying against her jawbone.

She flattens her tongue to the roof of her mouth so she won't snag the loosening flesh and grabs hold of it. The tweezers don't catch it. She moves to a coarser hair, tries again, but it slips away from the brushed steel. Dammit, these were her best tweezers, unfailingly reliable, so she knows Jenna must have got hold of them, must have used them to bend a wire, fix an earring or flatten a clasp—some small, urgent task that has ruined forever the grip of their faithful slant tip.

Cheryl tosses them onto the bed, clicks the compact mirror shut and heads for the front desk. The woman who runs the place, Dawn. Hard to tell but she's definitely older with that white gold hair. And even a woman that fair has to have a pair of decent tweezers.

She finds Dawn in the kitchen, mixing the next morning's muffins. Blueberry oatmeal, same as this morning's, and Cheryl realizes it must be the same each day—homemade muffins, boxed cereal, two kinds of bread beside the toaster. A carton of eggs by the microwave with poaching pods and instructions posted nearby for soft, medium and hard. A jug of orange juice, a few pieces of fruit in a bowl. Coffee on, teabags ready. A nearly effortless spread.

Not hard to run a place like this, Cheryl thinks, though her impression had not been as favourable when she and Jenna arrived, already aggravated because they'd missed the turn in the dark and

gone ten minutes too far before Cheryl realized her mistake and
turned around. Their bladders full and their patience exhausted and
then to find out they weren't expected—that the reservation Cheryl
had made and paid online was somehow lost in the ether.

Jenna hitting peak anguish at the news of no wifi but settling
down again after she discovered a hardwired computer in the
common area. It was so slow that Cheryl knew it must be dial-up
technology, but after the drought she'd just survived, even Jenna
was grateful for a few drops of rain. By the time Cheryl had warmed
up a few bowls of lentil soup, Jenna was basking in the harsh glow
of her social network.

She complained between spoonfuls—only some of the pictures
loaded and video didn't work at all—but her voice was subdued,
lacking any of the rage it had carried all the way here. Cheryl
couldn't tell if she was tired, or if the kid was actually ready to
admit defeat.

Tired, it turned out. Today Jenna's in high umbrage over the
crawling internet, and Cheryl's already had to tell her twice to stop
banging on the keyboard. If you break it, you'll pay for it, she'd
threatened, and then gone back to her room wondering if that was
the kind of threat the Egg Lady would sanction or condemn.

So, Cheryl says when Dawn doesn't look up from her batter,
weird request.

Even though she's startled, Dawn's plastered a full-on fake hospitality smile across her face when she turns to Cheryl.

I don't suppose you could lend me a pair of tweezers for a few
minutes?

Dawn doesn't hesitate, doesn't even blink. Just says, Of course,
but not in the woman-to-woman way Cheryl would like. Dawn puts
a ready-fit lid on her bowl of batter and leaves through a side door
that must lead to her private quarters and Cheryl thinks *four more
days of this.*

Four whole days out here in the middle-of-fucking-nowhere, Jenna face-and-eyes into that computer. No TV, no Netflix, no one to talk to. It's just ten o'clock on the first day and already Cheryl feels like packing up the car and moving on to somewhere more interesting. Whatever she was expecting at Graceland, it wasn't this. It was something more kitsch, more populated. An aging Elvis cult, maybe, or a desperate dive full of quirky characters.

She's got her equipment with her, her camera and tripod, battery packs and memory cards. Ready for anything. But this place is an absence of anything. There's nothing going on here, no way to even spin something interesting. She's already considered and discarded the idea of doing a chronicle of the lives that time forgot.

She heads back through the lobby, stands in the doorway of the library. Jenna is immersed. From this angle, Cheryl can't tell which social media account she's scrolling through, but at least she doesn't look distressed, isn't bashing at the keyboard and swearing or crying. In fact, she looks bored, and Cheryl realizes it's the best she can hope for.

And anyway, wasn't that the whole point of this trip, to take the edge off? Well the edge is certainly off.

Dawn finds her there and hands her a long pair of tweezers—the longest, pointiest pair Cheryl has ever seen. Cheryl coils her fingers around the cold steel, nods thanks and then says, I swear, I'd have time to run the world if I weren't busy getting rid of unwanted hair.

She ignores what comes from behind her then—Jesus, Mom. Embarrassing much?—and sees a twitch at Dawn's mouth that might actually be a real smile if she'd let it out. She doesn't though. She just says, Those are tight enough to hold even the thinnest flower petal, so they should do the trick.

The sun is blasting through the window nearby, illuminating Dawn's face and Cheryl can see now that Dawn doesn't have a single whisker, just has that barely-there pale down lying flat to her face.

Hey kid, Cheryl says. You can't sit there all day. Get dressed so we can go out somewhere.

You go ahead, Jenna says, and her gaze stays fixed on the screen, eyes wide and barely blinking.

Nope, you're coming with me.

Jenna's expression doesn't change, but all the same Cheryl hears the sneer in her daughter's voice when she asks where they're going and why she has to come along.

I'm sure we can find something interesting.

For you maybe. Jenna's words wrapped in a snarl. She spikes the enter key twice, hard and harder.

And because, darling, Cheryl's says through gritted teeth, we can probably find cell service, maybe even some wifi.

That's got Jenna's attention, yanking her up out of her snarling slouch. Cheryl leans quickly toward Dawn, asks in a low tone if that's possible, if there's cell service and wifi within reach.

Dawn nods and then she's stepping away, taking herself out of this scene. Fleeing the familiarity of it, the way this woman reminds her of Andrea, how the daughter is a haunting of herself at that age—two disparate lives colliding, making Dawn feel disoriented and clumsy. She needs to get back to her muffin mix, to do something so rote it steadies her.

But Cheryl doesn't let her break away. She follows Dawn, asking in a confidential undertone if she has kids.

Dawn tells her no, no kids, and she's still moving away, a soft-stepping flight, when Cheryl says, That's why your skin is so smooth—it hasn't been wrecked by the heartache of children.

Just leave the tweezers at reception when you're done with them, Dawn says over her shoulder. She picks up her pace then, keeps walking, all the way to her living quarters, shuts the door behind her and sits down hard on a chair at the small dining table that doubles as her desk and glares at the bright red couch she bought last year.

It's too big for the room and now everything's off balance. She uses a big toe to force the shoe off the heel of the other foot. Changes her mind and reaches down to pull it back on, grabs her cigarettes and marches through her tiny bedroom to the sliding glass doors.

Outside, it's colder than she expected but she doesn't bother to go back for a coat. She takes one deep pull after another, watching the smoke boil out of her mouth, thinking about the heartache of children, about the last time Tara came home.

Came unexpected, let herself in and called Dawn—actually called downstairs, landline to landline—and asked her to come up to Andrea's bedroom. Dawn had gone reluctantly. It wasn't quite eight months since Andrea's death and the room hadn't let go yet of that smell, of infirmary and grief. The only place Dawn wanted to be in that room was facing into the closet, where the smell of real Andrea still clung to her cottons and wools.

But now Tara wanted to clean out that closet, to take some of her mother's things for herself and bag up the rest for donation.

I just wanted to know, she said when Dawn appeared in the doorway, if there's anything you want from the jewelry box or the closet?

She presumed that Dawn hadn't already been through it all, hadn't already taken what she wanted—her favourite earrings, a scarf, a blue wool cardigan, rough and pilling and still pungent with Andrea.

Dawn stayed in the doorway, fingering the small rose gold rose on a chain that she wore—a birthday gift from Andrea years earlier—and shook her head. No, she said, I don't need any of it. But I appreciate you thinking of it.

They stood looking at each other for a long second like they were standing on opposite sides of a river with no bridge between them. Tara was a few years older now than Andrea had been when Dawn had moved into this house. She couldn't make out any of the baby that Tara had been, but she could see Andrea lurking in the shape of her daughter's jaw, the way Tara's thighs pressed together and her calves bowed away, and Dawn wondered how you could know someone their whole life and still feel like a total stranger.

A total stranger who was taking it upon herself to dig through Andrea's possessions.

Let me help with this, Dawn said. It's too much for just you.

They sorted through Andrea's drawers and closet together. Tara built a small mound on the bed of things she wanted to keep—scarfs and purses and a pair of boots, an old blouse, all the photos in their envelopes and two empty photo albums. All the rest they put in garbage bags to be dropped off to charity. When Dawn asked if there was anything in the house that Jacob might want, Tara assured her that he wasn't sentimental like that.

He only likes new things—whatever's the trendiest and the most expensive.

That was true, he'd always been like that. Just like his father, Andrea said. If Dawn took the kids out shopping for Andrea's birthday, Jacob would always want to buy the highest-end, most expensive brand of whatever they were getting. Only he wasn't paying, and Dawn clocked a lot of hours over the years wrestling him down to the mid-range. She wondered if that was why he left so young to go stay with his father—if he was tired of all the sacrifice, of having to settle for good-enough.

When the closet was empty, Tara gathered up her small pile of souvenirs and thanked Dawn for her help. Looking around the room one last time, Tara teared up then swiped at her eyes impatiently. I try so hard not to do that, she said, because I know Mom would just tell me to quit moping around and get on with it.

And then she drove away, leaving three garbage bags still sitting open on the bed, and Dawn still thinking that's exactly what Andrea would say.

Her cigarette has burned down to the filter, half of it smoked by the wind, and there's a hollow ache beneath her ribcage when she pulls in the last draw.

She wrenches the door open and charges for the phone. Calls Jerry. Skips hello and gets straight to it—Your online reservation system is shit, Jerry. I got two guests and I was totally unprepared for them.

DAWN'S JUST PASSING THE RECEPTION DESK WHEN SHE HEARS the clacking of the keyboard so she knows one of them—the mother or the daughter—is in the library. She hesitates, looks down at the half-finished mat in her hand, the bottle of wine she's been whittling at for the past hour. She could just go back to her room but she can't bear spending the evening holed up in there. It's become her habit in the long months alone to treat the library as an extension of her space, to keep the woodstove roaring and sit near it while she struggles to get this mat she's hooking to look like it does in her imagination. She's got the grey expanse of cracked limestone more or less how she wants—rippled ledge, a slight deepening to signal a crevice leading off to one corner—but she's struggling with the flowers, two on a single stem, and she's close to ripping them out, trying over or else abandoning the damn thing altogether.

Maybe she should try a different flower, start with the buttercup—its open simplicity and uniform, sunny yellow. The Kraft dinner of flowers, familiar and understood. Why keep trying to fashion the peculiar pinwheel cant of the four-petaled Long's braya, all those knotted tongues at its centre? It's not even the prettiest flower, though Dawn loves it best for its rarity, for its tenacious hold on the limestone barren. For all the peril it finds itself in.

She should just stick to her pressed flowers. Even dead, desiccated and trapped under glass, a blossom goes on looking like it did—paler, severed from its body, but still a close enough resemblance to what it was in life. The Long's braya, under glass, remains unmistakeably itself.

Not that anyone would ever recognize it. Every time she puts a guest in the Long's Braya room, she sees the question in their eyes, how they're trying to sort out the syllables they've just heard. At least when they ask outright, she can show them the pamphlet with the pictures of the flower, say, See, this one—it's rare now, endangered. After that, they might remember the name, Long's braya, when they come back to ask for more towels or to let her know they're checking out earlier than expected.

Still, she's taken two of them, those near-extinct flowers. Cut them off in their prime. She needed one to press and frame to hang on the door to the room she'd named for it, another to pin down her design for this mat. A photograph might have done, but it's her first mat, and she wants it to turn out better than just okay. She wants it to be worthy of the Wednesday women.

The whole thing, everything, looked better when she was here alone—when every damn light in the place wasn't blazing, wasn't sending her electrical bill sky high. And maybe it's that, or maybe it's the chill in the air that makes Dawn wish for kerosene lamps, for sconces surrounded by a warm yellow glow. She'd read once, in some novel she's otherwise forgotten, that humans crave firelight, that modern notions of it, so devoid of smoke and soot and danger, are a romance born of instinct. After she'd read that, Dawn bought two hurricane lamps and a dozen pillar candles, but she's never burned a single one. There's no point in the summer months, when it stays light so late into the night. And why bother when the only light people ever come to the library looking for is the kind that beams strong and steady from the computer monitor, like it does now.

She takes another quiet step forward and sees it's the mother at the keyboard, the daughter nowhere in sight. Dawn feels a rapid release of tension. There's enough friction between the two of them to light every room in Graceland. She'd sensed it when they'd checked in, and she'd hesitated, wondered if putting them side by side in Long's Braya and Lady Slipper, an adjoining door between, was the right idea. But later she'd heard them laughing down there, so she figures they must have thrown open the door and found some common ground.

Dawn starts to back away, deciding she'll go back to her room after all, but she's cast a shadow that's caught Cheryl's attention and the woman looks up from the computer, one eye reflecting its blue screen.

Dawn reverses into forward. Sorry to disturb you. Do you mind if I light the fire?

Dawn's voice has the desired tone—the one she learned first from Margaret then perfected in a seminar the province offered on good travel management. But the smile she offers feels like nausea, and she lets it fall away fast.

Doesn't matter—Cheryl's not looking at Dawn's face. Her eyes have fallen to the wine in Dawn's hand. What a great idea, she says. Mind if I join you?

And it's Dawn's own voice that sounds pleased, that offers to go get another wineglass. But there's treachery in that voice, too, and she knows it's just a hangover, the bitter aftertaste of all the bottles she split with Andrea over the years, progressing from sweet to dry, from white to rosé to red like they knew they were on a darkening journey.

It's a bad habit, Dawn knows, and she reminds herself to knock it off, to stop filtering everything through Andrea's absence. Still, she's relieved when Cheryl tells her she doesn't like wine, but she's got a bottle of scotch in her room.

SPENCER THINKS HE WON'T TELL HIS COLLEAGUES WHAT HE'S doing, won't tell them he'll be staying on the island while they drag themselves to the airport at the crack-of-dawn for a flight home.

He'll just let them figure it out on the plane, maybe worry that he's slept in and missed it. Worry all the way home— Where's Spence? Has anyone heard from Spence? He didn't make the flight.

Fret and anxiety, maybe sending him emails over the whole long weekend and waiting for the ping of his reply, getting worked up about it before they finally hit the staff room on Monday morning, look up at the whiteboard above the coffee machine and see he's booked a few days off.

Or maybe they don't give a damn. Maybe they figure Spencer is Spencer's own problem. He supposes he'll be able to tell by the number of messages he gets.

Knock it off, Menard. That's what Janet would say to a scheme like this, did say plenty of times back when she thought he was worth the effort of getting angry at. She'd tell him to stop trying to make people prove they cared when it was obvious they did.

Her belly round when she said it the first time; her face round, too, all of her like a ripe apple and she'd never wavered, not even when the hospital sent them home with that huge tiny responsibility like they could be trusted to know how to keep a newborn alive. Sometimes, like when she deposited their infant son in his arms, he worried that it was just the way she accepted him, mean streak and ugly past and all, that made him love her so much. But in the year they've been apart, really been apart this time, he's discovered that it's all of her he loves. Every ounce and bulge and scrap. And if he'd been more certain of it and of her, it wouldn't have gone in the shitter and he wouldn't have this keen ache that's worse than his knee on the dampest day, worse even than anything he'd been dealt in prison.

So he'll tell them, tell Sue and Dave—but not yet. Not until after a few rounds have eased some of the irritation of the annual meeting, of all that posturing and powerpointing and blather. For three days they've been in it with Redempt-Ed staff from across the country, fifteen of them packed into a musty, windowless conference room in St. John's. Everyone growing more and more leaden from the oily conference muffins, more and more bitter from drinking lukewarm battery acid that the hotel passed off as coffee. Tonight, the provincial reps had planned ahead and made their own dinner reservations—someone tracking down a recommendation, best seafood in town—but they'd neglected to invite the head office staff to join them.

And really, that's fine. Sue spots a taxicab in the parking lot and Spencer takes the front seat, asks the driver to take them to the best authentic Newfoundland bar.

Not a tourist place, Spencer says. We want a place where the locals go.

I know a place, the cabbie says, where there's no kissing of the cod.

His accent thick with Eastern Europe so Spencer thinks he heard wrong.

Ten minutes later they pull up to a downtown curb and the cabbie points to a painted sign, takes the bill Spencer gives him and hands Spencer a blank receipt. They're on the sidewalk in the drizzle, the cab just taillights moving away, before they realize the bar's entrance is down a steep flight of concrete stairs, cigarette butts swirling in puddles on every step.

Spencer's knee, always so much worse in damp weather, is bawling and he has to hang onto the iron railing, glad the others are behind him and can't see his face. At the landing, he fishes out his cigarette case, the polished steel reflecting the red light from the bar's Open sign. Sue and Dave stop abruptly, flanking Spencer, and he gestures at the butts littering the ground. Might as well make like the locals, he says, flipping open the case to see he's got just two left. He's usually so disciplined—rolls five smokes every morning and that's it, his daily limit. But the anxiety of this trip, all of it, has him rolling a few extra. He's sure he had six or seven in here this morning.

Sue and Dave stand like obedient children beside him. You guys go ahead, he says, cupping a hand around the flame of his lighter. I'll catch up.

But they don't go ahead. They wait, Sue looking down the stairs at the street below and Dave looking up, both watching cars sluice by as if the view from this narrow alley is exactly what they were hoping to see tonight.

Sure doesn't look like the commercials, Dave finally says.

Spencer takes a last drag, drops his cigarette in a can of sand that's set out, he assumes, for just that purpose. Sue pulls open the heavy wooden door of the pub but they let Spencer take the lead and he likes that—likes knowing that even limping this bad, he's the closest thing they have to feeling secure.

Inside, the pub is dim, its low ceiling pressing down on dark walls hung with everything they could find to hang on them. A hodgepodge of mismatched chairs sit empty and the dearth of locals somehow adds to the claustrophobic effect. Dave starts to suggest they find a different place, but Sue cuts him off. I got the first round—what are you drinking? she asks.

Thank god for Sue. Spencer is sick and tired of complaints, of taking shit over every lousy bit of this trip. Planning this meeting was like everything else in his job—too many details, too few resources, too little fun. They'd had to stay at an inexpensive hotel on a commercial artery, far out on the outskirts, nowhere near the downtown they'd all fallen for over the internet. Nothing nearby but chain restaurants and a mall with all the same stores everyone recognized from whatever city they'd come from.

A dozen people complaining to Spencer—three days of solid complaints, morning to night—and he could see there was plenty to complain about. The sun hadn't shone once and the wind was wet and still as bitter as winter. Even the guy from Saskatchewan complained about the cold. Overhearing him, the server who cleared their plates after the last buffet lunch had shrugged and said, Sure, it's not even April. Come back in July.

The rancor shifted, then, from the weather gods to Spencer, that asshole Derek from Alberta calling down the table, Christ, don't you even look at the weather when you organize these things?

Hey, Spencer had said, holding up two hands splayed in surrender. I'm not the guy in charge. This wasn't my call.

He wanted Harve to take note, but the prick was looking at his phone. Probably reading up on the latest trends in charismatic leadership or else buying some slick app to automate his farts. Harve had a digital agenda up his in-charge ass and absolutely no interest in face-to-face conversation with the troops. Thank god he was leaving even before the last meetings wrapped up—earliest exit possible, and Spencer knew Harve always planned to travel alone so no one else knew he got to fly first class.

Sue sips her wine and suggests after drinks, maybe a walk around to see the downtown.

No fucking way, Spencer says. Sue knows all about his bum knee and Dave doesn't need to, so he settles for yet another nod to the shitty weather. It's pissing down rain, he says.

Right, Sue says. But Christ, Spence, we haven't seen anything since we got here.

We went on that bus tour—

Are you kidding? Sue's just halfway through her second glass but she's starting to look pouty, her lips haloed with the stain of merlot. We skirted around downtown, drove up a big hill in the rain and then drove back down, she says. And the bus was damp and overheated and it stunk of puke. It sucked, Spencer, it sucked.

So not a five-star rating then? Hey since we're trashing things, he says, employing his best deflect and distract move, let's talk about the worst presentation of the week.

Dave leaps in. Ontario hands down, he practically shouts. You can't beat two hundred tiny little words on every slide and a presenter who reads them verbatim.

Sue nods in agreement. The worst, absolutely.

Hang on, Spencer says. Is a bunch of words really worse than three words, bullet-pointed?

I think so, Dave says, but his tone says he's wavering.

Oh, right, that was worse, Sue says, tipping her wine glass up and her head as far back as it will go.

You meditate on these three words while I drone, Spencer says. He watches the last shivery drop of cheap Merlot slide toward Sue's mouth. Wait, I know, he says, stroking the beard he's grown in the last few months. It was a haiku.

Sue's laugh so large and sudden that her wine-stained teeth are visible, all at once.

It lifts Spencer's spirits, knowing he can still make her laugh even in the pissing-down rain, that they're still friends. He's been edgy about that for a month, ever since the last trip, when she'd said too much and he'd rewarded her with stony silence for the rest of the drive home from Sudbury.

Neither of them has ever mentioned it, but it's been there all the same, a distance he didn't want to explain, or jolly his way through. But now that they've been through the wars together, he feels bad for not letting her in on this little trip he's about to take, this big secret he's been keeping. He's tempted, just this minute, a couple of beers under his belt, to tell her the bald truth of what he's up to but he can't, not in front of Dave. And that's why Dave is here, why Spencer asked him to come along tonight—to keep Spencer from getting too comfortable and spilling it all. Jinxing everything that was suddenly possible—the whole pantload of a future running out in front of him, all his debts paid. And Janet and Denny, that reconciliation he's dreaming about, the three of them under one roof again.

Hey Spencer— Dave is holding both his palms out on either side of his empty pint glass like he thinks a baby is about to drop from the ceiling and it's his job to catch it. Why do they always hate us so much by the end of the meeting?

Dave isn't young enough to still be so fucking green.

Because Dave, Spencer says, they hated us that much at the start of the meeting. He hands Dave his empty glass. It's your turn to buy.

I gotta hit the can, Dave says, fishing in his back pocket. Here, use my credit card.

Spencer eyes the card, thinks goddamn cashless generation.

Go ahead, Dave says, you don't need a PIN, it's one of those you tap.

Dave thrusts it toward him a little too aggressively, and that insistence makes Spencer pull back, makes him shake his head and say I'm not using your card. He hears the distrust in his voice.

Dave doesn't retreat. What's the problem?

You never know, Spencer shrugs. Something might happen, a fraudulent charge and suddenly you're remembering the ex-con who had your card for five minutes. I'll use cash.

Dave chuckles like he's uncomfortable, shrugs and walks away, slipping the card back in his wallet as he goes. Sue says Jesus Spence—

He puts up his hands. I know, he says, and he does. This is one of those examples Janet would use to prove that he's too wary, too walled up and on his guard. Look Sue, Spencer says. Identity theft's a big charge—forgive me if I'm not taking that chance.

I don't care about that, she says. I mean Jesus, I can't believe you booked us on a five-a.m. flight. You hate mornings.

Spencer's up and ready to head for the bar, but he figures now is as good a time as any. I'm not on that flight. He tries hard to sound sheepish, to tamp down his giddiness. I'm staying in Newfoundland, heading to the west coast. I've got an old friend out there I'm dying to see.

Cheryl sets her glass down on top of the field guide to northern flowers. Dawn placed that book on the coffee table more than two years ago and she's certain no one has ever bothered to thumb through it since. Dawn eyes the glass, ice cubes bobbing in scotch, anticipating how long before it starts to bead with sweat, the air warming now that the fire's roaring. She waits until Cheryl picks up the drink to slide the book aside and put a coaster in its place.

Dawn would smile to take the sting out of the criticism if Cheryl was paying attention, but just now she's looking at the books on the shelf to her right—Sir Wilfred Grenfell's autobiography and *Grenfell of Labrador* and *Adrift on an Ice-Pan*—and she doesn't set the glass back down. Instead, she cradles it close to her chest and points to that gathering of books.

I should tell Jenna these are here. She bought Grenfell's autobiography at the gift shop today and she's holed up in her room with it.

She likes history?

News to me, Cheryl says. I thought as soon as she hit a signal, she'd be lost in her phone. Instead she used it to take pictures of every plaque in that museum, and then she scrolled through, reading them over on the drive back.

It had been Jerry's suggestion. After Dawn had finished chewing him out over the reservation system, she told him she had bored guests, a mother and her teenage daughter, and what was there to do this time of year?

Send 'em to see the good doctor, he'd recommended.

It was the other grand adventure story at the tip of the Northern Peninsula, much more recent than the Vikings but no less fabled. The good doctor was Wilfred Grenfell, an Englishman who came to treat the ailments of the fisher folk and Labrador Inuit and hung around to build a small empire on compassionate service. Doctors on dogsleds, Jerry called it when he'd dragged Dawn off to see the display a few years back, though what he'd wanted were more pictures of the legion of young nurses who braved the northern wilds to tend the malnourished and the afflicted.

Doc's always in, Jerry had said over the phone, and people do love stories about suffering.

These two are suffering enough just being together, she'd said. But Jerry reminded her that Grenfell's story had the kind of suffering that felt good—far away and told through the lens of someone with a plan to fix it—a kind of balm for the agony that gets dished up every day in high definition. So she'd handed Cheryl and Jenna a brochure and sent them off to the Grenfell Historic Society in St. Anthony, which gave Dawn a few hours to get to the grocery store and get used to the idea of sharing her space.

Now Cheryl wants to know if anyone's *done anything* with Grenfell, tried to breathe life into this story, made a documentary or—?

Cheryl's sitting on the couch and Dawn on the matching loveseat, the two pieces set perpendicular to form an L that frames the woodstove, arms touching at the tips. A matched set from a moving-away sale, hardly used. The Grenfell books, too, leftovers from someone else's life. Dawn has to turn before she can extend her arm to them, use a flat-handed sweep to indicate *all of these*.

Ah, Cheryl says. I guess he's been done to death.

Is that what you do?

Do things to death? Cheryl laughs. You've been talking to Jenna.

There it is again, the edge that reminds Dawn of Andrea. She watches the other woman finally set her glass on the coaster, says, I meant do you make documentaries?

Dawn had seen the equipment when it came in, all those black cases, a tripod. The daughter prickling—Mom, I thought this was a vacation—and Cheryl swearing she was only bringing it in out of the cold.

Yes, I make films—but not history. Too dangerous these days.

Dawn has no idea what she means, but the way Cheryl says it, reaching for her bottle, feels like a gate slamming shut.

Full glass in hand, Cheryl resettles herself, tucks her feet up under her and leans on the arm of the couch. I used to work in TV. I directed the PI *Files* until we were canceled. She surveys Dawn over her glass while she drinks, sees there's not a gig of recollection. The reality TV show, you know, about private investigators?

Still not a clue. Right, Cheryl reminds herself, no TVs, so she tries a different angle. We did an episode in Newfoundland a few years ago that sparked some controversy. You might remember it— Dawn shakes her head.

We followed an investigator, little weasel of a guy the insurance companies hire to spy on claimants, guys with back injuries out cutting wood or riding snowmobiles, that sort of thing. We got about a million complaints. People from Newfoundland said we were making it look like you were all a bunch of crooks. People from the rest of the country said they couldn't understand the accents. We figured we'd have to use subtitles next time, but we never got back here.

Cheryl can tell Dawn is only pretending to be interested, and she thinks she might as well be talking to a vacant lot. Anyway, nobody liked those insurance stories—too much sympathy for the subjects—so Cheryl says, Cheating spouses, that's what our audience wanted. More cheaters, more desperate confrontations.

Really? Dawn says, and Cheryl can't tell what the hell is going on under that controlled surface, or if anything's going on at all. It makes her wonder if her radar's broken, if that's just one more kind of transmission that won't be received in this backwater.

Really, Cheryl says. People loved it, even though it was always the same ending. She offers a sampling, deadpan: Honey I'm sorry. It was all a mistake, it's you I love.... God, how many times can you do that story?

There it is, a ripple across that smooth surface. Dawn slides two fingers down the stem of her wineglass and back up and Cheryl sees her do it, knows she's struck a chord. Knows there's a story hiding underneath.

Just once, she says, I wanted someone to say, ever so calmly, well you caught me. But nope, always the begging and the sobbing, every damn time.

And you put this on TV? Dawn asks, and she's no longer gracious.

You don't clock even a few years in reality television without having a speech ready for this particular kind of judgment.

Listen, Cheryl says, all kinds of people give up their privacy for a chance to be on TV—that's the actual reality of reality television. Anyway, the spouse who hired the investigator was always thrilled to be chosen, and why not? We did their hair and makeup and wardrobe, and they got to look their best while they stuck it to their cheating spouse.

I just can't believe— Dawn is clutching her wineglass and her eyes are trained on the far bookshelf, on a little pile of rocks set at its dead centre. I mean, exposing people like that.

Cheryl shrugs. People have their reasons for wanting to be exposed. And if they changed their minds, we had ironclad contracts.

She chuckles at that, but Dawn obviously can't see the humour in it, in any of it.

What, you've never had a cheating partner you wanted to stick it to?

Dawn shakes her head. I've never been married, or even close to it.

Cheryl's radar kicks in then, full force. But he was, she says. She doesn't have to wait for an answer. So how long did it go on?

Dawn swirls the last bit of wine in her glass, watching it. Making a decision. Ten years, she finally says. Right through my thirties.

Cheryl's heard worse—heard twenty years, even thirty. Wow, she says, you must have really loved him to waste a whole decade on him.

Dawn drains her glass, refills it in one smooth rotation and she's remembering just how perfect that decade was. Two dates a week, always in the cloister of her apartment, her bed, her shower—candlelit dinners, no one tugging at their sleeves, no to-do lists or fights over his mother. Great sex and Bryan always out the door before it got too late to head upstairs and hang out with Andrea.

But Dawn knows that's not the story Cheryl wants. She's angling for anguish and Dawn's trying to decide whether to accommodate that desire. Wondering how many stars it might be worth. She hasn't answered the last question and already there's another being cast: Did you work with him?

No, Dawn says. I met him at a party.

I wanna hear all about it, Cheryl says. Just let me run to the bathroom and track down more ice.

When she's gone, Dawn lays a heavy junk of spruce on the fire and watches the flames lick up around it. She hasn't thought about Bryan in so long, can't picture him anymore, can barely recall the details from those ten years together. She can only remember how it started, Andrea charging downstairs on a Thursday night, clutching a videotape to her chest. You have to come to a party with me on Saturday, she said. I need you to be my Louise.

Your Louise? Dawn knew exactly what she meant.

People are always telling me I look like Thelma— Andrea held the video up beside her face— but the costume won't work without a Louise.

Dawn considered Andrea, how little she actually looked like Thelma, like the actress Geena Davis, though she'd concede there was something in the snap of Andrea's eyes and the fullness of her mouth.

But I don't look anything like Louise, Dawn said. She hated Halloween parties and Andrea knew it.

That's the thing about costumes. A wig and the right clothes, a few props—people imagine the rest. C'mon, please? Andrea held the video box over her face. Come upstairs, she said, tilting her head to peep out. Watch it with me and you'll see how perfect it is.

As soon as the movie had ended and the credits began, Andrea turned to Dawn, all shiny-eyed. You see why it has to be you now, right? A rounded popcorn husk was curled around her incisor like a gold cap.

Dawn's hand was still clapped over her mouth where it had landed when the movie pair launched off the cliff. She held it there, stared at Andrea, at that golden husk, and knew she'd lost the battle.

On Saturday night, Andrea knotted a bandana around her throat, hauled it off, twisted it and started again, saying I want this to be perfect.

Dawn couldn't take it anymore. She flicked Andrea's hands away, said, You know they died, right?

That's what makes it so great. They had the guts to go for it and not surrender. Now bend over so I can tie up your hair.

Then Andrea crammed that awful nylon wig on Dawn's head and dusted her face and white tank top with brown eyeshadow to approximate desert dirt. She handed Dawn a pair of sunglasses to hide her blue eyes and stood back. Geez Louise, she whispered.

The party, when they arrived, was more subdued than expected and almost no one else had bothered to dress up. Dawn could feel Andrea deflating fast as they shed their coats, but as soon as they walked into the living room, someone saw it—saw Thelma and Louise—and Andrea was back on top, back in character. Eventually, though, she noticed that lack of costumes and wondered aloud why there were so many slackers at this party.

Hey, we're all just extras in your movie.

That was Bryan from across the room, and remembering it, Dawn can see his face now, can picture how he looked that night.

Can still hear Andrea whispering, That's him—that's my JD.

Dawn saw it, too, the vague resemblance to Brad Pitt. And maybe if Andrea had made a move, had done more than just brush past him once—and maybe if there hadn't been a game of liar's dice on the go, Dawn standing half the night at Bryan's elbow dressed up as someone else, she might not have asked Bryan to come outside and look at the stars with her.

When Dawn woke up the next morning, he was gone. The room was still dark and thick with the smell of exhausted booze and sex and she was wide awake. She remembers that, the way her six a.m. skin zinged with the sweet prickling of getting laid, how she started to feel giddy, started letting herself fall into the throes. But then she remembered Andrea's face, how she'd looked when she found Dawn and Bryan on the back stoop, pressed together in a kiss, Bryan's fingers tangled in the nylon knots of Louise's wig.

Sick then—sick all morning while she waited for Andrea's response to that betrayal. When she heard the thundering foot-steps coming downstairs, Dawn kicked the wig under her bed and hugged her arms to her chest like a shield. And then Andrea was in front of her, ablaze with excitement. Guess what? she said. He's married—Bryan McKinley. He's *married*.

But Dawn already knew that. She knew all about it and she said so.

Andrea took a step backwards and her mouth puckered, her lips rounding into a silent *oh* before arriving at the syllable she wanted. Cool.

And just like that, Andrea was all in. They went over that cliff together.

Dawn looks down into the wood box but decides against commit-ting to another log. She's sitting on the loveseat finishing her wine when Cheryl settles back into the couch. So was he worth it, your married man, Cheryl asks. Did you love him that much?

But Dawn's not sure. She couldn't tell then and she certainly can't tell now how much of her passion for Bryan was genuine and how much was fed by the gasoline that Andrea's interest poured on the fire. Maybe Dawn did love him, at first, but she suspects it would have burned out fast if it hadn't been so fun to share—every conversation and carnal detail, all the foreplay and every damn thing he ever said about his wife.

Dawn was on the Pill by then and it dulled her appetite, but she made sure the sex was wild and adventurous just so she'd have a story to share with Andrea at the end of the night. When email replaced phone calls, Dawn showed them all to Andrea, who analyzed their content and hooted over their salacious yearning.

The few times Andrea had a lover herself—a woman Andrea met during the month she tried working out at the gym on a free trial membership, a new electrician at the paper mill—Dawn listened to Andrea's details and tried hard not to show how much she resented the intrusion. They weren't like married men, those women—even if they were also meant to be secrets. They wanted relationships that couldn't be contained in tidy boxes, and they sprawled into the house and took up more space than Dawn could bear. But those invasions never lasted more than a handful of months, and the conversation always swung back to Bryan.

Eventually, though, even his emails got dull and even Andrea grew tired of being a spectator in someone else's romance. By the time the affair was over—Dawn's choice, not his—a new millennium had begun, and Dawn and Andrea were making plans to visit Vegas. Dawn thinks now that she barely noticed Bryan was gone.

I don't think I loved him, she finally tells Cheryl. I think I just liked the attention.

She knows it's not the answer her guest wants, but Cheryl doesn't react, doesn't even seem to have even heard. She's looking into her glass of ice, lost in her own story.

I checked in on Jenna, Cheryl says, and even her voice is different, fragile around the edge. She's asleep with that book on her lap.

She pours a healthy dose of scotch over the ice and the frost on it dissolves into a shine.

The firelight reflects off Cheryl's face, off the glass in her hand, and whatever Dawn thought before, there's no Andrea in this woman now. She's just a stranger sitting near a stranger, and Dawn's glad for the surfeit of wine flowing through her, the way she doesn't feel that absence.

Cheryl looks over at her. Can I ask how old you are?

Fifty-six, Dawn says, and as far as she's concerned, it's the true answer. She's let go of those few years she had to sacrifice, released them without a struggle. They belonged to someone else, some-where else, and since she had no plans for them anyway, she figures they're better off thrown back in the pot for someone else to make good use of, if that's how it worked.

It's awful, isn't it?

Dawn looks around trying to spot what she's missed, the awful part.

I mean getting old. Middle age, perimenopause, all that bullshit. I feel like I'm looking into the abyss. It's as if we just— here, Cheryl includes Dawn in a sweeping hand gesture— we just fade away and disappear.

Dawn doesn't say anything while Cheryl studies her, tells her it's great that she doesn't dye her hair. It's brave, she says. People are so dismissive of grey-haired ladies, right?

Dawn thinks about Sylvia, about her bright white hair and hot pink lipstick, her presence so absolute she could never be dismissed. But then she thinks about the other women at the Wednesday group and how long it took for her to tell them apart.

Cheryl sets her glass down on the table and circles back to where they'd been.

When you were with your married man, did you talk more about his relationship with his wife than about your relationship with each other?

Dawn laughs. If the question's meant to inflame her, elicit some kind of epiphany, it's a few decades too late. Andrea nailed that one right from the start, assuring Dawn the mistress always played the marital counsellor.

It's all we ever talked about, she tells Cheryl.

Trust me, that doesn't change even after they leave their marriage. The first wife is a cross we all bear. Cheryl stirs her ice cubes with a finger, then says, I lived with someone for six years, and it was like she was always in the room. Anyway, he's moved on, so all I can hope is that I'm the spectre haunting his new relationship.

Cheryl takes a deep gulp and wraps both hands around her glass. So—did you ever meet her, the wife?

The sudden shift reminds Dawn of turning her ankle on an uneven piece of rock, but she doesn't wince. This is, after all, the best part of the story.

Yeah I did, she says. I painted their house.

Cheryl stares at her, wide-eyed, and Dawn lets her gape awhile before she shrugs like it was nothing. Someone recommended me, what could I do?

And he was okay with that?

I think he thought it was funny.

That's not true. Bryan thought it was a calamity. It was Andrea who thought it was funny. Andrea thought it was a scream, and that probably kept the affair alive another few years.

What was she like?

His wife? She was nice. She had good taste.

Cheryl untucks her legs and stretches them out onto the couch, settling in like she expects they'll talk all night now. But Dawn can feel the alcohol trudging through her and it isn't that warm wine-singing anymore. It occurs to her that she has guests and guests have expectations, boozy chats aside, and that she's the one who has to get up in the morning and make sure those expectations are met.

She stands up, empty wineglass in one hand, empty bottle in the other, and says goodnight. Leaves her guest with a full drink and a dying fire.

What colour? Cheryl calls after her from the couch.

Dawn turns in the doorway. Dove grey, she says. Every room, with a blood red accent wall in the dining room.

Nice, Cheryl says. Nice.

WHEN DAWN SEES THE SUV AT THE FAR EDGE OF GRACELAND'S parking lot, she senses something terrible has happened. It's nothing specific, just a feeling like a faint whining in the distance, and there's no reason to feel it. Nothing about the new vehicle, its silver body bleeding into a silver sky, suggests menace. But there's something about the way it's parked, crooked and urgent, that holds Dawn in her car, looking across the expanse of empty asphalt to this newcomer. The front end is nosed diagonally toward the building, one rear tire resting beyond the asphalt where the ground slopes steeply into the rise that hides Pistolet Bay.

And maybe it's just that, one wheel higher than the rest so the whole thing is off-kilter, that makes Dawn feel queasy. That and the wet wind, the sheet of clouds obliterating the sky. The way spring always comes on here, the sun climbing higher but not warmer, a slow absence of snow that creeps like a desolation across the ground.

Or maybe it's just the last of the red-wine hangover that dogged her all morning, that sent her out walking the only trail she knew wasn't still ankle deep in snow and muck. It was that or watch Jerry fiddle with the reservation system—an aggravation too much for her to bear.

She's tucked her car beside Jerry's truck, the motel entrance practically right in front of her. But when Dawn finally gets out, she walks right past the entrance toward the SUV like she's caught in its gravitation pull. She sees it's a rental, a Ford Escape, before she heads inside.

Jerry's reading the newspaper. When she walks in, he folds it up into an approximation of its original shape and slaps it down on the desk. You see that letter in the *Western Star*? he asks by way of a hello. Fella from Alberta had a lovely time on the island ten years ago, so he wants to be sure we don't change a thing before he's got a chance to come back.

Dawn nods and peels off her gloves. The heater fan in her old car is shot, so she has to clench and unclench her fists to loosen her knuckles and get the blood back into her fingertips. She knows Jerry's working up to something and there's no point saying anything until he gets where he's going.

Everybody loves the past long as they're not stuck in it, he says. Maybe we should all get a touch of the scurvy, a bit of beriberi like the good old days, just to make it more authentic for the tourists.

Shut up Jerry, Dawn says, looking around the empty lobby. You're bad for business. She hears Margaret in her tone and it almost makes her smile, but then she remembers the suv.

Everything okay here?

Sure, I figured it out, he says. Reservation notices should come direct to your email now. Course you have to actually check your email—you know that, right? It's not magic.

That's not what you said when you set it up, Jer. Dawn drops her gloves on the reception desk. You promised those reservations would come tumbling in and tap me right on the shoulder.

And they would, if you'd get yourself a phone and turn the notifications on.

Last thing I need, messages popping up at all hours, asking me what's for breakfast. Dawn points her thumb in the general direction of that hulking suv. Who's this?

You've got more company, Jerry says. Fella just checked in for a few nights—paid cash, up front, for the first two.

Dawn turns to look out the window, even takes a step toward it to get a better view though she doesn't know what it is she's looking for. She can't see so much as its shadow from this angle. She pulls off her toque and rakes her cold fingers through her short hair, hoping for the dread to lift. It doesn't.

When I saw the rental, I thought maybe those other two, the mum and daughter, that they'd had an accident.

Jerry studies her. That's a strange leap to make.

It's a strange time of year for drop-ins. He belong to somebody nearby?

Jerry shakes his head. Spencer's the name, he says. Doesn't sound local but he wasn't saying much. I put him down in the Blue Suede Shoes.

Give it up, Jerry, she says.

Jerry hates that she named the guestrooms after the flowers, their namesakes pressed and framed and hung beside each door. He says the names are too obvious, too on the nose, and he's forever rebranding the rooms. People, he's always telling her, expect a little more Elvis.

Dawn made it clear right from the start that she has no intention of heading down a path that leads to Lonesome Tonight at Heartbreak Hotel and anyway, it's only the Americans who arrive expecting Elvis. Everybody else just wants a clean room, a wifi password and a map, and they're willing to settle for two out of three. But Jerry keeps it up, calling the Blue Flag Iris the Blue Suede Shoes and the Lady Slipper the Hound Dog. She's noticed, though, that he can never keep his Love Me Tender straight—that sometimes it's the Long's Braya, sometimes the Harebell.

You gave the big room to someone alone?

Smoker, wanted a door to the outside, Jerry says. He clasps his hands together and smirks. But you understand all about that.

Jerry's in some kind of mood today that Dawn can't figure out. She wants to tell him to go light up, take the edge off—wants to tell him again that quitting hasn't exactly done him any favours in the charm department, even if it has been more than a decade. But Jerry won't give her the opening.

Something off about that guy, he's saying. Real stiff. Hesitated about giving me a name, wasn't interested in talking about what brought him up this way. I just—I got a vibe.

Not a *vibe*, Dawn says. She has a soft spot for people who won't rise to Jerry's insistent chit-chat. A softer spot for people who pay cash directly to her rather than paying credit to some giant, ethereal cyber-company that's never lifted a finger to run this place.

Any new reservations on the system?

Not soonish or even upcoming, Jerry tells her. He looks sheepish, a little crestfallen even. Nothing but the ladies who are already here. Sorry.

So much for tourism, Dawn thinks. She slides past Jerry so she's at the desk and he's just leaving.

I guess it doesn't matter what room you put this new one in. It's not like I'll fill up.

You never know, girl. It is Easter weekend.

Shit, it is. Dawn hadn't realized—and why would she, the way it moves around? She's got no reason to mark it anymore—no kids around expecting chocolate, no family dinners to tag along to. No suitcases to pack. These days she only keeps track of the significant holidays: Victoria Day in May, which kicks off tourist season, Canada Day, which opens the floodgates, and Labour Day, which turns the faucet back off. Thanksgiving, too, that last gasp when families come home and can't be accommodated. Two years ago, Thanksgiving had filled all her beds and stuffed her fridge full of leftovers—pie plates covered in tin foil that all got left behind when the crowd cleared out on Monday morning.

I wonder if the new guy's here to join that mother and her daughter, Jerry says. Something about the way he looked around when he checked in, like he was expecting a welcome. She say anything about that?

Dawn tries to remember what Cheryl said, exactly, the night before—the small fragments that were about her and not about Dawn. The parts that aren't obscured by a red wine fog. There was a man flitting in and out of the conversation, Dawn remembers that, but she's pretty sure Cheryl didn't mention someone was coming to join her. Even a handful of glasses in, Dawn thinks she would have picked up on that.

She tells Jerry she doesn't think so, that it's a mother-daughter adventure thing. Then she looks at the long tweezers on the reception desk where Cheryl left them and says, Then again, she has been making an effort to look her best.

Jerry reaches around the desk to snag his coat off the back of Dawn's chair. Well I hope he's the good kinda surprise. You don't need any drama out here—especially if we get the weather they're talking about.

Bad? Dawn asks. Jerry's always on her to check the weather, check the weather—but she forgets. She still thinks of weather as the thing you see outside the window and not something coming your way. It's screwed her over more than once.

Worst case scenario, it's the snowpocalypse, he says. But you know how that goes. Weather forecasts are all about ratings and clicks now. I did bring some wood around from the shed just in case, and you probably want to get more in.

He plunges an arm into his coat, says the temperature is supposed to stay close to the line, so maybe most of it will come as rain. Hope so, since I won't be anywhere nearby to come plow you out.

Dawn asks where he's headed, though she can guess the answer. But Jerry doesn't respond, not right away. He zips his coat first, watching his hands accomplish the necessary maneuvers. And then he doesn't look up to meet her eye when he says, I'm driving straight to Port Saunders now. Not back until Monday.

He's in a hurry to leave, heading for the door and Dawn smiles at the back of his head. A romantic long weekend, then?

When Jerry turns, his expression is flatly serious but his cheeks flush, so Dawn knows he's trying to tamp down some kind of excitement.

Meeting the family, he says. Nancy's got her son and daughter in law coming for Easter with the kids.

She crosses her arms. This is moving pretty fast, don't you think Jerry?

We're celebrating four months already next Saturday.

The way he says it, so plainly awestruck, makes Dawn laugh.

Big anniversary plans?

We'll see how this weekend goes before I make any absolute commitments.

His hand reaching for the doorknob as he says, Or ask her to.

Dawn lunges after him then, ducking around the desk and catching a fistful of coat sleeve just as he's stepping over the threshold. Jesus, Jerry, she says. Four *months*. You can't possibly know—

He steps back, lets the door close, turns to put his hands on Dawn's shoulders. Something in the gesture says settle down, be quiet and Dawn's father flashes through her mind. For a second, she expects to be scolded. Instead, Jerry says, I waited a lot of years to find this, Dawnie, and I'm not wasting any more time. Not any at all.

AFTER JERRY'S GONE, AFTER SHE'S WATCHED HIS PICKUP DIS-appear from the lot, Dawn stands behind the desk and runs over a checklist in her head.

If there is snow—big snow, the kind that keeps people inn-bound—she'll need to have enough on hand to keep everyone fed and warm.

She's only responsible for breakfast. The website's clear about that, but Dawn's discovered no one reads it, not thoroughly. People show up empty-handed and hungry, asking what time the restaurant opens, and they get agitated when she hands them a map with all the nearest—though not near—restaurants starred. In her second year, she realized it wasn't good enough and she started stocking fruit and granola bars just to manage the worst of the low blood sugar.

But three guests for Easter weekend and a snowstorm coming— that's a new frontier. And will they expect something special for Easter? Is she supposed to hide treats, colour eggs, cook a ham? Well she won't be doing that. She's got enough eggs and bread and sugar to get through it, and worse comes to worse, she can share the canned soup and frozen pizzas she's got stocked to feed herself.

Jesus, Good Friday. So there's no point even worrying about. Snow or not, it's too late. Everything's already closed.

Dawn looks out the window at the gathering gloom. Good Friday. She tells herself not to think it—it's best to break the habit in this new silence that's come—but she can't help it. She goes right back there. Back to Good Friday, the day Dawn and Andrea always left on vacation, wherever it fell on the calendar.

It was all Andrea's doing, a birthday wish as she was staring down forty-five. We need to have some fun before it's too late, she'd said, get ourselves laid in a foreign land before we're too old. Mexico had been her first choice but Dawn, thinking about borders, said she wouldn't go anywhere they'd have to worry about everything that passed their lips. She had Andrea at diarrhea, at the impossibility of sexy romance with strangers if their guts were falling out, so they bought cheap seats to Las Vegas. That seemed equally ripe with possibilities and turned out to be plenty foreign enough.

At first they tried to rise to the outrageous excess of Vegas, gorged themselves on booze and buffets, a couple of overwrought shows and high stakes card games. Andrea wouldn't gamble but she liked to stand behind Dawn at the blackjack table and watch her win big and then lose it all in the turn of a card. That's where they were when Andrea spotted Coralee. Dawn was watching her luck dwindle and then Andrea was drifting toward the bar, suddenly intent on a different kind of lucky. Dawn never understood how Andrea could tell, just from looking, that she'd found what she was looking for, but when it was clear she had, Dawn feigned interest in a forest firefighter from California. As soon as Coralee led Andrea to the elevator, Dawn abandoned the bar and the firefighter. She went back down to the table and lost and won and lost again while Andrea got what she came for.

Adequate but disappointing, Andrea reported over the brunch buffet, and Dawn said, Me too. Let's rent a car.

Dawn crosses her arms on the desk and lays her head down against the long bone of her forearm, her eyes closed as she replays that first drive out into the desert, how breathless the indescribably alien landscape made them feel. They'd cruised south through the Mojave, then north. Parked and hiked into the Valley of Fire, everything looking dead from the car but alive beneath their feet, spring pulsing up in yellow and red flowers.

Dawn had smuggled home a wealth of small desert flowers—of desert globemallow and brittlebush—pressed between the pages of a novel she knew she'd never finish. Those blooms must still be there. She presses her eyes together tight, trying to think where that book might sit on her bookshelves now, the flowers inside waiting, perfectly preserved.

Down the hall, a door opens and shuts. Dawn lifts her head from her arms. Listens. The footfall is slow and unusual. Dawn takes a step sideways behind the desk so she can see this newcomer that has Jerry so wound up.

He's tall and broad—from this angle his shoulders seem to fill the narrow hallway. Dressed in black, jacket to jeans, and a dark cap pulled low that throws a shadow so she can only make out a salt-and-pepper beard. Absolutely nothing menacing in his slow gait—a slight limp like there's a stone in his shoe—or in the way he stops to study the pressed lady's slipper on the wall.

Dawn unfolds one of the small maps marked with restaurants, grocery stores, attractions. She pulls on her hospitality smile, clasps her hands. Waits.

He's stalled again, looking at the floor now while a gloved hand searches a pocket, emerges holding something shiny and silver. He takes two more steps before he looks up. And then he freezes like he's caught in a children's game of statue.

Welcome to Graceland, she says. I'm Dawn. Is everything okay with your room?

Ethan peers steadily out the tiny window, trying to focus on the horizon, the distant end of rippling cloud. Trying not to think about how close the man beside him is, how close the seat in front of him is, how ridiculous it would be to panic in an airplane. They'll be down soon and he'll have plenty of room but right now, all he can do is long for an envelope of space, a place to put an arm straight out in any direction without coming up against something else.

Thick cloud has concealed the ground the whole length of his trip, all the hours east from Toronto to St. John's and now every bumpy minute of this last northwest leg. The heavy blanket keeps Ethan from catching even a glimpse of coastline or landmass— whatever it is they're flying over—and cottons his anticipation.

He's leaning deep into the curving body of the small plane, banging his forehead into the oval window with every pluck of turbulence. His back is starting to ache from being twisted and hunched, but it's the only way to avoid colliding with his seatmate.

The guy's massive, tall as he is broad—a man who'd reached one burly arm up before takeoff and, without even straining against his seatbelt, caught and pulled shut the overhead bin. Ethan had lowered the armrest between them then, meaning to establish a firm boundary, but the neighbouring arm had massed on that border and spilled over it; every few minutes, the elbow made an incursion into the country of Ethan's ribcage.

What Ethan had wanted, when he'd picked this window seat, was a view—was to see from overhead the continent's rough edges stretched wide, the scrappy coastline and piney hills he'd seen online. What he wanted was to know what he was heading into.

Finally the plane begins to descend and Ethan draws in a deep breath, closes his eyes as the clouds press in against his window. He doesn't open them again until the wheels drop. They're beneath the clouds but too low now for a vista. It's just treetops and ground and Ethan's breath catches—he can see how close they are to earth, how far the wheels are from the runway's paved lip. Can see they're going to touch down too soon, tumble out of control. He braces for the impact. He's still working through it—still imagining how he'll triage twenty-odd bloody, broken passengers all by himself—when the plane rolls to a stop at the terminal building.

The pilot comes over the PA, apologizes again for the delay out of St. John's that made them more than an hour late. But we're just in time to beat the weather, folks, he says. Welcome to St. Anthony.

It's not what Ethan expected of an airport with the three-letter code YAY, though what exactly he thought he'd find he's not sure. Something more festive, maybe. Instead, he's looking at what appear to be trailers joined at odd angles, held together by duct tape and one-by-fours that look like they were nailed up in a hurry. It makes Ethan think of the developing world, though he knows that's not fair. He's spent some time in Africa—just out of school, sure he would find some way to be useful that he never found—and none of those airports ever looked this haphazard.

Ethan unbuckles. Next to him, the big man hunches out into the aisle, still stooping though his head's got plenty of clearance. Ethan stays in his seat but leans toward the aisle, asks the man how far from the airport to downtown St. Anthony.

Gotta be thirty or forty klicks. No, more than that. I don't know for sure. The man jerks his head back like he's indicating some army behind him. We go the other way.

Forty kilometres? Ethan says. I guess that's a pricey cab ride.

Though the man is probably no more than Ethan's thirty-five years, he eyes Ethan like he's a newborn calf. Can't think that I've ever seen a taxi here before, he says, but there's a car rental.

The wind catches Ethan with a sharp right hook when he steps from the shelter of the plane onto the stairs. It isn't the force of it but the noise of it, a kind of layered clatter that seems to be coming from all directions at once. And something else on top of it, a thwacking that makes him turn his face right into the pelting rain—or ice, it feels more like ice—to see a long strip of duct tape has come loose from the terminal window and is now whipping the vinyl siding.

After he picks his suitcase up off the luggage belt, he looks around. He could take in the entire rabbit warren of the terminal at a glance if it weren't for the plywood hoarding erected to block off the security areas. He pulls out his phone, turns it on. He's got no signal, and it takes a minute to connect to the airport's wifi. Longer to load his email. Finally, two messages. One from the hospital, telling him where to be on Monday morning. The other from Pauline, which he doesn't open, doesn't want to read. Not now. Figures he'll let her know he got here safe once he gets into St. Anthony proper, settles in, gets a handle on his situation. He's not about to give her the satisfaction of hearing him sound adrift, displaced.

There's a little kiosk open and he realizes he's been hours without more than a bag of pretzels, so he makes his way over, eyes a turkey sandwich. It's cut on the diagonal and set in its triangular packaging so its guts are revealed. At first he thinks it's gone off, crumbled and moldy, but then he leans in closer and sees there's some kind of dressing and herbs pressed in with the turkey, so he picks it up and asks for a large coffee, adds milk.

Coffee in one hand, sandwich in the other and luggage stacked and resting against his thigh, Ethan looks around. There doesn't seem to be anyone else in the airport, and for a second he thinks it might be later than he realizes, that he might have got the time difference wrong. But there's still daylight washing across the floor from some glassfront around the corner, so he's okay. He has time to sit down and breathe.

He puts the sandwich in his bag to eat on the drive and starts in on the coffee. Hot enough, anyway, but it's not great coffee, even as kiosk coffee goes. He drinks it all anyway, hoping it will reignite the anticipation that left him hundreds of miles behind. Then he considers his empty cup for a full minute before he drops it in a waste can and heads to the men's room. It's only there, while he's washing his hands, that he realizes he's stalling, delaying the moment when he might have to admit he's made a mistake.

He shakes the water from his hands. Time to see where he's landed.

But when he looks around for the car rental place his seatmate mentioned, scanning the walls for a backlit banner, a recognizable logo, he can't find it. He turns a full circle twice and is almost to the point of asking someone before he finally spots a small sign at waist level.

There's a young woman behind a small counter with too-long bangs and a set of keys in her hand. She drops them when Ethan leans against the counter and asks for a vehicle.

Did you reserve? She's looking at a torn-in-half piece of lined notebook paper. I don't have it here, she says.

On the paper, there are four distinct lines of text scrawled in blue pen. All four are struck through with red ink.

I didn't know I'd need a car. I just arrived—I'm the new scan technologist at the hospital.

Ethan hears how that sounds, like he thinks he's important and she should, too. Like he thinks everybody in this little place is anticipating his arrival.

Sorry my love, she says at a quick clip. Got nothing for ya. Last car on the lot won't do—tires are bald and this weather's coming from St. Anthony.

He stares at her, trying to make sense of what she said at such breakneck speed. It takes some deciphering even to catch Anthony, the way she strangled the *th*.

Tires, bald. He got that part.

She's looking out the window with a sour expression on her face so he turns to look, too, sees the snow coming down thick now.

Is there another way for me to get there?

Nope. Shuttle's just left. Everybody's in a hurry to get off the road tonight.

A shuttle. He hears that loud and clear.

Wish I'd known. He laughs at himself then, his grand adventure off to such a blundering start. Guess I'll have to take my chances with that car you've got.

She looks at him for a good, long second like she's weighing whether it's worth her time to argue, then takes his license and writes down the information. Every few seconds she shoves out her bottom lip and blows a hard stream that ruffles her bangs, shifting them slightly away from her eyes.

Ethan asks if the car has GPS and she shakes her head. He takes his iPhone from his pocket, but before he can even open the app she's shaking her head again. That won't help you much, she says before she even looks up at him, not until you're practically on top of the St. Anthony anyway.

Then she points toward the window. It's not hard. Go right out of the lot, left at the highway and stay on it until you get into town. You'll either see your hotel, or somebody there can tell you how to find it.

He looks where she's pointing. He can just see the parking lot, the thick snow that's starting to clot on the cars, but he can't see the highway she means though he tilts his head this way and that, trying to get a bead on it.

His attention is brought back inside by the short barrel of a man who sidles past him, slush dripping from his hair and his coveralls as he passes.

Hey Jack, the car rental clerk says without looking at the man. I'm goin' now, before the arse comes right out of her. She turns her attention back to Ethan. I'm telling you, those tires are shit. I shouldn't even give you this car. Take it easy.

She lays the keys in his hand and then she's done with him.

SPENCER IS SITTING IN THE SUV ON A ROAD THAT'S SOMEthing between gravel and pavement and rock, looking out at the water and he has no idea what he's doing, or what he'll do next. He left Graceland and hit the highway with no fucking clue where he was going. He didn't look at the map, didn't head for the restaurants she said might be open, just flung the car around the curves and when a new road appeared—maybe five minutes, maybe five years into the drive—he took it.

He'd had hours on the drive up the peninsula to get used to this coast. Astounded at first by how much the topography reminded him of northwestern Ontario. Then, his agitation growing, deciding it was similar but stunted. That it lacked even a whiff of majesty, like God had taken a beginner's course in fashioning rocks and trees but they'd all turned out misshapen and scraggly. That God must have moved on, tried again further west, finally hitting His stride only when He got to the Rockies.

And then the water came back into view and Spencer drew a breath so deep he wondered if he'd been holding it for a long time.

Leaving Graceland, he'd wanted that water again. Wanted the ocean to rise up and give him back his breath, but for the longest time all he saw was low marsh and ponds, the beleaguered spruce getting sparser and more bent. And then finally there it was, big water and soon after that, a place to stop, a little convenience store and café where he bought some kind of Saran-wrapped biscuits, two little jars of jam and a coffee to go. He drove on from there and took this narrow side road toward the water. Got out and walked around long enough to have a smoke. The ground was rock and muck and the steady breeze coming off the water felt like a cold shower, bracing first and then just unpleasant, and it blew tiny embers off his cigarette like it was a sparkler.

He gave up on the outdoors then, climbed into the passenger seat and unwrapped the biscuits, which turned out to have raisins lurking inside. So he chucked them out the window and now he's eating partridgeberry jam out of a tiny jar. He's got no spoon, nothing like a tool, so he's just sucking the jam off his finger and looking out at the water, remembering the time he took Denny fishing, how disappointed the boy was when they didn't catch anything but weeds. Thinking about Denny in his bright orange life jacket, and then not thinking about him. Thinking about Janet, and then not her either. Wondering if there's an extra charge for cleaning if he gets jam all over this grey upholstery, but deciding he doesn't give a flying fuck about that.

Then he's going back over it again, what just happened at Graceland and what the hell he should do now.

When he'd arrived at the motel—no screwing around, four-and-a-half hours straight there from Deer Lake with just a quick stop for food and a piss—he'd been supercharged. So damn nervous and excited he'd practically driven right into the motel trying to park. Sat behind the steering wheel for god knows how long, looking at how incredibly blue the sky was. Then stood, smoking a cigarette to steady himself, wanting to walk up over the small rise he'd parked against just to see what was on the other side. But he was too nervous, too busy watching the windows for any signs of a face.

Finally he'd pulled his bag off the passenger seat and said, Showtime. Said it out loud to gun up his courage. His knee didn't hurt so he knew adrenaline was doing its job, and he figured that would get him through. He didn't even pause when he got to the entrance, just flung the door open and sauntered in, thinking steady, steady, don't spook her.

Flung the door open, fully expecting her to be right there on the other side, waiting for him.

Behind the reception desk, a short, wiry man with a bristle of grey hair and big smile punching dimples in his face stood up and said, Welcome to Graceland.

In every daydream, every possible scenario Spencer had imagined since he'd seen her face on the website, not once had he considered this. Her absence.

It threw him off, made him awkward. He'd spent half a lifetime with shady characters, so he knew when he was acting like one, but he couldn't help it. Couldn't stop looking around like she might pop out from behind a wall at any second. Couldn't stop wondering was this guy her husband? No way, he thought, though Spencer had to concede she'd surprised him before.

Anyway, what did he know? Maybe she wasn't the Dawn M. Taylor whose name was on the title. Maybe she just worked here—worked for the Taylors. Or had, once, around the time they were taking pictures for the website. In the few pictures he'd seen online, she was working—she was behind the desk or hauling in wood or folding towels. Most of those photos were taken from far away or from behind, but that one, the first one he saw—her face. Turned slightly, looking off toward something else but close enough to be sure—or almost sure—that it was her.

At the front desk, Jerry had asked for a name and address, but Spencer had shaken his head. I'll pay cash, he'd said.

Sure, Jerry said and handed him a card and a pen. But I need a name and address—don't worry about the license plate number.

Spencer couldn't think fast enough, his head whirling as he took the pen, so he scrawled just Spencer and then added a made-up, bullshit address in Toronto. While he wrote, fast and sloppy, Jerry plunked an old school credit card machine on the counter, the kind that used carbon imprints.

Spencer shook his head again, took out his wallet. Laid two hundred and twenty dollars on the counter, the bills smooth and seamless, fresh from the bank machine that morning.

I still need a credit card, Mr.— Jerry flipped the card around and peered at it. Mr. Spencer. It's just for incidentals, just in case. You know how it is.

And Spencer did know, but all the same he missed the days when you could slap a few twenties on the counter and get a bed for the night, no questions asked.

Out came the Redempt-Ed business card—Harve's executive privilege card, left with Spencer to settle up at the hotel in St. John's. It was a stupid move, an asshole move, the kind of thing they taught you not to do in the most rudimentary of Redempt-Ed classes. Spencer hated that he'd done it—hated that it felt so convenient, so much like it was what he'd planned to do all along and he just didn't know it.

Although now, swiping the last of the jam out of the little jar and looking out over the endlessly rolling, riffing, darkening water, Spencer couldn't think what possible harm it could do. It wasn't even out in the airwaves, just an imprint on carbon forms. He'd ask for that back when he checked out.

Still, it only added to his agitation as he dragged himself to the room at the furthest end of the hall. There wasn't another soul in the place besides the goofy guy at the desk, and as far as Spencer could tell, there might not be another soul for many miles.

He was wiped out, bled dry. So deflated it was almost defeated. He knew he should take a shower and get something to eat but even that felt like too much, so he laid down and let himself consider the terrible reality: she wasn't here and maybe she never would be. Maybe she didn't work here anymore, if she ever had. Maybe he'd made some stupid assumptions based on a who-knows-how-old photo on a website and he'd come halfway across the fucking country just to be disappointed.

He could ask about her—but how? He was trying to figure that out, phrasing and rephrasing careful questions, when he fell asleep. Deep asleep, out cold for two hours. And while he slept, the world changed. Gone was the cobalt sky that had hung over him the whole day, such a relief after the drizzle of St. John's. A solid blanket of clouds had moved in and waking up in that dreary light, Spencer was hungry. He figured he better skip the shower and find some food, so he pulled on a cap and sauntered down to ask Jerry where to go.

Only it wasn't Jerry behind the desk anymore.

Spencer peers out the windshield. To his right, the water looks more and more like black ink. To his left, the clouds are darker, looming close to the ground.

But he doesn't register that. Doesn't even see the cold spit that's starting to filter from the sky. He just sees her face, the face behind the desk at Graceland.

He'd looked right into the face that had haunted his dreams for decades, and there was no doubt left for him now. It was her, right there in the living flesh. Her, looking back at him. But what he saw in those familiar blue eyes has shaken him worse than anything he could have anticipated.

She didn't recognize him.

She'd looked him right in the face, and she was looking at a stranger.

DAWN HAS PRIED THE FLOWER FROM HER RUG HOOKING, blossom to stem, and now there's bits of nylon all around her, scattered across her lap and her red couch, and she's looking at the hole she's made and thinking she's done too much damage, there's no fixing it. She's tempted to keep ripping until every last scrap of limestone is destroyed, too—until even the bright yellow frame along the edge is gone—but she can't see any value in the effort. Not when there's a garbage can under the sink.

She sets what's left of the rug on the arm of the couch, thinks maybe if she ate something it would lift her out of the hole she's been dropping down into since Cheryl and Jenna came back from their outing, sour expressions on both their faces.

Dawn crosses the floor. Four steps and she's in her kitchen, which is just a single wall, small appliances lined up on a short span of countertop, a sink and a refrigerator. She drops two slices of bread into the toaster, plunges the lever and watches as the filaments bloom to crimson.

Thinking how apologetic Cheryl had looked when she stopped at the reception desk, the way her cheeks went scarlet when she said, I guess we've seen what there is to see around here, and I know there's probably no refund if we paid online— she'd paused long enough to let Dawn correct that misapprehension, then continued— but I think we'll be checking out tomorrow.

Dawn knows she could have been more graceful, or at least smarter. Definitely smarter. She could have fanned the brochures across the desk, said, There's plenty more to do, let's find something. She could have offered a credit for the two nights—Come back in the summer!—instead of letting Cheryl wrangle the promise of a partial refund. Once Cheryl had headed off, Dawn propped the ring-for-service sign next to the remote doorbell. By the time she shut off the desk lamp, she could hear squabbling down in the library.

She flicks a toast crumb off her plate toward the sink and watches it fall to the floor. No reason to be upset about it. She knows from experience that people who check out early never leave a stellar review, but the refund can't hurt and anyway, Dawn would like to have the place back to herself long enough to sort out this new quiet.

Right, she'd forgotten about that other guest, the newcomer. He is weird, just like Jerry promised, but he doesn't seem like he'll be much trouble. Judging from his monosyllabic replies, how he couldn't wait to grab the map she handed him and get the hell out, she figures having him around will be a lot like being alone. Plus, he's at the other end of the building. She'll just have to keep the music down.

It's hours too early for bed and she can't bear the destruction still strewn across the couch, not right now, so she grabs her cigarette pack and heads outside.

When she slides the door open, she sees the whole world has changed.

IT'S ONLY WHEN ETHAN TURNS OFF THE AIRPORT ROAD AND onto the highway that he starts to feel alive again. It's the swerve of the little car on the snow-slicked road that does it—flings him out of the doldrums that pursued him off the plane, through the dismal airport and into the parking lot, where he threw his big suitcase in the trunk and looked for a brush to clear the snow. When he couldn't find one, he cleared the car windows and mirrors with his bare hands and his jacket sleeves. The snow was hard to get ahead of, one side building back up while he cleared the other. His hands were numb by the time he started the car. Flicked on the wipers to discover only one blade, the driver's side, was good for anything.

Ethan considered going back inside and handing over the keys then, but it was already dusk and the snow seemed to be coming down thicker and faster than before. He couldn't see waiting an hour for a cab that would come after dark, if it came at all.

Besides, isn't this what he told Pauline he was after—an adventure? Something different, someplace else. And maybe this won't turn out to be the right someplace for Ethan, but at least it's a start, a launch pad, the first place that offered him a job.

The car fishtails when he takes the corner. He lifts his foot off the accelerator, keeps a firm hold on the wheel with one hand and drops the other—but there's no need to shift into neutral. He's in full control again and sure he's driven in worse. The road's a plane of white, snow erasing the pavement, but he can see where it ceases to be the road—the ledge that gives way to jagged tufts of grass and weeds, the gentle slope off the shoulder. There's virtually no other traffic on the road, so he can stick close to the centre.

And he's taking it slow because she wasn't kidding. These tires really are shit.

SPENCER SITS LOOKING OUT TO SEA, STEWING, UNTIL LONG after the sea disappears, obliterated by the snow that coats the vehicle, making him feel encased. A confinement that feels more like a respite than a punishment. It doesn't hurt that he's got the keys in the ignition, can leave whenever he wants. But he doesn't, not right away—not until he realizes that he's hungry and tired and making this harder than it has to be.

It isn't complicated. He'll have her alone, in the middle of nowhere, and if she still doesn't recognize him, he'll make sure she does.

He brushes off the car and sets out for Graceland at dusk, deciding against food, telling himself to focus on why he's come. When the high, bright headlamps on the suv hit the snow, they turn it into a crazed lightshow that makes it hard to focus on anything but where he's headed. Anything but keeping the highway under his wheels. Fuck, he'd done a piss poor job of noticing the terrain on his way out and now he has no markers, nothing to tell him when he's getting close.

He's keeping a lookout for any bright light that might suggest he's found Graceland, sure he'll see a sign.

ETHAN'S PICKING UP SPEED. HE'S FEELING IT, THIS NEW place. Even in the near dark, in the bucketing snow with no sign of civilization nearby, he can see how different it is. How it will be. Small enough to control his space, large enough to spread his wings. He'll be a stranger here, and the promise of that races up his legs and across his chest like an electric current.

The thrill of it, all of it—the masked road, himself a masked stranger—it's made him hungry. He reaches for the sandwich he set on the seat beside him, brings it up to the steering wheel so he can hold the package in one hand, open it with the other. He pinches a corner of cellophane and tries to wrench it free.

And then he's dancing. Whirling. Whirling so fast he can't focus, the sudden shot of adrenaline euphoric in the first instant, terrifying in the next.

There's no time to even form the syllables of those experiences— euphoria, terror—before the dance is over, a downhill rumble to a sudden, scraping halt.

When it all stops, he knows he's down the slope a short distance from the road. The car's facing the opposite direction, pointing him back where he came from, and it's canting on such an angle that he's leaning into the driver's side door. He moves every part of his body to make sure he's not hurt. He's not, but he's not sure he can drive himself out of this ditch, either. He tries to push open his door so he can roll out, get up and check just how stuck he is, but the door jams into earth, or snow, or something else he can't see. It won't open wider than a crack, won't let him squeeze through. He has to scramble over the centre console and push the passenger door open, and he has the feeling as he climbs out that he's climbing skyward, right into the clouds that are showering him with their fat, wet flakes.

He's left the lights on in case someone happens by, and the high- est headlight is climbing skyward, too, illuminating the falling snow and turning the whole world into a dizzying kaleidoscope. Ethan stumbles backward, has to grab hold of the side mirror to keep from falling.

He turns away from the bright beams, shuts his eyes to regain his balance. When he opens them, the snow seems to be falling with a more steady rhythm and he takes out his phone, uses the flashlight to peer under the car.

It's hung up on some little tree or shrub, something new but tougher than it looks, two branches spread like they're holding the car between them—and they are. He can see the front end is suspended and he can't believe he's done this. Can't believe he's hit the ditch.

All that planning, and here he is.

He shuts off the flashlight and peers at the phone's backlit screen. No service. It's like the understatement of all time and Ethan wonders what good it is, the roadside assistance he bought along with the rental insurance, if there's no way to get in touch.

He leans in the passenger door to get the keys, but he has to lie right across the seat, his feet sticking out, kicking air, to retrieve the sandwich from where it landed on the floor beside the brake pedal.

Ethan eats the sandwich, the whole thing and fast, and then he's walking. Trudging really, up out of the ditch and onto the road. There's nothing coming in either direction, not a headlight to be seen now that he's shut his off, and he's sure he hasn't passed anything in several miles, so he tramps off in the direction he was travelling.

There has to be something ahead.

His Blundstones were soaked through before he left the ditch, snow packed in around his ankles, and as he's walking the snow that's accumulated in his auburn curls begins to melt, and then to settle into his scalp, running in little rivulets across his forehead and down his neck. His coat is only water resistant, and its resistance is failing.

His wet ears are catching the wind and starting to ache, the left one especially, and Ethan cups his hands over both and walks with his head bent into the storm. He brought gloves and a scarf, but they're nestled in his suitcase in that half-submerged trunk. When his hands go numb, he stuffs them into his pockets, waits for his fingers to sting as they start to warm.

He's never understood it, the body's reaction to cold, how fast it moves to jettison appendages. He thinks about that for a while, and when he's cold enough, he thinks *so this is how I die.* He tells himself *don't give up, don't lie down, fight that temptation,* though he's not tempted to do anything but keep moving forward.

WATCHING JENNA FLIP THROUGH THE PAGES OF ANOTHER Grenfell book—flip through the *pages*, of an actual *book*—Cheryl regrets her promise to leave. She's sitting in the same spot she occupied the night before, the window behind her and Jenna on the couch to her left, and she's feeling more relaxed than she's felt since— Shit, maybe since ever.

There's nothing she has to do, and nothing she can do. They're just here together, with no pinging or chiming or ringing. No unfinished work and no schedule to keep. She takes a swig of her drink. It's like a movie that's all ambiance and no action, everyone just staring off into some foreign place called the middle distance.

Except she's staring at Jenna, and she can tell Jenna is feeling it, too, the way she's leaning into her book, caramel hair falling along her cheek and draping over her shoulder. Cheryl's following that hair to its natural end when Jenna looks up.

What? And she smiles, actually *smiles.* Why are you looking at me like that?

Cheryl leans toward her. You are so pretty, she says, wrapping her fingers more tightly around the glass in her hand. Really Jenn, you don't have to do those things to make boys like you.

Jenna's mouth drops, and the book drops from her hand, and what comes next is not so pretty.

SPENCER'S GOT A GRIP. THE SUV IS SLUICING THROUGH THE snow on the highway and he knows how to handle this now. He'll get back to the motel and he'll find her at the front desk or wherever she hides. Do that warm, amicable thing he does so well. Small talk. It's really coming down out there, and Lovely place. And then he'll ask, What was your name again? And she'll tell him some bullshit name and he'll say, Really, because you sure look like somebody I used to know.

And if she still has that vacuous look that says she doesn't know him—although it's inconceivable to him that she won't have recognized him by then—he'll spill it all. Who he is, who she is, and why he's there.

And he'll make sure he's standing between her and any quick exit she might try to make.

He's so caught up in his grand master plan that he only sees the lights of Graceland as he sails right past the turn. Jesus, you'd think they could have sprung for some kind of warning, a sign or a light beyond what's emblazoned way up on the hill. Barely visible in this fucking snow and vanishing, just like that, in the rearview mirror.

He slows gradually, taps the brake. He's careful. Too much on the line now to skid off the road. Waits until he's at a safe standstill to start a three-point turn.

One turn in, his lights sweep the figure ahead. He'd mistake it for a tree in the distance, maybe an animal on the road, if it wasn't waving two arms overhead like it was trying to bring a plane in. Jesus, not now.

Spencer reverses, backs up and swings until the lights fall off the figure and he can pretend he never saw it. Only he did, and now he can't unsee it. So he puts the car back in drive, rolls forward and opens the passenger door.

Where you headed? Spencer asks, hoping he doesn't have to go far to get this idiot home so he can get back to business.

Don't know, just got here.

The voice slurred, and Spencer can't tell if it's from drink or if the cold's penetrated the poor guy's jaw and frozen his tongue. Spencer doesn't get a chance to ask before the stranger clambers into the passenger seat and gets busy with the seatbelt. But he can't quite manage it; Spencer has to turn on the interior light. He watches for long enough to get frustrated before he leans over to help. Then he asks what the hell he was doing, walking down the road in this.

Hit the ditch, the guy says. Need to find a hotel. He tucks his hands into his armpits and finally looks at Spencer. I'm Ethan, the new guy at the hospital.

Spencer doesn't need the details, and he doesn't need a third wheel joining his party right now. But it can't hurt his cause to be seen playing the Good Samaritan.

Lucky I came along when I did, he says, and knocks the wipers up to full speed.

TEN SECONDS DOWN THE ROAD AND THEY'VE ALREADY arrived. So close to safe harbour—relief washes over Ethan as they pull into the parking lot. He'd have made it on his own, no problem. Still, he's grateful for the rescue, and he lets the other man help him from the vehicle, wrap a protective arm around his waist and lead him to the front entrance of the motel.

The place is lit up like an operating theatre, but the reception desk is dark and empty. Lights are on but nobody's home, the man says, more to that dark corner than to Ethan.

Ethan has the distinct feeling, just then, that he's not being supported as much as serving as a crutch, and he wriggles out from under the protective arm of his rescuer. Voices from down the hall reach his aching ears and both men start toward them, then freeze when a high-decibel scream boils out the open doorway, all of its syllables unmistakable.

Like you've never sucked a dick, Mom!

A girl storms through the doorway, hair flying, everything about her hellbent on fury. At the sight of the two men, she stops like someone caught in a freeze-frame instant. Her eyes meet Ethan's and he's not fast enough to look away from her reddening face. And then she's all furious motion again, flinging herself through a door and slamming it shut.

Neither man moves nor speaks. Silence settles around them in the bright hallway, broken by the faint scrape of a chair, the distinct clatter of a keyboard.

Ethan wonders where the hell he's arrived.

CHERYL SITS BACK IN THE CHAIR WAITING FOR GOOGLE TO load, listening to that old-time, familiar hum and hiss, the sound of dial-up, its slow speed taking her back to her twenties, back to when it all seemed like such a miracle: I wrote this letter today and you'll have it in minutes—before I wake up in the morning, your reply.

There's no patience, she thinks, in this new generation. And just thinking it makes her feel ancient, makes her think Jesus, Cheryl, listen to yourself. And then she does, and she hears what she just said to Jenna, all the prude judgment in it, and she's glad to be interrupted by a man coming through the door, blotches of wet across his black jacket like multiple gunshots.

There's something magnetic about him, handsome almost, full mouth set in a firm, red box. His beard is mostly grey, but his eyebrows are dark and drawn low and straight. Hat in hand, he's staring at Cheryl. And he's obviously disappointed.

Who are you? he asks.

Cheryl sits up straighter as she tells him her name.

You work here?

She shakes her head—I'm staying here—and now she's standing up because something in his tone told her to.

Oh, he says, me too. And I just picked this guy up on the highway—says he's the new doctor in town. Soaked right through and half frozen, needs some help.

And then the man turns, striding away with a sideways gait like one leg isn't right.

Cheryl follows him, leaves the Google box empty.

Dawn was just settling into bed with *A Farewell to Arms*, a battered paperback from her library that she figured might be worth a try. She wasn't getting into it, kept getting distracted by the notes scrawled in the margins of what had obviously been a school text. When the bell at the reception desk chimed, she was re-reading a paragraph that had been circled in blue ink, the word *foreshadowing* running beside it to the very edge of the page.

Now she's rushing a bowl of warm water and a fistful of washcloths into the library like some wartime nurse. Before she even hands them over to Ethan, sitting wrapped in a quilt in the big chair, she can see she's lost control of this. His wet jeans are strewn over the back of the couch, his socks and shoes perched on the baseboard under the window. And the other man, whatever his name is, is down on his knees lighting a fire in her woodstove.

As Ethan soaks a washcloth and puts it against his ear, the worst one—the one that looks shiny and taut, magenta fading to a sickly pale along the rim like the inside of a conch shell—Dawn tries to think of what clothes she has that might fit him. But even her flannel pajamas would be ludicrous on his sturdy frame.

She turns to the fire in progress, says, It'll light easier if you pull that side lever forward, Mr.—

She never loses a guest's name, not like this. He turns and looks at her with such intensity she can only think it's loathing.

Spencer, he says. Name's Spencer.

Right, of course. She gives him a taut nod and since she can see he's got the fire well underway, she turns back to Ethan.

My car's just down the road, he's saying, head tilted into the warmth of the cloth. If we can get something to pull it out.

Dawn doesn't need to look at the window to know that's not possible, not tonight. She says so, tells him she's got a room, points in the direction of the Harebell. You'll have to stay here tonight.

He drops the cloth back into the bowl and smiles up at her. Thanks, that's kind of you—but I insist on paying for it.

Dawn smiles, nods. Tags on a thank you like she means it, wondering if Cheryl is right—if maybe the grey hair is a mistake. If maybe it does make her look insipid.

After she's turned up the heat in the Harebell and folded down the bed, she pauses outside the Buttercup, her only vacant room tonight, and wonders if she should turn the heat on in there, too, just in case.

She almost wishes Jerry was around to see this, to see Graceland filling up at the end of March.

Spencer's standing at the big window, looking out at the snow falling in big, heavy clots. He can't believe it's turned out like this. Can't believe he finally found her and just when he thought he'd have her alone, there's a crowd—and he's just another face in it.

He's only half-listening to the woman behind him ply the poor doctor with twenty questions. He hears her why, why, why. Hears bald tires and bad roads. And when the doc says it was all just a stupid accident, a small moment of inattention, Spencer whirls on him.

That's what it always is, he says. It's always just one small moment of inattention.

And then here she is, walking in as if on cue. She's still every bit as slight and lithe and intense as she ever was, and he can see she's heard him but she doesn't look at him. She goes straight to where the good doctor hunches beneath his blanket, washcloths held to both ears.

It must be a registration card she's holding in her hand, the pen jutting out between her fingers. No need to make her half-frozen guest hobble all the way to the front desk in his bare feet. Man, she's all business, this one. And then Spencer thinks maybe she always was, and he was just too besotted to see it.

The poor guy's got his hands full with those two cloths, so she's filling the card out herself. Such service, such kindness—Spencer thinks he should just walk away, walk out the door, drive away into the storm and come back tomorrow when he's in a better frame of mind.

Then he hears the young guy say Ethan Turnowski, and Spencer almost laughs out loud. Jesus Christ, little Ethan Turnowski. This just got more interesting.

DAWN DUMPS TWO CANS OF CHICKEN NOODLE SOUP INTO A pot and twists on the burner, but she's thinking about small moments of inattention. She's thinking about a dark ring of desert dirt around a small crater in Andrea's breast, how easy it was to brush off. How that small crater would grow to swallow them up.

Painkillers. That was the other thing. The young guy wanted a pill to help with the frostbite pain, and then the older guy thought probably she could get them some hot food, too. And the way he said it, the edge of sarcasm laced with anger, she knew she'd offended him by not remembering his name. She'd repeated it all the way down the hall—Spencer, Spencer—and then stopped at the reception desk to check his card, find out if it was a last name or a first. But that's all there was, just Spencer, and so she's no further ahead than if she didn't know it at all.

She reaches up into the cupboard above the fridge, certain there's some Tylenol from the last time she had a cold. She feels around blindly, knocking travel mugs over until her fingers touch a pill bottle. Wrong one—it's Andrea's prescription for a sedative, a doctor's gift to cope with the anxiety of dying. The only time Andrea took one, she slept for fifteen hours solid. Dawn never let her take another one; she didn't want Andrea to be gone for so long before she was gone for good.

She finally locates the Tylenol. It's a year past expired, but she'll offer it anyway. Figures it's his choice, the chances he wants to take.

She stirs the soup and notices she's left the bedside lamp on in her room. When she goes to switch it off, she sees the Hemingway book lying on the pillow where she dropped it. She hadn't bothered to mark the page, and now she'll have to flip through to find that note in the margin, if she ever gets back to that book at all.

Just a single quiet minute before I lose my mind, that's all I want. Andrea used to say that when the kids were little—toddlers, barely out of diapers—always pulling at a pant leg, making some new demand. When Dawn heard that line, she always stepped in, took the kids out for a walk if the weather was nice, took them downstairs to draw pictures if it wasn't. Gave their mother twenty or twenty-five quiet minutes in her day just to breathe.

It's fine, she tells herself as she puts the book on the bedside table, switches off the lamp. You wanted guests who stuck around— well now you've got them.

THAT'S NOT WHAT I SAID. CHERYL THROWS HER HANDS UP IN frustration, leans back into the couch like she's been shot. At least that's how it looks to Ethan, who's loping in circles around the perimeter of the room, wriggling his bare toes against the wood floor. The pants Spencer loaned him are too loose and he has to hitch them up every four or five steps, but other than that—and other than his ears—he's fine. Recovered from his brush with the elements, though still fuming over his own recklessness.

Cheryl's recovered, too. She's leaning forward again, animated and trying a new angle on persuasion. I'm just saying you could tell it differently and it would still be the truth.

Ethan's not quite sure how they got here, how they moved from nice to meet you to discussing his mishap, from the insurance implications to this. Maybe it's the forced intimacy of being confined in this weird time-capsule motel, its mid-nineties vibe and the snow cascading down outside. Or maybe it's the general agreement that they're all half-starved. Whatever the cause, Ethan thinks the conversation has veered faster than usual into the philosophical.

You've got bald tires, icy roads, poor visibility— Cheryl's counting it up on her fingertips, bending each finger back like she's mounting a defense. Put the sandwich in, you're culpable, she says. Then she folds down her fingers like she's hiding away the evidence. Leave the sandwich out, it's bad luck in bad weather.

Ethan stops behind the stove, turns to confront Cheryl. But the sandwich *is* in there, he says. It's a fact—if I hadn't decided to eat a damn sandwich at that particular moment, I wouldn't have put the car in the ditch.

Cheryl puts two fingers to each temple like she's seen too many painkiller commercials. You're deliberately missing the point, she groans. All I'm saying is you have to consider your audience when you tell a story.

All you're saying, Ethan says, is that I should lie.

It's not *lying*. She pours herself another healthy dose of scotch from a half-empty bottle. It's crafting.

Ethan looks to Spencer, perched on the edge of the loveseat, but the older man is staying out of it, staring into the fire until Cheryl swings the bottle in his direction. Sure you don't want some?

Spencer's eyes hang for a second on the amber liquid, glinting in the firelight, before he shakes his head. Tells her again he never touches hard liquor. Gets up to get more wood for the fire.

Look, Cheryl says, offering the bottle Ethan's way, you don't have full control of what you say anyway. A message isn't just what a person sends out—it's what another person receives.

Ethan thinks about all the misinterpreted texts he's ever sent. About a message scrawled on a mirror. He looks at the proffered scotch and says, Sure, why not.

He settles back into the armchair with the glass she's filled and he's formulating a question about the surrounding area, what either of these two have seen of it, but Cheryl's still stuck in the same groove.

It's like making a documentary, she's saying. You edit out some things, you let the camera linger longer on others. She picks up her glass and takes a deep swallow. That's storytelling, not subterfuge. It's the same way your brain works, how it filters memories a certain way. If all the elements of a story are true—

Then it's a true story? Ethan says.

Exactly.

Ethan shrugs. I'm not sure it would hold up in a court of law. He watches Spencer close the stove door and when the man stands, asks him what he thinks.

Spencer laughs then, a sharp crack of mirth that shatters his stony expression. I think you haven't spent much time in a courtroom.

In the hallway, coming closer, the sound of clanking dishes, a waft of something sharp and salty.

Oh, are you a lawyer or something? Cheryl asks.

Or something, Spencer says, settling himself back onto the couch, his cheeks still ruddy from leaning over the fire and stirring the hot coals.

Like what? she asks. A prosecutor? A guard? A—what do you call it—a bailiff?

Spencer crosses his arms and looks her dead in the eye. A convicted killer, he says.

DAWN PROMISED TO COME BACK FOR THE DISHES, BUT AS soon as they've emptied their bowls and polished off every last cracker and every crumb of cheese, Ethan leaps up like he's on a mission, gathers all the dishes and carries them off to the kitchen.

Spencer takes that as his cue to leave, too, and he's on his feet, on his way to goodnight when Cheryl says, Hey don't go—it's still early.

Her arm out like a greeting or a hook, a welcome-aboard smile.

Usually when Spencer tells a woman he's a convicted murderer, that's it. End of conversation. The only ones who don't run for cover, in his experience, are the crazy ones who want to attach themselves to notoriety—and Janet. But this woman doesn't seem like either of those things. What she seems is insatiably curious. A hazard of her profession, he supposes, but he's not particularly interested in being the subject of her curiosity.

He says something about having to dig out tomorrow and he gets out of there as fast as his leg will let him. In the hallway, he pauses, listening to the clatter in the kitchen, trying to discern if it's one person doing the clean up or two. When Ethan emerges into the hallway, shutting off the light switch and hitching up the pants he's wearing, Spencer says goodnight to him, too.

Ethan ambles back to the library, meaning to grab a book and head to his room, but Cheryl asks, keeping her voice low, if he thinks it's really true. What he said, and she jerks her head to indicate the other he.

Ethan's not tired. He's the opposite of tired, still whirling from how his arrival has gone off the rails, so he settles down on the couch and takes the drink Cheryl offers, says he figures it was meant to be a joke.

He didn't sound like he was joking.

He didn't seem like a killer, either, Ethan says. Anyway, he did rescue me off the road and I am wearing his pants, so I'd like to give him the benefit of the doubt.

If only we had some kind of a— Cheryl puts her hand out, palm up, fingers curved as if holding a cell phone— a device that we could ask. And then she looks at the computer by the doorway and sits up like she's about to stand. I guess it'll have to be old faithful there to the rescue. Do you happen to know his full name?

No, Ethan says. And even if I did, I don't think we should be snooping.

Cheryl sits back, takes a long drink while she eyes up Ethan. She's wearing the same expression she had when she was exhorting him to deceive the insurance company.

It seems like the smart thing to do, if you ask me, she finally says. I mean think about it, what do we even know about each other? She drops her voice even lower. We're a bunch of strangers trapped in a snowstorm in the middle of nowhere—

The way she says it, ominous and thrilling, makes it clear she's not frightened in the least. Makes it sound like it's a movie, and she's excited to be caught right in the middle of it.

Why do we have to know anything about each other? Ethan asks. Hey, is your daughter okay?

The question takes Cheryl by surprise, chases away the elation she was feeling over the mystery of a killer in their midst. Reminds her that Jenna is still behind that slammed-tight door—sleeping? sulking?—who can guess. Cheryl had tried to rouse her when the food arrived, tapping gently on the door twice and calling out to her once, but the door had stayed firmly shut.

She's going through some stuff, she says.

Yeah, I saw her when I came in.

Cheryl covers half her face with one hand, eyes closed, and Ethan immediately regrets saying it. Then she uncovers and tells him it's teenager stuff. Ugly stuff, she says. And I'm the one who gets the brunt of it.

I'm sorry. How old is she?

Fifteen.

Tough age, Ethan says because he remembers it, not because he has a clue how to parent it.

Cheryl studies him. He's young—too young to have survived the war of raising a teenager—but he's got such a mature, wise way about him. And then she remembers that he's a doctor so she tells him the whole story—what she hasn't been able to tell anyone. How Jenna came to her sobbing after someone took a picture of her performing oral sex on a boy at a party.

It's apparently a thing they do, Cheryl says. Party favours, party tricks, I don't know. I've read about it online. Anyway, someone took a picture and sent it out, and it turned into a big thing—

Someone sent out a picture? Ethan didn't want to know any of this, but now he did. That's child pornography. He can be charged.

I know, right? I keep telling her that. Although it wasn't a he, it was another girl. Apparently the boy was somebody else's *boyfriend*. Here, Cheryl uses air quotes to make her point. And for Jenna, that seems to be the crux of the problem, as if nothing else in this is wrong.

Ethan, hit by a wave of fatigue, realizes his bare feet are ice. The fire's burned down to coals, and the heat is moving through those embers, making faces that disappear before he can focus on them.

Problem is, Cheryl says, she won't tell me who it was. She's clammed right up. I just don't know what to do. I mean, girls have killed themselves over things like this—

From behind them, a pad of footsteps, then a voice taking off, rising fast. Oh my god, you're *telling people*.

Cheryl whirls, sloshing the drink she's just poured. Jenna, honey—

God Mom, shut up about it—it was *months* ago.

It was *two* months ago—

Jenna plants herself right in front of the woodstove so she's facing Cheryl and Ethan. Just stop talking about it—

Honey, he's a doctor.

I'm not, Ethan says, but his objection goes unheard.

Oh, you're a *doctor*. The girl has focused all her scathing rage on him. So can you cure me, doctor?

Ethan looks down, studying his fingers for signs of frost damage.

Can you make it so I don't like sex? Or maybe— Jenna's moving in, closer and closer— maybe do some plastic surgery so my mother doesn't have to worry that the world will recognize her daughter as the girl who sucked a dick?

That last part a high-decibel shriek, and Ethan thinks this is where he came in. He gets up and he gets out, moving around the girl carefully so he doesn't brush against her. Leaves in a hurry and tries to stop his swollen, screaming ears from hearing anything more. But even after he's in his room, he can hear the two of them. They go at it for a long time after he's crawled under the blankets.

DAWN LURCHES OUT OF A DEEP SLEEP INTO THE DEEPER darkness. She has to spread her arms out at her sides, feel the cool sheets against her palms to know for certain she's awake. The bed trembles; it might be the wind that's buffeting the back of the building or it might be the fast hammer of her heart. She'd been trapped, wedged into some narrow crevice, arms pinned tight. Blind, her voice swallowed. And something else, someone coming toward her, a sloosh like slippers or like a whisper. That was it, that's what had startled her awake. A whispering close by, the words so clear in her dream but now so elusive.

She lies still, listens. There's no voice now, no one breathing nearby. There's just the raucous gusting of the wind and Dawn gathers the blankets up tight to her chin, extends one leg until her foot slides off the bed's edge. Turns to check the time on her bedside clock.

But there's no time, no numbers glowing red. No light at all. There's no power.

She sits up, lets the blanket fall away. The air on her bare skin isn't cold, just nighttime chilly, so she knows the power hasn't been out for long. But outside, the wind howls and it won't be long before it's whisked every scrap of heat from Graceland.

It's happened to her before, a power outage in a winter storm. Just never with a houseful.

She gets dressed as quickly as she can, using her fingers like antennae, locating the tag on her heaviest sweater so she doesn't put it on backwards or inside out. It's so utterly black in this room—no faint residue of light, no moonlit clues—that she has to move slowly to avoid colliding with something, has to concentrate on where she put things the night before so she can locate her coat hanging on the back of a chair, find the lighter in the pocket.

The flame is a shock of bright. She has to relight it four times before she locates the flashlight.

In the library, she tries several times to get a fire to catch and hold. The wind is whipping down the chimney, provoking the paper and kindling into a furious blaze and then blowing them out just as fast, filling the room with smoke when it does. After the third failure, Dawn gets worried about the smoke detector, how it might wake her sleeping guests before she's ready for them. She grabs a sturdy chair, climbs up and pops out the battery, glad she didn't install one of those wired-in systems with their permanent backups like she was supposed to.

It takes another two attempts but finally she gets the fire going, burning hot enough now to turn the tide on that downdraft. In the upper part of the windows, the part not occluded by snow, she see's a slight shift from black to dark plum. Before long, her guests will wake up into a nightmare, discover they're trapped in a freezing cold, buried-alive motel with no generator, just a dark hallway and no way to call for help.

If the power stays off, and that seems likely, she'll have to feed them in here.

She's bustling back down the hall with a pitcher of water from the water cooler and a basket of muffins, flashlight held in her mouth, when she realizes the woodstove will soon be hot enough to boil a kettle, fry an egg. Remembers that she's got two cans of baked beans in her own cupboard, and all those candles and hurricane lamps in the storage closet.

The sky is still a deep bruise, the wind still malicious, but with the woodstove raging and the lamps lit, the library is engulfed in a warm glow, firelight glinting off all the books and board games. This does not have to be a catastrophe. They might be trapped and powerless, her guests, but she can gather them in here, keep them fed and entertained. Make them grateful for this haven of safety and abundance while the rest of the world is smothered under snow and ice.

After this, there's no way they won't write glowing online reviews.

ETHAN WAKES TO A SEARING PAIN. WAKES TO ALMOST PERfect darkness, and it takes him a long few seconds to sort out where he is, to understand that he must have turned in his sleep onto his ear, throbbing now, misshapen under his fingers. He wants to have a look at it in the bathroom mirror but there's no light, no switch that works. He feels his way out into the hallway, intent on alerting the motel staff, but here she is coming down the hall with a tray of coffee mugs and spoons, a flashlight, everything spaced carefully across the tray so nothing clanks together.

Power's out, she whispers, motioning for him to follow her. When he does, he steps into a room that's warm and glowing, and Ethan has the sense he's been transported back in time. He thinks of old-time movies, of *Masterpiece Theatre* productions. It would be tranquil if this hadn't been the scene of so much tension the night before. If his ear didn't hurt so much.

Coffee's almost ready, she says, and then she sees it, his ear, and he can tell by her face it's awful. He takes her flashlight, goes back to examine it in the bathroom mirror. The right one isn't too bad, just crimson and a bit flaky. But the left—the left is a discoloured, misshapen mess with two fluid-filled blisters bulging out from what should be a hollow.

There's nothing to be done about it now. When he shows up for his first day of work, he's going to look like an idiot.

Back in the library, Dawn hands Ethan a cup of coffee and pours one for herself. They settle down in front of the fire. She asks if the Tylenol has helped at all and asks how far up the road his car is. He asks how long she's been running Graceland and what she did before that. In a few minutes, they've exhausted small talk and they're just as happy to sit in companionable silence, to watch the fire and listen to the wind.

After a while, Ethan sets his cup down, lays his head back and closes his eyes, and his breathing is so steady that Dawn thinks he must be asleep. She studies him. Even with that mangled ear, he's attractive in a way that makes Dawn briefly wistful for her youth, for all the life she never got around to having. But then she looks at this room and has the rare, acute feeling that this moment right now, this space and this light, is exactly the way she's always wanted everything to be.

It doesn't last long. Outside the window, the sky slowly shifts from dark to day. Then Spencer rambles in with his peculiar gait, upsets the fine balance without saying a word.

Minutes later Cheryl arrives, pale and blinking, and then Jenna, wrapped in the blanket from her bed. The girl is the only one who speaks— So what, now there's no power? Her voice an accusation, everyone else in the room implicated.

The sun has fully risen. The light coming through the snow-packed northwest windows is feeble, but it's more than enough to take the glow off the room, to wash away the gold tones that had made it feel so warm just an hour earlier.

And maybe it's just that, the dismal light in the room. Or maybe it's the early hour, the unrelenting wind outside, that makes all her guests so terse and churlish. When Dawn offers to make breakfast, the high tone of her forced cheerfulness grates against the stony silence.

She cracks an egg, then another. The third one crumbles along the edge; splinters of shell drop into the bowl. While she fishes them out, she notes her guests have staked out far corners of the room like mortal combatants. Dawn surveys them while she scrambles, churning yolks and whites into a pure yellow froth. Ethan peruses the bookshelves and Spencer stares out the window at what little sky there is to see, occasional glimpses of blue quickly obliterated by the snow that came down and is now being tossed up again in the wind. Cheryl's on the couch, arms crossed over the Nike swoosh on her sweatshirt, her head pivoting between the two men like she's watching a tennis match. Her daughter is stretched out on the adjacent loveseat, cocooned in her blanket and facing into the back cushion.

The only noise is the sound of Dawn's fork scraping against the bowl. The only warmth in the room is coming from the fire.

Dawn pours the eggs into the pan heating on the top of the wood-stove. Stirs the beans. When it's all ready, she hands each guest a plate and though they're forced to come together, they manage to sit as far apart as possible on the couch and loveseat. Which leaves Dawn to sit alone at the old oval table that fills out the alcove in one corner of the room—the table where she once imagined board games being played.

It's Jenna who notices her sitting alone, who brings a plate over and sits down across the table. This is really nice, she says, meaning breakfast, and her voice is quiet, like this is a confidential conversation she doesn't want the others to overhear. And then she asks Dawn where she lives in the winter, when Graceland is closed. When Dawn tells her, Jenna puts her fork down. By yourself? Don't you get lonely?

The way she asks it, with such grave concern, makes Dawn turn and look at the shelf of games so she doesn't tear up.

And then Jenna looks at the shelf, too, studies all the brightly coloured boxes stacked there. Says, Hey, can I do a jigsaw puzzle?

She picks one with eight hundred pieces—a lighthouse on a rocky shore—and she helps Dawn clear the table so she can get started.

THINK OF IT LIKE ONE OF THOSE 1970S DISASTER MOVIES, Cheryl says, where we're all thrown into some dangerous shit together.

She'd had the idea in the night. After the storm with Jenna had subsided, Cheryl was alone in the library, watching the snow tumble down and down and down. Realizing no one was getting out of here in the morning. On a whim, she'd tried the computer, typed in *Spencer murderer Canada*. It took forever to deliver results, longer to open a page. No photos would display—just blank spots where they belonged—but she had two likely possibilities, and she read enough to be pretty sure she knew which was the right one. By the time she'd climbed into bed, she had the whole piece framed up in her head.

Waking up to a power outage...well that's only sweetened the pot, added another element of peril. But she'll have to focus, keep it tight. Her batteries will give her three hours, closer to four if she's lucky.

She's got the tripod set up, the camera mounted and she's trying to decide what to do about microphones. Shotgun, she thinks—less intrusive than the lapels. No choice but to take them one by one. After breakfast and a few muttered apologies, the surprise of Jenna tackling a puzzle and Dawn, their awkward hostess, trying so hard to make everybody happy, a kind of genial truce took hold. Still, Cheryl doesn't think she can get everyone to sit agreeably around a boom mic and enunciate clearly.

You always travel with this much equipment? Ethan asks from where he's pouring himself another cup of coffee.

I always bring it along, just in case. You never know what you'll stumble into—

From the puzzle table, Jenna adds, Or what deep hole you'll fall into and get trapped in *forever*.

Ethan wonders if this is Jenna's wound—her mother's ambition, how it crowds the young girl out of the way. Or maybe it's preferable. Yes, he can see that, the way Jenna's shoulders have dropped since her mother found somewhere else to focus all that keen attention.

He drifts over to where Jenna's working on her puzzle. She doesn't look up, doesn't seem to care that he's standing there watching her. If she bears him any malice after last night's mayhem, it's not evident. She's not even here, not really. She's removed herself, he thinks, like she's not even occupying the same time and space.

He studies the puzzle in progress. She started the way everybody does—building the outside frame, cherry-picking the pieces with that tell-tale flat edge and arranging them by colour—and she's making good progress. She's already finished two sides.

Okay, let's do this, Cheryl says from across the room. You're first. When Ethan looks over, she's motioning to him.

I don't have a story, he says, and wraps both hands around his mug.

Everybody's got a story, Cheryl says. I just want to hear who you are, how you ended up stuck here in this motel. Nothing tricky.

You already know all that, he says. I came for a new job and I put the car in a ditch—

Stop! Come and sit here— pointing to the big armchair— and tell it to the camera.

I'd prefer not to, Ethan says, and he starts walking with no particular destination in mind.

I'll go first, Jenna offers, dropping the two pieces she's holding. I've got a story.

Nice try, but no way, her mother says. You're not in this one. At least not yet.

It strikes Ethan as bizarre, this banter between mother and daughter. There's not a hint of nastiness, no hangover from the night before, and he's left wondering how they managed to put it behind them so fast.

It's Spencer that Cheryl wants most, but he's gone to see if he can eke a wash out of the taps before the pressure has drained to nothing, so she turns to Dawn. But Dawn, spurred by some primitive instinct, is already scurrying out of the room on a hostess mission, the importance of which can't possibly match the speed with which she's undertaken it.

Cheryl flops down in the armchair she's angled so it's lit by the window, perfectly framed by the bookshelves behind. She's already shot as much B-roll as she dares on her battery power—interior shots, snow mounded against windows to highlight that idea of being trapped. Even a quick foray out the front door to capture the *magnitude* of the snow. She lasted maybe a minute out there, but it was enough to get shots of the cars buried nearly to their door handles, the drift mounding up over the hood of hers. And the wind—well that's a story in itself. It's raging, whipping the snow around. Snow in motion never translates well on film, Cheryl knows, but she's got a few powerful images and plenty of that raging sound. A story in itself, that sound.

Now she just needs an interview subject.

I DON'T EVEN KNOW WHERE TO START.

It's true, Spencer doesn't know. Now that the camera is facing him there are so many possible roads into this story, and he wants to take the best route to show what he wants to show, get where he needs to go.

Just start at the beginning, Cheryl says. Says it like she's talking to a rank amateur. And then she asks, Were there events in your childhood that affected you, that led you to become violent?

Spencer leans around the camera so he can see her face, find out if she's putting him on. When Cheryl doesn't lift her head, stays face and eyes into her viewscreen, he leans back and crosses his arms. Are we doing an episode for Oprah, he asks, or can we move on?

Okay, she says, one hand up like it can serve as her face. Where do you want to start?

I'll start at the beginning—nothing to do with my childhood. I was twenty-one years old, and I woke up alone.

Cheryl pulls back from the camera, looks him in the eye. Drop your arms to your side, please. You look really defensive like that.

It was a logging truck jostling past on the highway that woke him up, the sound of it like calamity in his swollen head. A shaft of early morning light punched him in the eye, made him wonder why she'd left the curtains ajar like that. He turned away from it, rolling over to face her, bedsprings squalling like a baby. And she was gone.

The door to the bathroom was half shut, so he figured she must be in there. He closed his eyes against the drums thudding in his head, punched at the pillow from underneath, trying to soften the rock-hard slab of it. Hungover as hell, taste in his mouth like camel shit in the Sahara. Wanting nothing more than to get back to sleep.

He almost got there, too, before it slammed into his mind. The night before, a kaleidoscope of splintered images—the bar, the knife in his hand. A good time gone bad.

Fuck. Wake up. We're in trouble.

Eyes open again, ears attuned to the absolute quiet. That was something, at least. Nobody here, nobody close. They were safe for the right now.

He closed his eyes to concentrate. To push through the fog, reconstruct the night so he could figure out how to fix the broken bits.

They'd met their connection, done the last deal. He was almost clear of it, the obligation—five drops, that was it. No pushing his luck. He'd stuffed the cash deep in the duffel bag and thrown it in the trunk and they'd driven back a few miles to the bar he'd noticed. There was a motel across the street where they could stay the night, but first he felt like celebrating.

When he suggested it to Rosie, she liked the idea, he could tell. She'd been sullen for the past week or more but now that the job was done she'd brightened right up. She was all smiles when she hung her jacket on the back of the chair and ordered a tequila sunrise. A party drink. He didn't know the drink, just knew the song, and he was surprised when it came to the table that a dive like this kept maraschino cherries on hand. But he was glad they did. He liked the look of that drink, how the colours were really just like a sunrise across the lake on a clear morning. And she looked so pretty drinking it. He felt boring with his plain old rye and seven but he toasted her anyway, promised her there were plenty more where that came from.

It was just about then the door opened. He noticed it because the sun came pouring in and raced right into Rosie's drink, illuminating it, turning the colours so psychedelic that he felt stoned even though he was straight. When the door closed it was like a shadow fell across everything, the whole place, and that shadow was those two dudes coming in, mismatched in size but dressed so similar it was comical.

He thought they might know who he was, the way they came right over. That they might be there to collect. A day early, but it wasn't exactly the kind of business that ran on a regular schedule. Maybe someone had noticed his car and sent over the boys.

That your Trans Am? the little one wanted to know.

Yeah, that's me.

Bitchin'. I've been thinking I might get one like it, except black. You had it for long?

Couple of months. Name's Slake—have a seat.

He wasn't interested in engaging in a long conversation about cars. He just wanted to get the business part of this over and get back to celebrating. The little guy oozed the kind of confidence that made Slake itchy, but the other one—older, bigger and stone silent—was hanging back like an enforcer, so Slake figured the smartest thing to do was to have a friendly drink.

As soon as the little guy's ass hit the chair, he extended his hand for a shake. Extended it to Rosie. Hi, I'm Pete he said. Smiling.

So many fucking shiny, straight teeth.

Slake saw his mistake right away. These guys weren't here to collect. They were all wrong for it. They were just a couple of cottager brats out looking for a little trouble to end the summer on. The best Slake could hope for was to turn them into customers, make a little more dough and get out clean. So he waited for the first beers to lube the conversation, then asked them straight out. Were they interested in hash? Ever done 'ludes? Pete said they weren't buying, not tonight, and the big guy just shook his square head and squared up his square jaw like he was making some kind of too-obvious point about his nature.

All this time Rosie was there, sitting next to Slake but somehow much further away. Leaning so far forward that her breasts in that tight little blue t-shirt were pressed flat against the table edge. Pete was talking and she was leaning forward, hanging on every word he was saying about his university dorm and the wild parties they had. Stories that only he found funny.

And then Rosie was talking about how she was going home to start college, maybe become a teacher—all kinds of shit Slake had never heard before. But sure, they'd have a few thousand bucks left after he paid off the boss and got free of it. He and Rosie could rent a nice place and he'd get a normal job, something in construction, and she could go to school.

He wanted to tell her that, right then. Problem was, she wasn't saying any of it to him. She was telling it all to Big Teeth across the table, and he was flashing all those gargantuan pearly whites at her and she was smiling back.

Slake drained his drink and said, Time to go, but Rosie didn't seem to hear him. And then that little fucker ordered a third round without taking his eyes off her.

Rosie got up to go to the bathroom. She was unsteady, stumbled a bit, and Slake remembered that they hadn't eaten, not all day, and it always hit her hard on an empty stomach. She was such a little thing—not short but slight—and he was looking around to see if there was a food menu when Pete leaned toward him and said, How much for that? I'd take a crack at her.

Slake stared at him, not reacting. Not sure he'd heard right.

Hell, I'll take her right off your hands.

Fuck you, Slake said, scraping back his chair to stand.

C'mon man, she clearly doesn't dig you, and you don't want any trouble, right? You pass her along and we'll keep our mouths shut— here, he implicated his friend, too— about the drugs you're dealing.

Your friend there doesn't seem to have any trouble keeping his mouth shut, Slake said. He threw some bills on the table, more than he owed, grabbed Rosie's jacket off the chair where she'd left it and walked away, careful to look solid, to watch them without looking like he was. Stood by the Ladies, wondering what the hell was taking her so long.

The waitress was already setting the drinks down on the table when Rosie came out. The door closed behind her and all she saw was her pretty new drink; she didn't see him. Didn't see Slake standing right there, waiting for her. So he took her by the elbow and said We gotta go—*now*.

She gave him a look then like she despised him. He saw it, felt it, but he figured it was just the booze gnawing a hole in her empty gut and he steered her out of that shithole.

Too late. The boys were already on their feet, following fast, that weasel Pete in the lead and looking like business. Hey Rosie, sweetheart, he was saying before her feet even hit the parking lot. You wanna ride with me?

And damned if Rosie didn't turn her head like that was a possibility.

Just get in the car, Rose, Slake hissed, but he could feel her hesitating and suddenly he was afraid. Fear like he'd never felt before or since, not for himself but for everything, for all of it, their whole world at risk and about to be obliterated.

He'd never actually been in a bar fight over a girl, but he had good instincts. He knew you had to strike first or strike out. Still, it was two on one unless she chipped in, and that didn't seem likely, so he pressed her jacket into her hand and pushed her off toward the car while he took out his knife to even the score before he even turned around.

Pete was right behind him when he did. Smirking, eyes all over Rosie—not even looking at Slake, like Slake was about as inconsequential as a gum wrapper. And Rosie, she hadn't carried on to the car. She was still standing within arm's reach, looking from Slake to Pete like she couldn't wait to see what was about to unfold.

Pete was alone in this after all, his pal not five feet away but looking more like he was waiting to catch a bus than looking for a fight. Pete, smirking, lips parted. Maybe something in his hand— Slake couldn't tell because the hand was in shadow. The setting sun danced off Pete's bared teeth. Slake wanted to knock those fucking teeth out so he threw a punch, only he punched with the knife hand, and that must have been a mistake because he wouldn't have done that. He's sure. He wouldn't have thrown the first blow blade first, so he must have forgotten he was holding it.

Pete raised his arm to protect his precious face just in time, and the blade sliced into his forearm, cut a long gash from elbow to wrist along the bone. Nothing lethal, not even a deterrent. Slake knew that much for sure. But Rosie saw it, saw the blade, saw how the blood was pulsing out where the wound was deepest. She dropped her jacket and pushed herself in between the men screaming, Stop, stop it!

Slake heard in her voice all the fear he was feeling, and he backed up a step.

Which left Pete enough room to grab Rosie around the middle with his bleeding arm and pull her tight to him like he could use her as a shield. In his other hand, Slake could see clearly enough now the blade of a pocketknife—not much, but enough if he used it on Rosie. Slake lunged then, all instinct—this is how it looks in his memory, a feral cat with claws unsheathed, an agile superhero—and stabbed just below the shoulder furthest from Rosie. That's where he was aiming, but Pete twisted and the blade barely caught the ball of his shoulder. And even as Slake felt his knife meet flesh and glance off bone, he was noticing that she wasn't struggling. Rosie was just leaning into that bloody arm across her middle and staring at him, at Slake, with loathing.

After that second meeting with the knife, Pete gave up. Gave up and dropped his own knife and released Rosie like she wasn't even worth fighting for. Fell to his knees and onto his side, holding just himself now, bloody palm pressed against his bloody shoulder. Rosie bent down to him but Slake grabbed her arm, meaning to get her to the car and out of danger.

She screamed again like there was something left to stop.

And Slake was telling her to shut the fuck up, to not look back as he pulled her away. But of course that's all she was doing, wresting away from him and trying to get back to where Pete was lying half on the concrete steps. And Slake didn't like the way Rosie was staring at the little fucker, crumpled there. Looking at him like he mattered.

One thing for certain—she wasn't moving forward on her own and Slake had to grab her by the arm and practically force her into his car, then snatch up her jacket and throw it at her. Lying in bed the next morning, he winced when he thought about it, how rough he'd been with her. How the booze and the adrenaline in his system made her screaming sound like a betrayal.

Shit. She was so quiet in there, in the bathroom behind the half-closed door. No water running, not a breath or a burp or a fart. Maybe she'd dozed off on the toilet, but more likely she was furious. She was in there with her arms crossed, and he knew he'd fucked up bad this time.

But he could talk his way out of this. That little puke had followed them out of the bar—at least the waitress would have seen it. And the other guy, the big silent one—the last thing Slake had seen as he scrambled into the car was Pete's sidekick walking away, heading around the dark side of the bar like maybe he had to take a piss. Like the prick lying fetal in a bloody mess had nothing at all to do with him.

If that other guy wasn't going to talk, and if Slake and Rosie got their stories straight—this little weasel had followed them out, pulled a knife first, grabbed her—they'd be fine. It was all self-defence. Slake just had to fix it with her, then find a way to fix the rest of it, get back to the meeting place and hand over the money he owed. And then everything would be okay.

His eyes were still closed and he was imagining that, talking his way out of this. Imagining how they could go home to Winnipeg and set up house and everything would be fine. He wanted to call out to her—to say words like sorry and fine—but everything was so heavy and trying to think of the right words to call out put him right back to sleep.

It was full-on morning when he woke up. He was still facing her pillow and she still wasn't there. He rolled over, grabbed his watch and checked the time. Ten-twenty. He sat bolt upright then, his head only thumping half as bad now. Jesus, they had to get back on the road.

He called out to her. Looked around to see the bathroom door still half open. Kicked her bloody t-shirt on his way to the toilet to take a piss. Picked that t-shirt up on the way out and looked around the room like maybe he'd missed her sitting somewhere off to the side.

Then he saw the chain was off the door and he knew he'd slept through her leaving. His first thought was that sometimes, she liked to go for a walk in the morning, stretch out before they got back in the car. But fuck, Rosie, not today. He'd have to pack up and find her and get to where they had to be.

His head back in full thud. Tylenol his next thought.

But when he looked for the big duffel bag that held the painkillers, held everything, he couldn't see it. Not in the room and not in the bathroom and he realized he must have left it in the trunk of the car. No, he remembered bringing it in. Knew he must have, because Rosie had changed her clothes.

That's when he looked under the bed and saw his things lined up in a neat row—his shaving kit and shampoo, a couple of bottles of beer. But there was no bag and no money and it made no sense, what he was looking at.

Where the fuck was it?

A hot-cold panic seized him. No bag, no money. Still he couldn't quite believe what he was seeing, and he thought maybe she was outside waiting for him, sitting on the hood of the car with the bag at her feet, the sun on her face. Waiting for him to pull his shit together and get out there.

It slowed him down a bit, thinking that. He moved more steadily, gathering up everything that tied them to this room. Thinking maybe he should take a shower before heading out, leave her sitting for just a little longer on the hood of the car. Getting bored. Learning her lesson about scaring the shit out of him.

A part of him just wanted to lay back down on that creaky bed and wait her out. Make her come looking for him. Because as long as he didn't go outside, it was still possible that she was there.

But it was ten forty-three now and he knew it was going to take them longer to get back there, to Sault Ste. Marie, than it had taken them to get here. Adrenaline had pushed his foot to the floor and they were lucky, just lucky, to have made it the night before without getting stopped. He couldn't get away with that in broad daylight—especially not if word was out, if they were looking for his car.

When he walked out of the motel, his car was there. Right there. He saw its back end as soon as he stepped out the door, the fin and the taillights—and that wasn't right. He'd parked it further around the side, put it where it would be invisible from the road. He was sure of it. But it wasn't invisible, it was clear as day, a dead giveaway, and he stepped back into the shadow of the doorway to think about that, fingered the keys in his pocket to make sure he had them. Tried to remember if they'd left again, if they'd gone somewhere in the night after he was so fucked up. But the night was a black, gnawing hole in his head and finally he decided it must just be the difference between night and day, the sun revealing what had seemed hidden in the dark.

When he got to the car, she wasn't there. Not sitting on the hood, not anywhere nearby. Slake unlocked the trunk but he already knew there was nothing in it, no duffel bag, just a small bag of hash that must have fallen from its hiding spot and was now lying in plain sight. He picked that up and hurled it into the bushes, and then he got in the driver's seat and he pounded on the steering wheel. Pounded on the wheel again, that time catching his wrist bone and shouting Fuck.

Considered going to the motel's reception and asking if someone had seen her, but he remembered the greasy clerk who'd rented him the room, how Slake had said he was alone and then given a false name. If he went back, it would only draw attention.

He punched the steering wheel this time, bruising the knuckles on his right hand, splitting one of them wide open. Then he punched the door with his left to even up the score, started the car and tore out of there. She had to be somewhere close by. He raced up the road a few miles, heading east, speeding and slowing, peering, and then he turned around and headed west. Looking for a sign, any sign, but the only one he saw was the sign in front of the motel he'd just left, faintly blinking Vacancy in the midday light. That, and the new speed limit signs. Ninety and ninety and ninety. Fucking new metric system.

He was doing about ninety in real speed, flying, and at one point he rolled down the window and shouted her name to the trees. Slowed and shouted it again. About five miles past the motel, on a hunch, he pulled off on a side road, an old logging road maybe, and drove until it got too narrow to pass. Stopped and shouted some more. His mouth dry, his throat dry. He went to the trunk, extracted the two bottles of beer he'd wrapped in his jeans. Grabbed up her bloody t-shirt, too, and walked a half-dozen strides to stand in a clearing.

Drank one of those Labatt's Blues in the clearing, calling out to Rosie after every third swig. Holding tight to her t-shirt like he was some kind of fucking bloodhound who could follow her scent.

Nothing, not even birdsong. She was nowhere.

It was slowly, slowly dawning on him that she was really gone. That she'd taken the money and she'd left—and who knew how long ago.

She was gone, the money was gone. And he was dead.

This wasn't small-time schoolyard stuff, selling a couple of pills or a dime of hash. This was the big leagues—these guys waiting for their money were connected, bikes and leather, and he'd been moving shit for them all summer and if he didn't turn over their share this time, they'd hunt him down and they'd kill him—maybe fast, maybe slowly.

He sat cross-legged on the ground drinking the second beer, and there was a part of his brain reminding him that every stupid thing he'd ever done—including taking on this job—was fueled by alcohol.

The rest of his brain screaming, Think! But that was all he could think—that she'd taken the money and left, and that he needed to come up with a plan.

There was no plan for this.

He had about sixty dollars and change in his wallet and two cigarettes left in this pack. He smoked them both, forgetting how far it was between stops out here, and after he sat on the ground for ten minutes or an hour, looking up at the sky through the trees, he climbed back into the car, threw the t-shirt over his shoulder into the backseat and headed west. Figuring that was the direction of home, so that's the direction she must have gone.

The main entrance to Graceland is the only way in or out of the building now. A wall of snow that stands as tall as Dawn has barricaded the side entrance, leaving just a thin transom of light. Dawn thinks it's probably good insulation, at least, from the wind. The patio doors off her bedroom have a few feet of clearance where the snow's carved back from the building—the vagaries of wind direction and roofline—but a wall's been built there, too, chest deep and blocking Dawn's path around the side, either side, of the motel.

But out the front entrance, just a coating of snow catches on the door sweep. The mercy of a southeastern exposure, the shelter of the dining room protrusion that guards the doorway. Dawn thinks, maybe for the first time ever, that some foresight went into the design of this place.

This isn't her first big snowfall here, just the first time she's had to step outside to shovel it herself, a handful of guests counting on her to break them free and no Jerry around to plow her out like he usually does. Once, in the middle of winter, she'd been three days in the motel, entombed and content, before Jerry showed up with his plow and about three weeks worth of groceries and toiletries, his eyes urgent like he thought he was delivering supplies to a village after an earthquake.

But he's plowing Nancy out this weekend and it doesn't even bear thinking about.

You picked a fine time to leave me, loose wheel, Dawn says—one of Jerry's old, old jokes—and then she sets to work. Thankful that she always keeps a shovel at her patio doors, inside and leaning behind the curtains she never sees reason to close.

Five steps from the building the wind catches Dawn and gives her a good push, the shovel in her loose grip twisting, taking her wrist with it. She turns her back to the wind, rubs her wrist to make sure it's okay. Keeps her head down and digs in.

Before long she's in drifts up to her pelvis, has to take the snow apart in layers, one shovelful at a time, the sun ferocious off the white of it. With every gust, shivers of fine snow settle on her bent-forward neck.

She's in a lather, breath coming hard, shoulders aching. Recalling another snow like this, how they watched it climb the windows for hours before it stopped, and Dawn pulled on extra socks and a sweater, headed out with Andrea into the late afternoon light. Cutting the snow into blocks, lifting them up to toss them onto the high dunes beside the driveway. Slow work, Dawn's arms and shoulders tiring. The wind still fierce, every other scoop flying back in their faces. She could feel her cheeks chapping from the blow-back, the snow melting on her overheated skin. They were almost clear when the snowplow growled past, dumping a waist-high berm at the end of the driveway. Andrea had held both her arms straight out then and dropped her shovel—just dropped it and let it fall. Walked away from it, pausing beside Dawn only long enough to say Valley of Fire.

They booked tickets that night to go back, but that time and every time after it, they abandoned Vegas immediately, driving out to stay in the dreamy little palm-treed desert town of Beatty a few hours away. Forsaking even the Valley of Fire with its tourists in favour of a landscape so parched and bare it offered a grander kind of exile, a new kind of sun-soaked ritual. They drove out into the desert, walked in deep and behind a rise or dune, they stripped off their clothes and laid down naked under that fierce sun, ignoring all the possible dangers. Let it burn into their marrow, melt the last of the frost from their bones. Seven years in a row they did that, always leaving on Good Friday. An annual habit that seemed, after just a few years, to have existed for all time, a lifetime of tradition crammed into seventy scattered days.

Dawn rammed the shovel into a dune and carved off a slab of snow almost too heavy to lift. If Andrea hadn't gotten sick, they'd be there right now.

But Andrea did get sick, and they raced from mastectomy to chemo to long months of radiation, beaming into her from a machine. Too sick that year to travel, but they were counting on the next. They thought it could be vanquished and then discovered it couldn't, that it had marched out in all directions despite the battery of poisons.

Before I'm worse, Andrea had said, we have to go back to the desert.

But Dawn shook her head, said something about staying close to home where Andrea could get help if she needed it.

Beyond help was the counter-argument. I need the desert, Andrea said. If anything can save me, that can.

It was impossible. The rules had just changed, passports required now to cross the border.

No way, Dawn said. Too risky. The bait and switch, working to convince Andrea that the risk was all on her.

Back and forth on that rope for weeks before Andrea saw how deep Dawn's adamant heels had dug in. Before Dawn saw her victory in Andrea's defeated eyes.

Dawn flung a shovelful off to her left, thinking what if Andrea had been right? What if Dawn had tried, found a way to get a passport. Taken Andrea back there, deep into the desert, and laid her down naked against the hot earth under that steady sun. What if that was the radiation that could have saved her?

Dawn stops to survey her progress, take a breather. She's barely cut a swath through the parking lot—enough room for one car to squeeze through—but she hasn't found the lane yet, let alone started to clear it. She sets the blade of the shovel down on the layer of ice that separates her from the pavement and she turns to face Graceland.

Graceland is gone. Vanished.

She stands frozen, trying to get a fix on it. Cold shards pepper her face, making it hard to keep her eyes open. The wind is blowing steady, threatening to pluck the toque right off her head, and the glistening maelstrom of snow coming off the roof of her motel has erased everything, turning her world into nothing but a turmoil of white.

CHERYL STOPS SPENCER COLD, LEAVES HIM HANGING, FROZEN in time, just outside of Sault Ste. Marie while she changes the battery in her camera.

Okay, she says, go on.

It's not like he's lost his place. He can pick up the thread easily—he's had a lot of time over the years to replay this story.

It was maybe half an hour before the scheduled meeting time and Slake was no clearer on what to do than when he'd left the motel that morning. So he stopped at a payphone just outside of town and called the only number he had, said he had car trouble. Fucking thing blew a gasket out on the highway, gettin' her fixed now but they gotta wait for parts.

Phone practically slipping from his hands, greasy with sweat and shaking.

No, everything's good. I got your money, it's safe. Two days from now, I'll be there. Sorry, man, just the car. Don't worry, I'm solid.

Figured he better get the hell out of there then. Headed back toward Sudbury and cut north, right back to where he'd come from. Maybe she was still at the motel, looking for him, wondering where he'd gone. She wasn't, but he checked in anyway. Why start something new, take a chance on another place? Got the key to a different room this time, then drove back to civilization. More than enough money left in his pocket after he filled the tank for a burger and a haircut.

Short, he told the barber. Clean cut like one of those TV dads from the fifties. Yeah, the mustache too.

Thinking of her fingers tracing that mustache along the outside of his upper lip and down past the crease in his mouth as the razor scraped him clean.

Headed west the next day, figuring he was on her tail. Trying to hold his speed and keep on the lookout, stopping when he saw places he thought she might be. Went all the way to Thunder Bay and walked the streets, one end to the other, in the evening. He hated that town but she'd always seemed to like it, so it wasn't a stretch to think that's where he'd find her.

Not a trace.

Up early the next day, thinking he should shed the car. Too recognizable—the guys would be on top of him any minute. A big network, tentacles everywhere. He filled up and pointed it toward home. Knew just where he'd ditch it not far from Kenora, a place that was hidden and safe. He could hitch the rest of the way and catch up to her at home. Get his money, go back and make amends. Then pick up his car. Easy.

The cops pulled him over not an hour outside of Thunder Bay.

By what grace Slake had thought to get that haircut he didn't know, but he was glad for it. Praying all kinds of thank yous to whoever was listening.

You alone, son? the officer wanted to know. Scrutinized his license, his face. Where you headed?

Some bullshit story about taking a last-minute holiday, heading back to university now. Did I do something wrong, officer? These new speed limit signs got me confused.

Cop smiling then, confiding. No son, nothing you did. We're looking for a car similar to this—got a report about an indian driving a Trans Am. He's got a young lady with him.

Slake shaking his shorn head, shrugging. Nothing to do with me.

The officer went back to his patrol car to run the plates, just in case. Left Slake steaming. Indian driving a Trans Am. Fucking Pete—must be how he'd described Slake when the cops showed up, probably a surfeit of whimpers and groans thrown in for effect.

Slake had never come up against it like that before. He was a lifetime into passing as white—his mother's insistence, the memory of what she'd suffered growing up Métis in Winnipeg's North End making her anxious and determined. But suddenly he grows his hair long and bam—he's another goddamned indian making trouble, needing to be scrutinized. Made him think Pete deserved worse than he got, worse than the blood loss and a few severed tendons, a bunch of stitches.

Raging so hard on that, hands gripping the steering wheel, that he didn't notice the officer standing at the window, ready to hand back the license. Ready, but seeing Slake's split knuckles, then stepping back a little to look around inside the car, Slake noticing only when the cop peered into the backseat.

Now what's this?

It was Rosie's bloody t-shirt that did him in.

OR ELSE IT WAS GETTING ARRESTED THAT SAVED ME, HE SAYS
to Cheryl, to her camera. Take your pick.

What happened then?

Lotta questions. Handcuffs, back to the station. I tried to tell them
look, he pulled a knife first, he was threatening my girlfriend. That
he'd grabbed her and bled all over her shirt, that it was his blood. And
then I shut up, because there's a hole you're digging and they want
you to dig it deeper. So I just kept my mouth shut, didn't talk except
when I asked for a lawyer. In the morning, they let me go instead.

He can see Cheryl's fooling around with the camera, zooming
in or pulling out or some shit, but he really doesn't care. He's been
talking a long time and there's still plenty more to come.

I figured I just had to get out of the province. Thought you
crossed a border and you were safe. Young and stupid—seen too
many movies, I guess.

Spencer chuckles and in that pause, Ethan gets up. He was listening earlier but now he's not. Bored, maybe. Just another old con's
twisted story of woe.

I remember I was so happy to see the sign, to see Welcome to
Manitoba, Spencer says. Thinking I was home free.

Ethan opens the stove to feed a few good-sized junks of birch
into the fire. Spencer watches him, watches the flames burnish the
other man's face, thinking what it is to be that young and fit. So sure
on your feet, of where you're headed.

But you weren't? Home free? Cheryl had swung the camera to
catch the action—more fuel for the fire—but she's got it pointing
back at Spencer now and she wants him to get on with it. He can
sense her impatience, can tell he's losing everyone's attention. He
needs to hurry this up, cut to the chase if he's going to get his story
on the record. On camera.

Hell no, they followed me home, he says. Maybe they switched
up, I don't know, but I caught sight of them a few times in the

mirror. Then they were gone and I thought I was okay. I ditched the car on a side street and took a bus across town to stay with a friend. The plan was to hide out until I got my money back. I went to Rosie's house to see if she was there—not knocking on the door exactly. More hovering in the bushes, watching. So stupid—

Spencer laughs, but no one laughs along with him. As far as he can tell, the only one who's hanging on his story is the kid. Every time he stops talking, she looks up like the screen is frozen, like maybe the cable signal's gone out. When he starts up again, she goes back to her puzzle.

I had no idea the cops were watching. They picked me up right there at Rosie's, literally dragged me out of the bushes. And that's when things got serious.

Spencer waits until he sees Jenna lift her head in his peripheral vision before he continues. Because see, they'd already decided that I'd killed her.

Cheryl lets that sentence hover for several seconds before she asks, Did you?

Spencer puts his hand up, meaning hang on, slow down, but Cheryl sees the way he shakes his head like he can't help it, and that shake is all denial.

So the cops haul me in— Before Spencer can get any further the door to the library opens, bringing a cold commotion of air with it and Dawn's voice, high and sharp, full of oxygen from outdoors. She's bundled in her black and puffy snowsuit, hidden inside its over-sized, snow-caked layers and saying something about the wind.

Cheryl curses and turns the camera fast, hoping to catch up to every other gaze in the room. But she's not fast enough, not sure her focus is sharp enough. Has to ask Dawn to repeat herself.

The wind's blowing it in faster than I can shovel it out, Dawn says. Her face is red as a beet, her toque pulled down to her brow line and covered in fast-melting snow. She's left her boots behind, peeled off her gloves, and she's watching her fingers catch hold of the zipper tab on her snowsuit. The room fills with the long song of its undoing.

When Ethan stands and says he'll take a turn at the shovel, Dawn tells him no. She points to his ears like a warning and says it's no use anyway, not until the wind settles down.

Only then does she notice the camera trained on her. Her eyes go wide and she pivots sideways, one hand splayed the way celebrities and suspects shield their faces.

It's fine, Cheryl says. Really, you're a natural beauty—you look great on camera. The pictures of you on your website are gorgeous.

But Dawn keeps her hand up and averts her face until Cheryl pans away—slowly, so she can get the whole tableau, this cozy scene set against Spencer's unsettling story. Then Dawn ruins the moment again when she asks if anyone's hungry, if she should find something for lunch.

Yes fine, Cheryl snaps, but give us some time without an interruption—we're just in the middle of something. The director in command of her set now, sending the crew off to fetch lunch and stay out of the way. Cheryl hopes the camera will serve as a repellant, will keep Dawn at bay. She doesn't have enough battery left to re-shoot anything.

Okay, she says to Spencer, sit back like you were. She's trying to compose the scene for a seamless edit, but he doesn't sit back. He stands up so she's shooting the buttons on his shirt and then the chair he's left behind. Time for a bathroom break first, he announces. Keeps moving away despite Cheryl's protests.

He follows the dark form of Dawn through the door that's just closed behind her, but Cheryl sees no value in capturing that shot. What she wants now is reaction. She's already framing this up in her head, the film she's loosely titled *Trapped with a Killer*.

So, she asks once she's got Ethan in focus. You're trapped in a snowstorm with a killer—

I think he's going to tell us he didn't kill her.

And will you believe him?

Ethan crosses his arms and looks directly into the camera. You're the one who says whatever story you tell on camera is true, Ethan says. So I guess it'll be true, won't it?

There's thump and sizzle as a log topples in the stove and then Jenna wades into the conversation. That's not what she means.

Cheryl sharpens the focus on her daughter, wants a clear record of Jenna jumping to her defense.

Since she's the one with the camera, she's the one who gets to decide. Whatever story *Mom* tells is true. That's what she means.

Hey, that's not fair— Cheryl steps back from the camera to defend herself, but she sees Jenna is fighting back a smile as she studies her puzzle, and she imagines Ethan, his back to her while he stares out the window, is doing the same, so she lets it drop.

Behind the bookshelves, faint but discernible, the rushing water of a toilet's flush, the kind of noise that usually goes unnoticed.

Now he's used the last flush, Ethan says—and he says it like it's a condemnation.

They all turn their attention to the door then, waiting for it to open, unwilling to be caught dissecting the story of the convicted killer in their midst.

SPENCER COMES OUT OF THE BATHROOM ACROSS FROM THE kitchen and thinks he'll step out for a smoke, centre himself before he gets back for his dramatic tell-all moment. But the sound of dishes clattering in the dining area draws him. She's got her back to the door, reaching up to lift a handful of mugs down from a cupboard. Still swaddled in her snowsuit. Her tiny hands, the way they stick out against all that puff, remind Spencer of Denny as a toddler and it sparks a keening in him so sharp he can hardly bear it.

She reaches up again, this time for plates. His instinct is to offer to help, but he can't risk it. Not now. He wants her to stay oblivious just a little while longer—long enough for him to get his story on the record before he draws her into it.

He backs away quietly, heads out the front for a quick smoke, keeping his back to the wind.

In the library, he settles himself into the big chair and sits stiffly while Cheryl repositions him until she's got him just where she wants him.

Where was I? he asks.

The police pulled you out of the bushes, Cheryl reminds him, tightening the focus.

Right. They'd sent that bloody shirt over from Ontario. That was Exhibit A, packed up in a plastic bag. They held it up to my face over and over. Taking shifts all night and day, back and forth, them asking why I'd killed her and where's the body and me saying, No, I didn't kill her, why would I kill her, I loved her? If I'd killed her, why would I go to her house?

I kept asking for a lawyer and finally one showed up. Guy was half-asleep most of the time. Hardly said a word except to ask if they were charging his client with anything. So they did—charged me with the kidnapping and murder of Rose Benson.

Kidnapping? Cheryl says.

Spencer holds up his hands like a question, like who came up with that idea?

We were in love, she came with me willingly, he says, but how could I fight it? Her family said she disappeared without a word, and that didn't seem like her. Her friends said they didn't know a thing.

So I stuck to my story—I didn't kill her. I told them over and over about the bar fight. Told them this guy Pete, that's his blood. Figured even if I went down for that, it was better than what I was facing. But either they didn't look too hard or Pete had clammed up and skulked off to whatever party school he called home, because they never did find him. Waitress in that bar made a statement—recognized the picture of Rosie they showed her, the mugshot of me. Said all she could recollect was that I'd dragged Rosie out without letting her finish her drink.

Damning, Cheryl says, and has to remind herself again to shut up.

Rosie's stepmother identified the shirt as hers. So they had me, and other than my own mother, I had nobody on my side. You know after awhile, even I started to think maybe it was true. That maybe I had killed her. That I'd done something that night—got rid of her and the bag and I just couldn't remember it.

So you confessed?

Shit, Cheryl thinks. She hadn't meant to give away anything, hadn't wanted him to know that she'd read up on him the night before, even if she was proud of herself for having figured out which murderer he was. Anyway, he doesn't seem to notice. He's just barreling forward.

Confessed, yeah, to murder—but not kidnapping. Kidnapping with murder is first degree.

He looks over and sees Jenna and Ethan are both fixed on him now. Rapt.

I had some leverage, Spencer says. They wanted a body, and I wanted a deal. So I told them I'd killed Rosie and thrown her down into a deep crevice, down where she'd never be found, but I was so high I couldn't remember where or when. I got my deal—second degree murder—and they got their case closed.

How long did you serve?

Fourteen-year sentence, nine years before I got parole.

That's a long time, Cheryl says.

Nine years for murder? Ethan chimes in. That's ridiculous. It's nothing compared to the sentence your victim got.

Spencer ignores that, answers Cheryl. Long time, he says. Especially if you didn't kill anybody.

Not that he'd ever been totally sure about it, not until recently. As the months and then years ticked by and she never showed up, he weighed the evidence against himself. The night was a complete blank spot, the car wasn't where he remembered he'd left it the night before. It started to seem possible, after awhile, that he'd thrown his Rosie into a dark hole between two rocks. And then it started to seem likely.

Oh, so now you do remember it wasn't you. Then who killed her? That's from Ethan, his voice even and hard.

Spencer looks over at the impervious wall of judgment he's run up against a million times before. The same expression Janet's father wore the day they met. His whole life's work has been to try to shift that expression, to knock its wearer just a little off their high perch.

Nobody killed her, he says. It was Pete's blood on the t-shirt—

So you didn't kill her? Let's talk about that, Cheryl says.

Oh c'mon. This is bullshit!

Every head turns then toward Jenna, who's got her arms up in exasperation, a puzzle piece pinched in each hand.

Hello—DNA. They could tell whose blood it was.

Spencer smiles. He almost feels sorry for the poor kid, stuck listening to old-time stories like his. They didn't know about DNA back then, he tells her.

Really? Jenna looks at her mother for confirmation. Cheryl's trying to keep the conversation in focus, but she lifts her head long enough to say it was a prehistoric time, even before CSI.

Ethan jumps in. Of course they knew about DNA—it just wasn't used in evidence yet. I'm not sure when they started that, maybe the nineties?

Late eighties, Spencer says, his voice certain. They started using DNA as evidence after I was paroled.

Oh, Jenna says, arms at her side now. Sorry. Then she goes back to the business at hand, to making sense of which pieces are sky and which are sea.

Cheryl swings the camera to Spencer, checks her focus again. Can you repeat that they didn't use DNA as evidence until the late 1980s, and by then you'd been paroled?

Spencer complies but he says it fast, anxious to get back to the main point of his story—

But Cheryl sidetracks him again, wants to know if he ever asked them to re-open the case.

Why would I? I'd already lost ten years of my life. I was out, still young and looking to the future. I wasn't interested in returning to the past.

He's thought about it a million times, but who knows if that t-shirt even still exists, bagged and tagged in some evidence room somewhere. Besides, he'd confessed—not to blood on the shirt, but to tossing his girlfriend into a crevice. There was no way he could prove he hadn't.

Also, Ethan says coldly, and Cheryl tells him to speak up as she trains the camera on him. Also, he says loudly, you get parole because you accept responsibility, isn't that the way it works? And aren't you putting a lie to that process right now?

Shit! Cheryl steps back. My battery's gone.

You got another one? Spencer asks. I've got some important things to say.

Save it, she says. We'll have to wait until the power's back on.

DAWN DRIVES THE KNIFE HARDER THAN SHE NEEDS TO, cleaves the apple in half and then half again. Carves out the core, but not elegantly. The knife's too big, the cuts it makes too square. She drives into another one, just missing her finger. Steps back and tells herself to settle down. But the anger that started with being dismissed from the library smouldered until it settled on Jerry—Jerry, putting pictures of her on the website. Now it's raging, and she can hardly wait until the power is on so she can call Jerry, interrupt whatever romantic interlude he's in the middle of and cut him to ribbons.

Can hardly stand the idea of carrying these neatly arranged tuna sandwich triangles into the library, smiling.

But that's what she does, strips off the ridiculous coveralls that have her overheating and arranges the apple wedges on a separate plate, walks down the hall with a plate balanced on each palm like some servant girl in her master's house.

She walks in without pausing, without even trying to avoid interrupting some precious moment in movie making—but the camera's off and Cheryl is sitting idle next to Ethan on the couch. Jenna is still bent over her puzzle. Dawn holds the plates aloft and considers the room; with the table covered in puzzle pieces, she's got no clear surface to set the food on.

It's only Spencer who's noticed her come in, who sees her problem. He crosses the floor until he's right in front of her and reaches out to take a plate.

Something about his hand, his wrist. Something whispering at the back of her mind.

Dawn goes to make room on the coffee table. She wants to drop off the sandwiches and leave without a word, but she's trapped in the role of local hostess when Cheryl asks how long this could go on. Everything about her tone suggests she holds Dawn responsible for the weather, the lack of highway plows and the failed wires.

Wind's dying down, Dawn says, so hopefully they'll get the power on soon.

And then she's walking away, only half turning her head to ask if there's anything else she can get. But she's through the door without waiting for anyone to formulate a response.

ETHAN NIBBLES ON AN APPLE SLICE BUT HE HAS NO APPETITE. Even with the camera off, Spencer's holding court, setting himself up to be the hero of the piece and Ethan's watching Cheryl and Jenna—especially Jenna—eat it up.

That kid's got enough turmoil without some ex-con manipulating her emotions.

What this country needs is more programs inside our prisons and fewer inmates, Spencer's saying. But the system's going the wrong way. Tough on crime really means more punishment and less hope for rehabilitation.

Ethan moves to stand behind the loveseat so he's between Spencer on the couch and Jenna at the table. It's a fantasy, he says, that every violent offender can be redeemed with a little loving care and a few literacy classes. This is something he does understand—bad wiring in the brain.

I didn't say everyone, Spencer says. And then he shuts up. He knows better than to engage with someone who's been hurt personally. All he's got is a body of research, facts and figures and insider knowledge—a victim has the hammer of all that pain, all that umbrage.

Ethan doesn't let it go. And what about the victims, how long their sentences go on? What about justice for them?

Spencer can't let that lie. So what you want is an eye for an eye. Well then be honest, because you're not talking about corrections or justice—you're talking about vengeance.

I'm talking about public safety.

Interesting, Spencer says. I didn't take you for a hardcore conservative.

Ethan just wants people to be held responsible for the things they do. If that makes him a conservative, fine. The man who'd held him captive, abused him—he was out on parole for three months before he did it again to some other child. Ethan's parents thought they'd shielded him from that news, but he was thirteen by then. He could read the goddamned newspaper.

But Ethan's not thinking that, not exactly. He's just thinking he's glad to be wearing his own pants today.

Spencer has him in his sights. *Ever had a patient who you thought had no hope of recovery, doctor?*

I'm not a doctor, Ethan says emphatically. *I'm a medical scan technician.*

Jenna and Cheryl both turn on him, identical expressions on their faces, a simultaneous accusation. *I thought you were a doctor!*

He throws his half-eaten apple wedge back onto the plate, starts to move away but Spencer pins him down with a look. *I'm sure you know what I mean,* he says. *Sometimes a patient surprises you, even when you've written them off.*

Ethan thinks about his father at that keyboard, coming to life character by character after everyone else thought it was over. *Sure,* he concedes, *but that's an anomaly—that's not something you build a system on.*

He heads for the firebox and snatches up another split log, but Cheryl protests, says it's already too hot in here.

It would be great to get this conversation on camera, Spencer says to Cheryl. *This is important stuff.*

Let's see what happens, she says through a yawn. *Can't do anything until I've got power, and now it's too late in the day anyway. We have to wait until morning for the right light.*

She stretches out on the couch and drags a blanket off the arm-rest to cover herself despite the heat. She could make the light work if there was a story here, but there isn't. It's all backstory and moral blathering. She wanted tension and a collection of imperiled characters. Instead, she's got a debate about social justice and a plate of tuna sandwiches.

It's Jenna who finally eats one of the sandwiches, her chewing and the fire's incessant spit and crackle the only noise in the room. And it's Jenna who finally speaks, asking Spencer what prison was like. Spencer isn't sure if this is something he should talk about now, or wait until the camera's back on, so he asks Cheryl if it's okay.

Sure, she tells him, that one could use a little scared straight. And with that, she turns into the couch and closes her eyes.

It's not a good place to be, he tells Jenna. For one thing, it's unbelievably boring and monotonous, the same routine day in and day out—

That doesn't sound so bad, Cheryl mumbles into the couch.

It's hell, every minute, following orders and trying not to make waves, trying to avoid the simmering violence day in and day out. But okay, so you want the gruesome? Spencer looks down at his hands, spreads his fingers wide and studies them like he's counting up grievances, picking his best-of. Finally, he talks about how the guys he owed all that money to sent someone to lay a good beating on him, smashed his kneecap and broke his femur. How long he was left to lie in the yard with his blood seeping into the ground before anyone official bothered to come out and help him.

Ironically, the best part of my incarceration, he says, was the few months I spent in the infirmary. Best drugs in the place, plus I got to read some good books, think about my life without interruption.

He sees Ethan cross his arms, sees the hostility in that.

Anyway, Spencer says, it was an interesting time to be in prison.

What do you mean? Jenna asks.

Well there were a lot of celebrities, a lot of big names walking the yard, he says. Carlou, Farquharson. Ted Macky, the famous con artist who, as he liked to tell it, almost took down the central bank.

Spencer can see none of them have a clue. Can see he runs in different circles and this is all just nonsense, but he's going somewhere he doesn't mean to be going and he can't seem to stop the train.

Stu Whitbourne—I shared a cell with him for a while. Nicer guy than you'd expect.

Jenna wants to know who Stu Whitbourne was. She, at least, has the excuse of not having been close to born yet when that story broke.

Spencer smiles. Stu was a famous musician—Canadian famous, anyway—a folksinger, mostly. Big deal in the seventies, had a couple of hits. Then he murdered his brother and sister so he'd inherit everything.

Spencer likes the way the girl's eyebrows go up, how she's all ears now and not a smidge of retreat. Reminds him of Denny, the way you can see the wheels whirring in his head as he's gathering up something new and intriguing.

Poor guy was pretty drug-addled, he says. Did a ham-handed job of it, really—deserved to get caught. And if you ask me, the inheritance wasn't close to enough to risk the life sentence.

Who else?

The way Jenna asks it, all genuine interest and encouragement, feels to Spencer like permission to keep going. Like it's not his fault, he's off the hook for the bomb he's about to drop in this close, overheated room.

Oh, some of the radical anti-establishment guys they'd nailed on ridiculous charges—bounced cheques and parking violations. Proudflower and James, guys like that. Used to hold court in the yard, talking revolution, the end of capitalism. Spencer laughs. I guess now they'd all be running for office, he says.

And then he stops, let's the silence build while he pretends to think. It's a trick he learned from Bax.

And Garry Mitzencor, I was in with him.

Spencer's still addressing Jenna but keeping a peripheral watch on Ethan. Notorious pedophile, he says. Of course I didn't have a lot to do with him—guys like that, they keep them apart from the rest of us.

Spencer's not sure what he expected would happen when he dropped Mitzencor, but it was more than nothing, and nothing is what he's seeing. Ethan doesn't move, doesn't even fucking blink.

Doesn't colour. Spencer has survived and thrived by knowing how to read slight shifts in expression, in body language. But there's nothing here to read. If Ethan even registered what Spencer said, he hasn't shifted one iota.

And then Spencer's ashamed, and he feels himself shrinking, a slackness taking hold, and he can't tell if he's deflated or relieved.

Ethan stands up and says he's going to help with the shoveling.

Spencer looks at him full on, at the scabby cauliflower stuck on the side of the poor guy's head. Cover your ears, he says.

Ethan turns, looks not quite at Spencer but over his head. No point, he says. The damage is already done.

DAWN STARES DOWN INTO HER DARK FREEZER DRAWER, HOPing for a forgotten miracle, for anything she can cook to please this crowd and turn the tide on what's amounted to a terrible day, a terrible stay for all of them. She moves aside a stack of pizza boxes, stares down into the shadows. She's letting all the cold air escape, but the room's frigid enough now not to worry about that. Frigid enough to start worrying, instead, about pipes freezing.

Even without a flashlight, she can see there's nothing down there—nothing she could roast over a fire or stew in a Dutch oven. Just a single leathery pork chop and a bag of frozen peas. She lifts the peas out, massages the bag to break them up, hoping they're not too freezer-burnt, then drops them back into the drawer and kicks it shut, hoping no one gets hungry any time soon.

Her fingers are still numb and the sun's on its way down. She'll have to light the kerosene lamps soon, make sure the fire's stoked, but all she wants to do is to crawl under a blanket and close her eyes, wake up alone and not feel so lonely.

In the library, she finds Cheryl has done just that—has pulled up a blanket and gone to sleep, leaving Jenna alone with Spencer while Ethan takes a turn outside.

Dawn was obliged to hand over her shovel, but only because Ethan had insisted. She offered every protest she could think of—you're a guest, you're not dressed for it, your ears—but he'd said, I have to do something. I can't sit in there and listen to any more of that crap. Then Ethan told her what the conversation was about, that Spencer was a convicted murderer, that he'd killed his girlfriend and done time. But now that he's got a camera pointed at him and a captive audience, Ethan said, he claims it wasn't him after all.

Dawn didn't know what to say to that, and Ethan didn't seem to expect her to say anything. He just took the shovel from her hand and set off to work his way toward the lane that led to the highway.

And now this—the teenage girl sitting across from a murderer, both of them hands and eyes into a damn jigsaw puzzle while her mother snores softly on the couch like she's oblivious to the danger she's left her daughter in.

Dawn has to hand it to Jerry—he knew there was something sinister about this guy right from the start. She steals a look at Spencer while she lights a kerosene lamp, hoping to glimpse what it was that Jerry saw. There's a flash, a kind of gut-punch of a feeling, but it's fleeting, gone before she can grab hold. Still, it's something, and she can't just leave Jenna here unattended, so Dawn pulls up a chair and sits down next to the girl. Studies the table, trying to make sense of all the pieces in front of her.

When the power comes back on, the sun is setting and the three of them are still bent over the puzzle, trying to discern shades of blue and grey in the flickering glow of the kerosene lamps. They have no idea the power's back, not until Ethan tromps in and says the yard light just came on. He flicks the switch inside the door and the room floods with light.

Suddenly the puzzle, nearly completed, is awash in light and Jenna almost rears back, blinking like she's come out of some deep fugue. She looks around, runs her eyes along the bookshelf and maybe something there reminds her or maybe she's been thinking about it in the quiet, but she says, Hey, it's Easter tomorrow.

Suppose it is, Spencer says.

He's been watching Dawn for this past hour, trying to will her to look up and see him, but she wouldn't. She wouldn't even favour him with a glance. He pushes away from the table, stands. Right now, he says, it's time for a smoke. And he heads for the front door— doesn't even bother with a jacket, his limp barely noticeable at the speed he's moving.

Cheryl rouses herself on the couch and asks Ethan what it's like outside, if it seems possible that they'll be able to leave in the morning.

I've shoveled the rest of the parking lot and all the way down to the highway, Ethan says. As soon as they plow the road, we're home free. And then he remembers Pauline. Remembers that he's been gone two days without a word, and he should tell his mother that he's alive. He goes to the computer and boots it up, stretches and shakes loose his shoulders while he waits for it to spool through its opening chords.

Dawn blows out the kerosene lamps and stands for a minute in the middle of the room, thinking how everything looks different, looks hollow and cheap, with all the overhead lights blaring. She tells them they should all make sure the heat's turned up in their rooms and plug in anything that needs to be charged. Hopefully it'll stay on, she says, but who knows. I'll throw some pizzas in the oven right now.

She doesn't make it out the door before Ethan calls out to her, tells her there's no internet connection.

She checks the cables, fools around as much as she knows how, but she can't make it work so she heads down the hall to reception and picks up the phone. All she hears is dead air.

THE WIND'S NOT BAD, HE'S DRIVEN IN WORSE, BUT IT'S STILL
kicking up enough snow to blind Jerry on the open stretches—and
that's mostly all there are, open stretches. His tires are solid, big
monsters with heavy tread, but the road's slick, the snow on it polished to a sheen of ice by a day of sun and wind. There's a single lane
that's been plowed down the centre but that's blowing in, sometimes completely filled. He's got the telephone poles for a rough
guide, and he's telling himself slow and steady. It'll take him four
hours to get there at this rate, but he can't risk picking up speed.

He shouldn't have left, should have listened to his instincts. He
knew there was something about that guy, something off in the
way he was acting. Something dangerous. It dogged him all the
way from Graceland to Nancy's, looming like a bad hangover. Jerry
couldn't shake the feeling even during supper, and finally he gave
into it. Booted up his laptop and tried Googling Spencer and Ontario
online, but what the hell was the point of that? He'd waded through
about a hundred and found nothing, no resemblance at all, before
he gave up and went back to Nancy and her son Stockton, resumed
instead the hard work of trying to get her forty-year-old youngster
to warm up to him. Jerry was sticking to stories by then because
asking questions only led to curt replies. Told all his best stories,
aware that Nancy was the only one laughing—laughing even though
she'd heard them all before.

Nancy had warned Jerry—had said her son was a hard case, a
curmudgeon from the day he was born. Jerry thinks now that she
understated it.

Jerry flicks on the high beams but it's a mistake, a blinding one,
and he flicks them back off. Redials Graceland from the hook up on
his steering wheel.

He's been phoning Dawn all day. Just checking in to see how
you're doing up there, that's what he planned to say but he couldn't
get through. It rang and rang, no one picking up, no answering

machine. No reply to his email either. He figured the storm had knocked the power out—it made sense, and there was nothing he could do about it. But when he tried again this evening, there was no ring at all, just a fast busy signal, the sound of it like an emergency. Like alarm bells that woke up an idea he didn't even know was inside him. He went back to the computer and this time, he searched for her. Searched her name from the time before she was Dawn, a name he knew by accident and had hoped was long forgotten.

He was sitting with his laptop in the living room. Nancy and her son were talking in the kitchen. He could hear Stockton say something about his father barely cold in his grave, and Nancy telling him she had a right to be happy.

Sure Mom—but this guy? Come on, you could do better.

Jerry didn't hear how Nancy responded to that. Suddenly he was looking at the face of the man he'd checked into the motel—a man called Spencer Menard. A murderer. And set right next to his picture: an old school photo of his victim.

Jerry leapt up, told Nancy he was going. Made up a story about a cousin in critical condition, laid it on thicker than he needed to and he could see she didn't believe him.

Jerry, just stay, she'd said, and her voice held a kind of please that was sincere, but not begging. Stockton just needs some time but he'll come around, you'll see. And if he doesn't, well I don't care.

Jerry kissed her quick and hard then, but he stuck to his story. It's a family emergency, I have to get there.

He could see tears welling up in her eyes so he turned fast and walked away, walked out and climbed into his truck, thinking it was a good thing he'd plowed the driveway earlier.

Thinking what was the point of it anyway, trying to love one woman if your head was full of another.

Jerry's call doesn't connect. The truck fills with that beeping again, fast and furious, and the sound of it and the snow flying at the windshield are enough to crank Jerry's heartrate up to bust. When he jabs the button to hang up, he jerks the wheel, feels the truck start to glide sideways on the polished ice. Then a rear tire catches on the drifted snow and that's the break he needs to set things straight.

He's remembering another icy night at the end of '77—or maybe they'd already slid into '78. Didn't matter. It was miserable driving and he stopped at the first place he could. Had a coffee and a burger, went to the bathroom. Came out and then he was looking into her face—unmistakeably her, leaping right off the wall at him.

Her face. Dawn's. His Dawn. *Missing.* The police looking for anyone with any information. He'd torn down that poster and taken it with him, kept it on the seat next to him all the way back across three provinces, wondering what she'd done or who was after her, what he'd have to ask to find out. Wondering whether he should just pull over and call the cops.

And then he walked into the Blue Iris and saw her wrapping the cord around the old Hoover.

She didn't see him. She was just kind of singing to herself, looking relaxed and happy, and he decided right then that he would never tell a soul about that poster, and if he ever saw another one, he'd rip it down and throw it away, too.

Since then he's never asked anything, or hardly anything. Never let himself dig around, even after Google made it so damn easy. Figured at first that it was her business, that she'd talk about it when she was ready. Then he let it slip into some dark recess in his mind. What did it matter? So much time had gone by that he was surprised he could even dredge up the name Rose Benson. But there it was, like it had been waiting inside him for all these years.

Jerry accelerates gradually and his tires hold the road. He's hurtling through loose, blowing snow. The way it's coming at him, smearing into white lines that part as he races past, reminds him of the way the stars blur when the Enterprise switches to warp speed on *Star Trek.*

Warp speed ahead, he mutters. Mutters it, over and over, a mantra to keep him steady at the helm.

SPENCER SIDLES UP BEHIND JENNA, WHO'S STANDING IN THE hallway peering into one of the frames.

A lot of dead flowers on display in this place—what's that about?

It's the sort of thing Spencer would say to Denny, partly just to amuse himself and more because he could count on Denny to come up with something hilarious, his brain always working so fast to make sense of the senseless world. But Jenna doesn't go that way. She just says I think they're pretty, and her voice is matter of fact, laced with an edge that might be earnestness and might be accusation. Spencer can't tell if she's being contrary or if she just doesn't want to offend their hostess, who's cleaning up in the room behind them.

I like its name, lady's slipper, Jenna says. It's just what it looks like.

Spencer leans toward the framed flower, tells Jenna his mother showed him one as a kid. I leaned down to look, he says, and a bee came right out and stung me on the nose.

Seriously?

Hurt like hell. But my mother called this something else. She called it a moccasin flower.

And Dawn, passing behind them, empty plates in one hand and empty cups in the other, pauses for just the instant it takes to hear bee sting, to hear moccasin flower.

To hear the other slipper drop.

SPENCER TAMPS THE LAST OF HIS TOBACCO INTO THE ROLLER with his finger, slides the tube in, taps the filter on the table to pack it a little more tightly. Then he lays it alongside the others. They're all too loose, the seven smokes lining his silver case, and they'll burn too hot and fast. He should have seen this coming, this running out, should have known he'd be smoking so much more than usual and brought extra. In the morning, he'll have to go buy a pack, pay the toll for ready-made. Or maybe he'll ask Cheryl to pick him up one when she drives Ethan into town to see about his ditched rental—force her hand, make her admit that she has no intention of coming back here. Spencer's sure that's the case, that she won't let him finish his story on camera, get to the big reveal. That she'll never even use what she's already filmed.

He heads down the hallway to smoke in the shelter of the front entrance.

When he first saw that camera, he couldn't believe his good fortune. Third-party documentation, a professional storyteller. So easy. Fuck.

He takes a deep drag and wonders why he thought telling his story would turn out differently this time. He's back to square one, back to the original plan and at least everyone else will leave tomorrow and leave him to it.

His cigarette is gone in a gust. He drops it, thinking he's going to have to do this the hard way. Then he sees the light go on in the dining room and he decides he's too impatient to wait that long.

Dawn's suited up—dressed in her snowsuit, the balaclava folded back over her head, mitts in one hand and the shovel in the other. If she can't get her car out fast, she can probably walk to Wanda's—it's a fifteen-minute drive so what's that, three hours, maybe four on foot? She's fit, not feeling any signs of age. Her body hasn't betrayed her yet. And if the highway's been cleared now, maybe she can flag down a passing car.

But she doesn't even make it out of the dining room—he's there, looming in the doorway. Slake. And the minute he appears she knows he's come for her. She'd tried to convince herself this was some kind of weird coincidence—stood looking in the mirror at her silver hair and lined face, thinking maybe it was disguise enough, that maybe he didn't even recognize her. But she'd seen the way he looked at her.

Is there something you need, Mr. Spencer? she asks, the hospitality in her voice pulled taut, the shovel held out in front of her, its blade resting lightly on the floor.

He's moving toward her, blocking her way forward, and she doubts that if she turned and fled, she'd make it to her room, door shut and locked, before he was on her. Anyway, it's the one door she didn't replace with something more solid—the only door without a deadbolt.

Sit down, he says.

I don't understand, she says. Wishing she'd pulled the balaclava over her face earlier.

I think you do, Rosie. He's right in front of her now. He tugs the shovel from her hand before she can react, tosses it across the floor so it lands in front of the counter where the microwave is still blinking from the power outage.

Sit down, he says again. We're going to have a talk. And he marshals her toward the corner booth.

Dawn sits, thinking maybe she can talk her way out of this. He takes the seat across from her and then there they are, staring at each in the corner booth like lovers in a romantic restaurant.

Where's all my money, Rosie? As he asks it, he's looking around like it might be hanging off the walls.

She shakes her head. I don't know what—

Oh Jesus, I'm sitting in it. This is my money, right here—isn't it? This little empire you built with that wad of cash you stole while I was getting my knee kicked so hard it bent backwards, steel pins half down my leg. My spleen removed.

I'm sorry that happened—

Happened because of you, because I owed money I couldn't pay.

She looks down at the table. Notices it's got a coat of dust that needs to be wiped clean.

Anyway, he says, I'm not here about the money. Although you know, Rosie, that was a lot of money back in those days. And you were a smart girl—I expected you to make something more than this out of yourself. And then he looks around the room again. Please tell me you at least lived high on the hog until the dot.com craze ended.

She's waiting for Andrea to make an appearance, to put something razor sharp and cunning into her mouth, but it's Margaret who claims her tongue.

I have worked very hard to build this, she says. If you don't like it, you can just get out.

Spencer leans back a little, throws up his hands like he's conceding the point. Hey, I don't care about the money anyway. That's not why I'm here.

Look, I'm sorry, she's says, feeling like she's got the ground under her now. But I really don't understand why you're here, Spencer— that's your name, right?

You goddamn know it is.

And then it twigs for him. Maybe she doesn't. She knew him back when he went by Slake—a nickname he acquired on a camping trip with his cousins, all of them barely out of high school and Spencer so wasted he kept trying to tell them there was a lake right there. S'lake, s'lake, he kept saying. Or that's how they told it, and they never called him anything else for years. Not until they wrote him off entirely when he went to prison.

The world thinks you're dead, Rose, he says. And they think I killed you.

He's looking at her close and he can tell she's surprised, that she didn't know about that. It makes him feel softer toward her. It makes him feel hopeful.

I lost ten years of my life—more than that, way more—and all I'm asking is that you come back with me and show them you're alive. Let them see I didn't do it.

She looks away from him. Looks down at her hands and then out the window for a long few seconds before she meets his eye again.

Do you want a glass of wine? she asks.

Spencer leans closer then leans back, studying her. Trying to figure out if she understands what he's just said. He decides this is some kind of conciliation, that she's getting ready to negotiate.

You got any beer?

She nods and gets up.

Keep that door open, he says, and don't try to leave.

She points out the window to her car, sitting right outside and blanketed in a thick dome of snow. Where would I go? she asks.

DAWN DASHES FOR HER BEDROOM, FOR THE PATIO DOOR. Slides it open just wide enough to squeeze through, but the snowdrift surrounding her exit is too high. She can't fight her way through that drift—she'd likely smother before she got very far. And if she tries to go the other way, skirt tight along the building to the far side and cut through the cleared parking lot, he'll see her out the window. She could probably outrun him, but she's in her socked feet. Her boots are at the front entrance and her runners are tucked there next to them.

She slides the glass door shut, goes back inside and makes enough noise that she knows he won't come looking for her.

CHERYL TURNS THE PAGE ON THE TWO-YEAR-OLD GUIDEBOOK she pulled off a shelf—and there it is: Graceland in all its glory. A full-page ad, photos taken to make the place look bigger, more opulent. More interesting. *Graceland*, the ad reads, *where the old world meets the new.* And at the bottom of the page *The perfect launch pad for your adventure!*

Cheryl pretends to gag, turns the page. Turns another—then turns her head to watch Jenna, who's standing at the table breaking up the puzzle she spent all day constructing. She looks younger than she has in ages, and Cheryl can't decide if it's the light in the room, or the sudden interest in puzzles, or just the lack of heavy eyeliner that's causing it.

They've been here four days, and they've had an adventure—but they haven't talked. Not really. Cheryl's hasn't managed to raise any of the big issues, to have the conversations she imagined so they could move on. Move away.

It's impossible to tell, Cheryl says, what a place is really like from one of these guides. I think we'll have to get to wifi—then at least we can see ratings and comments before we book something.

Can't we just stay here for our last day? Jenna asks, dropping pieces into an open box.

No way. I'm sure we can find something better than this.

Jenna pauses, her palm full of puzzle. I like it here.

Cheryl spies Ethan slipping into the library—and even in this light she thinks she can make out a faint flush creeping over Jenna's face. And Cheryl thinks oh no, the time to leave was yesterday.

Thought you'd gone to bed, she says to him without taking her eyes off her daughter.

He points at the computer. Just hoping to get an email out—is it working yet?

Nope, we're still cut off from civilization, she tells him, but Ethan comes all the way in anyway, skirting the couches—goes straight to the table and starts to help Jenna scoot puzzle pieces into the box she's holding below the lip of the table.

Cheryl throws the guidebook toward the coffee table like it's a Frisbee, but the paper's slick and it skates over top and lands on the floor. She shrugs, watches Jenna tuck the puzzle box back on the shelf. Then the girl hesitates, looking over the other boxes, and reaches up.

Don't even think about starting another one, Cheryl says.

Jenna turns with a game in her hand. Hey, can we play Clue?

A little too on-the-nose, don't you think? Cheryl says, and it's Ethan who laughs, who says, Colonel Mustard in the library with the candelabra, *that's* who killed her!

Jenna breaks into a wide grin and now she really looks young, looks like she did back when she was content to be Cheryl's sidekick, full of high spirits and shenanigans. But when Jenna sets the game on the table, Cheryl sees the girl's face is shifting—maturing so fast it makes Cheryl think of those time-lapse photography projects some parents do with their children, the years racing past in a minute, infant through adolescent to adult. The same face but changing shape, all the world accumulating in the eyes.

I don't get it, Jenna finally says. And she's looking at Ethan. I mean, if he confessed that one time but he didn't do it, then couldn't he just say that? Couldn't he just say it wasn't true—I didn't kill her. If he didn't, I mean. Because there's still no actual *proof* that he killed her, right?

Cheryl can see Ethan weighing his answer and she wants him to hurry up, to shut this down, but there's something in Jenna's expression that holds her own response at bay.

Ethan places eight fingers on the edge of the table—gingerly, like he's about to play a concerto—before he says, Once you give in, once you agree to be the thing they want you to be, you can't come back from that. They've already made up their minds. If you sign off on it—even once—you're done.

Jenna's expression changes again and Cheryl can see her retreating from Ethan. She gives him the pursed, indulgent half-smile that she often gives Cheryl, the one that says she knows better.

But if it's not the truth, Jenna says, then it's just what they think. You just have to convince them it's wrong.

Ethan laughs, and Jenna retreats even further, but he isn't looking at Jenna anymore. He's looking out the window, focusing on a point where a shaggy spruce top meets its end at the bleak twilight sky. Their minds, your mind, he says. After a while, it's all the same.

Jenna steps back from the table, crosses her arms. So what, so you just let other people say who you are?

Or you find new people, and a new place to be.

Exactly, Cheryl says. You go somewhere new.

Jenna looks from her mother to Ethan. You guys rehearse this?

And now she's the teenager Cheryl brought to this middle-of-nowhere nightmare, and Cheryl feels her shoulders relax as she's overtaken by a yawn.

Ethan looks over at the computer, then out at the darkness that is falling, erasing even the closest trees. Anyway, he says, I guess we'll hear what kind of evidence he has to the contrary when the filming resumes in the morning.

His words a question now for Cheryl, who stifles another yawn and shakes her head.

Fuck that, she says. Guys who say they didn't do it are a dime a dozen. There's no story in it—no tension, no menace. And certainly no market for it.

And then she's up on her feet. Okay Jen, time for bed. Her tone is like the lid slamming shut on a laptop.

DAWN PUTS A GLASS OF BEER IN FRONT OF HIM, SLIDES AN ashtray to the middle of the table. Sits down with a glass of wine still in her hand.

Look, he says, I know what I'm asking for is huge. But listen, I have a little boy now. I don't want him to grow up thinking his dad is that guy, that murderer.

She takes a small sip of her wine, eyes fixed on the beer he lifts to his mouth.

Is it okay? she asks. It's been in my fridge for a while.

It's fine. Look, Rosie—

Dawn, she corrects him, focusing on her hands as they draw out a cigarette and light it. Go ahead and have a smoke, she says. We'll make an exception tonight.

You never had children, did you?

She blows a plume of smoke toward him before she answers. None to speak of.

He's not sure what that means, but he pulls his silver case from the pocket of his sweater, slides out a cigarette. On a whim, Dawn leans forward and lights it, her eyes meeting his.

It's amazing, he says, how little you've changed. I knew right away it was you.

She drops the lighter on the table. I think you've mistaken me for someone else.

He taps his ash. I'm sure I haven't. I did some checking, you know, after I saw your picture. There's no trace of you before the eighties—nothing, not a single vital statistic that I could find. And I paid a guy who specializes in finding people who don't want to be found.

Dawn lets a slow smile creep across her face. She's practically thrilling—she's been saving up for this for so many years. That's right, she says. I moved here from the States, from Pennsylvania. Tell your guy to look it up.

Spencer takes a drag, blows a few perfect smoke rings toward her.

My dad used to do that, she says, and that part is her own true story.

Yeah, my kid loves it, too. Bad role modelling, I suppose.

Spencer takes a deep drink of his beer. So how about this, Dawn. We do a DNA test, just to be sure you're not her.

She sips her wine. Why would I?

Because I've already collected half a dozen of your cigarette butts, so it'll just save us some time.

Her cheeks are flushing, but he can't tell if it's the wine or if it's because he's got her on the run now.

She slides a finger around the rim of her glass. And what would you compare this DNA to? Have you got the hairbrush of a dead girl from decades ago?

He crushes his cigarette in the ashtray. Better, he says. I've got a dead girl's sister.

I don't have a sister.

As soon as it's out of her mouth, she hears what she just said. The admission in it.

I mean I have two brothers, back in Pennsylvania. She says it fast, and then lifts her glass. Feels the tectonic forces, the plates shifting beneath her.

Your stepmother brought your sister to my first parole hearing, he says. She wasn't much younger than the young one down there. He points over his shoulder. Pretty girl, looked a lot like you with darker hair, ringlets. She made a good impression, growing up without her big sister. I'm sure she was the reason I spent two more years in that hellhole.

Spencer lifts his beer and drains the glass, three big gulps. Tips it back and takes the dregs, all of it.

Dawn tries to catch up, to dodge the image of that girl and her ringlets. Loops back around to you've mistaken me for someone else, but it sounds forced now and she knows she's lost.

Knows he knows it, too.

He sets the glass down and says, So how about it. Will you come back with me, or do I get those DNA tests done? Either way—

Dawn lights another cigarette and waits. Sips her wine. Rolls her toes under her feet. Watches him reach for the lighter, fumble when he tries to pull out another cigarette.

She points to his empty glass. Another one?

He shakes his head, then struggles to line the flame up with the business end of his smoke. His eyes are glassy.

I have a little boy now, he says.

You said.

Rosie, please. His voice is thick, whiny. You owe—

She leans forward. I don't owe you anything.

She smokes her cigarette, finishes her wine. Watches his head start to bob on his neck like it's not quite anchored there. He tries to flick his ash but misses the ashtray and then he drops the cigarette on the table and fumbles, trying to pick it back up.

All the things you did, she says finally. Fuck, Slake, I watched you *kill* somebody.

I never fucking killed nobody, Rosie. I'm not that guy.

His words so slurred she can barely catch them. She leans toward him. You got everything you deserved, she whispers.

I know, he says and his tongue is thick, tears pooling in his eyes. I know I wasn't a good guy. But Rosie, I never meant— He's overtaken by a coughing fit. And then he straightens up and for an instant, he seems like he's in control. Rosie, please, I changed. I got a little boy.

His head bobs again, chin dropping to his chest, eyes closing for long enough that she's surprised when he emerges again. But he doesn't speak.

C'mon, she says. Let's get you to bed. She stands up. We'll talk about it in the morning.

And for whatever reason, he complies, struggles to his feet—and that's what it is, a struggle. She can see his legs want to betray him and she has to steel herself to touch him, to wrap an arm around his waist and let him lean on her.

The hall is dark and he keeps stumbling. She lets him. Helps him bump against the walls, cajoling him along in a louder voice than necessary and then switching to a whisper to tell him again that he's wrong, that she's not who he thinks. Riling him up until he's shouting nonsense, banging his fists on the wall. And it's perfect timing, how he says I should kill you now just as Ethan and Cheryl come out of the library.

Dawn apologizes for the noise. I don't know how he got like this, she says. How he got so drunk. Jenna appears then and Spencer twists free from Dawn. Stumbles backwards into the wall, into the Long's braya in its frame.

It's the resurrection, he slurs, and he lunges forward, his face inches from Jenna's as the flower hits the floor, glass shattering into a thousand tiny shards.

Jenna stands paralyzed, clearly terrified, but Ethan's got his hands on Spencer, is pulling him away as he shouts, She is risen! He keeps repeating it—*she esh rishen*—low and thick like a record on a slowing turntable, and Dawn's certain she's the only one who hears the words.

Dawn and Ethan wrestle Spencer into his room and shove him onto the bed, hold him there. He shuts up then, lies down like a recalcitrant child and he's out in seconds.

At least he's on his side, Ethan says, pulling one arm forward to make sure he stays that way. He'll probably survive the night.

Then Ethan asks Dawn what the hell happened.

I don't know, she says, her hands splayed, shaking. He came down to my room like that and started raving. Thanks for your help. I'm really sorry—this isn't the sort of thing that usually happens here.

Not your fault, Ethan says.

I'll clean up the mess. You get some sleep.

She doesn't turn to look back at the bed, not until Ethan has left the room. When she does, the light streaming in from the hallway casts her long shadow across the still body and off into the corner of the room. She sees him then, sees Slake asleep just as she left him all those years ago—a kaleidoscope of images, all that fear rising up in her—and she wonders how she didn't see him yesterday.

But the scene's not quite right. She edges closer, close enough to take his hand. Tugs him until he's stretched out flat on his back.

DAWN LIGHTS A CIGARETTE. SHE CAN'T STOP PACING, WALK-
ing from table to table in the dining room like she's the busiest
waitress in the world. Trying to figure it out, what to do now. She
knows she's only bought herself some time. Even if everyone here
thinks that man is just a raving lunatic, he'll wake up eventually, and
he'll wake up straight. Groggy maybe, hungover, but all there and
ready to talk. And so what if they don't believe him—the roads will
be open and he'll have the whole world for an audience.

He's finally caught up to her, and she's done.

She grabs a cloth from the sink, wipes the table where they'd
been sitting, then stands at the sink with the water running, taking
one deep drag after another from a cigarette.

Those things'll kill ya, you know. The voice startles her, sets her
heart to hammering even though she recognizes it right off.

Jerry, what the hell are you doing here?

I'm getting you out of here, he says. My truck's on the highway,
about a quarter mile down, tucked back in the service yard. They
managed to plow that out, at least.

But why—?

She looks at him bewildered, the ember of her cigarette twirl-
ing circles in the dark. He waves away the smoke to make the
point and says, I'm glad you're okay. I know all about it. He hasn't
hurt you?

She studies Jerry for a long minute. There's just enough light
shining through the window to see him clearly. To see he really does
know all about it.

Not yet, she says, but he plans to. He's made that clear.

Well c'mon then, let's get you far away from here before he has
a chance.

Both of them keeping their voices quiet, talking in rushed
undertones.

It's no good, Jerry—there's no point. Dawn's arms swing around as if they're trying to take in the whole of it, all of Graceland and everything else. I can't just run away from home.

Sure you can, he says.

And then Jerry takes both her wrists. Just this once, Dawnie, he says, you need to dance with the one that brung you.

He stands so close that she realizes, maybe for the first time, that he's no taller than her.

She wrenches her hands loose. Jerry, she says. You're not getting it—he'll just find me again. And anyway, I got nowhere to hide, not anymore.

She sits down at the same corner table where she'd sat across from Slake—Spencer—and crushes out her cigarette.

Okay, Jerry says. He sits down, too. Then let's go to the police.

And tell them what? That I've been living under an assumed identity and now it's caught up to me? She hugs her arms close to her body. Jerry, they'll take everything and then they'll lock me up. Stolen identity, she says. They won't let that go.

You tell them you were scared, that you ran for you life. Jerry reaches across the table to take her hands, but she keeps them tucked where they are, under her armpits, and lets the tears boil up in her eyes.

There's something else, Jerry. Something I never told anyone.

His hands flat on the table, all ears now. She swears she can see those ears beneath his grey stubble turning like satellite dishes to catch the signal.

He killed a guy. I watched him, and I never did anything to stop him or turn him in.

Jerry pulls back so his hands are his own, balled up in fists, knuckles matched with knuckles.

Help me, she whispers, and then for a long time there's no sound but the occasional puff of wind, blowing its last breaths outside the window.

Where is he now?

She looks sheepish, maybe playful. Jerry can't tell which but it surprises him, the way her expression changes. I crushed some tranquilizers, some old pills of Andrea's, she says. Into his beer. He's out cold.

Nice work, he says. And here I thought you needed a rescue.

Jerry picks up the metal case lying on the table. What's this?

Those are his, she says.

He opens it and sees the cigarettes lined up and leaning crooked behind the clip. Rolls his own I see, he says, and snaps the lid closed again.

Another long silence before she speaks. Jesus, Jerry, what were you thinking putting pictures of me on the internet?

I guess I thought it wouldn't matter, all this time later. Jerry twirls the silver case in a slow circle on the table, then looks up at her. You know they've been there for two years. And the way he says it, it sounds like a defense but he means it as an accusation. Means how come you never even looked at the website I made for you.

You really fucked me over this time, Jerry. She drives her fingers through her hair and pulls them around along her throat, leaves them up against her jaw like a hangman's noose. I might as well just let him take my life.

Stop that, he says. I kept you safe all these years, didn't I? I'll think of something now.

I don't think you can fix this one, MacGyver.

She starts to stand, thinking she might feel better if she moves around, but the heavy weight of exhaustion draws her back down. And then she looks like she might start to cry for real, but she doesn't. Jerry watches the crisis blow across her face and then he looks outside at the sign he'd been so proud of, the red script pronouncing *Graceland*, the small lettering underneath that she'd insisted on and he thought ruined everything: *of the north*.

He picks up the cigarette case, weighs it in his hand. You really got him knocked out cold?

She nods. I practically had to carry him to bed.

Get me those pills then, he says, and he pockets the silver case.

JERRY SLIDES ALONG THE BACKSIDE OF GRACELAND AND INTO Dawn's bedroom through the sliding glass doors. Comes through to the dining room still walking on tiptoes.

She's sitting at the corner booth in the shadows just where he left her. Just where he told her to stay though he's been gone much longer than he expected. It was harder than he thought it would be, getting that going.

He pulls the balaclava off his head and hands it back to her.

You stay right here and wait until the smoke detectors in the hall go off, or at least until you can smell the smoke. He peers down the hallway. It'll go fast when it goes, so you have to get those ladies up and out fast, you understand me?

Jesus, Jerry, what did you do?

Dawn stands and steps out of the shadow, steps into the light coming through the window and Jerry thinks her face has hardly changed since the first time he saw it when she climbed into his truck. Exhausted and anxious like it was that day, but every bit as lovely.

He puts a hand on her shoulder and it steadies him. Still, he feels like he's looking down on her from a great height.

I cut you loose, he says, and for a minute he thinks he might kiss her forehead. You, and me too.

And just before he's out the door, he turns to say—a conspirator's whisper—I was never here tonight. You never saw me. He doesn't say I'll never be here again, but he figures she's a smart girl. Figures she gets it.

And then he's gone, though he doesn't go far. He hangs in the shadows outside where he won't be seen but where he's close enough to help if he's needed. Stands there long enough to see how it all plays out. To see Dawn and the ladies make it out safely—and then a young guy, someone he didn't know about, too.

And when Jerry can see they're all safe, he heads for his truck.

On the highway, he looks back one last time to see it go up. To watch the sparks fly, pinpricks of light against a smoky sky.

ETHAN HAS TO SHIFT HIS HIPS, LIFT AND TWIST TO EXTRACT his seatbelt from underneath him. When he's got it fastened, he looks up to watch a young woman wrestling her carry-on down the aisle. It's a duffle bag, too wide for this narrow plane, and he's surprised they let her bring it on. He sees her spot his scabby ear, sees her dark eyes opening wide, but she looks away fast when Ethan catches her eye.

He's got used to that these last few weeks.

He pulls out his phone, checks his email but there's nothing he wants to see. There's just a piece of spam that slipped through the filters—the syntax of its promise of eager companionship so off-kilter he finds it endearing—and another message from Cheryl that he doesn't open.

He drops the phone to his lap and leans across the empty seat next to him to look out the window, wondering if he'll get lucky and no one will show up to claim that seat. Wondering in the next instance what it is that Cheryl wants from him.

She'd called him a few days ago, said she was coming back and she wanted to see Ethan, to show him something. To get him on camera. But Ethan's no more interested in a dead killer's story than he was in a live one, and he told her so. But he didn't tell her he'd be gone before she arrived.

Maybe there's something he doesn't know, some new development. He's been avoiding the news for more than a week, trying to settle into his new role, but he can't see any harm in satisfying his curiosity while he's waiting for take-off. It's an escape, at least, from trying to figure out his next move now that he's resigned his job. Now that he's unemployed and homeless.

Ethan enters a quick search. The headlines don't give away anything he doesn't already know but he picks a story from a few days after the fire and scrolls through it.

One man was killed when fire broke out at a motel in the early Easter morning hours. He skims over the story, grazing *Graceland (no relation to the famed Memphis attraction by the same name) is located on the highway...* and *Investigators believe the fire was caused by careless smoking.* Ethan already knows the facts, went over them with the police and again with the insurance investigators. Out of his mind drunk, he told them both. It's amazing that he even managed to light a cigarette.

There's a video, too—*Filmmaker Cheryl Hayworth, who was staying at the inn, shot this dramatic footage of the fire*—but Ethan hasn't watched it. He isn't interested in reliving the experience, and he has opinions about filmmakers who are more concerned with getting their equipment out of a burning building than looking after their terrified kid.

Still, he's not averse to a small scrap of glory. He scrolls back up to find his big moment in this story.

There it is. *Motel guest Ethan Turnowski, 34, escaped the inferno through a window, then went back in to try and rescue the deceased, but was driven back by the fire.* Underneath that, a link to another story—a newer story—the headline bold and centred on the line underneath: *Motel fire hero no stranger to narrow window escapes.*

Old news, all of it.

Ethan switches back to his email, deletes Cheryl's message unread. Then he holds his thumb on the button until he feels his phone shudder and shut off. He leans his head back, listens as they close the plane's door. Disappearing, he thinks, would have been easier if he'd just stayed where he was.

DAWN STEPS OUTSIDE WHAT'S LEFT OF GRACELAND ON A moonless spring night, closes the door securely behind her. Another step and a gust of wind catches her, rushing up into her face and then rolling over and past her.

She's not supposed to be here. She's a trespasser, not allowed in. The building's condemned, half consumed by fire and the rest destroyed by smoke. On the breeze, there's an acrid smell of char and something else—something more pungent and longer lasting that she doesn't bother to name.

She lights a cigarette and listens to the sound of caution tape fluttering, the whine of tires on the highway coming closer. The headlights from a passing vehicle bisect the parking lot and then catch on the motel sign, illuminating *Graceland* and *of the north* for a flash before moving beyond it. Before everything is swallowed again in darkness.

Dawn takes a last drag and lets her cigarette fall, crushes it under her heel before the wind takes the butt off. Picks up the bag of what she's managed to salvage. It's not much to show for a lifetime of accumulation, but it's heavy on her shoulder and she has to resettle the weight to carry it.

She looks up. Sees a hundred stars dotting the sky, and then a thousand more. Holds her breath and waits, eyes fixed until she finds it—finds one single point of light dodging between those stars, moving in a steady line across constellations she's never learned the names of.

She watches that satellite fly, silent and small, until it disappears from sight.

Playlist

This is the soundtrack for *We All Will Be Received*—songs that filled the space into which I was writing. Some are referred to, directly or indirectly, in the novel. All served as inspiration, and wove into and around the lives of the characters and their stories.

"Thunder Road" – written and performed by Bruce Springsteen on *Born to Run* (1975).

"Hound Dog" – written by Jerry Leiber / Mike Stoller, performed by Elvis Presley (1956).

"Don't be Cruel" – written by Elvis A. Presley / Otis Blackwell, performed by Elvis Presley (1956).

"Adam Raised a Cain" – written and performed by Bruce Springsteen on *Darkness on the Edge of Town* (1978).

"Mustang Sally" – written and performed by Mack Rice (1965).

"I Can't Untie You from Me" – written and performed by Grayson Hugh on the soundtrack from *Thelma & Louise* (1991).

"Don't You Need" – written and performed by Melissa Etheridge on *Melissa Etheridge* (1989).

"Secure Yourself" – written by Amy Elizabeth Ray / Emily Ann Saliers and performed by the Indigo Girls on *Indigo Girls* (1989).

"Graceland" – written and performed by Paul Simon on *Graceland* (1986).

"Heartbreak Hotel" – written by Mae Boren Axton / Thomas Durden / Elvis Presley (1956). Check out Lisa Dillan's amazing cover on *Love Me Tender - The Quite Quiet Way* (2012).

"Meeting Across the River" – written and performed by Bruce Springsteen on *Born to Run* (1975).

"Something in the Night" – written and performed by Bruce Springsteen on *Darkness on the Edge of Town* (1978).

"Wildflowers" – written by Dolly Parton and performed by Dolly Parton, Emmylou Harris and Linda Ronstadt on *Trio* (1987).

"Iris" – written by John T Rzeznik and performed by the GooGoo Dolls on the soundtrack for *City of Angels* (1998).

"One Light Left in Heaven" – written by Jim Cuddy / Greg Keelor, performed by Blue Rodeo on *The Things We Left Behind* (2009).

Acknowledgements

I'm eternally grateful to Jessica Grant for her tremendous insight and enthusiasm, and the long conversations that shaped and enriched this novel. Many thanks to Shaun Bradley for generous and wise guidance, and to Rebecca Rose and James Langer for their faith in a book that was not yet written.

Thanks to Christine Clouston for careful reading and insider knowledge, to Rhiana Chinapen for offering crucial intel on equipment and what the filmmaker is worrying about, and to Brenda Leifso and Lauren B. Davis for long online talks about writing, redemption, truth, and darkness.

Thanks to Robert, Fiona, Zuz, Maria, and Gerald for the loan of lovely and silent surroundings, and for abiding friendship.

Funding from the Canada Council for the Arts and Arts NL gave me the gift of time to create a story out of an idea.

Gratitude to the many visionaries whose work in the 1960s and 70s connected us all in this big web, and to the internet itself for being there when I need to know stuff. You're not all bad.

Most especially, thanks to Russell and Isabelle for putting up with me through those long months, and for all the great meals and kitchen debates.

ALSO BY
LESLIE VRYENHOEK

Short Stories
Scrabble Lessons

Poetry
Gulf

Fiction
Ledger of the Open Hand